Pledge of Authenticity

I know that the facts presented in this book are true and that the principles of successful aging really work because they've worked for me, and they've worked for many other men and women whose stories fill this book and without whose inspiration I could not have written it. Writing this book helped me to lose 75 pounds, to adopt a healthier diet, and to exercise more vigorously than I did in my teens; now, at age 56, I look and feel years younger. In my experience, when you surround yourself with examples of healthy aging you cannot help but have a little bit rub off on you. Let some of it rub off on you, too. My hope is that you will experience important changes in your own life by reading this book, studying the examples of spunky eldsters, doing the exercises at the end of each chapter, and applying the principles of the successful aging in your thinking and behavior.

*– **Richard Kownacki, Ph.D.** August 4, 2010*

**Cover Photo: Joseta Barker celebrating her
eighty-fifth birthday. See Preface.**

Richard Kownacki, PhD

DO NOT GO
GENTLE

Successful Aging for Baby Boomers
And All Generations

IAgeHealthy Publications
Wichita Falls, TX • Asheville, NC

iagehealthy.com
2910 Kemp Blvd., Suite 210
Wichita Falls, TX 76308
billing@iagehealthy.com

Credits

Dylan Thomas, "Do Not Go Gentle into That Good Night," The Poems of Dylan Thomas, [lines 1-3], (New York, NY: New Directions Publishing, 1957), used with permission.

Etta Clark, Growing Old Is Not for Sissies: Portraits of Aging Athletes, parts 1 and 2, copyright ©1987 and 1997. Excerpts used with permission.

George Vaillant, Aging Well, (New York, 2003, Little, Brown and Company). Excerpts used with permission.

Harvard Health Publications, Harvard Medical School. Excerpts from the Harvard Heart Letter, July 2004, used with permission.

Ray's Boathouse, Cafe & Catering (6049 Seaview Avenue NW, Seattle, WA 98107-2690, 206-789-3770). Quotations used with permission.

Roget's International Thesaurus, 4 ed., revised by Robert L. Chapman, (New York, 1977), quoted with permission from HarperCollins Publishers.

Oliver Seikel quoted with permission.

Steve Silva of SilvasLifeSteps (www.silvalifesteps.com, 615-243-6311), gave permission to use quotations.

Biblical quotations are from the King James translation.

Front cover photograph used with permission of Joseta Barker, Bud Cole, and West Tennessee Skydiving (901-255-1725).

Harley-riding granny photo used with permission of Joseta Barker and Carl Wyatt.

Fifty percent of the profits from the sale of this book will be donated for charitable purposes to benefit needy elders—through programs like Meals on Wheels and other worthy causes.

ISBN: 1451555253
ISBN-13: 9781451555257

Disclaimer

This book is not meant to be a substitute for medical treatment or mental health care. Reading this book does not constitute entering into a professional relationship with Dr. Kownacki. If you need medical care or psychological services, please consult with an appropriate health care professional in your area. Always check with your personal physician before starting any new exercise program or before making major dietary and nutritional changes. Making any kind of change in your life involves an element of risk. You can minimize the risk by getting more information, planning well, consulting with knowledgeable sources, and practicing moderation in all your behaviors.

Contents

Acknowledgements

The title of my book was inspired by "Do Not Go Gentle into That Good Night" by Welsh poet Dylan Thomas (1914-1953). The poem was written for his dying father, urging him to rage against death. For me, the following are some of the most poignant lines from this poem:

> Do not go gentle into that good night,
> Old age should burn and rave at close of day;
> Rage, rage against the dying of the light.

I'd like to dedicate this book to my father, who died at the relatively young age of 57. Dad never went gentle about anything in his life. In some ways, he embodied the Socratic ideal that the unexamined life is not worth living. He was opinionated, outspoken, and critical of the powers that be—people, government, institutions, religion, God—nothing was beyond questioning. Dad's example encouraged me to think for myself. Reading and learning were an important part of life, and early on I learned the value of a good book. One of my first memories is when, at age four, Dad dropped me and Mom off at church and said, "Okay, Jean, take that kid in there and get him some religion. I'm going to the Carnegie Library to get a book by Sigmund Freud and find out why you're all crazy!" I know what you're thinking—that experience influenced me later to choose psychology as a career. There's no doubt about that. However, first I got interested in biology and anthropology, but that's probably Dad's influence too. Dad made us attend Mass until we were 15, even though he only went to church about once a year on Christmas or Easter. He made a token appearance, always sitting in the back pew, so he could sneak out early and go back to the car to catch up on his reading. Once I caught him reading Charles Darwin's *On the Origin of the Species*. He didn't see any conflict between true religion and science. "Kids need a basic religious education," he said. "Otherwise they grow up to be total animals."

My mother taught me that it's okay to have fun and enjoy life, so that at age 56, I can still feed the ducks without being embarrassed about not acting my age. My grandfather taught me the value of charity, and to his dying day, he always bought an extra bag of groceries for the less-well-off neighbors, tapping into his tiny mill worker's salary. My sister, Debra, continues to inspire me by being bold, assertive, and just plain tough—traits she was forced to develop from being the only girl in a family of four boys. My brother Bob encourages me with his patience, fortitude, and ever-present sense of humor. Ron provides contagious enthusiasm for his love of Nature and the great outdoors. Mike continues to impress me with his persistence and ingenuity.

Mary Kownacki, my wife, made valuable contributions to this book. She's been a sounding board for ideas and concepts, offered anecdotes and insights into aging issues, and contributed clever snippets of wisdom from her *Little Book of Just Becauses*. She has also practiced the principles of successful aging by reviewing this book while working out on our home treadmill. Mary teaches me patience, kindness, and love for animals. She continually shows me how to be gentler with myself and everybody else. I dedicate this poem to her, from my *Halfway Haiku* collection:

Late Marriage to the Cat Lady

She took in strays.
He immediately felt right at home.

I want to thank my Uncle Jim for some sound advice about further education and the aging process. During a family reunion, I told him I wanted to go back to college to become a psychologist but complained that I'd be 40 years old before I could get in. He just smiled and said, "Well, how old will you be if you don't do it?"

Dr. Jack Moore helped educate me about humility and prepared me for acceptance into a doctoral psychology program.

Dr. Will Shadish, my dissertation adviser, mentored me in theoretical issues like statistics and research design but kept me practical minded with advice like, "You might not want to wear your Alfred E. Neuman tie pin when you go on psychology job interviews."

For reviewing portions of the manuscript and offering critical feedback, I wish to thank Mary Kownacki, Debra Kownacki, Debbie Lawson, Dr. John Ozone, Father Raphael Moore, Edward Bartosh, and Bob Balch. My brother Ron provided photographic support.

I am grateful for the books and teachings of Pema Chodron, American Buddhist nun. The greatest thing the nun taught me with her take on Zen and meditation is that I no longer have to run away from the world or myself. I can stay put and enjoy the spectacle, which is like having my own personal three-ring circus. The teachings of Thich Nhat Hanh continue to inspire me with practical application of the Buddha's living-in-the moment philosophy, so that even the most tedious chores can be a delightful adventure.

I want to thank everybody else I need to thank for whatever they did to help me along the way, but either I don't have enough room or I can't remember who they were and what they did.

I am grateful for the rich and varied sources of information about aging, without which this book could never have been written. These include personal testimonies, newspaper and magazine articles, books, scientific journals, government publications, videos and DVDs, and the World Wide Web—the Internet, which brings knowledge of the entire world and the whole of history conveniently into our homes. I wish to thank all of the spunky eldsters for setting a brilliant example of successful aging and for sharing their experiences with us. I am indebted to the scientists, researchers, writers, photographers, journalists, and media personnel who have opened new vistas on the prospects of aging. I am grateful for the rich database from which to draw abundant examples, colorful quotations, and a never-ending supply of new and important information about how we can grow old successfully. I am especially grateful for two wonderful books by Etta Clark, *Growing Old is Not for Sissies: Portraits of Senior Athletes,* parts 1 and 2. Photos and stories of Clark's spunky eldsters have been a profound inspiration to me for the past five years. Similarly, *Aging Well,* by George Vaillant, MD, has been indispensable in reshaping my outlook about aging.

Preface

The Skydiving Granny from Trenton, Tennessee

The skydiving granny on the cover is my mother-in-law Joseta taking her first skydiving lesson—to celebrate her eighty-fifth birthday. When she became a grandmother, Joseta didn't want to be called *Grandma* because it made her feel old. She asked her grandchildren and everybody else to call her *My*, short for my mother's mother.

Joseta presented a videotape of her skydiving adventure to her four children for Christmas. They were quite surprised by her aerial exhibition; some must have thought perhaps it was time to check her into a nursing home. However, Joseta isn't senile. Fifteen years a widow, she lives alone in a fair-sized house on a couple of acres of land on the outskirts of a small town, Trenton, Tennessee.[1] She cooks for herself, takes care of a dog, feeds the birds, plants a small garden each year, and keeps busy around the house. Joseta's interest in life and her level of activity are much greater than many individuals decades younger. She's a responsible member of her community. Although a prominent member of her church who does volunteer work at a nursing home, she's not an attention seeker. She keeps busy and active, but she is by no means athletic; she doesn't even exercise regularly. She's not particularly concerned about what she eats, just so long as she gets some cheese and a candy bar every day.[2] She thoroughly enjoys traveling and doesn't hesitate to get in the car for a 100-mile trek to the nearest big city (Memphis) or hop on a plane to visit relatives halfway across the country or even join a few friends for a two-week trip to China.

Joseta is basically an ordinary person who chooses to be exceptional in a few areas of her life. As such she demonstrates that all of us are capable of doing extraordinary things. I remember shortly after Mary and I got married, Joseta took the whole family on a river rafting trip to celebrate her seventy-fifth birthday. It was a moderately rigorous trip, and it certainly wasn't something you would expect from a septuagenarian family matriarch. As Joseta floated down the river in an old inner tube, she appeared peaceful and content, free from the troubles and concerns of the world. There was a childish gleam in her eyes and anybody could tell that she had not carried her worldly anxieties into the wilderness. Here was a woman who clearly understood how to stay in touch with her own joy and how to celebrate life fully.

When I got Joseta's permission to use her picture on the cover this book, I asked her what she thought was the secret to successful aging. She replied, "Don't just sit at home. Get out and do things. Keep interested in life. That's what keeps you going." As you will see throughout this book, keeping active is a vital part of successful aging. A lot of current research on aging demonstrates the wisdom of this philosophy of *use it or lose it.*

It is very important to learn how to get pleasure and enjoyment from the simple things of life. After all, what's the point of living a long time if you're not happy? Happiness is important at any stage of life, but the aging process provides a unique opportunity to increase the quality of your happiness. My Aunt Margie expressed it fittingly at Dad's funeral, when she had just turned 65: "When you get to be our age, you don't know if you're going to live another 20 minutes or 20 years. That adds a certain zest to the process of living." Similarly, an 83-year-old psychologist stated, "My seventies were interesting and purely serene, but my eighties are passionate. I grow more intense with age."[3] The approaching end of life can be a catalyst to intensify your gratitude and appreciation for the process of living. In Aunt Margie's case, she lived 20 more years. She moved from Pittsburgh to Florida and traded in her snow shovel and tire chains for a bathing suit and sun hat, and she had immense fun in her senior years.

Joseta knows how to have fun. She recently sent us an e-mail attachment entitled Maxine's Living Will. You have probably seen the cartoon character Maxine, a cantankerous old gal with sly wit and clever insights into issues of aging (and just about every other subject about which one can have a strong opinion). Maxine's Living Will proclaims that if she ever gets so sick that she can no longer request a piece of chocolate candy, then it's definitely time for relatives to pull the plug![4] In other words, it's important to maintain a high quality of life until the very end. (Check out the Maxine.com Web site, which features Maxine holding her *I love my attitude* coffee mug, and take a side trip to Hot Flash Central to hear her gripe about the world.)

Attending outings with Joseta and her older sister, Aunt Ruth, made a lasting impression on me, and I got to rethink seriously what we can and can't do in old age. Studying the lives of successful seniors and struggling with my own aging issues motivated me to take a closer look at American values on the subject of aging and to examine what scientific research on the subject of aging has to say. In so doing I continue to learn important things about the aging process, the true meaning of the counterculture, and the place of the baby boomers in history.

We are fortunate to be living during a unique period of human civilization. There have never been so many older people alive at any one time, and there have never been so many elders living remarkably exceptional lives. Many believe that the 1960s and the era of the counterculture was a pivotal time in history because the enormous number of youthful baby boomers helped to define what it meant to be young. Today is another pivotal time, and the rapidly aging baby boomers will have a second chance to make a major contribution to history—this time by helping to define what it means to grow old.

Introduction

The Challenge We Face

Many, if not most Americans today, including the baby boomers, are inadvertently limiting the length of their lives and the quality of their senior years because of poor lifestyle choices. We have become a nation of couch potatoes. This is no longer a quaint metaphor but a literal fact: America now has the highest rate of obesity of any country in the world. The state of affairs has become so grim that the United States may become the first affluent nation to experience a decline in life expectancy, according to the calculations of a team of medical researchers published in the *New England Journal of Medicine.*[1]

There are many factors that contribute to unsuccessful aging—obesity, smoking, addiction, sedentary lifestyle, unhealthy diet, overeating, depression, disease and disability, health problems, and even prejudice against old people. The good news is that all of these things can be overcome by lifestyle changes—especially shaking up our attitudes about what it means to get old.

Today we are at a crossroad. Will Americans take charge of their health and well-being or continue to spiral downward in a tailspin of self-imposed destruction? Seventy-seven million baby boomers are advancing toward retirement status over the next twenty years. Time will tell. When they were young, baby boomers transformed society in the image of youth. As they advance in age, will they revolutionize the standard of aging? Will they become the heroes of their own lives or merely the victims?

This book addresses aging issues that affect baby boomers and members of all generations. Middle-aged individuals can stave off serious decline, young people can learn to prevent future age-related problems, and elders can slow down or even reverse existing deterioration. Baby boomers are of unique interest because they comprise over one-quarter of the U.S. population. Every day they grow older, rapidly increasing the elderly population. By sheer size and potential influence, the boomer generation raises challenging issues about aging. What will happen as baby boomers surge like a tsunami into the retirement phase of life?

My goal in writing this book is to summarize what I think is the truth about aging, identify the factors that contribute to successful and unsuccessful aging, and share the motivation I've found to make lifestyle choices for empowerment to live a full and meaningful life—at any age. Today, we Americans basically have two choices in how we deal with aging: either keep doing what we're doing or make a serious commitment to lifestyle changes. The first option leaves us doomed to a dismal future of progressive deterioration and a distressing, limited life in our senior years. The second option opens up a world of opportunities to enjoy the aging process as one of the happiest times of our life. I urge you to choose the second option; learn to surf the silver tsunami and recognize age as the culmination and fruition of your entire life's work, and the opportunity to finish all those things you started in your youth.

Grow old along with me!
The best is yet to be,
Robert Browning, "Rabbi Ben Ezra"

This book examines the subject of aging in the United States today from a personal perspective, combining some of the latest scientific research and my professional experience as a psychologist. I've blended facts and evidence with my own experience, opinions, and insights, and I've also shared some of my own theories and explanations. As a recovering perfectionist, I found inspiration in the words of Tai T'ung, author of the thirteenth-century *History of Chinese Writing*, "Were I to await perfection, my book would never be finished."[2] Please accept my book as a work in progress, just like my life.

Do Not Go Gentle focuses on the concerns of aging Americans, but its scope is truly global, as are the problems with aging that it addresses. Scientific studies from all around the world are cited, and I hope that you will find this book useful whatever your national origin or country of residence.

The book can be read from start to finish or individual chapters can be read in any order, according to your needs and interests. Chapter 1 discusses my experience of being out of shape and feeling over-the-hill at age 50. This motivated me to study the lives of spunky elders who seemed to defy the standards of growing old, which led to the discovery of the principles of successful aging. Chapter 2 summarizes the scientific evidence of the benefits of exercise. Many chronic diseases and conditions associated with aging can be prevented or lessened. Exercise can extend your life, reduce the impact of age-related decline, and improve your physical, mental, and emotional functioning. Chapter 3 outlines the psychological benefits of exercise and explains why I got motivated to practice psychology for the health of it. Learn how to become the hero of your own life by making healthy lifestyle choices and taking responsibility for your physical, mental, and spiritual well-being. Chapter 4 examines why America literally has become a couch potato nation and how baby boomers are the least healthy age group. Readers are invited to make an honest appraisal of their lifestyle and health risks. Assess where you are with the stages of change model. Chapter 5 argues that the lap of luxury is way too soft, because the ease and convenience of modern society creates diseases of lifestyle which threaten Americans with premature death and unhappy retirement years. Learn how to overcome denial and resistance to lifestyle change—a prerequisite for successful aging. Chapter 6 demonstrates that it's never too late to change your whole life around. Even if you become sick, incapacitated, or disabled you can still modify your lifestyle to prevent further decay and even improve or restore functioning. You can never get too old or too decrepit to improve, and even minimal amounts of exercise are beneficial. Chapter 7 discusses the psychology of reaching bottom. You can use illness or personal tragedy as a springboard for personal growth and development or make a midlife crisis work for you. Chapter 8 dares you to be inconvenienced and regard exercise as an act of cultural rebellion. Go against the flow of modern society's ease and convenience by finding ways to incorporate more activity into your daily schedule. Bicycle riding is recommended as a fun, economical way to stay healthy and improve the quality of your life in multiple areas. Chapter 9 shows how to conquer over-the-hill syndrome and not use age as an excuse for not living life fully. The remarkable achievements of spunky elders can shock us into sensibility and help us develop a new attitude towards aging as a remarkably creative, productive, and socially valuable time of our lives. Update your concepts of aging: you don't have to become decrepit, you can remain active all your life, you don't have to succumb to depression or senility, and you can remain healthy and keep your body in tip-top shape. Chapter 10 urges you not to become an old fuddy-duddy and shows how anything in life is possible. Model your life after elders who have aged successfully. Spunky eldsters do not use age as an excuse. They remain full of vitality, stay creative and innovative throughout their entire lives, and make the best of diminishing resources. Chapter 11 shows how to become a real-life space cowboy. Dare not to be decrepit and stay young in spirit. Prove that age is no barrier by defying old age stereotypes. Overcome fear of aging and learn why creative blossoming in old age begins in midlife. Chapter 12 describes the real fountain of youth, discovered by practicing a lifestyle that promotes optimum physical, mental and spiritual health. Exercise, good nutrition and positive lifestyle factors can reduce the degeneration of old age and help you look younger and live longer. I share my own experience of applying these principles of successful aging. I invite boomers and members of all generations to begin a journey of discovery which will propel them into a stage of life more fulfilling than they every dreamed possible.

Chapter 1

Growing Old Is Not for Sissies

When I turned 50 years old, I performed my stereotypic, aging American male duty and bought a shiny new sports car. Unfortunately, the car was so low to the ground that getting in and out of it left me with a severe backache. Nobody was very sympathetic to my suffering when they saw that I was driving a Corvette. My 16-year-old nephew complained to my brother Bob, "Gee, Dad, how come these old guys get all the nice cars?" Bob replied, "Well, son, I guess it takes that long to save up enough money to buy one." Driving my little sports car brought back memories of being a teenager, which is probably why we older guys drive them! I remember watching the Jack LaLanne exercise show on TV when I was a teenager. I read those Charles Atlas ads in the comic books: "Hey, all you 98-pound weaklings! Get in shape so the bullies don't kick sand in your face on the beach!" Back then the paperboy used to pick on me all the time, so I got with my best buddy, Bill, to join a gym. Before long I had built up a set of beefy biceps. The next time the paperboy gave me a hard time, I took a deep breath, flexed my muscles, and stood him down in the aisle of the high school bus. After that he never picked on me again, and everybody started calling me Herc. It was great. That was my earliest experience of personal empowerment, and when I first realized that I could positively influence my life through significant lifestyle changes. It felt really good and was a tremendous boost to my self-esteem—something desperately needed during those angst-ridden teenage years. I remember telling Bill as we hitchhiked home from the gym one day that I felt like I could "tear telephone poles up by the roots!"

The 1950s exercise gurus promised that you could get into peak physical condition with exercise and good nutrition, no matter how out of shape you were. That sort of thing sounds fine for a young person, and obviously in my case it worked. But what are you supposed to do when you're 50 years old and you haven't been inside a gym since high school? Surely, you're over the hill and there's not much more you can do except keep coasting toward the crypt.

At 50 I literally felt a half century old. I was 75 pounds overweight, took medication for high blood pressure, suffered from aches and pains all over my body, and experienced shortness of breath and chronic fatigue. I got winded walking up steps. Just cutting the grass in our small yard was a big chore. I had to take pain medication afterward, or I'd feel sore all over for days. Eventually, I got to the point where I needed to take the extra-strength, time-release formula before I started to cut, and even then I'd still be miserable afterward. I thought this was just the normal course of aging, and it seemed like everybody else I knew about my age was going through the same thing.

I was feeling pretty depressed and hopeless, until I saw a poster on the wall of a local health food store. The poster portrayed an older guy flexing his well-developed muscles, with a physique that would make younger men jealous. The caption read Growing Old Is Not for Sissies. That got my attention. After some searching, I discovered a book of the same name by Etta Clark,[1] which is full of photographs and testimonials of aging athletes. The poster featured John Turner, a 67-year-old psychiatrist who lifts weights and does a lot of walking to keep in shape. He attributed his health and physical fitness to a lifetime of vigorous exercise. "Exercise is necessary to full enjoyment of life, body, and mind," he told Clark. "I think physicians have a responsibility to sell health at least as much as they sell pills."[2]

I didn't know what to make of all this. My initial reaction was excitement, followed quickly by shock, suspicion, and disbelief. It was all very confusing. A 67-year-old man with a bodybuilder's physique was contrary to everything I believed about aging. After all, 65 is the retirement age established by Franklin D. Roosevelt back in the 1930s in conjunction with Social Security. At age 65 you're officially a senior citizen and entitled to discounts in restaurants and movie theaters. Younger people are supposed to offer you their seats on public transportation and airlines let you board early with the first class passengers, parents with young children, and people with disabilities. At 65 you qualify for Medicare, which presumably you're going to need by then because your body will be all worn out. By age 65, you've lived your life and paid your dues to society through a lifetime of hard work. You've earned your retirement; it's time to draw a pension, put up your feet, and catch up on your reading. You can play golf or go fishing every day if you like, or else sleep in late and just lie around the house in your undies and watch TV. If you're really energetic and have enough money, you can take long vacations on tropical beaches, tour the country in an RV, or go on ocean cruises to exotic locales.

Why Don't They Act Their Age?

Those are the kinds of things I envisioned as part and parcel of the senior citizen's lifestyle. Vigorous physical exercise was definitely *not* part of the picture, especially weight lifting, which struck me as oddly incongruent behavior for a 67-year-old man. However, the longer I studied the subject of aging, the more contradictions I found to my preconceptions about what it means to grow old. Before long I confronted a growing body of evidence that large numbers of senior citizens just weren't behaving the way I thought they should! Unconsciously I was thinking, "Why don't they act their age!" But my rational mind could no longer ignore the mounting evidence that just because you get old doesn't mean you have to become feeble and decrepit.

In *Growing Old Is Not for Sissies* Etta Clark documents the active lives of several dozen senior athletes who have kept fit and trim well into advanced age by vigorous exercise and fitness. Take the case of Joe Bruno, who swam across San Francisco Bay when he was 83 years old. Crossing San Francisco Bay is a major achievement for swimmers of any age, on account of its frigid water and treacherous tides. You would think that for an 83-year-old it must have been a formidable challenge. Apparently, however, it was old hat to Joe Bruno who swam across the bay every year since he was 21 years old. Clark commemorated Bruno's sixty-third annual crossing with a newspaper article provocatively titled "My

Grandfather Can Swim Laps Around You!"[3] Moving from the water to the ice, we find 71-year-old John Morris, who plays in a senior ice hockey league twice a week. Everybody on his team, the Diamond Icers, is over age 60. Each year they compete in the Snoopy World Hockey Tournament—yes, organized by Peanuts cartoonist Charles Schultz in the 1970s. Morris's motto is, "You don't wear out; you rust out—from lack of activity."[4] On the beaches of Hawaii, we find Woody Brown, an 83-year-old surfer who's something of a local legend in Maui. His training regimen is going to bed early and not using alcohol, tobacco, drugs, or soda pop. He follows a vegetarian diet and "tries not to overindulge in sex."[5] (I'll discuss this thoroughly later in the Sex and Drugs and Rock-And-Roll for Senior Citizens section.) Suffice it to say here that *Growing Old* contains a nice picture of Woody with a big grin, holding his eight-foot surfboard, standing next to his six-year-old-son, Woody, Jr.! Clearly, the pursuit of peak physical fitness, including an active sex life, is not only for the young. According to Steven Austad, a biologist who studies aging, "there are reliable reports of men siring children at age 95."[6]

Senior fitness is not the exclusive domain of aging male athletes. There may be more robust and athletic female seniors because women live longer, and some of their feats surpass those of their male counterparts. Ella Peckham, age 86, was the oldest female competitor to swim in the 1985 Masters Olympics in Toronto.[7] Peckham swam in nine events and she set nine world records! At age 75, Sister Madonna Buder set a record as the oldest women ever to complete the Hawaii Ironman triathlon. She crossed the finish line at one minute before midnight, after nearly 17 hours of grueling activity—beginning with a 2.5 mile swim, followed by a 112-mile bicycle race, and ending with a 26-mile marathon! These all-day triathlons require the strength, discipline, and endurance of an Olympic athlete. Sister Buder, who has competed in over 300 triathlons, holds the well-deserved title "the Iron Nun." Her motto is "Never give up and never slow down."[8] Doris "Granny D" Haddock walked across the entire United States, a distance of nearly 3,200 miles, when she was 89 years old. Granny D was not an athlete, just a little old grandmotherly type from New Hampshire who decided to do something grand instead of sitting at home being depressed after her husband died. When she completed the 14-month journey, which took her across the Mojave Desert and the Appalachian mountains, she wrote: "The walk, I must say, improved my health. ... I finished the walk twenty years younger than when I started. It was good for my arthritis and emphysema."[9]

All across the country and around the world, we find an increasing number of men and women in their sixties, seventies, eighties and even nineties, who are in excellent health and have better physiques than many men and women decades younger. However, most of us don't see older people this way.

"Surely these must be exceptional people," you may be thinking, "Peak performance in old age is not for the average Joe like you and me." It's easy to come up with a litany of negative rationales. Carl Rogers, a humanist psychologist confronted such pessimism head on by asking his students questions like "Who's going to become a famous psychologist?" When nobody raised their hand, he continued, "Then who's going to become a famous writer? Artist? Scientist?" After there was still no show of hands, Rogers challenged his protégés further, "If not you, then who?" Why don't we become exceptional people? Who is to say we can't? We are held back so often by our own critical and limiting self-image. Perhaps we should ask ourselves why don't we believe we can become exceptional, and even more importantly, what keeps you and me from believing that we already are exceptional? Low self-esteem and negative self-image cripple young and old alike.

I had pretty low self-esteem, with respect to myself as an aging man, when I started writing this book. By the time I finished writing it, my self-esteem had improved tremendously. I developed a more positive self-image by learning the truth about aging, practicing what I learned as part of my life, and enjoying the benefits. You can do the same thing. One of the major reasons I wrote this book was to share my experience so others might also discover the delights of successful aging.

Spunky Eldsters

Our language is full of negative imagery and disparaging verbiage to describe the elderly. According to *Roget's Thesaurus,* synonyms of *old age* include decline of life, an incurable disease, the downward slope, the shady side, winter of one's days, decrepitude and infirmity of age, debility, feebleness, dotage, second childhood, and senility. Similarities to the verb *age* include decline, fade, fail, sink, waste away, dodder, totter, shake, wither, wrinkle, and shrivel. Then there's seen better days and one foot in the grave, before we come to the adjectives like past one's prime, overblown, overripe, over the hill, along in years, long in the tooth, sinking, and wasting. And don't forget these common terms of disparagement: stricken in years, decrepit, infirm, debilitated, feeble, rickety, worse for wear, moth-eaten, moss-backed, tottering, rickety, prune-like, mummified, and senile.   (There's a lot more, but I'm getting depressed just thinking about it!)

As part of the growing movement for a *new gerontology,* I propose two new terms. We talk about young people as *youngsters,* so why not apply the terms *oldster* and *eldster* to elderly people who are defying the traditional definitions of old age and not going gentle about the aging process? I was surprised to find that the term oldster is already in the dictionary, although I can't recall ever seeing it in use. *Merriam-Webster* simply defines oldster as "an old or elderly person," so I'll use it freely as a variant. Everybody else of advanced age status can be called elders, seniors, or older people—terms devoid of negative emotional content. We have to be careful how we use words because words that have a common meaning may convey very different emotional tones.   Bertrand Russell illustrated this with a clever conjugation: "I am firm; you are obstinate; he is a pig-headed fool."[10]

Surfin' U.S.A. Senior Style

I became so motivated by the spunkiness of these agile eldsters that I began researching the subject of successful aging. In 2006 I was invited to present my preliminary findings at the annual conference of the Texas Psychological Association. My colleagues got a real kick out of seeing a picture of 83-year-old Woody Brown on the beach with his son and giant surfboard, while I played the Beach Boys' song "Surfin' U.S.A" and discussed why we all need to update our attitudes about aging. While putting together the presentation, I looked up Jack LaLanne to find out when he died. To my great surprise (and delight), not only wasn't he dead yet, but he was healthy, active, and still preaching the gospel of exercise and good nutrition. He's like that battery ad bunny—there's just no stopping him.

Jack LaLanne opened the first modern health spa in the United States in 1936. I remember trying to keep up with the callisthenic routines on his TV exercise show as a kid and getting a kick out of seeing him with his two German Shepherds. He's still on television. I watched him just the other day selling juicers and still promoting the potency of good nutrition and vigorous exercise as a way to health and longevity—using himself as a prime example. He talked about being "a skinny and sickly 16-year-old" until one day he attended a health lecture and decided to join a gym and start eating fresh fruits and vegetables. At the psychology conference, I showed a picture of LaLanne doing fingertip push-ups at age 91, and then asked the audience how many of them could do fingertip push-ups—now or at any age? In an interview for *Life Extension Magazine*, LaLanne told a reporter that he got motivated to take good care of his health because his grandfather died from heart disease when he was 50, and he wanted to prove "your genetics [don't] control your longevity" but rather "you control your life."[11]

Be Careful of Expert Advice

Ironically, when Jack LaLanne began promoting resistance training at his gyms in the 1930s, scientists and fitness experts were genuinely convinced that weight lifting was bad for your health. According to Jan Todd, a sports historian from the University of Texas at Austin, "during the first two-thirds of the twentieth century... most athletes, male and female, eschewed weight training because it was considered by coaches and physical educators to be detrimental to athletic performance."[12] Today expert opinion is totally reversed. Weight resistance training is encouraged as a fundamental part of the conditioning programs for most men's and women's sports because it enhances muscular endurance, improves overall ability, and reduces susceptibility to injury.

Even more surprising is the fact that most of the experts back then believed that cigarette smoking was good for your health! That's why you see so much smoking in the old movies from the 30s, 40s and 50s—the growing influence of the tobacco industry on American advertising also played a part. The late forties radio show *NBC Mystery of the Air* ran ads that included claims like "According to a nationwide survey: More doctors smoke Camels than any other cigarette."[13] Cigarette smoking in America reached its peak for per capita sales in 1963, and it wasn't until 1964 that the surgeon general first issued a report declaring that cigarette smoking is hazardous to your health.

So much for the experts' advice! This only goes to prove that just because everybody believes something, that doesn't necessarily make it true. My mother taught me that truth when I was a kid. Whenever I wanted to do something crazy she always asked, "If everybody else jumps off a bridge, are you going to jump off, too?" That's why I tell everybody to make up your own mind about things. Don't just trust the opinions and advice of experts. Look at all the evidence and think it through yourself. Above all, experiment with making healthy changes and see what happens. The best proof of successful aging principles is to see them come true in your own life.

Health and Fitness Are Possible at Any Age

What has impressed me most about Jack LaLanne over the years has been the amazing feats of strength and endurance he performed after he turned 40. In 1957 at age 43 he towed a 19-foot, 2500-hundred-pound cabin cruiser six and one-half miles across the Golden Gate Channel in San Francisco. When he was 47, he swam the entire length of the Golden Gate Bridge underwater, twice! When he was 60 years old, he swam from Alcatraz to Fisherman's Wharf while handcuffed and with his feet shackled. At age 70, he swam one and one-half miles (the "Queen Mary Mile") while towing 70 boats, with a person in each boat, while handcuffed and with his feet shackled. LaLanne's motto has always been, "Anything in life is possible."[14] His life has been a demonstration of the truth of that philosophy. With a lot of hard work and a positive outlook, you can accomplish anything you want to in life—no matter what your age.

Now I don't want to give the impression that successful aging requires you to jump out of airplanes, tow rowboats with your teeth, or pull off Evel Knievel stunts to prove to relatives that you're still alive. There are plenty of more pedestrian activities. For a little exercise, you might just go down to your local bowling alley. That's what 93-year-old Ed Longner does. He won the bronze medal in bowling at the 1988 Arizona Senior Olympics, and he didn't even start bowling until he was 75. Longner attributes his longevity and fitness to moderate exercise and a vegetarian diet. He also stands on his head five minutes a day and calls it *reverse aging*.[15] You can buy his handstand gadget off the Internet for about $100.

I am spotlighting the remarkable achievements of these spunky elders to emphasize the importance of exercise and fitness, and to demonstrate that physical activity is possible at any age. I expect that you will be surprised by some of the things these elders are doing. That's a normal reaction. I was quite shocked when I came across them, and that's why I'm discussing them throughout this book. My belief is that we sometimes have an urgent need to do something out of the ordinary to shake ourselves free of old habits and preconceptions. When we experience a major crisis like an automobile accident, a heart attack, or a stroke, we are shaken out of our lethargy. But why wait for a catastrophe? Experience something out of the ordinary today. At least read about other people who have— because you can always learn from and be inspired by real-life heroes of fitness and human achievement.It's worked for me, and it can work for you too. It keeps working every time I look at a picture or read a story about one of these spunky eldsters.

Who says you can't get better with age?

<table>
<tr><td align="center">**Age 50**
265 pounds</td><td align="center">**Age 56**
190 pounds</td></tr>
</table>

Back to the Gym

Studying the lives of these aging athletes and spunky eldsters convinced me to join the local gym and get myself back in shape. By exercising on a regular basis, I lost weight, built up my muscles, and increased my energy level. My blood pressure normalized, so I got off the medication (with my physician's blessing). I could climb steps without getting winded, and I wasn't dead tired and ready to go to bed as soon as I got home in the evening. In fact, I didn't need as much sleep, and I felt more rested and vigorous when I woke up in the morning. I even started going to the gym at 5:00 A.M. three days a week. The irony of exercise is that when you put out effort, you get back more than you gave in terms of increased energy, stamina, endurance, and vitality—in addition to improved health and a heightened sense of well-being and personal empowerment.

A Journey of Discovery

Without knowledge action is useless, and knowledge without action is futile. Abu Bakr[16]

Applying the principles of successful aging greatly improved my health and vitality, which motivated me to read more books and study the body of psychological and medical research on gerontology. The more I learned from the research, the more I applied what I learned to my own life. It was a snowball effect but in a positive direction. A vast body of scientific evidence, combined with my personal experience, convinces me that aging should be seen as a continuation of human development and that it need not be a steady decline into decrepitude.

It was an exciting journey of discovery, and the results have been more rewarding than anything else I've done. It's given me new life, fresh hope, and a sparkle of liveliness more intense than anything I've felt since I was 20 years old in the winter of 1974 and trekked off from the icy hills of Western Pennsylvania to the sunny beaches of Southern California. My hope is that you, too, will learn to become the hero of your own life's story by practicing the principles of successful aging.

Activities and Solutions: How to Use This Book

After you read each chapter, I recommend you spend some time thinking about what you have learned. In the Activities and Solutions section at the end of each chapter, I offer a few suggestions to help you apply the principles found in the text. There are also a few lines to record your impressions and make notes.

For chapter 1, describe your reaction to the picture on the cover of this book. What were your initial thoughts and feelings about an 85-year-old woman going skydiving? What was your reaction to learning about a 67-year-old weight-lifting psychiatrist? A 76-year-old nun who races in triathlons? Why did you buy this book? How do you expect to benefit from reading it? What are you willing to do to age successfully?

I encourage you to obtain a copy of *Successful Aging for Baby Boomers and All Generations: THE WORKBOOK,* soon to be released by **IAgeHealthy** Publications. The workbook contains many useful questions, practical applications, activities, and motivational exercises. It is designed to help you implement the ideas presented in the book and to derive maximum benefit from them. My website, IageHealthy.com, also provides practical guidelines for applying the principles of successful aging.

Reading about the principles of successful aging is not enough. You have to apply what you learn and make it part of your lifestyle. The good news is that we all have the power to make changes in our own lives and daily activities during which we interact with other people. In a paradoxical but pleasing fashion, when we change ourselves the whole world sometimes seems to change around us.

You might keep a journal or diary and jot down your impressions of the facts and ideas presented in the book. Or come up with ideas and solutions of your own. Writing things down increases your chances of success, and so does sharing your goals with supportive others.

Studying the text and workbook with another person or in a small group will increase effectiveness. Working with other people has psychological advantages. You gain moral support by sharing your own experience, get inspired by the experience of your peers, increase accountability by sharing goals, and obtain positive strokes for your achievements.

Notes:

_____

_____

_____

_____

_____

_____

_____

Chapter 2

Why Should I Jog When There's a New Car in the Garage? Exercise for Disease Prevention

It's crucial to adjust our thinking to accept the truth: Many chronic diseases and much of the decrepitude in old age are not a normal part of the aging process; instead, they are the result of physical inactivity and poor lifestyle choices. All the experts now agree with this assertion, including the U.S. surgeon general, the American Heart Association, the American Medical Association, and increasingly so, most gerontologists. Unfortunately, many Americans don't realize they possess tremendous power to improve the quality of their lives. The good news is that lifestyle changes like exercise to promote fitness can reduce the impact of age-related decline and help you maintain a high level of health and fitness throughout your lifetime. More importantly, exercise and fitness in themselves can extend your life, minimize the chance of disease, and improve your physical, mental, and emotional functioning.

How One English Grandmother Stays Fit

Over the years, you've probably watched a few of those British TV shows on PBS, so you doubtless have some ideas about how an elderly English woman is likely to spend an afternoon of leisure. She might bake a batch of scones for tea with her friends, take a bus across town to visit a relative in the hospital, or maybe go for a leisurely stroll to a local park bench and feed the pigeons. If she's more adventurous, she might even turn into an amateur sleuth and solve a murder mystery in the neighborhood—while she's baking scones, visiting a sick friend, or sitting on the park bench feeding the pigeons. (We know all about those British eccentric types.)

Well here's something you're not likely to see on television, even in a quirky PBS sitcom. Eighty-four-year-old Marguerite "Gran" Elsley of York, England, opted for a rather unconventional form of exercise when she became the oldest participant in the Annual World Naked Bike Ride in London in June of 2005.[1] If you're squeamish, have no fear; the event's advert proclaims: "Full nudity not required—go as bare as you dare." The coordinators were proud to proclaim that in 2005, they had 250 riders, and nobody got arrested!

In 2009 the Naked Bike Ride was held in 70 cities and 28 countries throughout the world—it's no local curiosity.[2] The Naked Bike Ride is advertised as "a peaceful, imaginative and fun protest against oil dependency and car culture."[3] Gran Elsley told a reporter, "I'm now a fit and healthy 84 year-old, and I love being free from the restrictions of clothes. I also revel in living a car-free life. By remaining very active, I benefit from the pleasure that always follows exertion."

Keep on Trucking for Health and Fitness

Gran Elsley is truly a spunky eldster who demonstrates that you're never too old to get a little exercise, and you can even rebel against convention while you do it. (That certainly appeals to my own Inner Hippie!)

There are many different ways to exercise and keep physically fit. Your choice of activities is virtually without limit. You can choose traditional activities and go fishing, play golf, or just walk around the block. If you're on vacation, you might take long walks on the beach, and most cruise ships have jogging trails on the top deck, as well as tennis courts and sometimes a rock-climbing wall. You can march in a demonstration if you're still a political activist—maybe even join the Raging Grannies, the group of senior citizens who travel around the country to stage protest demonstrations. You can exercise in conventional ways by walking, jogging, running, bicycling, swimming, lifting weights, or more unconventional ways like hang gliding, skyscraper stair climbing, and, of course—naked bicycle riding. Less strenuous forms of exercise such as yoga and tai chi are also beneficial. The important thing is to keep on truckin', as we used to say in the sixties. Even if you've never exercised before, it's not too late to make a change, and you're never too old to get into shape.

Healthy Aging: Scientific Evidence of the Benefits of Exercise

All diseases run into one—old age. Ralph Waldo Emerson

A healthy physical and emotional lifestyle seems to be of even greater value to older people than younger ones. Rowe and Kahn, *Successful Aging*[4]

One of the reasons we dread old age so much is because it's considered synonymous with devastatingly poor health. It's a sad commentary on our attitudes about the aging process that aging experts need to make statements like "aging is not a disease."[5] Although Emerson had a somewhat dim view about diseases of old age, he intuitively recognized the importance of taking care of yourself when he said, "The first wealth is health."[6] The truth is that many of the diseases we believe to be an inevitable part of aging really are due to poor lifestyle choices. Therefore, we can avoid them by making healthy lifestyle changes.

If you consider that there is a direct correlation between inactivity and disease, early death, and many diseases and chronic health problems, then it follows that activity could reverse the process. Most diseases and conditions that are either caused or aggravated by inactivity can be prevented or even reversed by physical activity and exercise; this includes heart disease, which is the leading cause of death in America.

"Physical activity is essential to healthy aging," according to the Centers for Disease Control. "As an older adult, regular physical activity is one of the most important things you can do for your health."[7] In *Keep Fit for Life,* the World Health Organization (WHO) recommends physical activity, combined with sensible diet and healthy behaviors (like not smoking or abusing alcohol and drugs) as "essential for our health and well-being."[7] WHO advises everyone, especially the elderly, to "be physically active on a regular basis and include exercises that strengthen muscles and improve balance."[8]

It is vital that we continue to exercise and engage in some type of regular physical activity as we age. We may be able to get away without exercise when we are young, but it becomes increasingly important when we get older. It's no longer just fun and games or a way to keep yourself looking good—although it still serves those ends very well. In many ways, continued exercise and physical fitness are fundamental elements of successful aging. In a very literal sense, maintenance of health and well-being of the aging human body depends on regular exercise or physical activity. Here's a summary of the scientific evidence of the benefits of exercise:

- Exercise slows down the biological aging process.
- Exercise strengthens the immune system, which increases resistance to disease by reducing the risk of infection.
- Exercise can delay or prevent age-related decline by keeping our hormones in balance and lowering our body mass index.
- Exercise is one of the best ways to win the battle of the bulge and avoid or overcome obesity.
- Exercise can help prevent or reverse diabetes.
- Exercise can reduce the risk of heart attack, stroke, and cancer—three of the leading causes of premature death.
- Exercise can reduce the risk of chronic diseases like hypertension, cardiovascular disease, osteoporosis, and arthritis or help reverse their course.
- Exercise can help prevent Alzheimer's disease.
- You can never be too old or decrepit to benefit from exercise, and even small amounts of exercise are beneficial.
- You can incorporate exercise into other activities of daily living, like walking the dog or shopping at the local mall.

Exercise Slows Down Biological Aging

I'm here for one reason and one reason only—to show you how to feel better and look better so you can live longer.[9] Jack LaLanne, 1951

Nearly 60 years ago, Jack LaLanne became a regular feature on television with the *Jack LaLanne Show*, where he began with a beaming, "Happy Monday morning to you," or some variation of that greeting. LaLanne has always been a man ahead of his time, advocating the benefits of exercise years before physical fitness became a media craze. Today, the evidence of scientific research has finally caught up with the intuitive wisdom of this twentieth-century pioneer of health and wellness.

"Exercise can slow down the rate of aging," according to Carolyn Aldwin and colleagues.[10] Analyzing a vast body of scientific studies, the research team found a strong relationship between healthy aging and various psychological factors and health habits. Smoking, obesity, hostility, depression, and anxiety are *aging accelerators,* which actually seem to increase the rate of biological aging. In contrast, exercise is an *age decelerator,* and it decreases the rate of biological aging. Emotional balance, good social support, and low-fat, high-antioxidant diets also slow down the aging process. Heart output decreases with age, but physically fit elders have 50 percent greater cardiac output than elders who aren't in good physical condition. Exercise promotes healthy aging through improved physical health. Aerobic exercise strengthens your heart muscles, improves cardiovascular function, lowers cholesterol, and increases lung capacity. Weight resistance training is beneficial in late life because it slows down calcium loss from the bones and improves body flexibility, balance, and muscle strength. When you keep physically fit, you're less likely to fall—one of the major reasons seniors end up in the hospital and often in nursing homes.

Exercise Increases Natural Immunity to Disease

Exercise improves the functioning of our immune system and helps protect us against a wide variety of diseases. Moderate exercise can enhance the functioning of the immune system in a number of ways; it releases more antibodies, increases the total number of white blood cells, natural kill cells, and T cells, and in many other ways improves our body's natural functioning to either protect us from getting diseases or make us better able to recover from diseases that we already have.[11]

Cold and Flu Prevention

People who exercise regularly don't get as many cold or flu symptoms as those who don't exercise. Randomized studies have shown that 40 to 45 minutes of brisk walking each day can cut your sick days in half, according to David Nieman, director of the Human Performance Lab of Appalachian State University.[12] Over the past 20 years Nieman has gotten similar results with studies of both young and older adults.

How Healthy Is Your Spit?

Exercise and physical activity increase the level of salivary immunoglobulin A (IgA), which is considered to be our body's first line of defense against many types of infection. Many researchers believe this is why athletes and exercise enthusiasts regularly get fewer colds and oral infections than their couch-potato neighbors. Studies repeatedly show that the higher your level of IgA, the lower your risk for infections, and vice versa.[13] However, we have to be careful not to overdo it because too much exercise can lower our immunity.[14] Coaches, trainers, and sports doctors have known for years that serious athletes "have a heightened risk of colds and other respiratory illnesses during the weeks leading up to their major competitions."[15]

You might be thinking "Big deal! What's so great about not getting the common cold or the flu?"[16] Plenty, especially if you're elderly. Most adults get at least one cold a year. The common cold is the "most commonly occurring human illness" and it costs Americans $40 billion a year,[17] according to Blue Cross. The common cold costs more to treat each year than migraines, asthma, COPD, and congestive heart failure— making it uncommonly expensive and "a significant clinical and economic burden on society." These figures don't include the cost of personal misery, which we all know from experience. Just think back to the last time you had a "common cold" and suffered from 7 to 14 days from a runny or stuffy nose, coughing, aches and pains, fatigue, and general misery.

The flu is also a serious problem, affecting about one in five Americans every year, causing enough problems to require hospitalization of 200,000 according to the Centers for Disease Control.[18] According to the CDC, "people aged 65 and older are at highest risk for complications, hospitalizations, and deaths from influenza."[19] Despite advances in antibiotics, about 36,000 Americans still die every year from the flu, and most of them are elderly.

It would seem that the common cold and flu can be uncommonly serious threats to your health and well-being, increasingly so the older you get. Most of us grew up chanting the preventive medicine maxim, An apple a day keeps the doctor away. Now we need to add something like, Walking each day keeps cold and flu symptoms at bay.

It Pays to Practice What You Preach

One of the satisfactions of writing this book was discovering the results of research in a certain area, and then actually experiencing those results in my own life. As one of many examples, I saw my own immune system improve after a major increase in my weekly aerobic activity. In the summer of 2008, I discovered the enjoyment and benefits of bicycle riding. I began cycling about 50 miles a week, which translates into three to four hours of moderately vigorous aerobics exercise. That was in addition to my weekly workout regime of going to the gym three days a week, for about 45 minutes of weight training and 45 minutes of jogging. When winter time came around, I found myself sniffling one day. I assumed I was getting a cold because for as long as I can remember I've reliably gotten two colds every winter. Each cold caused me at least one week's worth of misery. However, after a couple of days of sniffling the symptoms went away. The same thing happened again about six weeks later. When I finally came down with a cold, the symptoms were so muted that my wife, Mary, had to point out how much I was sniffling and sneezing and "looking like I had a cold" before I realized it. I didn't miss any work or cut back too much on activities and only experienced a bit of the typical yep-I-got-a-cold symptoms for about two days. It would appear that the increased aerobics activity strengthened my immune system to the point where my body fought off two colds and only marginally succumbed to a third one. It was very gratifying to see the results of implementing the *Do Not Go Gentle* philosophy, and it helped motivate me to continue writing this book.

The effects of regular exercise and a healthy diet seem to be cumulative. During the second winter after I began riding my bicycle 50 miles a week and eating a vegan diet, I never even came down with the sniffles. I believe the cold germs weren't able to break through my healthy immune system. And 2010 was the winter of the swine flu epidemic. I also did a record number of ADHD assessments on small children, many of whom were sniffling and sneezing all around my office. Seeing improvements like this firsthand in my own life is more convincing than reading the most carefully crafted scientific studies, and it convinces me beyond doubt that exercise and a sensible diet really do make a drastic difference in your health. That's why I invite you to try out the principles of successful aging for yourself. Don't just read about it or take my word for it. Besides, if you don't like a healthy lifestyle, you can always go back to being a couch potato and junk food junkie. Just keep your medicine chest stocked full of all those cold remedies and make sure you have plenty of sick leave for the days you'll be missing from work.

Exercise Delays or Prevents Age-Related Decline

Age isn't the limiting factor people think it is, especially in endurance. We've tested 70- and 80-year-old athletes who have cardiovascular fitness levels similar to an average college student. Dr. Hank Williford, exercise researcher[20]

Both aerobic and anaerobic exercise can slow down the rate of aging. Handbook of the Psychology of Aging[21]

Exercise is important at any age, but even more so as we get older. As we advance in age into our senior years, our bodies undergo changes in body mass and metabolism. Two things that customarily have been attributed to normal aging processes happen to aging human bodies. First, hormonal changes make us more prone to get diabetes, and the incidence of diabetes increases sharply with age. Second, muscle mass tends to decline while body fat increases, resulting in increased body mass index (BMI). The increase in BMI is associated with decreased longevity and increased mortality from heart disease, stroke, cancer, and most other diseases customarily associated with old age. The good news is that current research demonstrates how both factors are not inevitable consequences of aging but more the result of aging combined with not taking care of yourself through proper exercise and nutrition while you age.

Can You Win the Battle of the Bulge?

One of the most well-established facts of biological gerontology is that with aging, muscle mass decreases and fat mass increases, while the metabolic rate decreases. In other words, as we get older, we get fatter and more out of shape even though we eat less. Isn't that the truth!? Up until recently this has been considered a normal part of the aging process, attributed to decreased metabolism because of declining production of growth hormone. What this means in practical terms is that there's not much you can do about it except eat like a bird. In the film *A Prairie Home Companion*, Garrison Keillor jokes about taking on a new diet when he became a senior citizen—one meal and two light snacks per day.

Fortunately, recent research shows that we're not powerless against the forces of aging debility. A Swiss research team from the Medical University in Berne concluded that "regular physical training seems to prevent changes in body composition and fuel metabolism normally associated with aging."[22] Thirty-year-old men who never exercised were compared to 70-year-old men who either never exercised or who jogged an average of 18 miles a week for the past 10 years. As you would expect, the sedentary older men had the highest body fat with the least amount of muscle mass and the lowest ability to burn fat. Fat-burning metabolism in the older men who exercised was lower than the younger men but much better than the sedentary elders. The big surprise was that there was no difference in the body mass of the exercising elders and the sedentary youngsters. In other words, 70-year-old fitness buffs have essentially the same body mass as 30-year-olds who don't exercise!

The conclusion is clear—exercise is crucial in old age. You may be able to get by without exercising when you are 30, but your body really suffers from the sedentary lifestyle at age 70. There are several perspectives here, of course, depending on your age. If you're a 30-year-old couch potato, it can be a wake-up call to realize that you have the body of a 70-year-old man who keeps fit. From the fit elders' perspective, it is humbling to know that you really have to work your butt off (literally!) to keep your body as fit as a 30-year-old who does nothing at all. If you're a 70-year-old couch potato—well, you probably need to reserve a bed at your local nursing home.

How are the baby boomers faring in the battle of the bulge? Not very well at all, according to the American Hospital Association, and the prognosis for their retirement years is quite grim.

The Pending Boomer Diabetes Epidemic

Exercise is part of a healthy lifestyle for everyone, and it's especially important for people with diabetes. American Diabetes Association[23]

The American Hospital Association (AHA) makes some gloomy predictions in their provocatively titled report *When I'm 64: How Boomers Will Change Health Care.*[24] According to the AHA, by the year 2030, when all the boomers have reached age 65 and are officially senior citizen boomers:

- One out of three boomers will be obese.
- One out of four boomers will suffer from diabetes.
- One out of two boomers will have arthritis.
- Six out of ten boomers will suffer from more than one chronic health problem.

Baby boomers are being diagnosed with diabetes 17 years younger than their parents' generation. It seems that the boomers are doing everything in larger measures than their predecessors—including contracting the diseases of old age sooner!

Diabetes can strike at any age, but it is a well-known fact that the incidence of diabetes increases steadily with age. For example, currently at age 65 about 8 percent of seniors have diabetes, whereas 25 percent are afflicted at age 85. If the AHA prediction is accurate, then three times as many boomers will suffer from diabetes as their parents' generation did at retirement time!

Getting diabetes will guarantee that you age unsuccessfully. Diabetes results in a 10 to 15 year reduction in the average lifespan and is listed as the sixth major cause of death in the United States today by the American Federation for Aging Research.[25] Moreover, diabetes contributes to death from heart disease, stroke, and kidney failure—listed as the first, third, and ninth causes of death by the Centers for Disease Control.[26] Diabetic elders are in the hospital two to three times as often as elders without the disease and use primary care health services two to three times as much.

Is contracting diabetes inevitable? Not in the least. The risk of getting diabetes increases with age, in part because of Americans' tendency to put on fat and also because our bodies become less efficient in processing sugar. Fortunately, exercise improves insulin action and can reverse age-related declines in hormones.[27] Exercise is one of the best ways to avoid getting type 2 diabetes (which accounts for 90 to 95 percent of all diabetes) or to reverse diabetes if you've already got it. The American Diabetes Association strongly advocates exercise and asserts that *"type 2 diabetes can be prevented through modest lifestyle changes and losing about 5 to 7 percent of body weight."*[28]

According to studies in the United States and China by the World Health Organization: "Relatively moderate changes in lifestyle, especially increasing physical activity and improving diet, are sufficient to prevent the development of almost 60 percent of type II diabetes cases."[29] A team of Canadian researchers found that either aerobics training or resistance exercises (like weight lifting) can be "an important part of diabetic care," but both together "results in better blood sugar control after 6 months."[30]

How a Wyoming Man Beat Diabetes

The good news is that in most Type 2 cases, diabetes can be prevented or at least controlled, through diet and exercise. American Association of Retired Persons[31]

Les Engelter, a retired teacher and principal from Sheridan, Wyoming, enjoyed good health throughout his career life, boasting, "I visited my doctor as little as possible."[32] Then one day his doctor informed him that he had high blood pressure, high cholesterol, and blood sugar abnormalities. Further testing indicated early stage diabetes. He dreaded the diagnosis because his father suffered miserably from diabetes. "I remembered what the disease did to his body over time," he told AARP.

Engelter didn't take the bad news lying down. He got more exercise, increased his vegetable intake, and reduced the carbohydrates and sugars in his diet. "If I wasn't in the grocery store reading labels, I was out walking my neighborhood, trying to bring my blood sugar level down," he wrote. Self-management through lifestyle changes paid off. In 8 months, he lost 30 pounds and at his follow-up annual physical learned that "I had reached nondiabetic status!"

"I am healthier under my new regimen," he told AARP readers, "and I also learned to really appreciate broccoli!" What more can be said? Except that Engelter is AARP Wyoming's state president, and he plays the accordion for nursing home residents in his spare time. And he will probably avoid going into a nursing home himself by paying attention to the principles of successful aging.

Regular Exercise for Chronic Disease Prevention

Physical activity is at the crux of successful aging. Rowe and Kahn, *Successful Aging*[33]

Adults, by engaging in regular physical activity, can promote and maintain health, and reduce risk of chronic disease and premature mortality. American Heart Association[34]

Inactivity leads to loss of bodily flexibility and causes bones to become thinner and more fragile. Sedentary individuals are more likely to develop bone and joint problems like osteoporosis and arthritis. Regular exercise can protect against degenerative conditions like osteoporosis and thinning bones.[35] All the major authorities recommend exercise, and the earlier in life you start, the greater your chance of avoiding late-life problems. A recent article in the *British Journal of Sports Medicine* announced: "Vigorous physical activity in children is likely to stave off knee osteoarthritis in later life."[36]

Regular exercise can reduce blood pressure, lower weight and reduce obesity, and decrease the risk of coronary heart disease. According to the Center for Disease Control's website on diabetes, "moderate weight loss and exercise can prevent or delay type 2 diabetes among adults at high-risk of diabetes."[37] Manson and colleagues studied 90,000 middle-aged women over an eight-year period and found that vigorous exercise at least once a week lowered their risk of developing diabetes.[38] Regular exercise can reduce blood glucose levels, cholesterol, and body fat—it can even lower the risk for some types of cancer.

According to the World Health Organization, regular physical exercise helps to prevent or reduce hypertension and osteoporosis.[39] It can also reduce the risk of lower back pain, help manage problems with chronic knee and back pain, and reduce the risk of hip fractures in women. Regular physical activity "helps build and maintain healthy bones, muscles and joints and make people with chronic, disabling conditions improve their stamina."

Jobs that require more exercise can actually be better for you. In a study of nearly 400 longshoremen followed for 22 years, those who burned more than 8,500 kcal per week had a "significantly lower risk of coronary heart disease" than workers in positions that required less energy.[40]

Alzheimer's and Exercise

Regular physical exercise is probably the best means we have of preventing Alzheimer's disease today—better than medications, better than intellectual activity, better than supplements and diet. Dr. Ronald Peterson, Mayo Clinic director of Alzheimer's research[41]

What about Alzheimer's disease, that dreaded fear of seniors everywhere? First the bad news. The Alzheimer's Association has predicted that 10 million American baby boomers will develop Alzheimer's disease—that's one in every eight. The good news is that aerobics exercise can reduce brain atrophy and lessen the chances of Alzheimer's and other forms of dementia. A team of researchers at the University of North Carolina at Chapel Hill has discovered that individuals who maintain a high level of aerobic activity have healthier brains, with significantly less atrophy than individuals with a low activity level.[42] Many scientific studies have shown that elders who exercise or remain physically active have less cognitive impairment than elders who don't. Angelo Lunde, Mayo Clinic health education outreach coordination, summarizes "mounting evidence" from medical research in support of exercise and physical activity for Alzheimer's.[43]

1. Scientists have bred rats to develop Alzheimer's disease. Alzheimer's prone rats that are allowed to exercise have 50 to 80 percent less Alzheimer's brain plaque than sedentary rats.
2. Women age 65 or older who remain physically active experience less decline in mental functioning than inactive senior women. This is based on a longitudinal study of 6,000 elderly women who were followed for a period of 8 years.
3. You can lower your risk of getting Alzheimer's with as little as 30 minutes of moderate exercise several times a week.

Walk 50 Miles a Month

No one is too old to enjoy the benefits of regular physical activity. Centers for Disease Control[44]

Would you consider making a commitment to walk 50 miles a month? I know that sounds like a lot, but it breaks down to only 30 minutes a day at a brisk pace of three and one-half miles an hour. This is the advice of the *AARP Bulletin* for retirees.[45] What's in it for you by committing to these daily jaunts? You will increase your aerobic capacity and physical function and lower your risk of disability, arthritis, Alzheimer's, type 2 diabetes, heart disease, stroke, and cancer. You will lose about a pound a month and reduce your medical bills about $2,500 a year if you are overweight (like the majority of Americans). According to the Centers for Disease Control, walking 30 minutes a day "promotes psychological well-being," reduces depression and anxiety, and lowers your risk of dying prematurely.[46] Daily walking helps control weight and builds strong bones, joints, and muscles—which "helps older adults become stronger and better able to move about without falling."

A daily stroll can lower the risk of developing high blood pressure or reduce blood pressure that is already high. In a public health study conducted in Belfast, Ireland, 30 minutes of brisk walking 3 to 5 days a week lowered the blood pressure and decreased the waist and hip size of sedentary adults between the ages of 40 and 61 (the boomer generation, more or less).[47]

It seems that a daily stroll is a pretty good investment of time and energy—especially if you're retired (or even if you're not) and are looking for sensible activities to occupy your leisure moments.

Keeping Fit with Fido

Dog walking is a purposeful physical activity that may have health benefits for humans and canines. S.A. Ham and J. Epping, Centers for Disease Control[48]

Take your dog with you on your daily walk and double your pleasure—and your health benefits. M. Motooka and associates from Hokkaido, Japan, found that "walking a dog has potentially greater health benefits as a buffer against stress in senior citizens than walking without a dog."[49] Dog walking improves the functioning of the autonomic nervous system (ANS), which regulates heart muscles, internal organs, and the immune system. Dog walking is highly recommended for seniors because ANS function tends to deteriorate with age, and dysfunction of the ANS can contribute to serious disease and impair the quality of your life. If you can't walk the dog, don't worry, because Motooka found that "independent of actually walking, merely patting and talking to a dog also raises parasympathetic neural activity."

In their review of controlled studies over the past 50 years—titled "Is There a Scientific Basis for Pet Therapy?"—S. Giaquinto and F. Valentini from Rome, Italy, found "consistent evidence of the protective effect against cardiovascular risk, mainly through the moderate exercise prompted by walking a dog. Indeed, walking a dog may contribute to a physically active lifestyle."[50] This makes sense, because some people aren't inclined to exercise for their own welfare, but they might hoof it for the benefit of their four-legged friends. As a matter of fact, in a three-year study from Johns Hopkins University, R. J. Thorpe and colleagues in the Division of Geriatric Medicine found that "dog owners were more likely to engage in physical activity than non-dog-pet or non-pet owners."[51] (By the way, a lot of dogs are named Fido, which means "I trust" in Latin, because Fido was the name of Abraham Lincoln's dog.)

How About Those Mall Walkers

It seems like every time I go to the local shopping mall, there are more and more elderly citizens out doing their mall walking. Mall walking appears to be a very simple and convenient way to get a little exercise. But does it really work or is it just an advertising gimmick to get the elders out to spend their money? The *Canadian Journal on Aging* reports a pilot study of 52 sixty-six-year-olds that "supports the feasibility of and positive health improvements associated with mall walking."[52] The article concludes that mall walking and similar programs "should be considered as part of health-promotion programs, especially for the aging population."

A Temple University study found that "a brisk walk can reduce a variety of psychological symptoms such as stress, anxiety and depression" among the aging population.[53] Researchers followed 380 Philadelphia women for over 8 years, beginning when they were 42 years old. Postmenopausal African American women benefited the most from high levels of physical activity. This was not an organized program done in a health spa or university fitness center: "These women walked outside on city blocks or in shopping malls. Groups could organize to take walks after dinner. It didn't require going to the gym."

In other words, you can exercise pretty much anywhere, anytime. If you make it part of your daily routine, then you will develop healthy habits that will last a lifetime.

Exercise from A to Z (for all ages and inclinations)

Aerobics workout, amusement park strolls, apple orchard walking (any wooded area will do), acrobatics

Bicycling, ballroom dancing, bowling, bocce ball, badminton, ballet, bench pressing, baseball, basketball, backpacking, boating, beach walking, beach-ball tossing, bird watching, bronco busting, bull riding,

Calisthenics, chin-ups, cutting the grass, cleaning windows, camping, child care (counts as moderate to intense exercise with ADHD children), canoeing, cleaning the house, croquet, cycling, cross-country skiing, climbing hills, conditioning exercises, climbing trees, catching (baseballs, footballs, Frisbees, etc.), cave explorations

Dancing, digging, dog walking, diving, dog sled racing, dodge ball skirmishes

Elevator—Take the stairs instead, exercise a little or exercise a lot in every way you can; everybody should do it—EVERY DAY.

Football, Frisbee throwing, farming, field trips, flamenco dancing, flexibility stretches, flying a kite

Golf, grocery shopping (the bigger the store the better), gardening, gymnastics

Hiking, hula hoop twirling, hula dancing, handball, health club classes, horseback riding, hockey, hang gliding, horseshoe tossing, hopscotch

Intramural sports, ice skating, igloo building, ice hockey, isotonic workouts, ice sculpting, Iditarod dog sled racing

Jogging, jumping rope, jumping jacks, judo, jujitsu

Kite flying, karate, kayaking, kickball, and kickboxing stretches

Lifting weights, lawn work, leg lifts, low-impact aerobics, Latin dancing (especially the tango)

Mall walking, moving furniture or household items, mowing the lawn, marathon races, mambo dancing, martial arts, mountain climbing, museum visits (the bigger ones can be like a marathon!)

Nature trails, neighborhood walks or jogs

Olympic pool swimming, ornithological expeditions (bird watching hikes)

Push-ups, pushing a stroller, wheelchair, or grocery cart, Pilate's exercises, pogo stick, physical therapy, protest marching, parades, pecan picking (or you can gather any other kind of nuts—a lot of bending and stooping with this exercise)

Quality time with a friend while taking a stroll or doing any other light activity

Rowing, rope climbing, roller skating, racquetball, raking leaves, running in place

Swimming, stationary bicycle, stretching, skiing, stair climbing, scuba diving or snorkeling, surfing, sit-ups, soccer, softball, sports of all kinds, sweeping the floor, scrubbing floors, shoveling, shuffleboard, skateboarding, sexual activity, swap meet sauntering, stationary bicycling, spin cycling

Tai chi, trimming the hedges or trees, tennis, treadmill, trampoline, taekwondo, triathlons

Underwater swimming or snorkeling, unicycle riding

Volleyball, vacuuming, visiting a museum, visiting neighbors across the way and going for a walk with them around the neighborhood

Walking, weight lifting, water polo, water aerobics, window shopping walks, weeding, water skiing, washing or waxing the car, wrestling, wheelchair pushing, walking the dog, and waltzing

X marks the spot to add your own favorite exercise:

_____

Yoga, YMCA visits or activities, yard work of all kinds

Zebra watching on a safari walk, zoo walking

Activities and Solutions

Reflect on your experiences with exercise. Have you ever felt the direct benefits from exercise, through some type of major change in your life or other activity? What types of exercise do you like and why? Which are you willing to commit to on a regular basis?

Notes:

_____

_____

_____

_____

_____

_____

_____

Chapter 3

Psychology for the Health of It

You may wonder why I am taking so much interest in exercise and physical fitness. After all, I'm a psychologist and not a gym teacher or a trainer from the local health club. Besides, the world *psychology* literally means a study of the *psyche*, which is the Greek word for mind or soul. Shouldn't I be pushing positive thinking or talking about emotions, mental health, and all that touchy-feely stuff?

The fact is that modern psychology has developed many new specializations to accommodate our ever-expanding knowledge of human behavior. One of those specialties is *health psychology*, which is the application of psychology "to the promotion and maintenance of health, the promotion and treatment of illness and related dysfunction."[1]

Health psychology encourages individuals to be responsible for their health and wellness. Taking responsibility for the quality of your own life is one of the fundamental requirements for successful aging. When you increase your level of exercise and physical fitness, you help to assure the healthiness of your body, mind, and soul as you get older.

Discovering the tremendous benefits of vigorous exercise in later life convinced me to practice psychology for the health of it. My personal experience with the transformational power of exercise allows me to add first hand experience to the research findings. At two crucial times in my life, a commitment to exercise and physical fitness produced drastic improvements in my psychological state. As a teenager I was so out of shape that I couldn't even do a single chin-up. The gym teacher used to call me "Cow-nacki"—so I had to deal with both him and the paperboy picking on me. I felt embarrassed, humiliated, and powerless. After several months of working out at the gym I got physically fit and strong, and then I felt proud, confident, and powerful. Later as a mature adult of fifty, I was so overweight and unfit that I couldn't even climb into my new sports car. I felt depressed and defeated, and I pictured myself as an old and decrepit fuddy-duddy, well past my prime and way over the hill. After several months of exercise at the gym, I felt vibrant, alive, and exhilarated, and I adopted a new vision of myself as a healthy, athletic, and dignified man of middle age.

Personal experience greatly enhances my understanding of the research on aging and sickness. It's one thing to read about the devastating effects of illness and debility and how to overcome it; it's an entirely different matter to become ill or debilitated yourself and then actually to overcome the condition. You move from the realm of theory to a proven fact. There are some things in life that you can only know by direct experience. From simple events like the smell of a freshly cut lemon to more complex phenomena like falling in love for the first time or having a religious conversion, there is no substitute for direct experience. Intellectual knowledge and verbal descriptions are often shabby substitutes for the real thing. As Shakespeare put it, "There are more things in heaven and earth, Horatio, than are dreamt of in your philosophy."[2]

Personal experience is the reason I've included activities and exercises at the end of each chapter. Don't just take my word on the things I talk about. Try them out for yourself. Experience the benefits of successful aging directly in your own life, and then you will know the truth in a way that books can't teach you.

I highly recommend watching the movie *The Doctor* (1991). William Hurt plays a know-it-all doctor who develops throat cancer, and in the process of being a patient he learns about illness in a way medical school could never teach him. He gains humility, learns to live more actively in the present, and discovers the importance of relationships in our lives—things you don't learn from college textbooks.

Health Psychology and Exercise

There is no drug in current or prospective use that holds as much promise for sustained health as a lifetime program of physical exercise.
Walter Bortz, MD[3]

Exercise that promotes physical fitness is relevant to the psychology of aging for several reasons. The first and most important reasons is that there is a direct relationship between our physical, emotional, and mental states—which is what health psychology is all about. There is no separation between mind and body, because both influence each other. You can't do something good for the body, such as exercise, without seeing mental improvements—and vice versa. Physicians and philosophers from antiquity through the present day have promoted the body-mind connection. Volumes of scientific research indicate that abundant exercise leads to improvements in mental health and spiritual well-being. In his motivational classic *On Running*, Dr. George Sheehan, a heart specialist and self-confessed exercise enthusiast, advocates that we "begin with the body. The body mirrors the soul and the mind, and is much more accessible than either."[4] In *Health Psychology: A Textbook*, Jane Ogden concludes that "exercise is regarded as central to promoting good health both in terms of physical and psychological well-being."[5]

Every individual is ultimately accountable for his or her own state of health. When we recognize the interaction of physical, social, and psychological factors, then "the individual is no longer simply seen as a passive victim" and "the patient is therefore in part responsible for their treatment,"[6] according to health psychologist Jane Ogden. When we take an active role in our own state of health, many good things come about. Dr. Sheehan once confided to a colleague that most seasoned runners know how to treat athletic injuries better than most doctors: "The doctor is educated in the treatment of disease, not in health. This is a much more difficult subject. Health is the study of the universe."[7]

Second, exercising is something easy to do and the changes can be felt almost immediately. When you get physical, you breathe faster, get more oxygen to the brain, and you feel better. As runner-physician George Sheehan observed: "Running pays off, and it pays off today. Exercise gives instant and exhilarating effects."[8] Sister Madonna Buder, "the Iron Nun," told reporters that "heading to the finish line of the Ironman was an analogy to me of getting to the Pearly Gates—I think that is why I smile every time at the finish."[9]

Third, if you are physically fit, you are more likely to have good mental health. There is plenty of evidence to show that exercise and physical fitness are linked to high self-esteem and positive mental states. When you exercise, you are taking positive action to change your life, and this increases self-confidence. Exercise and activity take your mind off worries and problems. I learned this firsthand while in grad school: Ten to fifteen minutes of muscle relaxation exercises before bed rejuvenated me better than a full night's sleep without the exercise. When you are physically active, you are not sitting on the couch feeling sorry for yourself. When you take action, you gain a sense of personal empowerment as soon as you put your first foot forward. It's hard to stew in hopelessness when you are walking around the block, and it's difficult to be totally despondent when you are working out at the gym. If nothing else, the activity takes your attention away from morbid thoughts.

Fourth, exercise and physical fitness may be a necessary first step to continue growing in other areas. Psychologist Abraham Maslow discovered a hierarchy of basic human needs.[10] Physiological needs like diet, health, and physical fitness must be satisfied before you can satisfy psychological needs like self-esteem, love, etc. Generally, our needs must be met in order, from the lowest to highest.

Finally, a profusion of scientific research demonstrates clearly that exercise and physical fitness are vital to maintain a healthy body, mind, and soul as we age.

Healthy Body, Mind, and Soul for Successful Aging

I feel much stronger after I'm surfing than before I go. Woody Brown, 89-year-old surfer[11]

- It's never too late to start exercising or increase your activity level, and you can still derive benefits regardless of your state of mental or physical health.

- Exercise improves the mind and emotions as well as the body.
- Psychological factors enhance the functioning of the immune system, which leads to better health and greater happiness.
- Exercise improves mental functioning, raises self-esteem, and increases your general satisfaction with life.
- Exercise can reduce negative emotions like anger and hostility and improve your general sense of well-being.
- Exercise improves mental health. It can prevent depression and anxiety disorders or reduce the severity of these conditions.
- Exercise is beneficial at any age but increasingly important as we grow older. It can increase longevity and improve the general quality of your life in many ways.
- In short, exercise helps you look younger, feel younger, and think younger at any age.

Improved Self-Esteem

Exercise and physical fitness seem to go hand in hand with high self-esteem. There is abundant psychological research showing that people who exercise a lot and keep physically fit have higher self-esteem than those who don't.

Of course, the question arises what comes first? There's logical sense in believing that if you have high self-esteem, you will be more prone to exercise and take care of yourself and be more physically fit. On the contrary, if you have low self-esteem, you won't care about yourself enough to exercise.

However, it is clear from several controlled, randomized scientific studies that exercise and physical fitness can generate self-esteem and reduce negative emotional states. In a review of research over a 10-year period, Plante and Rodin found that "exercise improves mood and psychological well-being and enhances self-concept and self-esteem."[12] Another review found that exercise "reduces anxiety, depression, and negative mood, and improves self-esteem and cognitive functioning."[13]

Exercise may indirectly improve self-esteem by first improving your physical fitness. In other words, when you exercise you lose weight and get healthier, and it is because of these physical changes that your self-esteem improves. Abby King and her research team from the Stanford University School of Medicine found that exercise generally leads to improved body satisfaction, which in turn leads to greater self-esteem and confidence.[14]

Reduction of Negative Emotions

Negative emotions, especially anger and hostility, can have a detrimental impact on health. In a well-respected review of 45 research studies, Miller and colleagues found that *hostility* was a risk factor for coronary heart disease above and beyond other factors like age, sex, high BMI, excessive alcohol consumption, smoking, high anxiety or depression, high caffeine consumption, and high blood pressure.[15] Yikes! Better get some anger-management counseling before you keel over from a heart attack. By the way, death by heart attack was a commonly used measure of the outcome in the studies.

There is a strong correlation between exercise and level of depression. As you might expect, getting more exercise and physical activity is a good way to reduce negative emotions. In study after study researchers have found that depression is strongly correlated with inactivity, whereas people who exercise more tend to be less depressed.

Exercise is effective in reducing anger, hostility, depression, and anxiety. Exercise is good for preventing or reducing the severity of most of the chronic health problems that are associated with aging. It is also a well-proven method to enhance your psychological health and mental well-being.

Old Age and Depression

Old age is a shipwreck. Charles DeGaulle
Life is one long process of getting tired. Samuel Butler

Many people believe that depression is inevitable with old age. Not so, according to psychiatrist George Vaillant, who boldly proclaims that *"successful aging is not an oxymoron."*[16]

In *Aging Well*, his longitudinal review of nearly 1,000 elders, Dr. Vaillant concludes: "The majority of older people, without brain disease, maintain a sense of modest well-being until the final months before they die. Not only are they less depressed than the general population, but also a majority of the elderly suffer little incapacitating illness until the final one that kills them."[17]

According to the U.S. National Library of Medicine's *Medical Encyclopedia*: "Physical exercise programs involving walking or other forms of aerobic exercise can reduce depression in older adults."[18] Timothy A. Rogge, MD, a psychiatrist who contributes to the *Encyclopedia*, especially recommends "group-based physical exercise programs involving walking or other forms of aerobic exercise."

Exercise reduces depression in people of all ages, but it is especially beneficial to the aging population. Depression is a significant cause of disability among the elderly, and disabled elders are also more prone to become depressed. Among the general population, anywhere from 8 to 20 percent of people over 65 living in the community report symptoms of depression and the rate is nearly doubled (17 to 35 percent) for seniors in primary-care settings like hospitals and nursing homes.[19] Fortunately, relief is just a short walk away—literally. And you don't need to join an expensive health club, invest in budget-breaking exercise machinery, or trek off on a wilderness expedition to get it.

Dr. George Sheehan affirmed that becoming a runner at age 45 helped him over the slump of "middle-aged melancholia."[20] Researchers at Duke University found that a moderate amount of regular walking "was equally effective as medication after 16 weeks of treatment," according to a five-year study of elderly individuals suffering from major depressive disorder.[21] Researchers selected 156 individuals between the ages of 50 and 77, and randomly assigned[22] them to take antidepressant medication, participate in aerobic exercise, or do both. The exercise involved walking around a track for 30 minutes three times a week. All three groups of patients "exhibited a significant decline in depressive symptoms." Patients who got the medication showed more rapid relief from symptoms initially, but after 16 weeks "exercise was equally effective in reducing depression."

A survey of British elders from the University of Portsmouth found that walking your dog on a daily basis "can ward off depression."[23] Elderly dog walkers were able to "stay physically fitter and maintain social contacts," compared to elders who didn't enjoy the great outdoors with their canine companions. Even "if they were feeling low, they always felt better once they were outside," and afterwards they enjoyed a "better overall sense of well-being" and ended up "feeling happier."

Psychological Factors Enhance Immunity

Positive emotional states may promote healthy perceptions, beliefs, and physical well-being itself. Peter Salovey, Yale psychologist[24]

Until about 30 years ago, medical researchers believed that the human immune system operated independently of other bodily functions—especially psychological factors. In the mid-nineteenth century, Louis Pasteur discovered that germs can cause disease, and ever since the *contagion theory* has shaped modern medical practice. According to this theory, sickness is due to the invasion of germs, and healing takes place when medications kill the germs. Quite simply, when you get sick, you go to the doctor to get some pills, then you take the pills and get well.

However, germs are around us all the time and many people who are exposed to them don't become ill. Why do some people get sick and others don't? Scientists have discovered that some people are more immune to disease than others, and so mere exposure to germs does not guarantee that anyone will get sick. There are many factors that affect the functioning of our immune system. An ever-growing body of scientific research demonstrates that our beliefs, emotions, mood, and stress levels can directly effect the functioning of our immune system.[25] A new discipline has sprung up, called *psychoneuroimmunology*, which is basically a fancy name for the old concept of mind over matter, or positive thinking.

The science of mind over matter has literally come of age within the lifetime of the baby boomers. In study after study, researchers have found that positive mood is linked to better immune system functioning and greater health; this also means that negative mood is linked to worse functioning of the immune system and poorer health.

Dr. Peter Salovey and his colleagues summarized the scientific research that "examines the influence of emotional states on physical health."[26] I think it was appropriate that this review was published in the January 2000 millennial issue of the *American Psychologist* because this line of thinking is future oriented and represents a sharp break from the nineteenth and mid-twentieth centuries' contagion theory of disease. It is becoming increasingly clear that our emotional states can have a direct effect on immunity and illness. On the dark side, for instance, "negative emotional experiences cause one to be more vulnerable to illness," according to Salovey.[27] For example, older women who cry more have more health problems, according to Labott and Martin.[28] People who are depressed report more sickness than people who aren't depressed. Negative moods stimulate the production of more cancer cells. On the bright side, positive emotional states are associated with better health, especially improved immune system and cardiovascular functioning. Positive moods inhibit the proliferation of cancer cells and speed healing.

The Biochemistry of Laughter

Humor is especially beneficial, according to the findings from a series of experiments by Professor Kathleen Dillon and her colleagues from the Department of Psychology, Western New England College in Springfield, Massachusetts. Humor increases the level of immunoglobulin A (IgA) to help us fight off infections. Dillon showed groups of students either a humorous videotape or a serious film. Students who watched the silly movie showed improved immune system functioning, but students who watched the serious film did not. Dillon also found that the students who routinely used humor as a way of coping had greater immunity protection than those who didn't. Dillon concluded that "the use of humor as a coping style in everyday life" may help to "enhance immunity in the long term."[29] A follow-up study tested her theory about the protective function of humor. Breastfeeding mothers with better humor coping got fewer upper respiratory infections than mothers who didn't use humor to cope—and so did their babies! It seems that the humor-loving moms had very high levels of immunoglobulin A (IgA), which got passed through their breast milk, so their infants developed greater immune protection. In a similar study, Labott and her associates found that IgA levels can change in direct response to our emotional states; IgA levels increased when college women watched a funny video but decreased when they watched a sad video.[30]

The old school of gerontology research emphasizes that our immune system experiences a sharp decline as we get older. If so, then we all need to laugh a lot more as we age. Indeed, perhaps the increased use of humor among the elderly reported by some researchers is nature's way of protecting us?

Simple Solutions to Common Aging Problems

You'll always be young if you have old friends. Miss Mary's Durn Good Therapy Guidebook

Here are some pain-free and nonsurgical solutions to common aging problems, based on the real-life experiences of the author and his wife.

Problem: You wake up and see a new wrinkle in the mirror.

Solution: Find another mirror.

Problem: People you know make nasty comments about your appearance.

Solution: Get new friends.

Problem: You wake up with a new ache or pain.

Solution: Stop doing what you were doing the day before. It's like the patient who complains: "Doctor, it hurts when I do this," to which the doctor replies, "Well, don't do that!

Laughter Yoga and Elder Humor

A light heart lives long. Irish proverb

Indian physician Madan Kataria promotes the practice of *laughter yoga*. He and his protégés have formed laughter clubs all around the world. The clubs are very popular in Japan, which has the longest-lived people and the largest elderly population of any country in the world. There are currently 33 registered laughter clubs in Japan, where group leaders have brought activities into senior centers and nursing homes. According to Dr. Kataria's website: "It's the aged who report maximum benefit from laughing. They respond dramatically to laughter sessions and the exercise can transform their state of health." Laughter might even slow down the advance of Alzheimer's.[31]

For her dissertation research, Dina Rebeca Madrid conducted an experiment to study how humor affects the immune system functioning in older adults.[32] She found that 15 minutes after receiving a "humor intervention," a group of elders had more lymphocytes (white blood cells) and T suppressor cells (cancer fighters) than a group who didn't get the intervention; the humor effect lasted for at least 24 hours.

I love the irony of this line of scientific investigation. It proves that watching silly movies is not just first-rate fun, but it can also have a seriously positive impact on your health and well-being. This type of research refutes the old adage that if something feels good then it must be immoral, illegal, or bad for you. How often can you do something you really, really enjoy that's actually good for you? Maybe physicians need to play the Comedy Channel or the Cartoon Network on their office TVs instead of the news network or soap operas? Especially since the scientific research shows quite clearly that stress and negative emotions reduce the effectiveness of our immune systems.

We ignore the humorous dimension of life at our own peril. So the advice I give to everyone is lighten up or else! Lighten up or else you won't be as healthy as you can be. Lighten up or else you won't have a full and satisfying life. My wife has been on my case for years not to watch serious movies after working all day in a stressful office. She absolutely insists on watching a comedy show or silly movie in the evenings after she's provided eight to ten hours of psychotherapy. (As you might expect, we have all eleven seasons of *Frazier* on video, and last year for Christmas Santa Claus brought Mary the complete series of *I Love Lucy* on DVD.)

The Breath of Life

The secret of longevity is to keep breathing! Sophie Tucker—Last of the Red Hot Mamas (1884-1966)

Comedians are unwittingly helping all of us extend our lives. Perhaps health care insurance should start paying our way to visit the local comedy club or buy us tickets to see the funny movies at the neighborhood theater.

Hearty laughter is similar to aerobics exercise because it increases respiratory rate. Aerobics exercise is beneficial for many reasons. It strengthens the muscles used in respiration, increases lung capacity, and circulates more blood and lymph fluids, which improves immune system functioning, reduces the chance of infection, and promotes healing. Getting more oxygen to your brain can create a feeling of relaxation and well-being.

The simple act of breathing is something most of us take for granted. Yet for many Americans, breathing can be a challenging experience because of asthma and lung disease, allergies, sleep apnea, or even the common cold. Air pollution in urban areas also takes its toll. Lung capacity and functioning generally decline with age. "The effects of aging on the lungs are physiologically and anatomically similar to those that occur during the development of mild emphysema," according to the *Merck Manual of Geriatrics*.[33]

Maximum lung capacity is called *peak flow*. Peak flow is measured by breathing out as hard and as long as you can. Greater peak flow is associated with a lower death rate among older individuals and is associated with cardiovascular fitness and a high level of physical and mental functioning.[34] That's a good reason to stay physically fit and active as you get older. So get out there and ride those bicycles, go to the gym and pump that iron, or dance in the streets if you wish! Go to a studio wrestling match or a local ball game and shout your lungs out. You'll feel a lot better than if you just stay home and watch the evening news. If you do stay home, at least watch a funny movie and experience the health benefits of a good belly laugh.

Spirituality and Exercise

It is exercise alone that supports the spirit and keeps the mind in vigor. Cicero, Roman philosopher (died 43 BC)

Exercise can enrich one's spirituality. It is an important component of a life that is balanced physically, emotionally, mentally, and spiritually. The ancient Greeks knew this, and that's why they created the Olympics games and promoted gymnastics as an integral part of the educational process. Twenty-five hundred years ago the philosopher Plato wrote that "lack of activity destroys the good condition of every human being, while movement and methodical physical exercise save it and preserve it." The renowned Roman physician Claudius Galen (131-201 AD) promoted exercise as one of his Laws of Health, together with breathing fresh air and eating proper foods. He also wrote a book called *The Best Physician is also a Philosopher.*

In modern America we still require exercise in the primary schools, but not at the university level, and most adults have dispensed with exercise all together. That's too bad, because we never lose our need for physical activity. It can even help to restore our sense of spiritual well-being when experiencing a midlife crisis.

When Dr. George Sheehan took up long-distance running in midlife he was going through an existential crisis. "I had lost my sense of purpose, my faith in what I was doing, my caring for creation and creatures," he confesses in *On Running.*[35] He found new meaning and purpose through vigorous physical activity: "In the creative action of running I become convinced of my own importance, certain that my life had significance." For Sheehan, running promises "the development of maximum physical capabilities which in turn helps us to find our maximum spiritual and intellectual potential." Sister Madonna Buder, the "Iron Nun," discovered vigorous exercise in midlife and it became a realization of her faith. She became a nun at 23 and began running when she was 47, upon the recommendation of her priest, for "spiritual enrichment." By age 79 she had competed over 300 triathlons and won a wall full of medals and trophies. Some folks have questioned whether Sister Buder's passionate dedication to athletic competition is contrary to her faith. She told ABC News, "Who says I can't be in the church and doing God's work out everywhere I go?" According to Sister Buder, there is no conflict between her activities as a nun and as an athlete, because "there is no limit, no boundaries to when and where you can commune with God."[36]

The relationship between sports and spirituality has attracted "unprecedented academic interest" in the first decade of the twenty-first century.[37] Richard Pengelly, a former Olympic athlete, teaches a new course titled Sport and Spirituality at the University of West Australia. York St. John University in England recently established the Centre for the Study of Sport and Spirituality. According to Gordon Preece, PhD, Senior Lecturer in Sport History and Exercise Science at Victoria University, Melbourne, Australia: "The grace or aesthetic excellence of shared bodily exercise can help eradicate a passive sense of entertainment that distracts us from coming to terms with the 'junk' of our alienated, mortal bodies."[38] This concept is expressed in a more experiential fashion by Eric Liddell, the protagonist of the 1981 film *Chariots of Fire*: "God made me fast, Jenny, and when I run, I feel God's pleasure." The enjoyment of athletic excellence is "a pre-echo of eternity" and "a signal of transcendence," according to sociologist Peter Berger.[39]

The ancient practices of Tai Chi and yoga can improve your life on multiple levels—physically, psychologically and spiritually. In a review of 81 comparative studies, Ross and Thomas found that "in both healthy and diseased populations, yoga may be as effective as or better than exercise at improving a variety of health-related outcome measures."[40]

When spirituality is combined with exercise, it can reduce the risk of chronic disease. A Johns Hopkins University study of African American women aged 40-plus found that church involvement and "spiritual strategies" were more effective than self-help groups in reducing cardiovascular risk.[41]

Exercise can enhance the quality of life for people with chronic illness. Professor Eileen Hacker of the University of Illinois at Chicago found that "exercise improves quality of life in people with cancer [and] the research literature provides strong support for the physical and psychological benefits of exercise."[42]

Go Take a Hike: Psychological Benefits of the Great Outdoors

I think I cannot preserve my health or spirits unless I spend four hours a day sauntering through the woods and over the hills and fields. Henry David Thoreau[43]

Exercise improves the mind and emotions as well as the body. I once went on a Sierra Club outing to the Davis Mountains with a gentleman who explained why he went on regular nature hikes. As best I recall, he said something like this: "I used to go to psychologists and counselors, but now I just take a wilderness trip once a month with the Sierra Club. That's all the therapy I need."

It seems my Sierra Club associate was really onto something. Dr. Simon Crisp, an Australian psychologist, has been researching Wilderness Adventure Therapy for 15 years. He and his mental health associates take groups of adolescents on three- to five-day outings that include bush walking, cross-country skiing, white-water rafting, rock climbing, caving, and camping. Outcome research demonstrates "wide-ranging benefits for up to two years for a variety of mental health and behavioural disorders."[44] Wilderness Therapy compares well to state-of-the-art treatments for depression, such as cognitive behavioral therapy and antidepressant (SSRI) medications; it "produces equivalent rates and degree of symptom reduction in severely depressed adolescents." That says a lot for the healing power of old Mother Nature! Of course, Wilderness Therapy is much more than just sitting around looking at trees and birds. Activities are therapeutically designed to enhance social interactions, stimulate problem solving, encourage risk-taking, develop assertiveness skills, and build trust and self-confidence.

Bottom Line: Live Longer and Better

You don't get old from age, you get old from inactivity. Jack LaLanne[45]

Regular physical activity, including aerobic activity and muscle-strengthening activity, is essential for healthy aging. American Heart Association[46]

One of the best reasons to exercise and keep physically active is that it will help you live longer and better. According to the World Health Organization, "physical inactivity is estimated to cause 1.9 million deaths globally" every year, and about one-quarter of a million of those deaths occur in the United States.[47] On the other hand, regular exercise increases lifespan. A study in the April 2008 issue of *British Journal of Sports Medicine* claims that "a regular programme of aerobic exercise can slow or reverse the functional deterioration, reducing the individual's biological age by 10 or more years."[48]

It has been well-established that exercise increases the lifespan of rats, for instance, and compared to their sedentary colleagues, rats free to run and exercise live about 15 percent longer.[49] Rats are used in scientific research because they have a short lifespan, and you can quickly find out what happens when you make changes in their living habits and conditions.

People, of course, are not rats. The next best thing to rat studies are longitudinal studies. Longitudinal studies look at large groups of people over a period of many years. A longitudinal study of nearly 17,000 Harvard graduates, aged 35 to 70 found that people who burned 2,000 kcal per week lived an average of two and one-half years longer than those who exercised less than 500 kcal per week.[50] To burn 2,000 kcal you would need to do the equivalent of brisk walking for about five hours.[51]

Real-Life Time Travel

How many times have you wished you could go back in time to repeat an experience that you handled poorly, except this time get to relive it with the wisdom and knowledge that you have now? Unfortunately, time machines haven't been invented yet. The closest thing to time travel in human behavioral research is a longitudinal study, which allows you to compare the lifestyles of the survivors to those who died at a younger age and find out what worked to keep them living longer. This is exactly what was done by psychiatric researcher Dr. George Vaillant, in *Aging Well: Surprising Guideposts to a Happier Life from the Landmark Harvard Study of Adult Development*.[52] I've described Vaillant's study in-depth here because it is a landmark of aging research, and I will cite it time and time again in this book.

Vaillant used subjects from the Harvard Study for Human Development, which has been called "the oldest and most thorough study of aging ever undertaken."[53] Nearly 1,000 men and women were first interviewed as teenagers or young adults, beginning in the 1930s, and they were checked up on at regular intervals throughout the remainder of their lives. The Harvard Study used three separate groups of subjects: 268 well-to-do Harvard grads, 456 poorer inner-city men, and 90 middle-class intellectually gifted women. This allows researchers to draw conclusions about the relationship between aging and factors like gender, education, intelligence, and social status.

Dr. Vaillant interviewed the Harvard Study subjects when they were 70, 80, and even 90 years old. *Aging Well,* the summary of his research, contains a wealth of information that challenges the decrepitude model of aging and portrays a much more inviting picture of old age.

Among Vaillant's many findings is that physical activity, including exercise, is one of the major predictors of successful aging: "Men who exercised at age 50 were more likely to be alive, happy and healthy at age 75-80 than men who didn't exercise at age 50."[54]

Midlife Predictors of Successful Aging

It is important to develop good habits in midlife because the positive changes you make can have a major impact on how successfully you age in your elder years. Dr. Vaillant was surprised to find that much of healthy aging is predictable, and even more so because the factors are controllable.[55] Several factors, if present at age 50, strongly predict making it to age

80 and living a high quality senior life: exercise, no tobacco, little alcohol, a sustained and supportive relationship, adaptive coping style, and education. It's interesting to see what factors *don't* predict successful aging. It doesn't matter how long your parents and ancestors live because sometimes the ancestors are healthier than their descendents. It doesn't matter if your folks were poor, died young, or had a rotten marriage. Your folks might not have been rocket scientists, and your family life might have been terrible. These factors are associated with unhappy young adulthood—but not old age! It seems that over time we work out the problems of our youth.

The men and women studied by Dr. George Vaillant are the older generation of the baby boomers—their parents and grandparents. This generation tends to be healthier, as a whole, than their offspring—as we have seen. The spunky elders of the Harvard Study can serve as role models of successful aging for their boomer juniors, which is desperately needed because of our current obesity and health crisis.

Public Education Isn't Working

The government has been trying to educate the American public about the need for weight loss through lifestyle changes, including exercise, diet, and proper nutrition. As part of the new millennium effort, *Healthy People 2010* was launched in January 2000 by the Department of Health and Human Services (HHS). One objective was to reduce obesity to no more than 15 percent of the American population by the year 2010. A midcourse review of progress in January 2004 indicated not only lack of progress but "a trend for the worse."[56] The rate of obesity among American men age twenty and older *increased* from 20 to 28 percent and from 25 to 33 percent among women in the same age group. Especially disturbing was the fact that 60 percent of Americans with diabetes were obese—a 50 percent increase!

"Americans live in an environment that promotes obesity," concludes the HHS, and this heads the list of reasons why national health is going downhill. We face abundant food in ever-increasing portions, decreased opportunities for physical activity, massive advertising campaigns by manufacturers who promote less healthy foods (compared to tiny budgets for agencies that promote health), and "faddish diets (e.g., low or high carbohydrate, low fat, high protein) that are not based on sound scientific evidence."[57]

The Carrot and the Stick

Those who do not find time for exercise will have to find time for illness. The Earl of Derby[58]

When you stop to consider the tremendous health advantages of exercise and physical fitness, you might wonder why people aren't knocking each other out of the way as they rush to their local gym. Evidently, education about the benefits of exercise is not enough. People are far from logical, especially when it comes to their decision-making. Social psychology provides another reason—perhaps the most salient—why the dangling carrot of exercise bliss fails to motivate us to take better care of ourselves. It's a regrettable truth that we are influenced more by the negative consequences of our unhealthy behaviors than by the expectation of positive outcomes of good health. Princeton psychologist Daniel Kahneman won a Nobel Prize in 2002 for his influential work in *prospect theory*. When given a choice, time and time again "people are generally more motivated to avoid potential losses in the present than to secure potential future gains." [59] To put it bluntly, we generally respond better to the stick of pain than to the carrot of reward. Practically applied, this principle means that health education is more successful when it focuses on the problem. As an example, Meyerowitz and Chaiken's research on AIDS education (1987) found that people are more likely to adopt health-promoting behavior when the emphasis of education is on "potential health losses" than on "long-term health benefits." [60]

The Journey Continues

Life is like an onion: you peel it off one layer at a time, and sometimes you weep. Carl Sandburg

I'd like to tell you that I am so highly educated and nobly inspired that I am an exception to the rules governing mass behavior—but I'm not. Although I discovered a vast body of scientific evidence testifying to the benefits of healthy living, I still got much of my motivation to change from bad news at the doctor's office: high blood pressure, excess weight on the scale, high cholesterol and triglycerides, dangerous levels of PSA, etc. Learning the principles of successful aging was a slow and difficult process. I had to overcome a lot of resistance—half a century of accumulated misconceptions, cultural prejudices, and partial truths. Doctoral studies in psychology biased me to favor genes and biochemistry as the chief determinants of health and aging; I was far from convinced that lifestyle factors—especially simple things like getting more exercise or changing your diet—could make much of a difference. A greater challenge was to overcome the boomer hubris that my generation is the biggest, the bravest, the strongest and the best in *everything*, and that we all should expect to stay healthy and live to be 100 without putting any special effort into it.

It was a rude awakening to discover that so many boomers were in such poor health—and I was one of them! Nevertheless, learning the truth about boomer health and the reasons for our national obesity epidemic was crucial to overcoming my denial and resistance. Recognizing that I had a problem was a major step towards finding a solution. It also satisfied my historian's quest to understand how we became a couch potato nation and why the lap of luxury is way too soft (chapters 4 and 5).

Activities and Solutions

Watch the movie *The Doctor* and discuss your reaction. Have you ever been in a situation which forced you to realize that you didn't know what you thought you knew? Have you ever been humbled by a health or life crisis? Do you believe you are responsible for your own health and wellness? Discuss your views about the mind-body connection. In what way(s) do you take responsibility for your health and wellness?

Notes:

_____

_____

_____

_____

_____

_____

_____

_____

Chapter 4

The Couch Potato Nation

The United States is the best place to be if you are sick—but one of the last places to be if you wish to remain well. George Sheehan, MD, cardiologist[1]

The United States is the richest country in the world, and Americans spend more on health care than anybody else. Paradoxically, American health ranks much lower than most other affluent nations—and it's getting worse, especially because of obesity. Even more ironic is the fact that baby boomers are the most obese of any age group, despite all the hoopla about the boomer exercise mania. However, we must be careful to avoid stereotyping boomers; they're not a uniform group but highly diverse in their beliefs and behaviors—basically, they represent a microcosm of America and the world.

The Affluent Society

Millions of G.I.s returned home from World War II, and "the biggest war in history was followed by the biggest baby boom," writes Harvard historian Gerard DeGroot in *The Sixties Unplugged.*[2] Between 1947 and 1964, 77 million Americans were born into the world's most affluent society. On October 26, 1953, at 5:30 A.M., I entered their ranks.

Baby boomers grew up during a time in history when the United States enjoyed undisputed status as a global leader in industry and economic pursuits. I was barely one year old in 1954, when President Dwight David Eisenhower praised American world supremacy: "We are richer, by any standard of comparison, than any other nation in the world."[3] After World War II, the United States became "the most powerful of world powers" according to historian Donald White in *The American Century: The Rise and Decline of the United States as a World Power.*[4] We had not only the most powerful navy and air force but also the largest number of commercial ships and airplanes in the world. We had the largest industrial output—producing more oil, steel, cotton, and other vital products than any nation on earth.

What was the impact of this unbelievable prosperity on American society? It ushered in an era of domestic peace and the greatest affluence for the largest number of people in the history of America and the world. "The experience of nations with well-being is exceedingly brief," according to economist John Kenneth Galbraith in *The Affluent Society*. "Nearly all, throughout all history, have been very poor. The exception…has been the last few generations in the comparatively small corner of the world populated by Europeans. Here, and especially in the United States, there has been great and quite unprecedented affluence."[5]

After World War II America enjoyed an economic security unknown to the post-Great Depression era generation. Good-paying jobs were plentiful, and the American dream of raising a family in your own house with a new car in the driveway became the reality for the burgeoning ranks of newly affluent middle class suburbanites. Between 1950 and 1980, 83 percent of the American population growth occurred in the suburbs, and that's where most of the baby boomers grew up, becoming essentially the first generation of modern suburbanites.[6] My family was part of this exodus. In 1958 we left a run-down Italian neighborhood in Pittsburgh and migrated upriver to the plush green foothills of Beaver County. I was five years old when my parents bought a small tract home in a spiffy new housing development in the little town of Baden, Pennsylvania. Everybody else seemed to have the same idea because every house on the block had two or three kids, and they all seemed to be about the same age. Growing up with that many little kids running around was a real-life *Our Gang* follies, except that we weren't dirt poor. We could even afford to eat out. One of my earliest memories of suburban life was going into the new McDonald's down on Ohio River Boulevard, where you could get their advertised three-course meal for only forty-seven cents: a hamburger, french fries, and chocolate milkshake. Life was mighty good.

During the 1950s, Americans enjoyed the highest standard of living in the world. Yale historian David Potter summarized our position in his 1954 book, *People of Plenty: Economic Abundance and the American Character.* "We have, per capita, more automobiles, more telephones, more radios, more vacuum cleaners, more electric lights, more bathtubs, more supermarkets and movie palaces and hospitals, than any other nation. Even at mid-century prices we can afford college educations and T-bone steaks for a far higher proportion of our people than ... anywhere else on the globe."[7]

Throughout the twentieth century, health care improved by leaps and bounds with superior sanitation, especially better water supplies to control communicable diseases, safer workplaces, improved diet and nutrition, and synthetic vitamins and nutritional supplements. Medical researchers discovered antibiotics and cures for infectious diseases and childhood diseases. The world's first wonder drug, penicillin, was synthesized in 1950, and Jonas Salk introduced the polio vaccine in 1955. The 1950s was an especially fertile time for medical advances, witnessing the first open-heart surgery, kidney transplants, pacemakers, and artificial values and hearts.

I don't remember getting sick too often as a child, but when I did I sure hated to have to go to the doctor's office and get a shot. And I certainly had no gratitude for the fact that the medicines in those needles were miracles of modern science. With the maturity of an adult perspective, of course, I still sometimes lack gratitude for scientific and technological progress because I tend to take the conveniences and comforts of modern life for granted. The truth is that as a result of these advances, there was a drastic decline in infant and childhood mortality, and fewer deaths from infectious diseases and chronic conditions throughout the lifespan. Consequently, more people have been living to maturity and a larger percentage of the population is staying alive into advanced old age than ever before.

A Senior Citizen Nation: The Aging American Population

Will the longevity granted to us by modern medicine be a curse or a blessing? George Vaillant[8]

The average lifespan has increased substantially over the past century. In 1900, you had about a 50 percent chance of living to be 50 years of age.[9] Today most American's will live into their seventies. The average lifespan is about 77 years—and this may reach 83 by the year 2050.[10] According to the MacArthur study, 75-plus is the fastest growing age segment of the American population.[11]

The percentage of senior citizens has increased enormously over the past century. In 1900 only four percent of Americans lived to be 65 or older.[12] By the year 2000, this increased to 12 percent. In 2030, when all the boomers are senior citizens, it is predicted that 20 percent—one in five Americans—will be 65 years old or older.[13]

Growth of U.S. Senior Population

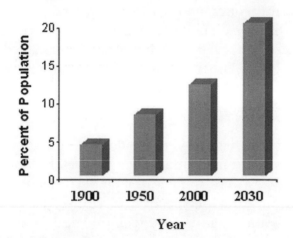

Year

Increasing Number of Seniors

In 1900 there were about 3 million seniors, which increased to 33 million by the end of the twentieth century—11 times as many![14] By the year 2050, the U.S. Census Bureau (2004) estimates that 21 percent of the U.S. population will be 65 or older— that's *87 million of an estimated 420 million Americans.* In 1900, the entire population of the United States was only 76 million![15]

Born into this senior-heavy milieu, baby boomers have the potential to become the longest-living generation in the history of the world. Walter Bortz, MD, author of *Dare to Be 100,* makes a bold claim: "There is now sufficient fund of data and experience to allow baby boomers—and of course, younger generations—to plan their hundredth birthday party with calm assurance, prepare the guest list, and muster enough respiratory reserve to blow out all those candles."[16]

What is the likelihood that you will live a full-century life? The odds have become more favorable over the past 100 years—over four times as likely as it was in 1900. Based on actual statistics from the U.S. Census Bureau, Hobbs and Damon found that an American born in 1879 had only a one in 400 chance of living to be 100, but someone born in 1980 had a one in 87 chance of becoming a centenarian.[17]

Projected Rise of U.S. Centenarians

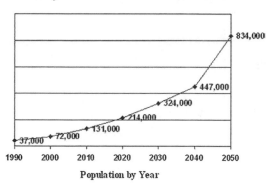

Population by Year

Unexpected Perils of Prosperity

Basically, you die earlier and spend more time disabled if you're an American rather than a member of most other advanced countries. Christopher Murray, World Health Organization[18]

We don't have a **health** *care system in America; we have a sick care system.* Tom Harkin, U.S. Senator[19]

Unfortunately, not all the experts are equally optimistic. In 2005, a team of medical researchers published an article in the *New England Journal of Medicine* with the ominous title "A Potential Decline in Life Expectancy in the United States in the 21st Century." Olshansky and colleagues[20] predict that the United States will become the first advanced nation to experience a decrease in the average lifespan, largely due to the epidemic of obesity currently sweeping the nation, combined with poor lifestyle choices that are eroding American health.

What happened? Basically, the luxuries and comforts of post-World War II American have proven to be a mixed blessing. Half a century later, all of those T-bone steaks have made the arteries of aging Americans more clogged than the Los Angeles freeway system at rush hour. The convenience of the automobile and the sedentary nature of modern life have resulted in a crisis level of inactivity and slothfulness that threatens our physical health and longevity. Convenience foods from our supermarkets have replaced the healthier whole foods diet of yesteryear with fatty, sugary, and chemical-laden synthetics that deprive us of proper nutrition and slowly poison our bodies.

Ironically, while the most affluent generation in American history grew up with an unprecedented culture of abundance, it simultaneously began to succumb to new diseases of lifestyle. Consequently, the United States has become one of the least healthy among the world's affluent countries.

How does our nation rate half a century beyond the 1950s? Here are some well-documented facts about the United States in the first decade of the new millennium with which you may be familiar:

1. The United States is still by far the richest nation in the world. The U.S. Census Bureau estimates the country's 2008 resource value at 187 trillion, 739 billion dollars.[21]
2. The United States still has "the largest and most technologically powerful economy in the world."[22] As of August 2008, per capita income was highest in the world—$46,000.
3. The United States continues to lead the world in science and technology.[23] The United States employs 70 percent of the world's Nobel Prize winners, houses 30 of the top 40 universities in the world, and accounts for 40 percent

of the world's total expenditures for scientific research and development.

4. The United States has the most expensive health care system in the world. We spend more per person on health care than any other country in the world—nearly double the amount spent in the United Kingdom and twice the average of thirty of the world's most affluent countries. Per capita spending on health care has increased more in the United States than in any other country in the world since 1980, almost doubling from 8.8 percent of the gross domestic product (GDP) in 1980 to 16.0 percent of the GDP in 2007.[24]

You would think from these statistics that Americans should be the healthiest, longest-lived people on the face of the earth. On the contrary, the United States has become one of the sickest countries in the world. Here are some sobering statistics that are also very well documented and with which you may not be familiar:

1. The United States was the very last affluent country in the world to legislate health care for all of its citizens.[25] The Health Care Reform Bill was passed into law just before I sent this book to press. South Africa established universal health care in 2002. Less-developed countries like Mexico, India, most countries of South America, and the even the tiny island nations of Trinidad and Tobago all had universal health care before the United States. "Lack of health insurance causes roughly 18,000 unnecessary deaths every year in the United States," according to the Institute of Medicine of the National Academy of Sciences.[26] *The New York Times* asserts "there is a growing body of evidence that, by an array of pertinent yardsticks, the United States is a laggard not a leader in providing good medical care."[27]

2. The United States ranks only thirty-seventh in the world in terms of quality of health care, according to a report by the World Health Organization,[28] which compares 190

countries. The United States ranks below the Dominican Republic and Costa Rica and just above Slovenia and Cuba. The World Health Organization is an agency of the United Nations, whose objective is to monitor and protect the health of people in every country in the world. WHO's quality of health care rating is based on four criteria: fairness in the way people pay for health care, how people are treated by the health care system (dignity, confidentiality), responsiveness of the system to people's expectations, and providing for the welfare of the population. "The disparities in access to care and health outcomes are very much greater in the United States than anywhere else from which there are reasonable data," according to Bruce Vladeck, PhD, from Mount Sinai Medical Center.[29] Furthermore, "there are considerable pockets of the population for whom access to health care and the effects of health care status are much more similar to those of poorer and less successful Third World countries than they are to those of the rest of the industrial world."

If American health care were graded on a school curve basis, we would be considered B- students. For the money we spend, we should be getting an A+. American longevity would get about the same grade rating.

3. The average American lifespan is 77.9 years, which is ranked only thirty-first in the world out of 177 countries compared; one lower than Denmark and one higher than Cuba. Japan heads the list at 82.3 years.[30] This is based on United Nations data, comparable to data from the U.S. Census Bureau which estimates the average life expectancy in the United States as 77.8 years.[31]

4. The United States has the highest obesity rate of any country in the world.[33] Thirty-four percent of American adults aged twenty and older are obese.[34] Obesity rates doubled between 1980 and 2004.[35] "Obesity has become an epidemic," according to Steven K. Galson, MD, acting

surgeon general of the United States.[36]   According to Joel Fuhrman, MD, who has helped thousands of diabetic and obese patients lose weight and live normal lives: "Obesity is a more important predictor of chronic ailments and quality of life than any other public scourge."[37]

5. Baby boomers have the highest rate of obesity of any segment of the American population. Approximately 40 percent of boomer-aged men and women, compared to 30 percent of younger and 32 percent of older Americans, are obese.[38]

Obesity Rates by Gender and Age Group

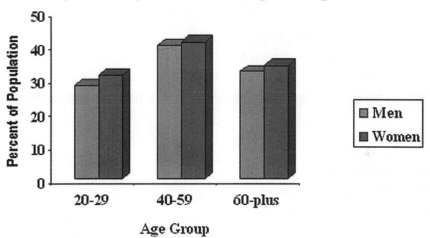

These are broad based statistics from the Centers for Disease Control, an agency of the U. S. Department of Health and Human Services, whose objective is to monitor and protect the health of our nation.[38] In a separate study, Leveille and colleagues directly compared baby boomers to the generation immediately before, born between 1926 and 1945. They found that "members of the baby boom generation were more obese, and became so at younger ages than their predecessors."[40] Obesity rates ranged from 14 to 18 percent among the older generation, in comparison to 28 to 32 percent among the baby boomers.

Years of Life Lost Due to Obesity

Obesity is one of the greatest threats to successful aging. You just don't find too many morbidly obese seniors because most obese individuals die before getting that old. I've done a lot of work in nursing homes, and I've seldom seen morbidly obese patients of advanced age. However, I have seen quite a few morbidly obese younger and middle-aged people in nursing homes—they had become so sick and incapacitated from excess weight that they needed nursing home care, and most of them died prematurely.

A recent study in the *Journal of the American Medical Association* estimates that obesity reduces an American man's life by as much as 13 to 20 years. "Years of Life Lost Due to Obesity" was the compelling title of the study.[41]

Race and Gender Effects on Longevity

Kevin Fontaine, PhD, and colleagues analyzed data from national surveys of nutrition, disease frequency, mortality, and life expectancy from 1971 through 1999. They calculated the risk of dying premature as a result of obesity. There are race and gender differences. Whites with a body mass index (BMI) of 23 to 25 or blacks with a BMI of 23 to 30 are likely to live the longest. In sharp contrast, severely obese white males will likely die 13 years younger, trimming 22 percent from their expected lifespan were they not obese. Severely obese white women will likely die eight years younger. Severely obese black men and women run a similar risk. Age differences also exist, and "for any given degree of overweight, younger adults generally had greater years of life lost than did older adults." Severely obese young black males are at the greatest risk and may shorten their lives 20 years. This is a sad testimony to the obesity epidemic that has so rapidly spread into the younger age segment of American society

How Did We Become a Couch Potato Nation?

Better health is an individual responsibility and an important national goal. Aristotle, Greek philosopher (384-322 BC)

The practice of engaging in regular physical activity is one which must be adopted broadly—by individuals and families everywhere—if we, as a Nation, are to make truly sustained progress in health promotion. Steven K. Galson, MD, acting U.S. surgeon general

Sadly, we have literally become a nation of couch potatoes. According to the U.S. Department of Labor[42] only 16 percent of Americans aged 15 or more engage in sports and exercise activities daily. In contrast, about five times as many watch television. It's therefore not surprising that 66 percent of Americans are overweight or obese.

According to the Centers for Disease Control (CDC) "physical activity is one of the most important steps older adults can take to maintain physical and mental health and quality of life."[43] Unfortunately, 60 percent of elders remain inactive, according to CDC statistics. Regarding Americans of all ages, only 23 percent exercise regularly and one-third remain completely sedentary.[44] Even our kids are way out of shape. According to the surgeon general, "nearly half of young people aged 12 to 21 are not vigorously active on a regular basis," and only about 19 percent of high school students get 20 minutes of physical activity each day.[45]

Regrettably, most aging Americans don't seem to appreciate the importance of exercise and good health as vital ingredients to successful aging. Only 48 percent of those over 65 said that changing health habits was an important preparation for aging, according to a survey by the National Council on Aging.[46] In comparison, 74 percent thought that preparing a will and building their savings were very important. Money and inheritance are certainly important issues when you get older. However, if you neglect your health, nothing else really matters too much.

Boomers and Exercise: The Bright Hope

Baby boomers are flocking to fitness centers in record numbers.
Colette Bouchez, medical journalist[47]

In contrast to the older generation, boomers are more likely
to value health and exercise. About 90 percent of boomers
are "making some effort to improve or maintain their health
through exercise and diet," according to Moschis and Mathur,
in *Baby Boomers and Their Parents: Surprising Findings about Their
Lifestyles, Mindsets, and Well-Being.*[48] However, 80 percent of
boomers' parents are making the same effort. Boomers are
exercising mainly to improve their appearance, whereas their
parents are motivated to exercise for better health. Furthermore,
there is a big difference between *making efforts* to exercise and
actually doing it. Only about 50 percent of boomers really get
out and exercise regularly. The Center for Disease Control
defines regular exercise for adults as "at least 30 minutes a day of
moderate-intensity activity on 5 or more days a week, or at least
20 minutes a day of vigorous-intensity activity on 3 or more days
a week, or both."[49]

Exercise Rates Decrease With Age

The bad news, according to the CDC is that there's a steady
decline in exercise rates as Americans get older.[50] Fewer and
fewer men and women meet the minimum requirements for
regular exercise at each age group. In general, men exercise
more than women—except during the middle age range
of 35 to 44, when 50 percent of both genders get enough
exercise.[51]

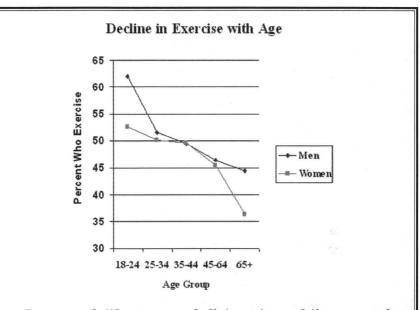

In general, 52 percent of all Americans fail to meet the recommended minimum standards of exercise. The good news is that overall exercise rates increased between 2001 and 2005, from a low increase of 0.2 percent among the 25- to 34-year-old age group, to a high of 7.4 percent increase among boomers aged 35 to 44.[52] So some of the boomers are getting the message.

Despite popular opinion, baby boomers aren't exercising any more than their parents, according to Moschis and Mathur.[53] The difference is that boomers are more likely to exercise at a health club or gym, whereas their parents tend to exercise at home or go for a walk in their neighborhood. The general pattern is that people exercise more at home as they get older: about one-third between the ages of 35 to 49, compared to a half of those 65-plus.

About one in five boomers is a member of a health or fitness club. "The boomer fitness market…has really exploded" over the past fifteen years, according to Colin Milner, CEO of the International Council on Active Aging.[54] There was a 180 percent increase in health club memberships in the 35 to 54 age range, with a massive 343 percent increase in members over 55.

Milner believes that better education among aging boomers about the link between exercise and health is partly responsible for this increase. "A lot of the problems we used to think of as being related to aging, we now know aren't related to aging at all," Milner told reporters. "They are related to disuse of the body, and boomers have finally begun to realize, 'Hey, we can do something about that.'"[55]

Poor Health—A Dark Side of the Boomer Mystique

If people are entering early old age in worse health, it doesn't bode well for society. Richard Suzman, National Institute on Aging[56]

I may be gone, but Rock and Roll lives on. John Belushi's (1949-1982) epitaph

Despite the promising exercise trends, boomers are far from paragons of health and fitness when looked on as a group. Statistics show that "the baby boomers are in worse health than previous generations of the same age," according to Moschis and Mathur.[57] Boomers are not only more overweight than older Americans, but they have also spent a larger portion of their lifetime being overweight. A disturbing increase of evidence suggests that the baby boomers "may be the first generation to enter their golden years in worse health than their parents," according to Rob Stein, *Washington Post* national science correspondent.[58]

In general, the obesity epidemic among boomers predicts poor future health because of an increased likelihood of premature death or disability from heart disease, strokes, and many of the other traditional diseases of aging. Most of the boomers are not yet old enough to experience the full ramifications of these severe health problems, but the forecast is ominous. We also need to keep in mind that some of the new medications that boomers are now taking at an earlier age than their parents may be forestalling the inevitable. Anticholesterol agents and blood pressure medications, which only came into vogue during the boomer generation, may be creating an illusion of good health. Many people would rather take a pill, because it is so much more convenient than eating healthy, exercising, and losing weight.

However, these medications treat only the symptoms of diseases and conditions caused by the abuse and neglect of our bodies. As medical researcher Dean Ornish, MD, explains, "if you don't address the underlying causes of a problem—any problem, including heart disease or obesity—then the same problem often comes back again."[59] Furthermore, boomers are developing less potentially fatal disease like arthritis, asthma, and diabetes and at an earlier age than their parents.

The National Institute on Aging has been following over 20,000 Americans age 50 and over since 1988 in the Health & Retirement Study.[60] The first group of boomers entering the study, born between 1948 and1953 was compared to their predecessors, born 1936-1941. The boomers rated their health less favorably than their predecessors and reported more problems performing routine tasks such as lifting 10 pounds or walking several blocks. Boomers reported more problems with chronic health problems like pain, high cholesterol, high blood pressure, and diabetes. They also reported more psychiatric trouble and problems with drinking. Baby boomers reported a higher level of stress than previous generations, with pressures like working two jobs, not getting enough sleep, greater job insecurity, and retirement planning concerns. Because of these stressors, many boomers become more socially isolated and don't have enough time to take care of themselves.[61] Furthermore, a RAND Corporation study found that disability rates have been rising fastest among the younger generation. There was a 40 percent increase in disability among Americans in their forties (mostly boomers) between 1984 and 1996—largely due to the increased rates of asthma and diabetes among the young.[62]

Baby boomers around the world are having problems, and American boomers are doing worse than British boomers but better than Australian boomers. Data from down under at the Australian Bureau of Statistics indicate that 51 percent are obese, two-thirds are "inactive or undertaking low levels of exercise," 25 percent still smoke, and 14 percent drink excessive amounts of alcohol.[63]

These facts contradict the popular image of baby boomers as a uniform group of health conscious, exercise savvy citizens. How do we reconcile the discrepancy? First, we need to realize that the baby boomers are not all alike and show tremendous diversity as a group. There were incredible extremes among the boomers during the sixties. We need to keep in mind that only a minority of boomers became hippies, for instance. Some boomers became war protesters and university demonstrators, but some of the boomers were among the police and soldiers who beat in their heads or shot them down during campus uprisings. There are even greater differences among the middle-aged boomers. Some boomers are exercise fanatics, while others are archetypal couch potatoes. Socioeconomic factors also contribute to boomer diversity; white male boomers exercise more than female and minority boomers, and the wealthier and more educated boomers take better care of themselves through exercise and improved health care.[64] As they age, boomers will become even more diversified as a group. We can expect a polarization, as more boomers become spunky elders than their parents, but more become worse off than their parents ever were; what statisticians call a bimodal distribution is likely. Some boomers will live to be a hundred; some have been long dead from drug overdose or lifestyle excesses—like John Belushi.

Why Do We Stubbornly Resist What's Really in Our Best Interest?

Just because you're a doctor doesn't mean that you know anything about health or that you do anything about your own health. Miss Mary's Little Book of Just Becauses

Those who are willing, Fate leads. Those who resist are dragged. Ancient Roman proverb

If exercise and physical fitness are such good things, you might wonder why everybody isn't actively taking much better care of themselves. In my private practice, I generally see three or four people a week for neuropsychological evaluations because they are having problems with memory loss. I refer them to their neurologist and other physicians for state-of-the-art medical treatment. However, I also routinely make strong recommendations for simple lifestyle changes, like exercising or eating more fruits and vegetables. I spend a lot of time talking to people about the principles of healthy aging, showing them the photograph on the cover of this book or pictures of other spunky eldsters. My patients (and their family members) listen politely to humor me, but they don't seem to take it too seriously. From their reaction, you'd think I was asking them to run in the Boston Marathon or climb Mount Everest.

Why do we stubbornly resist doing something that's really in our best interests?

The government has been active for years trying to educate the public about the need to take more responsibility for personal health care. Why do government efforts fail to motivate the American public to make lifestyle changes to reduce obesity? Mehmet Oz, MD, director of the Cardiovascular Institute of Columbia-Presbyterian Medical Center, maintains that the public doesn't really believe lifestyle changes can make a big difference in their health and well-being. Therefore, he argues: "The public turns to magic cures, pills, supplements, drinks, and diet plans that simply don't work or are unsafe. After a few failures they give up hope."[65]

I think most people have a genuine desire to take care of themselves, but they lack knowledge of the principles of health psychology: they genuinely don't realize that there is a link between lifestyle factors and physical health (see chapter 3). We have been culturally conditioned to leave our health care entirely up to the professionals. I'm thinking of that old car rental commercial that advertised "leave the driving to us." Modern life is like that. Things have gotten so complex, especially health care, that we tend to depend increasingly on professionals to perform services for us. We are encouraged to trust the experts more and more to make our decisions. We're bombarded by medication advertisements in the media, and there seems to be a pill for every modern malady. Who can keep track of it all? So we go on our merry way, not taking care of ourselves and eating all manner of unhealthy foods that wreak havoc on our bodies. When something goes wrong, we go see the family physician, who gives us a pill to treat the symptoms, without addressing the underlying causes—a lifestyle of overindulge and excess.

It's easy to get depressed and discouraged by all of the gloomy statistics about our poor health. However, all statistics are based on averages. The philosophy of *Do Not Go Gentle* is never to settle for average. Dare to be different. Dare to defy the odds and go against the flow. Rebel against the status quo of excessive comfort, convenience, and immediate gratification.

The good news is that you can regain control of your life and well-being by practicing the principles of successful aging. Each of us individually has the ultimate responsibility for our own health and well-being. If we rely exclusively on the government, our doctors, the professionals or anybody else to do it for us, it's easy to become complacent. Rebel against complacency and denial. In short, become the hero of your own life story.

Become The Hero of Your Own Life's Story

Will you be the hero of your own life's story or merely its victim?
Dr. Kownacki's Journals

Charles Dickens' novel *David Copperfield* begins with this sentence "Whether I shall turn out to be the hero of my own life, or whether that station will be held by anybody else, these pages must show." Throughout the novel, the protagonist contemplates his life in an attempt to answer that question. He reflects on his youth, reviews the trials and tribulations he's gone through, struggles to make sense of his experience, and strives to find happiness and meaning in his life, despite his unpleasant past. Essentially, it is the story of a man learning to take responsibility for his own life through a midlife crisis. It is an experience that many of us must go through.

At some point, and on some issues, you have to claim total responsibility for your own behavior. Your parents and family demand obedience while you are growing up, a spouse or significant other places claims on your time and attention as an adult, the boss has procedures and policies you must follow at work, and the government regulates you with rules and regulations throughout your entire lifetime. But at some point, on some key issues, you have to make decisions that are yours alone to make. At some point you have to totally dispense with all blame because you can't pass the buck anymore. In some situations you have to make choices, take total responsibility for your decisions, and accept the consequences of your actions. In short, we all have to learn how to be heroes of our own life stories.

Unfortunately, there is no magic formula to make lifestyle changes easy, especially when it comes to taking in more exercise or eating a truly healthy diet. A big part of the solution is basically to force yourself to do something that you really don't feel like doing. You have to decide to do something, and then you have to make yourself get out there and do it, even though you really don't want to. In AA and support groups, they call this "fake it 'til you make it." Some people call it acting on faith or acting *as if*. You really aren't totally committed to doing something with your whole heart and soul, but you know that there is a good reason to do it, and so you trust the process. Here is an area where social support is helpful. You can see other people doing it, get encouragement from them, and see the good results in their lives that came from doing it. That's why groups like AA and Weight Watchers are so effective. That's why in this book, I'm sharing my own experience and citing lots of examples of spunky eldsters who have successfully made major lifestyle changes. We all need more positive role models in lives, to counteract the ubiquitous gloom and doom and cynicism that pervade our contemporary news media and entertainment. We don't need more TV shows celebrating excess and self-indulgence, such as who can eat the world's biggest hamburger or largest bowl of ice cream. It's a welcome relief to watch programs like CBS's *Sunday Morning* or catch a glimpse of a *CNN Heroes* broadcast. It's refreshing to know that there are still a lot of people out there doing something good in their lives and trying to make the world a better place. When we see somebody else doing something grand and glorious, we know it's possible to achieve it and maybe we can do the same thing.

However, even if everybody else in the world is doing something, you still have to overcome your own inner resistance and inertia, then get out there and do it for yourself. Nobody can do that for you. I knew a woman who went to overeating support group meetings, and she struggled with this concept for years. She talked about how "I kept waiting for God to slap the sandwich out of my hand." This meant that she was waiting for divine inspiration or some type of infallible motivation that would miraculously make her like restricting what she ate. That never came. Finally, she realized that she had to make a decision, all by herself, to eat only three meals a day and force herself to stick with it. The magic was that once she took the first step and acted on faith, it got easier. It's similar to acts of courage. I've heard people talk about how they wished they had the courage to do something heroic. But when you talk to real-life heroes, they usually tell you they were scared to death, but they still did it. True courage is to feel the fear and do it anyway. In this sense, therefore, making any kind of serious lifestyle or behavioral changes takes real courage. When you commit to a program of discipline over a long period of time, you are becoming the hero of your own life's story.

A coworker of mine from the Light House for the Blind ran a counseling group for the young blind workers, which was called Personal and Social Adjustment. James was blind himself from diabetes, but he was really spunky and he worked largely on a volunteer basis out of dedication of service to help other blind people like himself. He heard a lot of griping from the trainees who didn't want to go to the group. One of the most common complaints was, "I don't feel like going." James offered a compelling challenge to that objection: "I understand your feelings. However, most of the work in the world is done by people who don't feel like doing it. So let's go start the group." In other words, you make yourself do it even though you don't really want to do it. You "fake it 'til you make it." Sometimes you have to force yourself to practice new behaviors in order to develop new habits. If you wait until you "feel like doing it," you may never get it done. You just have to get up, put one foot in front of the other, and get out there and do it.

Actually, much of our normal, everyday behavior is done the same way. How many people really feel like getting up in the morning and going off to work for eight hours—especially on Monday morning or after being on vacation? Truthfully, one of the reasons I go to the gym at 5:00 in the morning when they first open the door is to get it over with. If I put off working out too long, I might never do it. I know that the longer I put off doing something I don't really feel like doing, the less willing I am to do it. Therefore, I've developed a style of coping by doing the things I like doing the least first, and then the things I do later seem like a reward. This is a standard principle of behavioral psychology called the Premack principle, otherwise known as grandma's rule. Basically, you have to eat your vegetables before you get your dessert.

There is a lot of truth in Mark Twain's sarcastic proclamation that "the way to keep your health is to eat what you don't want, drink what you don't like, and do what you'd rather not." Much of our behavior is done out of a sense of obligation, duty, commitment, or necessity—emotions of yearning, desire, and joy are not necessarily present. Sometimes we do things to avoid punishment or negative consequences. How many people really want to drive the speed limit all the time? How many secretly speed a little if they know they can get away with it? How many people are cash-register honest if they know nobody is looking, and they can get away with cheating just a little bit?

Habit and custom account for much of what we do. When we commit to make a major behavioral change, we have to go against the grain of our habitual way of acting. At first it takes a lot of conscious effort and it's very difficult. Later it becomes easier, as a new habit sets in, and eventually it becomes second nature.

The good news is that we don't have to make a major change all at once. We go through several distinct stages of change when we're undergoing a life transformation such as stopping smoking, getting off alcohol and drugs, changing our diet and losing weight, or altering bad habits. Learning about the stages of change can help you overcome resistance, reduce your level of frustration, and let you deal more effectively with the transformation you are undergoing.

Stages of Change

We seldom make a major change all at once. Instead, we evolve into the change over a period of time, the length of which depends on the magnitude of the change. Essentially, it takes time and effort for us to change our attitudes about changing, especially when we are dealing with problematic behaviors.

Two psychologist professors, James Prochaska and Carlo DiClemente developed the *stages of change*[66] model while studying smoking cessation. Doctors Prochaska and DiClemente observed that patients were at different places psychologically with respect to their attitudes and commitments about making changes in their lives. The stages of change model is a good explanation of the way we progress from denial to transformation of our behavior patterns. Five basic stages of change have been identified, and different activities are useful for the successful transition of each stage.

The *precontemplation* stage is what we commonly call being in denial of having a problem. In this stage, we are not open to change because we don't even recognize that we have a problem. The way to break through denial is to take a look at where you are and make an honest appraisal of your behavior. Examine the reasons for your resistance to change—become open minded. You must be accepting of yourself as you are—wherever you are; only then can you begin to change. Education about how you came to where you are can be valuable. So is getting accurate information about the problems you may have.

In the *contemplation* stage, you recognize that you may have a problem or that there's something you need to do differently, but you are not yet fully committed to taking action to change things. This is commonly known as riding the fence. The important thing to do at this point is to find some way to open your mind. Continue with the activities from the precontemplation stage.

Increase your discontent with where you are now. Weigh the pros and cons of making a change, and gather and examine the evidence. Find some way to push yourself off the fence and take action. Often a life crisis can help to motivate us to move forward.

Action is the stage where you decide to change and start doing things differently. You have gotten over the hump of indecision, made up your mind to change, and started to practice new behaviors. Bravo for you! You have successfully overcome your resistance to change. Once you've made a decision to change, you may be surprised at how easy it becomes. You may experience a sense of relief and deep satisfaction. Resistance is a heavy psychological load and giving it up lightens your psyche tremendously. The German philosopher Goethe wisely observed that "until one is committed, there is hesitance, the chance to draw back, always ineffectiveness [but] the moment one definitely commits oneself, then Providence moves too. All sorts of things occur to help one that would never otherwise have occurred."

The *maintenance* stage is basically following through on your plan to change. Repetition and persistence are key elements to success. Sometimes the spirit may be willing, but the flesh is weak. In addiction terminology, it is at this stage that relapse may occur. Learn to deal with the temptation to practice old behaviors and avoid situations that tempt you to relapse. Learn to manage cravings and urges. For example, suppose you have resolved to eat only fresh fruit or vegetables for snacks. Hanging out in a candy store might not be a good idea. Don't keep sweets and junk food around the house. Having a support group or sympathetic partner can be crucial at this stage.

Relapse is the fifth stage of change. Many people quit smoking, drinking or using drugs forever. Others relapse but learn from their experience—take one step back then two steps forward. The same dynamics occur with other lifestyle changes. Most people require more than one attempt to make permanent changes in their behavior.

An Exercise in Self-Assessment

The unexamined life is not worth living. Socrates, Greek philosopher (469–399 BC)

At this junction, it would be useful to make a self-appraisal and see where you stand in the midst of the current crisis. Don't get mad and cynical. Redirect your distress about these gloomy statistics into meaningful action. Do some soul-searching work, and take stock of your problems and weaknesses; that's the first step toward change. Ask yourself questions like: How is your health? Do you have any chronic conditions or diseases? Are you overweight or obese? Do you exercise enough?

Apply the stages of change to an area of your life where you seem to be stuck, such as trying to lose weight, improve your physical condition, quit smoking, etc.

Notes:

_____

_____

_____

_____

_____

_____

_____

Chapter 5

The Lap of Luxury is Way Too Soft

We have designed a lifestyle of leisure and convenience that has become a threat to our well-being. The disadvantage of our modern way of life is that too much of a good thing can be bad for you, especially as you get older. Inactivity promotes diseases of lifestyle. The quality of our lives depends on exercise and physical activity, which is crucial for successful aging in all areas— physical, emotional, and mental. However, unrealistic optimism about our true unhealthiness and other forms of resistance discourage us from changing. Overcoming our resistance to making healthy changes is crucial for successful aging.

How We Got the Way We Are

Currently 60 percent of the world's population is estimated to not get enough physical activity. World Health Organization[1]

During the summer of 1969, the song "In the Year 2525" was number one on the Billboard chart for six weeks. I remember listening to the song repeatedly, and then for many years afterward because I was a teenage curmudgeon and the pessimistic lyrics fit in well with my cynical outlook. Zager and Evans's creepy ballad described a dystopian future for humanity. They predicted that in the year 5555 our arms and legs will be useless because machines are doing all our work. Admittedly, this is a grotesque caricature of the darker side of progress. Nevertheless, the theme of degeneration due to technological advancement is accurate. The sad irony is that it didn't take us 3,500 years to reach a crisis state of bodily deterioration. We've done it during the lifetime of the boomers—within the past half century. The ease and convenience of modern life have led to disastrous levels of inactivity that produce obesity and serious disease. The World Health Organization frames the problem broadly: "Industrialization, urbanization and mechanized transport have reduced physical activity, even in developing countries, so that currently more than 60 percent of the global population is not sufficiently active."[2] According to the Centers for Disease Control: "Physical inactivity increases the risk of dying prematurely, dying of heart disease, and developing diabetes, colon cancer, and high blood pressure."[3]

Sedentary Lifestyle and Inactivity Cause Obesity

People today are more sedentary than ever, and our level of inactivity has risen sharply since the 1950s. Our unprecedented low level of activity may be the root cause of the obesity epidemic. According to Louise Sutton, a lecturer in health and exercise science at Leeds Metropolitan University, people are actually eating fewer calories than in the fifties. "The real reason they are getting fatter is that they are not active enough."[4] Sutton found that the daily activities of people in the 1950s "were equivalent to walking three to five miles a day." Most of us today don't get that much exercise in a week. In the fifties people spent more time performing household chores, walking to shops, and engaging in outdoor activities. With the convenience and ease of modern living, people today spend most of their time at desk jobs or driving or commuting back and forth to work (the commute may be several hours a day in large metropolitan areas). The volume of traffic on the roads has increased as much as a fifteen fold since 1950![5] After work, since there's no time to cook, we stop off for fast food to eat in front of the TV for relaxation. According to a 2007 Nielsen survey, the average American watches 30 hours of television each week.[6] Our declining hours of leisure time are too often spent in front of the computer console, where we can do everything from order in more fast food to find a new mate through a computerized dating service. We have taught our children these same sedentary habits—so they are becoming obese at an alarming rate. Video games are now more popular as Christmas gifts than footballs, baseball gloves, and outdoor play items. I remember growing up in the fifties, how we would spend all day playing outdoors and come home in the evening worn out and ready to sleep soundly. Today children spend most of their free time playing video games or watching violent television programs and DVDs; yet we're surprised that they need to take medication to keep them from being unmanageably hyper and out of control. Our lifestyle of ease and convenience is clearly a mixed blessing, especially when it comes to long-term health and well-being.

Obesity Is a Bigger Threat Than Terrorism

Within the past 50 years, we've arrived at a crisis state of national decrepitude. Obesity is a bigger threat than terrorism, according to U.S. Surgeon General Richard Carmona. "Obesity is the terror within,"[7] he declared during a speech at the University of South Carolina. "Unless we do something about it, the magnitude of the dilemma will dwarf 9/11 or any other terrorist attempt." Is this an exaggeration? I don't think so.

Failure to exercise is not something to be taken lightly. Getting enough exercise is literally a matter of life and death. According to the World Health Organization, "more than one quarter of a million individuals die each year in the United States because of a lack of regular physical exercise."[8] Approximately 365,000 Americans died in the millennial year of 2000 directly from "poor diet and physical inactivity," according to the Centers for Disease Control.[9] This was 15.2 percent of the total deaths for that year from all causes. Compare this to smoking, which caused 18.1 percent of the deaths. The CDC makes an ominous prediction: "This proportion is likely to increase substantially in the next few years," adding, "the burden of chronic diseases is compounded by the aging effects of the baby boomer generation."[10] In a separate study the CDC discovered a 33 percent increase in deaths caused by poor diet and physical inactivity over a 10-year period, between 1994 and 2004.

"Overweight and obesity are literally killing us,"[11] according to Tommy Thompson, secretary of the U.S. Department of Human Health and Services. "Poor eating habits and inactivity are on the verge of surpassing tobacco use as the leading cause of preventable death in America."

Haven't-Got-Time-for-the-Pain Generation

Unlike for many diseases, the cure for obesity is known. Studies with thousands of participants have demonstrated that the combination of a dramatic change in eating habits and daily exercise results in weight loss. Joel Fuhrman, MD, *Eat to Live*[12]

Unfortunately, many people would much rather take a pill than change their lifestyle. It's a lot easier that way. The dominant attitude in America today about health care is to leave it up to the doctors. Eat what you want, do what you want, and then when your body gets sick, go to the doctor for a pill to fix it. Many boomers embrace this throw-a-pill-at-it approach toward health care because they grew up during a time in American history when the pharmaceutical industry came into full vogue. I remember watching the aspirin commercials with the 'I haven't got time for the pain' jingle. Tranquilizers were introduced in the 1950s and normalized during the sixties. The Rolling Stones critiqued their ubiquitous but questionable influence in the song "Mother's Little Helper." The neurotic housewife, troubled by the stress of modern life cries out, "Doctor please, some more of these," and "although she's not really ill, there's a little yellow pill." Millions of Americans cried for "more of these," not just to relieve anxiety and stress but to help manage depression, high blood pressure, pain from arthritis, high cholesterol, and an ever increasing list of medical maladies. Taking pills became synonymous with taking good care of your health.

Cholesterol Meds Hit the Playground

Cholesterol medications were introduced in the seventies, and their usage has become increasingly pervasive over the past thirty years. New guidelines from the American Academy of Pediatrics (AAP) advocate giving anticholesterol drugs to children as young as eight.[13] This advice is based on increasing scientific evidence that "damage leading to heart disease, the nation's leading killer, begins early in life." Sadly, this seems to be the response to the epidemic of obesity among children because the drugs would be targeted to children who are obese, have high blood pressure, or have high cholesterol. The AAP also discusses prevention, including serving one-year-olds low-fat milk, but emphasizes increased cholesterol screening.

Moynihan and his Australian colleagues[14] wrote in the *British Medical Journal* to express concern about "disease mongering," because "there's a lot of money to be made from telling healthy people they're sick." They accuse the pharmaceutical industry of "medicalising ordinary life" and are fearful that medical research as a means to identify illness is being replaced by "the corporate construction of disease."

Physical Inactivity: A National and Worldwide Problem on the Rise

The United States may be one of the leaders of global slothdom, but it is far from unique. "Largely preventable chronic diseases cause 86 percent of deaths in Europe," according to a press release by the World Health Organization.[15] "An estimated 80 percent of heart disease, stroke, and type two diabetes, and 40 percent of cancer, could be avoided if common lifestyle risk factors were eliminated." The seven leading risk factors were identified as high blood pressure, tobacco, alcohol, high-blood cholesterol, overweight, low fruit and vegetable intake, and physical inactivity.

Another disturbing irony of modern progress is that up until recently, the third world and less affluent countries had shortened life spans primarily because of communicable diseases—which the more affluent countries have controlled by good hygiene and modern medicines. However, that is rapidly changing, according to WHO statistics.[16] As of 2003 noncommunicable diseases caused 60 percent of all deaths and 43 percent of diseases around the world. The projected increase for the year 2020 is 73 percent of the deaths and 60 percent of the diseases. A longer life full of debilitating disease may not be an improvement over a shortened life with a merciful and rapid death from contagions.

Disney's Wake-Up Call to an Obese Nation

I recently watched a disturbing movie: *Wall-E*, a purported children's comedy put out by Disney, but it's really a wake-up call to an obese and overindulgent nation. Like many stories for children, it has two levels of meaning. You don't have to read much between the lines to pick up on the theme: human beings are destroying the planet and themselves in the process. Wall-E is the last of his kind, a trash-compactor robot, the only moving thing left on planet earth, which has literally become one enormous trash dump. There are no people left on earth, only the remains of their cities—and mountains of garbage. Wall-E cheerfully fulfills his robotic mission by building heaps of compacted trash that tower higher than the remaining skyscrapers of the desolate cities. Halfway into the movie, we discover what happened to all the people of the earth. The only humans left alive are the tourists aboard a gargantuan outer-space cruise ship, who escaped before the earth became too polluted to support life. After 500 years of living on a luxury liner, the people are grotesque, roly-poly sluggards, so obese that their fingers are too fat to grasp objects. They can only push buttons on the remote controls for their personal video screens, which seems to be their only contact with the world outside themselves—even though they're sitting side by side in mechanized chaise lounges. They are too fat and decrepit to walk anywhere, so when the captain falls out of his chaise lounge, he can't get back up by himself—a robot has to help him.

The movie is a disturbing caricature of one possible future, yet unfortunately elements of it are already here. When I went to school in the late fifties and throughout the sixties, the fat kid on the playground stood out as a rarity. Today obese and overweight children are commonplace and threatening to become the norm. The other day I was at a rural elementary school doing some counseling. Of ten kindergarten kids standing in the cafeteria lunch line, three were clearly obese. "Nearly one in four children starting primary school are either overweight or obese"[17] in the United Kingdom—which probably isn't much different than in the United States.

My wife Mary doesn't like to go to buffet restaurants anymore "because it's an invitation to overeat." I find it increasingly disturbing myself, and I try to avoid the lunch and dinner hour rush crowds. Sometimes it's so crowded that it's difficult to get in line and serve yourself in a calm and relaxed manner. I used to be one of the frenzied eaters and could easily get back into that pattern. I've jokingly talked about taking the "all you can eat" advertisement of buffet restaurants as a personal challenge. Sadly, there's more than a grain of truth beneath the humor. When I first started writing this book, I recall literally snarling at the bus boy as he tried to remove one of my unfinished plates of food from the table. I still have to struggle against eating mass quantities at the buffets, so I try to go to those kinds of restaurants only about once a month.

Why Do We Put up with It?

Would you get your dog up in the morning and give it coffee, cigarettes, and doughnuts? Jack LaLanne[18]

Let's put our cards on the table. I don't think we can place all the blame for our sad state of national health and well-being on failed governmental policies and junk food peddlers—although these certainly play a role. The real problem doesn't seem to be a lack of education. Most Americans know that their eating patterns are unhealthy and admit that they need to be more active. I've never met a person who thought eating junk food and watching TV all day long was good for you. Most of us are aware of the problem, but we still keep doing what we're doing. There must be some deeper reason why we allow ourselves to get sick and unhealthy. Psychologists are supposed to be pretty good at uncovering these unconscious motivations, so here is my stab at a solution: The concepts of *acceptable losses, optimism bias,* and *domination of culture.*

Acceptable Losses

The term *acceptable losses* is commonly used in military strategy. Military leaders talk about acceptable losses in combat, meaning how many lives are worth sacrificing to obtain some military objective. You don't have to be a four-star general to employ this concept. We all use it on a daily basis as a way of rationalizing the adverse consequences of our modern way of life.

Take the case of traffic fatalities. We seldom think of cars as killers, but the fact is that in the United States, every single year more than 40,000 people are killed in traffic fatalities.[19] Traffic death is a global problem. The World Health Organization predicts that by the year 2030 road traffic accidents will be the fifth leading cause of death worldwide—behind heart disease, strokes, COPD, and lung infections—ironically, a bigger killer than all forms of cancer.[20] As a point of comparison, consider that about 50,000 American soldiers were killed during more than 10 years of active combat in the Vietnam War. I'm certainly not suggesting that it's safer to go to war than to drive down the street, but the magnitude of deaths due to motor vehicles provides food for thought. Yet we take it all in stride as a normal part of our daily lives. Traffic deaths are an acceptable loss for the convenience of operating our motor vehicles. It's just part of the risk we're willing to take to maintain our lifestyle. We've gotten used to it and seldom give it a second thought, unless tragedy affects somebody we know. Last year my nephew was killed in a car wreck. That was close and personal. It was a terrible tragedy for family and friends, and everybody was very distressed for quite some time—but nobody stopped driving. An estimated 2,600 deaths and 330,000 injuries are caused each year in the United States by cell phone use by drivers, according to the Human Factors and Ergonomics Society.[21] Yet the use of cell phones by motorists is ever on the increase.

I lived in Los Angeles for seven years in the 1970s. One of my college professors, a biologist, used to caution us about how the air in L.A. was so polluted that you had the same risk of dying from lung cancer as if you were a heavy smoker just by living there, even if you didn't smoke. That concern stuck with me. But I didn't move from L.A. because of pollution. I considered it an acceptable risk. The increased risk of dying from lung cancer hasn't kept the Los Angeles population from growing by leaps and bounds over the past thirty years.

I believe that, in much the same way, the concept of acceptable losses affects our thinking about our diet, exercise, and health. Poor health and disease are an acceptable price that we are willing to pay for the conveniences of our lifestyle. We see the headlines in the evening news about the latest scientific study linking heart disease to high cholesterol, and then we go off and buy a fat-drenched, fast food meal of greasy burgers and wash it down with a cholesterol-rich milkshake. We read a newspaper warning about why we need to exercise to stay healthy, but we spend more time watching TV to unwind from a hectic day at the office. Our doctor tells us we have high blood pressure, so we decide to take a pill rather than join a gym and work out, and then stop taking it because we don't like the side effects. We watch our neighbors, friends, and family members get sick with diabetes, heart disease, or cancer, and wish they had taken better care of themselves. But we don't make any changes in our own lifestyle. We've become complacent in our lives of ease and convenience. The lap of luxury is way too soft.

Optimism Bias

There is another insidious factor at work that psychologists have identified as *optimism bias*. Everybody always thinks that the bad thing is going to happen to somebody else. That's one of the reasons we are willing to risk death or dismemberment on the highways. Nobody thinks they're going to become one of the statistics because everybody thinks they're an above-average driver. Of course, this is a statistical impossibility. Nevertheless, "in study after study, from the United States to France to New Zealand, when groups of drivers were asked to compare themselves to the 'average driver,' a majority inevitably respond that they are 'better.'"[22] Psychologists call this the optimism bias, otherwise known as the above-average effect.

Public radio star Garrison Keillor refers to his fictitious town of Lake Wobegon as the prototypical American community "where every child is above average." This would all be in good fun, except that people really believe it. In a recent review of this curious phenomenon, David Dunning and colleagues from the

Cornell University Department of Psychology concluded that because of "the imperfect nature of self-assessment ... people's self-views hold only a tenuous to modest relationship with their actual behavior and performance."[23] What a charitable way to put it! The above-average effect distorts our judgment in all areas of life. Students overrate their ability in the classroom, employees "overestimate their skill" on the job, and, most importantly for the subject at hand, "People are unrealistically optimistic about their own health risks" according to Dunning. Basically, we all think that somebody else is going to get sick and not us. This allows us to justify continued overindulgence and inactivity, until we get a wake-up call in the form of a serious illness and life crisis that cuts through our denial and forces us to realize that we have become one of the statistics.

Dare to Be Different: Rebel Against Unhealthy Culture

Just because everybody else is jumping off the bridge, does that mean you have to too? Every Mother's Maxim

One of the hardest things to overcome is simple inertia or force of habit. We become accustomed to living our lives the way we have been, and unless we experience a major crisis, there may be little incentive to change. The force of habit may be synonymous with what anthropologists call the *domination of culture*, which means the sum total of lifestyle practices of any given group of people. This basically means that we do things the way everybody else around us does them, the way our parents did and their parents before them. Americans eat with a fork; Chinese use chopsticks, etc. It's not based on scientific evidence, and it doesn't mean it's right or wrong. It's just a custom, but it's darn hard to go against the grain of culture. People may think you're strange or sometimes even want to hurt you for doing things differently.

Unhealthy cultural habits have become an integral part of modern life. We have become acculturated to driving our cars everywhere, and we automatically use the elevator instead of taking the stairs. We eat the standard American diet of high-fat, cholesterol-rich meats and dairy products. We practice an unhealthy lifestyle in many other ways without giving it a second thought—because that's what we've learned and everybody else around us is doing it. That's the domination of culture.

The *Do Not Go Gentle* solution is to dare to be different. Dare to be a cultural rebel. Rebel against the culture of ease and convenience. Dare to be inconvenienced. Dare to be a little uncomfortable because your life and well-being are at stake. Dare to take a good, honest look at your current lifestyle. The first step to making serious lifestyle change is to recognize that you have a choice to be different. Explore unconscious denial and resistance that may be keeping you stuck.

I'd Rather Be Beaten on the Head

All neurosis is caused by the avoidance of legitimate pain. Carl Jung
One of my favorite Monty Python skits is a parody of American TV game shows. John Cleese, as the emcee, offers the champion contestant a choice between curtain A—an all-expenses-paid cruise around the world or curtain B—being beaten on the head with a large hammer. There's a drum roll. In the background you hear the "Oohs" and "Aahs" from the audience, all the while the contestant is agonizing over her decision, "Ooh, aah, I don't know," and the audience is coaching her along, "Take the cruise. No, no, take the hammer." Finally there's a hush as the contestant announces "I think I'll take being beaten on the head." Then a man comes from offstage with a great big cartoon-sized hammer, wallops her good one on the noggin, and she smiles and passes out.

This is obviously a ludicrous example by intent. It illustrates the difficulty we have making good choices, even if something is really in our best interest, in contrast to something that may be harmful. You would say why in the heck would anybody ever make such a choice? It's much like a passage in the *Big Book of Alcoholics Anonymous*[24] that I'll paraphrase: "Sometimes the choice between living a life of happy spirituality or dying a miserable alcoholic death is not an easy one to make." The fact is that we make choices like that all the time, day in and day out, but they are very minor ones. The smoker who lights up a cigarette and exclaims, "Well, there's another nail in my coffin" is showing more awareness than most—unfortunately of a negative type. Vague promises to change our ways justify continued overindulge. An overweight individual gasps at the numbers on the scale, then pops another sugary snack while nodding, "Yep, I'm gonna hit that treadmill tomorrow."

Fortunately, it is possible to identify our areas of resistance and work through them. The good news is that learning why we unconsciously resist change can help to overcome our inertia. Making the unconscious conscious, as Freud conceived it, can be the first step toward a solution.

The Couch Potato's Catch-22

Seniors, middle-aged folks, and even young people often fail to exercise because they are out of shape, but they are out of shape because they don't exercise. That's the old Couch Potato's Catch-22. It's like the proverbial snowball plummeting downhill and picking up speed. The sad truth is that the more out of shape you are, the harder it is and the more painful it can be to get back in shape. All of which makes you even more unlikely to exercise or engage in physical activity. So you put off exercise and get further out of shape, and consequently you become even less likely to exercise. Then perhaps you make a trial run of exercise, sprain an ankle, and say, "See, I told you it wasn't worth it." The solution is to overcome your denial and resistance to change, then practice a sensible lifestyle of moderate exercise and healthy eating. (See chapter 6.)

Denial and Resistance to Change

Our research was designed to determine what is true, not what is easy. Dean Ornish, MD, integrative medicine researcher[25]

There are many, many reasons why people resist making lifestyle changes. Change can be disorienting. Behaving differently seems odd. You're not used to it, and it doesn't feel right. Other people might not like it. Making changes gets you uncomfortable and anxious, and the discomfort can easily be eliminated by reverting to your old behavior—or practicing addictions or other unhealthy coping methods. There are dozens of seemingly good reasons not to change old behaviors. Unfortunately, the source of our resistance is not often readily apparent.

Changing your life is not easy. Change requires practice, persistence, and a lot of hard work. Anybody who has ever quit smoking, drinking, or using drugs knows how difficult it can be to change simple bad habits, especially if they have an addictive quality. Sometimes we may lack knowledge of alternatives. Stereotypes and erroneous beliefs about aging and healthy living can keep us stuck in our old ways. Change can be scary. Many of us avoid stretching our comfort zones because of fear of failure or rejection. Depression, anxiety or emotional problems also may limit our ability to make successful choices. We must overcome many types of resistance to free ourselves from unhealthy behavior patterns.

Making up your mind to do something is vitally important, yet it's one of those things that is simple but not easy. Unfortunately, we often beat up on ourselves mentally and emotionally—or others do it to us. Well-meaning family members and friends may say, "Why don't you get a grip on yourself?" or "It's all in your mind" or "You really just don't want to change!" The sportswear commercials telling us to "Just do it" and the antidrug campaign advising us to "Just say no!" can oversimplify. Understanding the psychological underpinnings of resistance can help to unblock your potential to make effective and positive changes in your life. Once you become aware of what is blocking you, you are free to act differently.

Overcome Resistance to Get the Most Out of Your Life

There's no pleasure on earth that's worth sacrificing for the sake of an extra five years in the geriatric ward of the Sunset Old People's Home. Horace Rumpole, *Rumpole of the Baileys* BBC TV series

Rebel against the establishment of cynicism and blame that is now rampant in the media and our contemporary culture by learning to fight your greatest enemy: yourself. Conquer your own resistance to making effective changes in your life, especially when it comes to self-defeating or unhealthy habits. This may be the most important element of successful aging, because resistance to change can keep you stuck in old habits (or attitudes) forever.

1. Explore your resistance. Make a decision to be honest, willing, and open minded. Be open to the feedback of therapists, friends, family, and others.
2. Recognize that resistance is normal. You are not odd because you feel reluctant. Everyone experiences it at one time or another. It is just a part of the whole process of change. Be prepared to deal with it.
3. Take a look at your level of motivation for change. Why do you really want to make changes at this time in your life?
4. Make a list of the rewards of successful change. Rewards you can directly measure might include better health, weight loss, better sleep, more energy, need for less medications, etc. Intangible rewards include feeling better, freedom, peace of mind, and happiness.
5. Do a cost-benefit analysis. Costs should include things you have to give up like avoiding responsibility for your own life or the pleasure of indulging in your old behaviors. Benefits might include the rewards you have identified for successful change. Hopefully, you should find that the benefits of change are greater than the costs.
6. Take responsibility for your own change. Nobody else can make a change in your life but you.
7. Monitor your progress. Keep a journal or a record of the changes you make. Review your progress daily, weekly, or monthly. Discuss your progress with a significant other.
8. Find a progress buddy, somebody with whom you can share in confidence and compare notes about changes each of you make. A support group can be very beneficial.

9. Make a conscious decision to act differently. Feel the fear and do it anyway. "Fake it 'til you make it," if need be. Trust the process of change, even if it feels uncomfortable.

10. Practice persistence. Keep in mind what Dr. Albert Ellis says: "The most effective way to change old behaviors is to consistently practice new behaviors." Keep on keeping on. Take it one step at a time, one day at a time—like they say in AA. Just put one foot in front of the other. "This too shall pass." Thomas Edison tried thousands of different methods before he invented the electric light bulb. He said, "I knew I had to succeed, because I finally ran out of things that didn't work."

11. Develop a positive mental attitude. Our attitudes and expectations help to determine what happens to us. Henry Ford was credited with the statement, "Whether you believe you can, or whether you believe you can't—you're right!"

12. Be more aware of resistance in your thinking. Take the advice of Epictetus (55-145 AD), the Roman philosopher who taught the basic principles of what we know today as cognitive therapy: we don't get upset so much by things that happen as by what we think about those things. Read a book by Albert Ellis, PhD, who pioneered cognitive therapy through the development of Rational Emotive Therapy.

13. Begin with small goals. Remember the ancient Chinese saying, A journey of 1,000 miles begins with the first step. Learn to accept progress not perfection. Live in the moment, and focus on each day as it comes. The twelve-step program one-day-at-a-time slogan is a highly successful application of this principle.

Activities and Solutions

Identify your own areas of resistance to change, using the information provided above. Have you discovered any other reasons you resist change besides those listed? What are you willing to do to overcome your resistance? How will you go about it? Make a plan and stick with it. Consider keeping a journal or sharing your plan with a significant other to increase your accountability.

Notes:

_____

_____

_____

_____

_____

_____

Chapter 6

It's Never Too Late to Change Your Whole Life Around

It's never too late to start all over again. Steppenwolf lyrics

Many consider age-related changes irreversible...Fortunately, they are mistaken. Not only can we recover much lost function and decrease risk, but in some cases we can actually increase function beyond our prior level. Rowe and Kahn, *Successful Aging*[1]

Many of us neglect prevention until it's too late, and then we become sick, incapacitated, or decrepit. By then we've lost hope and become despondent. Fortunately, no matter how much you've declined, you can always turn your life around to prevent further decay and even restore or improve functioning. Ironically, we often do better at restoration than at prevention, and the crisis of reaching a bottom can lead to exceptional changes. Persisting with a program of moderate exercise and physical activity can lead to immense and sustained improvements in health and quality of life.

It's Never Too Late to Get Back in Shape

Nobody deliberately plans to get out of shape. Our decline usually comes about over a long period of time through a lot of little choices like "I think I'll have another piece of that pie for dessert" or "I'll just watch TV tonight and go for a walk tomorrow." Slowly but surely the damage is done. Then one day we wake up, look in the mirror and say, "Who the heck is that?" At that point it's hard not to feel depressed and hopeless, feeling that you're too far gone to change now.

Some of us hasten our demise by practicing bad habits like smoking, abusing alcohol and drugs, or compulsively overeating. What may start as occasional overindulgence for some people leads to greater and greater excess, until a point is reached where it seems impossible to go back and practice moderation. We've all seen the statistics: most diet plans are unsuccessful, the vast majority of people who quit smoking start back up again, and only a tiny percentage of alcoholics and addicts who go through rehabilitation programs succeed in staying abstinent.

Overindulgence was a defining theme of the baby boom generation, but it has become part of modern-day life for many Americans. We are starting to pay the consequences as a nation. The number of disabled Americans is increasing, according to a May 2009 publication of the Centers for Disease Control, with 21.8 percent of Americans reporting a disability.[2] Ten percent of disabled Americans report that they are unable to walk three city blocks or climb a flight of stairs. A sad testimony to our generation is that the number of disabled boomers (ages 45 to 64) is almost as great as the number of older disabled (age 65 plus)—17.3 million vs. 18.1 million. More than one-third of the people on disability in this country today are boomers, and that fraction is increasing. The CDC's prediction is grim: "Given the size of the baby-boom generation, the number of adults with a disability is likely to increase dramatically as the baby boomers enter higher risk age groups over the next 20 years."

There is good news. According to the same CDC report: "Increasing physical activity, and reducing or preventing obesity and tobacco use can eliminate some of the underlying causes of disability for some people and prevent secondary conditions in those already affected."

It's certainly difficult to make major changes after practicing bad habits for many years, perhaps for an entire lifetime. However, it's never too late to get back into shape. Sometimes it takes a major health crisis to get our attention.

Take the Stairway to Health and Fitness

When he was 30 years old, Steve Silva weighed 435 pounds and was so incapacitated that he could no longer do his job as a high school gym teacher. He could hardly make it back and forth to the mailbox. Less than 10 years later, he stood in front of the Eiffel Tower, where he beat the world record for running a vertical mile. "If I could go from having a death sentence to beating a world record," Silva told a reporter, "others might realize that it's never too late to make a big change."[3]

Silva was motivated to get in shape after the birth of his daughter, when doctors told him he was so "dangerously overweight" that he probably wouldn't live long enough to see her fifth birthday. Joining a weight loss program that stressed exercise to burn off calories, he took up a truly pedestrian sport—climbing stairs. Sometimes he climbed 30,000 steps a week. Slowly but surely he lost weight and got into shape. By age 40 he was in peak physical condition, weighing in at 180 pounds with a five-foot, eight and one-half-inch muscular physique.

I came across Silva's story 20 years ago and was so inspired that I clipped the article and put it in a loose leaf notebook I titled *Inspiration*. The notebook is still in my office waiting room, with a collection of similar uplifting personal testimonials, to motivate patients (and me!). When I was writing this section of the book, I looked for recent information on Steve Silva, and I almost gave up looking because I feared I would find some unpleasant news. That's because the overwhelming majority of people who lose a lot of weight gain it all back with interest after a relatively short period of time.[4] Before discovering his stair-climbing method, Silva, using conventional medical treatments like diet pills and shots, "lost 100 pounds on six separate occasions, only to regain even more each time."[5] It was a welcome relief to discover that Steve Silva continues to maintain a 235-pound weight loss after more than 20 years. Furthermore, at age 60 he planned to climb the Eiffel Tower again, in commemoration of the twentieth anniversary of his Outdoor Vertical Mile Record.

In 1992 Silva set a Guinness world record for outdoor marathon stair climbing. He climbed up and down the stairs of the 79-story Peachtree Plaza Hotel in Atlanta, Georgia, for nearly ten hours, taking in a total of 45,708 stairs. The year earlier he finished the Million Steps Climb with a vertical mile record at Giants Stadium in New Jersey, and a total of 1,335,545 steps climbed in one year's time.[6]

Silva worked 16 years as a senior national trainer for Health Management Resources in Boston, which is the group he joined to lose all of his weight. He eventually began his own company in 1992, Silva's Life Steps and "specializes in working with clients that have given up hope." [7] His own life example shines forth as a beacon of hope. Silva's 1987 Eiffel Tower record "drew international attention by demonstrating that it is never too late to begin leading a healthier lifestyle."

Steve Silva qualifies as a spunky eldster because he inspires us to take better care of ourselves. Like Jack LaLanne, Silva recognizes the larger goal of motivating others. That is also my purpose in citing all of these amazing stories—to inspire you with the spirit of commitment, persistence, endurance, and sheer spunkiness. Leading a healthier lifestyle is definitely within your control. You don't have to go out and break world records to get into shape, but if you manage to set the world on fire in the process of becoming fit and trim, bully for you. Beyond the accolades, the most important victory you will achieve is your own physical health and fitness. Besides, as we shall see, as we get older the desire for personal recognition and achievement tends to become less important than helpfulness to others and benefit to the human community.

Is There Hope for a Couch Potato Like Me?

You have to work at longevity. To live a long life, you have to work at living. Jack LaLanne[8]

Perhaps you are overweight, out of shape, and in poor health. Maybe you've been a couch potato for most of your adult life. This is especially likely if you are an American, and even more so if you're over 50, because (as we've seen in previous chapters) the national standard of health is disturbingly low. You might read about Silva's transformation and think it couldn't happen to you because he was still pretty young when he decided to get into shape. As for Jack LaLanne and some of the others discussed in this book, they've been exercising all their lives. So what chance do you have? It's easy to adopt a fatalistic attitude, give up hope, and stop trying—especially if you've previously been unsuccessful with attempts to stay in shape.

Fortunately, there is a reason to be optimistic. Even though some of the spunky elders in this book have been lifelong athletes, there are plenty of others who never took exercise seriously until later in life—sometimes not until after they became senior citizens or developed serious health problems.

It's never too late to get into shape. No matter how unfit you may be, improved fitness, exercise, and physical activity can reduce health problems and even restore functioning at any age. You can never be too old to maximize optimum health in all three spheres—physical, mental or emotional, and spiritual.

Staying Young at Any Age

Kenneth Cooper, MD, was the inventor of aerobics exercise, which he initially developed to keep astronauts physically fit while in space. At age 67 he wrote a provocative book titled *Regaining the Power of Youth at Any Age*. Cooper challenges the notion that "true happiness is possible only if we can maintain some illusion of agelessness." [9]   Cooper writes to people between the ages of 31 and 75 with his "easy-to-use manual for recapturing their lost or declining youthful vigor,"[10] advocating a combination of impact exercise, aerobics, and stretching. His exercise program is specially designed to counteract the effects of aging—particularly to prevent loss of bone and muscle mass, and maintain cardiovascular power. "Building bone mass is an essential part of maintaining the vigor of youth," he writes. "Lean body mass provides us with the power and strength we need to continue to move, lift, and maneuver in our older years as effectively as we did when we were in our teens or twenties."[11]

Cooper clearly practices what he preaches. In *Regaining the Power of Youth,* he skillfully combines personal experience, research knowledge, and wit. While writing his book, he suffered a mountain bike riding accident and smashed head first into a rock. He consequently "became even more a believer in protective helmets than in the past."[12] This incident validates the claims of his exercise and fitness program: although he was in his late sixties, he didn't break any bones and only needed a little aspirin at night for soreness.

Cooper's exercise strategy promises "boundless energy and stamina, emotional resilience and optimism, and agile reasoning, creative thinking, and comprehensive memory."[13] These are qualities we all need at any age, but when we can reclaim them in middle age, it effectively demonstrates the power of exercise as a bona fide agent of rejuvenation.

You Can Never Be Too Old To Start Exercising

- "Weightlifter Bob" Fusillo of Atlanta, Georgia, didn't start lifting weights until he was 67.He currently holds the record for oldest professional weight lifter. In August of 2007—at age 80, he traveled to Hungary for the World Masters Weight Lifting Championship of the International Weight Lifting Foundation. He has won dozens of medals, competing all over the United States and around the world. Five years after he took up the sport, he won a gold medal in the World Master's Championship competition in Glasgow, Scotland.[14]

- Seventy-two-year-old Ada Thomas didn't start jogging until she retired at age 65. She worked up to running 5 miles a day, entered a marathon at age 68, and won the women's division in her age group a year later.[15]

- Eleanor Hyndman began taking karate lessons with her grandson when she was 78, and two years later she won a gold medal in competition.[16]

- Eric de Reynier learned to hang glide when he was 75, and he was still sailing off the Big Sur cliffs at 81 when Etta Clark interviewed him for her book on aging athletes. Reynier took up the sport one day while he was riding his motorcycle along the beach, and a much younger crowd of hang gliders—mostly 50 years his junior, must have seen him as a kindred spirit, so they invited him to join them. He told Clark, "Individuals must make up their own minds about what they want to do."[17] What we do in our old age is a choice—whether to just stay home and read about other people doing things or take the risk and get out there and do it ourselves.

- When she was 60 years old, Annabel Marsh ran all the way from Boston to San Francisco with two companions to commemorate the first women's marathon in the 1984 Olympics. En route she celebrated her sixty-first birthday. She didn't even start running until she was 47, and since then she has run up and down Pike's Peak 8 times and completed 50 marathon runs.[18]

- Before 89-year-old "Granny D" Haddock walked 3,200 miles across the United States to protest against the influence of big business on government, she spent several months getting in shape. She gradually built up her stamina by walking 10 miles a day carrying a 25-pound backpack and being able to "sleep on the hard ground in a sleeping bag without crying about it."[19] She was also prepared to "thumb a ride," according to the advice of her 64-year-old son, who anticipated a time when she would "come to her senses and want to get home from the middle of nowhere." She summarizes her training experience: "Through all of 1998 I walked and walked, probably about eight hundred miles in all, wearing out one good pair of hiking shoes." Republican Senator John McCain later bought her a new pair of sneakers when she was running for U.S. Senate on the Democratic ticket. (Pun intended!) Who says the hawks and doves can't work together for a good cause?!

Exercise: A Timeless Classic

Research shows that it is almost never too late to begin healthy habits such as smoking cessation, sensible diet, exercise and the like. Rowe and Kahn, *Successful Aging*[20]

A sedentary routine shortens your life and increases your susceptibility to many diseases and conditions we generally attribute to old age, including mental diseases like depression. What better way to lose weight and get in shape than to increase your level of exercise and physical activity? This has been known throughout human history—well, at least as far back as the ancient Greeks and Romans, who were among the first "civilized" people to begin writing everything down. Hippocrates (460-377 BC), the venerable *father of medicine,* said that "walking is man's best medicine." The renowned Roman politician and orator Cicero (died 34 BC) wrote that "exercise and temperance can preserve something of our early strength even in old age."[21] Ben Franklin was so impressed with Cicero that in 1744 he published his treatise on successful aging, and it was read by many colonists, especially the founding fathers.[22]

Today, all of the leading authorities on aging agree that exercise, together with proper nutrition and related lifestyle factors, is desperately needed, especially among the aging population—which includes all of us baby boomers. The National Institute on Aging regards exercise as "one of the healthiest things you can do for yourself" in their exercise guide *Fitness Over Fifty.*[23] Two prominent physicians' organizations got together in November 2007 for a conference titled Exercise is Medicine. Members of the American Medical Association and the American Academy of Sports Medicine invited U.S. acting surgeon general Steven Galson, MD, to give a luncheon speech titled, "Encouraging Exercise as a Prescription."[24] Galson cited the first of several pillars of President Bush's HealthierUS fitness initiative: "Be physically active everyday." He encouraged all physicians to educate patients and to use "exercise prescription as part of medical care and treatment for patients."

Imagine your family doctor writing you a prescription for exercise instead of more pills! Although I'm not licensed to prescribe medicine, I do make recommendations in all of my psychological reports. Since I read about Dr. Galson's *prescribe exercise* campaign, I've developed a standard recommendation for reports sent to physicians who refer patients to me to test for memory problems:

"I strongly encourage the physician to consider prescribing exercise. That may seem like an unusual request, but the surgeon general recently met with a group of sports doctors and AMA physicians and advised them to *prescribe exercise* because it can produce improvement in functioning in most areas when conducted in a sensible fashion, particularly under supervision, and combined with conventional medical care. An excellent program is called Silver Sneakers, which is run locally through the YMCA. A recent two-year student by the Centers for Disease Control involving 5,000 Silver Sneakers participants showed they had *"significantly fewer inpatient admissions and lower total health care costs."* The Silver Sneakers program is *"designed exclusively for older adults who want to improve their strength, flexibility, balance, and endurance."* I recently spoke with a Silver Sneakers coordinator who was excited about the significant improvement in people's lives. Many of them are able to maintain and sometimes regain an active, independent lifestyle with supervised regular exercise, combined with lifestyle changes in addition to their regular medical care."

I talk with many of my patients about the importance of exercise, physical activity, and good nutrition as vital to their mental and emotional health. I show them pictures of my mother-in-law jumping out of an airplane, give out brochures about good nutrition and healthy aging, and share my own experience with getting into peak physical condition.

Exercise as a Presidential Initiative

The sovereign invigorator of the body is exercise. Thomas Jefferson

The inactivity and poor health of Americans has been a major concern of American presidents since colonial days. Thomas Jefferson promoted exercise, writing that "walking is the best possible exercise. Habituate yourself to walk very far."[25] John Fitzgerald Kennedy proclaimed: "Physical fitness is not only one of the most important keys to a healthy body; it is the basis of dynamic and creative intellectual activity."[26] According to the World Health Organization, health is one of the most pressing global concerns of every country in the world. "The health of people is always a national priority: Government responsibility for it is continuous and permanent."[27] In 2002 President George W. Bush began the HealthierUS Fitness Initiative, which was kicked off with a three-mile commemorative run. Bush invited members of his cabinet to run with him. The next day he met with residents of Marks Street Senior Recreation Complex in

Orlando, Florida, to promote physical fitness among senior citizens. He presented his Four Pillars of HealthierUS:

1. Be physically active everyday.
2. Eat a nutritious diet.
3. Get preventive screenings for early disease detection.
4. Make healthy lifestyle choices like not smoking and use alcohol only moderately.[28]

Scientific Evidence for Minimal Exercise

There's a growing body of scientific evidence that even minimal amounts of exercise can have a significant impact. For managing obesity and overweight, the American Society for Clinical Nutrition states that only 30 minutes of moderate-intensity exercise (such as brisk walking) per week is needed to "control body weight" but 60 minutes is needed "to maximize weight loss and prevent significant weight regain."[29] These figures are based on "a growing body of scientific evidence." This level of exercise will improve your cardiovascular fitness, and in turn reduce your chances of death from cardiovascular disease and most other diseases commonly associated with aging.

How Much Exercise Do You Need?

If you can't afford a half hour three or four times a week taking care of the most priceless possession, your body, you've got to be sick. Jack LaLanne[30]

The following guidelines are adopted from recommendations by the American Heart Association, the American College of Sports Medicine, and the Centers for Disease Control.[31] The recommendations apply to adults between the ages of 18 and 64. For individuals 65 or older or people with functional limitations or chronic conditions aged 50 to 64 to sixty-four, experts recommend the same exercise strategy as for younger adults *with an important difference*—they should focus on "activities that maintain or increase flexibility" together with balance activities to protect against falls. This means to do a lot of stretching. And of course, adjustments should be made to accommodate any physical limitations or disabilities, and your personal physician's advice should always be sought. Keeping a record of your activity and progress is helpful, and consultation with fitness professions is also encouraged. If you are new to exercise, then you should start below the recommended levels and work your way up.

Three areas are addressed: moderate-intensity aerobic activity, muscle-strengthening activity, and reduction of sedentary behavior. There are two levels of activity, based on the amount of effort you put forth:

Moderate-intensity aerobic activity—defined as about half your maximum effort, based on heart rate and breathing. Rate your maximum effort at 10; moderate effort is 5 to 6. At a moderate level of effort, you should spend two and one-half hours a week (150 minutes) doing aerobic-type activities, mixed with weight training. Do aerobics work about 30 minutes a day, 5 days a week.

Vigorous-intensity means pushing yourself to 70 to 80 percent of your capacity. Vigorous effort is measured as 7 to 8 points, where 10 points is your maximum effort. At a vigorous level of effort, you should spend one and one-quarter hours (75 minutes) doing the same as above. Do aerobics work 20 minutes a day, 3 days a week.

The Center for Disease Control emphasizes that you can space out your exercise—as little as 10 minutes at a time, and you will still get the desired results.

What can you expect for your efforts? Following these recommendations can "reduce the risk of chronic disease, premature mortality, functional limitations, and disability." Furthermore, greater effort yields more improvement, so seniors are encouraged to exceed the minimum recommendations to "further improve their personal fitness, reduce their risk of chronic diseases and disabilities, or prevent unhealthy weight gain."[32]

Calorie level approach. The gold standard of exercise is to burn 2,000 kcal per week. To burn 2,000 kcal you would need to do the equivalent of brisk walking for about five hours. Walking about half an hour will burn about 200 kcal.[33] Combine aerobics with weight lifting, use exercise bikes, stair-step machines, etc.

I keep a Schwinn Airdyne bicycle at home to use on days when it's too rainy or cold to exercise outside. The Airdyne combines upper and lower body exertion for a more complete workout. I remember reading years ago about one of the Pittsburgh Steelers who used the Airdyne almost exclusively for his training, and one of the Dallas Cowboys kept in shape mainly by doing sit-ups and push-ups—several thousand a day! So you don't need a lot of fancy equipment to stay in shape. What you mainly need is the willingness to put in a lot of hard work over a long period of time and not give up—practice persistence and determination. I remember a guy I used to know bragged to everybody about spending a lot of money on what was then the state-of-the-art home fitness exercise machine. A few months later, I saw the machine standing in the corner in his spare room, draped with laundry left to dry.

Practice Moderation

Everything in moderation. Inscription on the Temple of Apollo at Delphi.

Are you the kind of person who overdoes it? Do you go from one extreme to another—not do anything for weeks or months on end, and then madly dash off on an exercise frenzy? Perhaps you run three miles when you haven't exercised in six months, and then after the ordeal you feel so much pain that you don't exercise again for two years. I've been there and done that. Fortunately, over time I've learned the value of moderation. Admittedly, I don't always practice it faithfully, but I've gotten much better at it over time. Back in my drinking days, I used to say that I believed in practicing moderation in all things, including moderation—meaning occasional excess was okay. How we can rationalize and justify our bad behaviors! Today I've learned to recognize increments of progress because it really helps to pat yourself on the back every now and then for a job well done.

Moderation has been a guideline for healthy living for thousands of years. I got to see the 'everything in moderation' inscription at the Temple of Apollo at Delphi when I gave my first international Do Not Go Gentle presentation at the

International Psychology Conference in Athens in July 2007. I couldn't read the inscription, of course. Later I got Mary to take a picture of me in front of a Greek-lettered billboard, pointing to the sign with a quizzical expression. I added the caption "It's all Greek to me!" and use the photo for humor relief during conference presentations.

Unfortunately, so much of our modern life seems to be governed by the principle of excess. We can't really blame the baby boomers for this—it's a symptom of our affluent lifestyle. The boomers happened to grow up during a time in human history when technology and abundance converged to allow for a greater satisfaction of needs and desires than ever before. The boomers can learn a thing or two, however, from their successfully aging elders.

Boomeritis

A favorite topic of conversation for the 55-plus crowd is hospital visits and operations, such as what body parts have been surgically removed or altered and, more importantly, which ones remain and do they still work? Dr. Kownacki's Journals

The good news is that more boomers are exercising, but some of them seem to be overdoing it. Unfortunately, many boomers don't recognize their limits and end up pushing themselves too hard. The downside to vigorous exercise is that sports-related injuries are now the second major reason people go to see their doctor in the United States, behind the common cold. This situation is attributed to the boomers, and sports injuries have increased 33 percent among boomers over the past 15 years and cost 18.7 billion in medical care. According to a recent *New York Times* article, "boomers are flouting the conventional limits of the middle-aged body's abilities," resulting in torn ligaments and cartilage, tendonitis, arthritis, bursitis, and stress fractures. Hip and knee replacements are needed. Among medical personnel the term "boomeritis" is being used to describe this phenomenon.[34]

Orthopedic surgeon Nicholas DiNubile, MD, applauds the baby boomers as "the first generation who are staying active on their aging frames," according to an interview in the London *Daily Mail*.[35] Dr. DiNubile explains that "physical exercise is the best way to deter aging in many ways. But it has to be activity of an appropriate intensity and type, something many baby boomers are not prepared to accept." He acknowledges that the root of boomeritis is the boomer trait of excess. There seems to be a combination of hubris and rush (type A behavior); boomers are more prone to ignore the pain and warning signs of their body, and to keep pushing themselves until they get hurt.

How to Avoid Exercise Injuries

In the year 2008, more than 166,000 people between the ages of 45 and 64—the boomer generation—were treated for "exercise- and exercise equipment-related injuries," according to Reuters Health.[36] The good news is that as a whole, aging individuals in America today are "basically fitter and more athletic now longer into our lives than we ever were," according to Dr. Ray Monto, spokesman for the American Academy of Orthopedic Surgeon. He advises that the older athlete should take extra precautions. Get your doctor's okay before starting a new type of exercise, especially if you have a history of athletic injuries. Vary your routine from day to day and focus attention on increasing your flexibility. Dr. Monto strongly recommends yoga for older athletes. Practice good nutrition; take lessons in your sport; workout with a balance of aerobics, resistance training, and stretching; and set aside plenty of time to rest. Dr. Monto believes that most elder exercise injuries can be avoided by allowing "enough time to rest between tough workouts." Keep in mind that your body is definitely older, even if you've been keeping in shape. "You can't beat yourself up the way you did when you were 20 because it takes longer to recover," he cautions. Don't be part of the "tidal wave" of boomeritis injuries.

Peak Performance

Our period of peak physical performance generally lasts from the late teens through the early thirties. As a general rule, aging athletes are not capable of the same level of performance as younger athletes. Older athletes don't set world records for speed and strength. Professional athletes have to retire at a relatively young age not because of age discrimination, but because they can no longer compete with the younger athletes. The armed forces will not accept enlistees for active military service after age 35, because older bodies are not efficient fighting machines. Even the spunky eldsters cited in this book have experienced general decline over time. Despite their physical fitness, they don't have the same level of stamina, speed, or strength as they did when they were younger. That's why they have separate age categories for competitive sports. Spunky eldsters who still find the need to compete do so only against others in their age group.

The purpose of exercise changes as we age. Our focus shifts from external rewards like the praise and recognition of victory to inner rewards. Maintaining a peak level of fitness as we age becomes important for the intrinsic merits, such as personal satisfaction, health and physical well-being. For some it can be a way to negotiate a major life change, like the death of a spouse.

At age 83, Ivor Welch was distraught when his wife of 57 years died. He began going for long walks. Soon he was running, increasing his speed and distance, and before long he had the stamina to enter a marathon. By the time he was 90 years old, he had run five marathons and won a dozen trophies. He told Etta Clark that he "had no major participation in athletics" [37] until he started running at age 83.

An Exercise in Moderation

The journey of a thousand miles begins with the first step. Chinese proverb

It's important that you recognize your limits and work into an exercise routine gradually, starting with low impact and build yourself up, while simultaneously losing weight and/or improving your physical fitness. After five years of working out, I can easily ride my bicycle 25 miles Friday afternoon and another 25 miles Saturday morning without even getting sore—so long as I do some simple stretching exercises afterwards. But it took a long time to get to that point; I started with simpler activities, shorter periods of exertion, and worked up gradually over time. Here's what I did to ease into a workout routine without injuring myself.

1. Make a commitment to exercise.
2. Join a gym.
3. Hire a personal trainer for a few hours.
4. Make baseline measurements (weight, waist and body measurements—including stomach size, blood pressure, BMI, etc. This is the hard part!) Keep records in a lab book or bound journal (not scraps of paper) so they don't get lost.
5. Continue working out on regular basis three times a week. The fact that most gyms require you to pay for a full year's membership can be an incentive to stick with it. It was for me because I always want to make sure I get my money's worth.
6. Begin with low weight and low strain. When in doubt, do a little less.
7. Gradually build up the amount of resistance and total exercise time. Be careful not to load yourself up so much that you hate to work out. It's much better to do a little bit than nothing at all. It's better to space out your workouts—such as every other day—than to cram it all in on weekends.
8. Include all three types of exercise:
    a. Resistance training: Weight lifting and physical exertion exercises that build muscle strength.
    b. Aerobics activity: Exercises that build your heart and lung capacity such as jogging, bicycling, stair stepping, etc.
    c. Stretching: Activities that keep you limber, improve balance, and help to reduce injury.
9. Periodic follow-up measurements.

Guiding concepts: Lose the competitive edge; focus on the quality of the moment. After 50 you can't measure up to the youngsters in terms of speed and strength. That doesn't mean you have to give up on yourself. Follow the example of these spunky eldsters I've mentioned. Overcome your resistance to change. Get yourself getting motivated and stay motivated. If you insist on going for the gold, there are plenty of age-handicapped competitive sports and activities, so you can still try to be number one if that remains important to your ego.

Be Prepared

Yes, I was a Boy Scout. I also learned the importance of being prepared as the oldest child in a family of five siblings. I know that when it comes to exercising, having the right equipment can make the difference between whether you succeed or fail in sticking with a program. Nevertheless, I can still be stubborn and stay stuck in my old ways of doing things. One of my old habits was never to get rid of a pair of shoes until they are literally falling apart at the seams. I stubbornly insisted on wearing an old pair of tennis shoes for jogging, even though they weren't designed for jogging, because they still had a lot of good leather left on them, and I didn't like the look of running shoes. Mary finally convinced me to buy a pair of running shoes in a new, different style. Once I got beyond the appearance, I was elated because the shoes felt so good. I tore off jogging around the track like a giddy schoolboy.

The moral of this story is that just because you've been doing something all your life, doesn't mean you can't try something different. My 85-year-old mother-in-law, Joseta, isn't nearly as pigheaded as I am sometimes about things. A while back she was having problems with her yoga class, so she talked to the instructor. It turns out the blue jeans she was wearing interfered with her yoga stretches. After getting a pair of pants specifically designed for yoga, she was better able to participate and enjoy learning yoga. It really does make a difference if you have the right equipment for the activity you're doing.

Adjust Your Attitudes

I don't always get what I want, and sometimes I don't even get what I need. But thank God, I don't get what I deserve! Dr. Kownacki's Journals

Even if you take all the precautions and have all the right equipment, you are still likely to experience some discomfort during your exercise workout and feel soreness afterward, especially when you first start doing something new. This happens anytime you exert yourself beyond your customary level of comfort, when you use different sets of muscles, or when you do things that you're not used to doing. You can count on it. Some famous aging athlete said that anybody over 40 who doesn't admit to having a few aches and pains is a liar. Knowing what to expect and having reasonable expectations will help you stick with your program better. However, I don't believe you have to be masochistic. My person limit-setting method is to exert myself until it's a little uncomfortable, but not terribly painful, and then go no further. You don't want to hurt yourself and lose the opportunity to do something you really might need to be doing.

You can also anticipate resistance against sticking with your program, especially if you've been a couch potato for a long time. The inertia of not doing anything is very powerful, and it can take a lot of sustained effort to overcome. That's why the dropout rate is high for most exercise programs.

However, you don't have to be one of the statistics. When you realize that it's normal to experience resistance to change, you can deal with it effectively. It's when you expect everything to go peachy-keen smooth and painlessly that you get into trouble. When I was in graduate school and the going got rough, my adviser would rally me his maxim "If it was easy, then everybody would be doing it!" My fellow students had a darker motto, a quote from the German philosopher Nietzsche: "That which doesn't kill me, strengthens me."

Today, I still struggle with my own resistance, even after going to the gym faithfully three days a week (mostly) for the past five years. Sometimes I just plain don't want to do it, and there are times I haven't, but they've been few and far between. It sometimes helps to shorten your workout or to lower your effort level—rather than to skip it entirely. One of the reasons I go to the gym when they open the doors at 5:00 in the morning is to get it over with. I can usually think of several dozen things to do instead that would be more immediately gratifying.

Positive Addiction

If you can't practice moderation, apply your addictive behavior and spirit of excess in positive ways.

Reading this book, you may think I'm a bit obsessed with weight lifting and physical fitness. I am, but that's okay. It's good to be a little obsessed with some things like exercise, diet, and good mental health. These are healthy obsessions. In his *Positive Addiction,* psychiatrist William Glasser examines the lives of exceptional people such as sports figures or famous athletes who excel in their field—people who seem "almost superhuman" and who have "incredible self-discipline."[38] What drives them to perform so well and stick with their talent? Glasser doesn't think it is willpower alone but speculates that perhaps they "become addicted" to their sport. At first you have to work very hard and utilize discipline to develop extraordinary skill and talents— that's the willpower part. Over time you become addicted to your exercise or sport. The classic signs of addiction are evident— obsessive involvement and incredible pleasure from the activity. There's even an element of withdrawal—the unhappy feelings and mental distress that arise when you stop your addictive behavior. An activity is a *positive addition* when it is beneficial to you, it helps to improve you physically, and "increases your mental strength," says Glasser. "A positive addict uses his extra strength to gain more love and more worth, more pleasure, more meaning, more zest from life in general." In contrast, negative addictions such as alcohol or drug abuse "sap the strength from every part of your life." [39]

In his semiautobiographical tribute to marathon racing, *On Running,* cardiologist Dr. George Sheehan discusses why people run: "The neighborhood athlete is willing to let you in on the secret. ... There is a natural high to be obtained legally."[40] The expression *runner's high* is not a figment of the imagination of overzealous joggers or marathon runners. There is a physiological reason why exercise can be addictive. It's rooted in basic principles of brain chemistry. When we exercise strenuously, our brain releases compounds called *endorphins*. Endorphins are chemically similar to opium and opiates like codeine and morphine and work the same way. To put it bluntly, vigorous exercise makes us hurt, so endorphins kill the pain and make us feel euphoric. This is the biochemical reality behind the expression 'no pain, no gain.' Some people are naturally more sensitive to exercise euphoria. In the 1977 documentary *Pumping Iron*, Arnold Schwarzenegger compared a good workout in the gym to sexual orgasm. Regrettably, I've never gotten that same kind of rush from my own efforts at the gym. Which is probably a good thing because then I'd want to stay at the gym all day long!

Dieting Is Not Enough—Get Thee to a Gymnasium!

The Center for Disease Control conveys the shared opinion of the experts, who all agree that "overweight and obesity result from an energy imbalance."[41] That means we get fat and out of shape from "eating too many calories and not getting enough exercise." Metabolism, genes, culture, and socioeconomic factors play a role, but behavior and environment "are the greatest areas for prevention and treatment actions." It all boils down to a very simple solution: eat less and exercise more. Although this is a simple solution, it is not necessarily an easy one.

When we talk about eating less, of course, we get into the subject of dieting. Unfortunately, diets don't work. According to health and fitness researcher Kyle McInnis, "dieting is largely ineffective in maintaining initial weight loss as numerous studies suggest the majority of dieters regain all lost weight within 3-5 years."[42] Diets are doomed to failure by their very nature. When people talk about going on a diet, they intend to make a temporary change in their eating habits for the specific purpose of losing weight. After they lose the weight, they revert to their old eating habits. In a nutshell, diets don't work because they are a *temporary* solution to a *long-term* problem.

Some medical experts advise us mainly to change our eating habits to maintain physical fitness (e.g., Drs. Joel Fuhrman and John McDougall). Others extol the virtues of intensive exercise (e.g., Drs. George Sheehan and William Glasser). Still others recommend both (Drs. Dean Ornish and Kenneth Cooper), which is the position I take. In my experience, exercise and good nutrition are equally important, and you continually have to work on both for lasting change.

Successful weight loss occurs only by making a permanent change in your eating habits and exercise patterns. Short-term diets and New Year's resolutions to join the gym that last a few weeks or months aren't going to cut the mustard. Sure, they will work, but the results only last until you get back to your old habits of excess and overindulgence. I've done it myself for years, and I know that it's an exercise in futility (pun intended!). In my experience, I've found that you have to commit to a pattern of eating and exercising that you can maintain for your whole life. That's what making a lifestyle change really means. That's the only thing that will guarantee lasting change. You have to learn to eat in a way that you can sustain for the rest of your life. The same holds true for exercise—you must find a way to get the exercise you need in a way that you can stick with forever. To do that, it's necessary to maintain a healthy balance between moderate eating and moderate exercise.

Activities and Solutions

Assess your current state of physical fitness. Calculate your body mass index (BMI). Make an exercise plan, using the guidelines above. Write it down and follow it. Don't plan a program that is so difficult you won't follow it. Share your plan with at least one other person. This increases accountability. Follow through with you exercise plan for one month. Then weigh and measure yourself. Repeat the whole thing for a second month, and you will have established a new, stable exercise routine.

To calculate your BMI: A quick and easy way is the use the Body Mass Index Calculator on the website of the American Heart Association (www.heart.org), or a similar source, where you can just plug in the numbers and let your computer do all the work. If you want to do the math yourself, here's how. Multiply your weight in pounds by 703, and divide by your height in inches

(12 inches = 1 foot) squared. Formula: Weight x 703/ height^2. (Metric measure: Your weight in kilograms divided by your height in meters squared.) What does this mean? Below 18.5 is underweight; 18.5-24.9 is normal. 25-29.9 is overweight, while 30 and above is obese. BMI is a good measure of your general physical health. High BMI correlates with increased risk of heart attack, stroke, early death, and many common diseases. Lower BMI is associated with better health and increased longevity.

Notes:

_____

_____

_____

_____

_____

_____

_____

Chapter 7

Make Your Midlife Crisis Work for You

Turn your midlife crisis to your own advantage by making it a time for renewal of your body and mind, rather than stand by helplessly and watch them decline. Jane E. Brody, fitness writer and journalist[1]

Aging brings new challenges that can be seen as either crises or opportunities. Pursuit of excess and overindulgence will guarantee plenty of health and spiritual crises for the aging boomers. Fortunately, boomers have great potential, because they are one of the best educated and most affluent generations in history. However, it still depends on taking care of your body, mind, and soul. A commitment to regular exercise and activity will increase your likelihood of successful aging. The midlife crisis can be turned to your advantage as a springboard for even greater development, whether brought on by abuse or neglect of the body, unpredictable disease, normal aging processes, or unexpected life tragedy.

Generation Excess

Excess and overindulgence were chief defining characteristics of the sixties. Dr. Garry Egger (2008), Australian lifestyle medicine professor at Southern Cross University and a boomer himself, calls the boomer generation "Generation Excess."[2] He criticizes the boomers for abandoning ecology and conservation in favor of "scorched earth gluttony," which is depleting worldwide oil reserves and advancing the timetable for global warming. In *Shame on you, Generation Excess,* he raises the provocative question: "Am I, and my generation partly to blame as the generation that tried to warn against all this in the '60s and '70s, but then said 'wait for me' as the world took off again in the 1980s?"

According to Christopher Lasch, historian and social critic, modern Americans have lost their sense of community. "After the political turmoil of the Sixties, Americans retreated to purely personal preoccupations," he writes in *The Culture of Narcissism.*[3] Lasch argues that we have become indifferent toward the past and lost our historic sense of mission as a nation. We have become culturally bankrupt, absorbed in the pursuit of the individual, with narrow-minded self-gratification as the ultimate goal in life. "To live for the moment is the prevailing passion ...to live for yourself, not for your predecessors or posterity...it's a spiritual crisis," he asserts. Americans have "become connoisseurs of our own decadence."[4]

In my opinion, boomers are only partially to blame for our current crisis. Excess and overindulgence have become national traits for Americans, Australians, Europeans and people in most affluent countries around the world—and it's gotten worse over time. The parents of boomers as well as boomers' children and grandchildren have all adopted this same lifestyle. Unquestionably, boomers have tried to do it "bigger and better," but the entire population has cultivated a lifestyle of excess and overindulgence. We all have become part of the problem, and therefore we all must become active participants in a solution. A lifestyle of excess is now a deep-seated vein in our cultural makeup, and only deep-seated changes will solve the problem. We have to overcome the dominance of culture. (See chapter 8, section Dare to Be Different: Rebel Against Unhealthy Culture.) A midlife crisis can provide an opportunity to rebel against the culture of overindulgence.

My own experience as an aging boomer is that some of the chief counterculture values run counter to the principles of successful aging. Excess and overindulgence threaten us with poor health, unhappiness, and shortened lives. Many of my generation have made the same discovery, and more are realizing every day that too much of a good thing can be bad for you— increasingly so the older you get.

The good news is that it's never too late to make changes. Midlife is a good time to take stock of where you have been and to make midcourse corrections. However, sometimes it takes a major life crisis to get motivated enough to make the necessary changes.

Midlife Crisis Renewal

Take care of your body with steadfast fidelity. The soul must see through these eyes alone, and if they are dim, the whole world is clouded. Goethe

If Generation Excess is experiencing a spiritual crisis, then perhaps a spiritual solution is needed. For some people, exercise can literally be a life-changing and spiritually transforming experience. Dr. George Sheehan found long-distance running in midlife transformative. "At age 45, I pulled the emergency cord and ran out into the world," he explains. "It was a decision that meant no less than a new life, a new course, a new destination. I was born again in my 45[5] year."[5] Some of the spunky eldsters in Etta Clark's *Growing Old Is Not for Sissies* experienced a similar midlife renewal through exercise. Sister Marion Irvine went jogging for the first time at age 48. Some of the other nuns in her order "were put off initially by her skimpy running clothes— shorts and a T-shirt," according to Clark.[6] "But they came to realize that she couldn't very well run in her knee-length habit." Sister Marion began running competitive races only five months after her first jog, and two years later she entered a marathon and set a record for women in her age group. In 1984, after six years of running, she qualified for the U.S. Olympic Trials and ran against women half her age, setting a record for oldest woman ever to qualify in track and field. Sister Marion, who is principal of a Catholic high school, earned a fitting nickname— "the Flying Nun."

Back to the Future with Hope

Even if you aren't obese or haven't run yourself into the ground with a life of excess and overindulgence, you can still experience a crisis of health. TV and film star Michael J. Fox, a baby boomer born in 1961, was diagnosed with Parkinson's disease at the unseasonably young age of 30. At the peak of his Hollywood career, he was informed one fateful day that he had "a progressive, degenerative, and incurable neurological disorder."[7] Yet he proclaims that his disease is a "gift" and therefore, he is a "lucky man." He chose *Lucky Man* as the title of his autobiography. He goes so far as to proclaim that if you were to offer him a deal to take away the last ten years of his life, during which he has been struggling with Parkinson's disease, "I would, without a moment's hesitation, tell you to take a hike."[8]

The Psychology of Reaching Bottom

Behold, I have refined thee, but not with silver; I have chose thee in the furnace of affliction. Isaiah 48:10

How could anybody be grateful for the infliction of a devastating disease? Michael J. Fox is certainly no masochist. He freely admits to enjoying a self-indulgent and egocentric lifestyle as a Hollywood superstar before his illness. He makes it clear that he would not choose an affliction like Parkinson's nor wish it on anybody else. He became grateful because of what he learned from his disease, and the magnitude of what he learned far outweighs the pain and suffering caused by his disease. "Coming to terms with my disease would turn out to be the best ten years of my life—not in spite of my illness, but because of it."[9] The curious paradox is that sometimes a personal crisis turns out to be a blessing in disguise.

How does a person's life change so much for the better because of an illness or similar crisis? What can we learn from a life-threatening disease to make us bless rather than curse our affliction?

What Michael J. Fox learned is the wisdom preached by Isaiah 2,500 years ago. It is the same lesson many of us experience when we find ourselves back up against the wall by a major illness, traumatic experience, or other tragic occurrence in life. The way we cope is rooted in spiritual principles known to humans since the dawn of time. Isaiah and the Hebrew prophets understood this, and so did the writers of the New Testament and the sacred scriptures of all religions. Members of twelve-step recovery programs practice these principles to overcome addiction. Medical and mental health practitioners rely on spiritual healing, although few are insightful enough to admit it. Oncologist Bernie Siegel freely declares that "God and I both have a role in getting people well."[10] He clarifies further, "Four faiths are crucial to recovery from serious illness: faith in oneself, one's doctor, one's treatment, and one's spiritual faith." He adds that spirituality is the most important "although seldom totally achievable by most of us."

The good news is that a crisis in our lives, especially one which is life-threatening, can be a potent force for unleashing our true spiritual power. How does it do that? There seem to be several psychological factors that work together to bring about the transformation.

1. Honest self-reflection. A crisis forces us to be honest because the danger is simply too overpowering to ignore. We must honestly look at ourselves and abandon blame, denial, and all of our customary defense mechanisms. Honesty results in enhanced personal integrity, increasing our genuineness and decreasing superficiality. Suppose you have been overweight and physically unfit for many years. You always meant to do something about it, but justify being out of shape because you have a family history of longevity and are convinced that your good genes will prevail. Then you have a heart attack and suddenly, the rationalizations vanish, and you see very clearly that not taking care of yourself has landed you on the skids. Honesty clears your mind and allows you to identify the problem, which is the first step to change.

2. Open-mindedness. A crisis directs us to look inward because everything outside has become chaotic. We may have lost our job, money, status, power, family and friends, reputation, or health—all our former sources of security and identity are no longer there. A crisis disrupts our routine and forces us to question what we are doing with our lives and why we are doing it. The core of our identity gets shaken loose, and in a crisis we become forcibly open minded. We experience an existential crisis—because we all need a sense of meaning and purpose to exist as fully alive human beings. Paradoxically, loss of external security and deflation of our ego lead to the discovery of our true inner self. As Jesus expresses it in the Gospel of Luke (17:33), "whosoever shall lose his life shall preserve it."

Viennese psychiatrist Viktor Frankl survived the ultimate horror—imprisonment in a Nazi concentration camp, where he was stripped of all earthly wealth and every last shred of human dignity. In that state of abject worldly poverty he discovered "the last of human freedoms"—the power to "choose one's attitude in a given set of circumstances."[11]

3. Willingness to embrace community. The crisis impels us to embrace something outside of ourselves because we realize that we can't solve all our problems alone. Each of us needs other people, and we need to feel connected with something larger than ourselves. This can be a hard lesson to learn. In a crisis, we become willing to receive from others, and to listen and actually hear what they say. We are drawn closer to family, friends or supportive others, discovering real intimacy, sharing and caring, empathy and acceptance. When we receive the acceptance of others, we learn to practice unconditional acceptance of ourselves. Then we can practice selfless regard and generosity towards others.

4. Prioritizing spiritual values. Coping with a crisis helps us to prioritize the important things in our life. The prophet Isaiah didn't extol affliction to trick the Hebrews into grinning and bearing their misfortune. He was addressing a fundamental human experience from the position of spiritual wisdom. Suffering can produce many benefits that wealth cannot bestow. Michael J. Fox said that after he became totally honest and told the whole world he had Parkinson's disease, he experienced a "tsunami of goodwill."[12] He found freedom because he was no longer "driven by the need for commercial success." He continued with his acting career and actually did some of his best work after the onset of Parkinson's. On the eve of his retirement from the acting profession because his Parkinson's symptoms made acting impossible, he received the highest honor for TV acting, an Emmy.

Two Types of Conversion Experience

For the wisdom of this world is foolishness with God. I Corinthians 3:19

In the *The Varieties of Religious Experience*, psychologist William James defines two types of religious conversion experience: the *volitional* type and the *self-surrender* type. Volitional conversion comes about largely through the effort we make with our personal willpower. It is a "regenerative change" and it is "usually gradual, and consists in the building up, piece by piece, of a new set of moral and spiritual habits."[13] That's what I'm talking about mostly in this book, although my hope is that by reading and practicing it, you may get a glimpse of the other. In the self-surrender conversion experience "the subconscious effects are more abundant and often startling."[14] In extreme cases the experience comes across you like a whirlwind. The Apostle Paul was struck down to his knees on the way to Damascus by a blinding light. Moses witnessed the burning bush on Mount Sinai. In a more subtle form, this is the surrendering, the *let go and let God* experience of people in twelve-step recovery programs. We lose ourselves wholly and become "absolutely dependent on the universe," according to James. Sigmund Freud wrote one of the most vivid descriptions of this experience: "A sensation of eternity, a feeling as of something limitless, unbounded—as it were, 'oceanic.'" Ironically, Freud admitted that "I cannot discover this 'oceanic' feeling in myself."[15]

According to James, there is no fine line between these two types of religious experience. Few of us get to see the burning bush, but we all catch a glimpse of glowing ambers from time to time. I'm a big believer in balance. The age-old faith versus works debate is resolved by the fact that we need both all the time. Behind the desk in my office, I have a woodcut image of a man with a muscular physique pausing while rowing a boat to gaze up at the starry sky with a look of mixed peaceful release and rapturous ecstasy. The caption below the picture reads "Trust in God but keep rowing to shore."

William James wrote that religion is "the belief that there is an unseen order, and that our supreme good lies in harmoniously adjusting ourselves thereto."[16] Religious experience is "an essential organ of our life, performing a function which no other portion of our nature can so successfully fulfill." The ultimate meaning and purpose we give to the universe are ultimately religious, and how we act on that determines the quality of our experience in life. "When all is said and done, we are in the end absolutely dependent on the universe."

Spirituality and Psychology: Post-Traumatic Growth

We like to make elaborate plans for retirement, save up money in IRAs, invest in dream homes, make scrapbooks of travel destinations, and fantasize about how nice it's going to be when "our ship finally comes in." The problem is that the ship may never arrive. The Buddhist nun Chondra Pema offers an excruciatingly poignant metaphor, encouraging us to think of our life as an ocean cruise—a cruise on a boat that sets a course for the middle of the ocean in order to sink. The imagery is almost too grim to contemplate, but it's a stunning parallel to the reality of human existence.

The goal of such imagery is to help awaken us from our slumber, to encourage us to start living our lives fully in the present moment. We have to learn to find meaning in the process of daily living—not only in the ends for which we strive. A good chef learns to enjoy preparing and cooking a meal as much as serving and eating a gourmet dinner. If you gripe your way through a task and see only the tedium of your chores, then you probably won't have a positive mental outlook when you finish your work.

Spirituality is not without its earthly rewards. Individuals with spiritual beliefs are able to cope more successfully with major life traumas. This was the finding of Lyndal Walker's doctoral dissertation, which examined *posttraumatic growth* among survivors of breast cancer, spinal cord injury patients, HIV/AIDS patients, and survivors of accidents and natural disasters.[17]

Posttraumatic growth is a new field of study. Mental health professionals traditionally focused on the pathological outcome of trauma, with a goal to restore the sufferer to some type of normalcy. The focus of posttraumatic growth is on positive outcomes. There is a long tradition of seeing suffering as the source of psychological benefits. Two psychology professors from the University of North Carolina at Charlotte, Richard Tedeschi and Lawrence Calhoun have extensively researched this area and come up with surprising results. "In the developing literature on posttraumatic growth, we have found that reports of growth experiences in the aftermath of traumatic events far outnumber reports of psychiatric disorders."[18] We're talking about people who survived "critical life crises" like sexual assault, combat trauma, and hostage situations, as well as life-threatening physical illnesses like cancer, heart attacks, and HIV. Interviews with trauma survivors demonstrate many areas of positive growth experience, including "improved relationships, new possibilities for one's life, a greater appreciation for life, a greater sense of personal strength and spiritual development."

Brain Cell Regeneration

One hundred years of biology textbooks have taught students that adults lose brain cells throughout their lifetime, but new brain cells do not appear. That old paradigm has begun to shift. Researchers at Princeton University discovered that new neurons develop in the brains of adult monkeys throughout their lives. Elizabeth Gould and her colleagues discovered that new neurons appear in the cerebral cortex, the most advanced portions of the brain responsible for memory, learning, and complex decision-making.[19] Scientists have long observed this process of new brain cell growth or neurogenesis in birds and rats, but it was assumed that the brains of humans and more highly developed animals like monkeys were too complex for this to occur. The full implications for treating brain disorders and injuries remain to be seen, and neuroscientists tend to be conservative. The possibilities are exciting, nonetheless. Princeton engineer Steven Schultz wrote that this research "opens vast new areas that can be explored."[20] One possibility is the introduction of new brain cells into the memory centers and other key regions of the brain.

Researchers in Sweden and Denmark have pioneered brain cell transplants for Parkinson's patients. Embryonic brain cells are inserted into the regions of the brain that have been destroyed by Parkinson's disease and the new brain cells replace the diseased cells. So far, about 250 Parkinson's patients have been treated in experimental trials in various countries around the world, and they have experienced "pronounced improvement."[21] Scientists have shown that most of the transplanted cells remain unaffected by Parkinson's disease after more than a decade and "recipients can still experience long-term symptomatic relief."[22] Unfortunately, some of the new cells show signs of Parkinson's after an extended period of time. Ethical concerns have slowed down scientific progress in this area, however, and the whole debate over stem cell research is riddled with complex and controversial ethical issues.

Get Sick and Tired of Being Sick and Tired

There must be some other way to go through life besides getting dragged through kicking and screaming. Hugh Prather

Fortunately, you don't have to experience a life trauma to become spiritualized. Plenty of people are able to initiate major changes in their life simply because they get to the point where they are sick and tired of being sick and tired. The trials and tribulations of everyday life, with the occasional crisis, can be a springboard for tremendous growth and development. Even a minor crisis can get our attention and help us shift our priorities.

Most of us run our lives on a kind of automatic pilot, without much conscious effort. We may not necessarily be in a rut but get stuck in our old patterns of behavior. The equilibrium of our lives may not be comfortable, but at least it is familiar. Changing our behavior is hard, and we tend to avoid it, if at all possible. Sometimes we go well out of our way to keep things the same in our lives. The pain of a crisis can be a great motivator to change. Fear can serve a similar purpose. The fear of death and disease can motivate us to do things that we would never do otherwise. In this sense aging is good because the older you get, the more you have to face declining health and your own inevitable demise.

I know this firsthand from my psychology practice. Nobody gets up in the morning, looks in the mirrors and says, "Gosh! I feel great today. I'm madly in love with my husband, our children are polite and respectful, and I couldn't ask for a better boss. My life is so wonderful that I think I'll go pay some psychologist a hundred bucks to tell her how happy I am!" Nobody goes to the doctor because of their good health. People are motivated to get help by pain and suffering—reaching a bottom, as it's often called.

The transformation of suffering into spiritual satisfaction is not the exclusive domain of religious martyrs and saints. It is a fundamental human experience. Pain, both physical and emotional, is a basic source of motivation to change. However, most of us are willing to go to great lengths to avoid any form of suffering. Psychologically, we do this at our own peril. Carl Jung wrote that the origin of all neuroses is the avoidance of legitimate suffering. Healing begins when we are honest with ourselves and confront our legitimate suffering head on. Accept it for what it is. Many people believe that we have to wait until we are free from pain, suffering, and all bad habits to accept ourselves as successful human beings. Quite the contrary, according to humanist psychologist Carl Rogers: "The curious paradox is that when I accept myself just as I am, then I can change."

Suffering is a fundamental fact of human life. Suffering is so universal that the Buddha made it the first principle of his religion. What will we make of it? How do we deal with it? Do we let it overwhelm us and control our life, and transform life into misery and chronic despair? Or do we use it as an opportunity, a learning experience, and a challenge to cope to the best of our ability? When we rise to the challenge of a crisis, we learn a valuable lesson that we are not just passive observers but active participants in our own lives. That's the approach taken by the spunky eldsters quoted throughout this book. The good news is that each of us is capable of doing the same thing.

Take the Subway to Satori

Spiritual transformation doesn't require you to join a monastery, spend years in meditation on a mountaintop, or read lofty metaphysical textbooks until your eyes get blurry. All of us get to complete an unstructured course in spiritual discipline just by being part of the human race. You will inevitably obtain all of the opportunities for spiritual growth and development just by being part of a family, living with a spouse or roommate, holding a job, or just functioning on a day-to-day basis in modern society.

When an old high school buddy found out that I was getting married, he called to congratulate me and added, in his customary cynical style, that "marriage will force you to confront your own immaturities in a more unavoidable fashion." By golly, he was right. No matter where you go or what you do in life, it all boils down to a simple quest—learn how to be comfortable in your own skin and to live with other people and not drive yourself and everybody else crazy.

Here are a few of the basic principles behind successful habit change and spiritual transformation, based on normal, day-to-day life. You don't have to be a guru to apply them, but you can still take the subway to satori. The lessons of life are everywhere. As Simon and Garfunkel put it, "the words of the prophet are written on the subway walls."

Learn to Defer Gratification

Watch and pray, that ye enter not into temptation: the spirit indeed is willing, but the flesh is weak. Matthew 26:41

Why do we find it so hard to get motivated to practice prevention and take care of ourselves, so we don't reach a crisis state that forces us to change? I think it is largely because we give in to convenience and immediate gratification, rather than defer gratification to prudent, long-term self-interest. Overcoming the addiction to immediate gratification may be one of the biggest challenges to serious lifestyle change. Future well-being is pretty remote and far off—it may never even get here. In contrast, I know I can feel better now, for a short while, by overeating, drinking too much, smoking, etc., etc. Similarly, the problem isn't lack of knowledge. Let's face it, everybody knows that junk food is bad for you, and we're all aware that failure to exercise and being overweight and out of shape will do us harm in the long run. However, we keep doing what we've been doing and don't make any changes. Why? The bottom line is that we have developed bad habits that have become part of our modern culture. It's not easy to change the habits of a lifetime, and so "reversing the [obesity] epidemic will take concerted action by all sectors of society," according to the U.S. Dept. of Health and Human Services.[23]

A buddy of mine used to say "most of the work in the world is done by people who don't feel like doing it." That's why most jobs pay you after you've done the work and not before you finish the task. That's why you get your diploma after several years of toil and discipline and not right after you sign up for an evening psychology course. Sometimes I have to force myself to take the first step. Once you get the momentum, the rest gets easier the longer you've been following any program or discipline.

People in twelve-step recovery programs have to struggle with this issue big time. That's why they offer a standard line of advice to neophytes: the time when you least feel like doing something you really need to do—such as to attend an AA meeting or fulfill an obligation—is when you mostly need to do it. In other words, you refuse to indulge your resistance. You identify your resistance for what it is, but then you don't act on it. Sometimes you will find yourself doing exactly the opposite of what your old pattern of thinking is trying to get you to do. And that's okay. You may experience a tremendous sense of freedom from realizing that you are no longer a slave to your old habits.

Persist Until You Succeed

I will persist until I succeed. Og Mandino[24]

Persistence is the key to success in most endeavors. There's an old story about a young man frantically walking up and down the streets of New York City. He comes upon an elderly gentleman and asks, "Sir, please, how do I get to Carnegie Hall?" The wise old man nods his head, smiles and replies, "Son, you just have to practice, practice, and practice." I keep a copy of Og Mandino's 1968 motivational classic, *The Greatest Salesman in the World,* on my shelf of inspirational books. Chapter 10 deals with the theme of persistence, and I've read it repeatedly over the past 25 years, sometimes several times a day during trying periods of my life. Mandino's inspirational passages helped get me through some of the darkest days of doctoral studies and dissertation tedium. Mary once caught me chanting the 'I will persist' mantra and asked, "Are you working on your irritation again?"—a truly brilliant Freudian slip that I'm sure Robin Williams would have been proud to come up with for a comedy routine.

It's important to persist even in the face of obstacles, because things seldom work out according to our expectations. We need to keep focused on our long-range goals even when we're not enthusiastic about all of the hard work it takes to obtain them. A government agency supervisor once told me during a job interview: "You got a master's degree. That means you put up with a lot of things you didn't like doing and worked with a lot of people you didn't like working with, but you still got the job done. You'll be great working for us!"

Persistence is the key. Keep trying, and you will eventually succeed. Thomas Edison never gave up. A reporter once accused him of being a failure, because he made so many unsuccessful attempts to invent the light bulb. "I have not failed," he replied. "I've just found 10,000 ways that won't work."[25] Not giving up is an important part of coping.

There's too much cynicism in the world today, especially about the subject of aging. We need to look to the light at the end of the tunnel, realize that it's never too late, and understand that no effort is ever wasted, no matter how small. Effort and determination are always important. More and more as we get older, it's not the size of our achievement or results that matters, so much as the magnitude of our effort. One of my religion professors once told us an old Hassidic story that's always stuck with me. The story is about a farmer standing in the back of the temple one day. As the rabbi conducted the service, this farmer just stood there singing out the Hebrew alphabet. He made such a fuss that the rabbi had to go over and talk to him.

"Whatever are you doing, my good man?" The man stared down at the floor, embarrassed for a moment, and then explained how his father was so poor he could only afford to send him to school for two days. Consequently, all he ever learned was to sing the alphabet song. "I can't read the scriptures or prayer books or the psalms, but I figure if I just sing out the alphabet loud enough, then the letters will rise up to heaven and God can arrange them any way he wants."

Practice the Wisdom of Imperfection

If something's worth doing, it's worth doing wrong. Recovering perfectionist's motto

Don't worry if you don't do everything right the first time— or the second time or the thirty-seventh time, especially if you're practicing a new behavior and developing new habits. I still have to work hard not to beat myself up over minor failings and setbacks. I'm a big believer in the use of motivational adages and anecdotes to keep yourself on track. That's why I cite a lot of them throughout this book and during my *Do Not Go Gentle* presentations. Such as the metaphor about automatic pilot that was a favorite of the late Jack Boland, a Unity minister and motivational speaker. I used to think of automatic pilot as some type of invisible cable that guides the airplane safely to its destination. However, automatic pilots (or inertial guidance systems) are not perfect, and they accumulate errors over time. They require continual checking and rechecking to make sure that the plane stays on course. What this means, as Boland inferred, is that most of the time the airplane is off course, so it must continually make course corrections.

What a wonderful story about persistence in reaching our goals! It really helps to sooth my flagging confidence when I realize that even multimillion-dollar jet aircraft spend most of their time off course. I don't feel nearly so bad about my own minor setbacks, such as spending three years to write a book after going to a conference presentation in 2007 titled How to Write a Book in 30 Days. The automatic pilot metaphor is a good remedy for perfectionism and know-it-all-ism because it helps you to realize that you never can do anything that's absolutely perfect. Everything we do is a work in progress, and we must continually realign ourselves to our goals, following the guidance of our ethics, principles, standards, dreams, and ambitions. Getting back on track is the key. Like in Frank Sinatra's song "That's Life"—every time your find yourself flat on your face, you have to pick yourself up and "get back in the race."

Ease Into It

Easy does it. AA proverb

Any type of change in behavior involves risk. Especially with exercise, injuries can occur if you don't know what you're doing. Injuries can occur even if you are experienced. Health problems may demand the modification of standardized procedures. When it comes to physical fitness and personal wellness, one size does not fit all. It's always important to consult with your physician before starting any new exercise program. Learning the ropes from a trainer or person experienced in your form of exercise is also a wise move. The *Archives of Neurology* cites the case of a vertebral artery occlusion developing in a young adult shortly after doing yoga neck stretches.[26] An acquaintance of mine hurt his back doing yoga and had to see a doctor for severe back and hip pain. He was still receiving treatment a year later. I pushed myself too hard in a yoga class once, trying to keep up with the others, and hurt so bad I didn't go back. Fortunately, I discovered coffee yoga.

Try a Cup of Coffee Yoga

It was Christmas time a couple of years ago. Mary and I were waiting in line at the coffee shop of a local book store after browsing for holiday gifts. I spotted a unique item called *A Morning Cup of Yoga*[27] and secretly bought it for Mary as a stocking stuffer. In truth, I considered it something of a gag item and didn't think any more about it. I preferred to remember the book by my tongue in cheek retitling—*Coffee Yoga*. This is a play on words. *Hatha yoga* is one of the popular forms of yogic practice, so I really got a kick out of calling Mary's version *Coffee Yoga*. Then one day I saw Mary doing some odd stretching while standing near the coffee machine in our kitchen; she was following the book, which teaches a dozen or so basic yoga exercises that can be performed while waiting for your morning coffee to brew. Out of curiosity, I watched Mary do a few of the amazingly simple stretches. She later taught me some of them—which of course I resisted, still unprepared to take the book (or yoga) seriously. I didn't really see it as a genuine exercise.

After a few weeks, Mary told me about improvements she experienced as a result of doing her coffee yoga. She became more flexible and more limber. "It used to hurt to squat," she told me. Yoga greatly reduced the aches and pains from bending. "I could move in ways that I couldn't move before. I regained the capacity to be limber and flexible that I had as a younger person."

This yoga practice was beginning to sound like some kind of fountain of youth! Still halfheartedly, I tried out a few more of the exercises I'd seen Mary do; I even read the book a bit until I had a ten-minute routine. At first, the exercises appeared so simple and insignificant they seemed hardly worth doing. For example, one stretch is called Reaching to Heaven, and all you do is stand up straight, hold your arms over your head, and alternatively stretch each arm upward. That's like half a jumping jack, which I've never really considered being much of an exercise at all—I guess I'm a calisthenics snob! However, I discovered that I shouldn't let the seeming simplicity (or lack of ache) of some of these exercises deceive me. Small movements practiced consistently over time can yield big rewards.

The strange thing is that once I started focusing on the quality of the yoga movements, by being more fully in the moment while doing these simple stretching exercises, a new dimension opened up. That element of focus, of truly being still, of working on poise and balance was all quite a novelty for me. I began to perform each simple exercise wholeheartedly, concentrating totally on the experience rather than the outcome. Ironically, once I placed my attention on the process, the outcome took care of itself. I began to notice changes, subtle at first, but important and far reaching. For years, I had been plagued by a bone spur in my left big toe joint, an injury sustained from kicking a concrete wall while playing hand ball when I was 20 years old. The pain kept me awake at night, especially after an active day. I tried various topical creams and over the counter pain meds—which I really didn't like using. The best relief came from rubbing the toe and surrounding regions for 10 to 15 minutes with a vibrator. I wore out the smaller models and eventually operated one of those enormous thumper brands, with the gigantic head and two round balls on the end—the kind that looks powerful enough to relax a rhinoceros. Unfortunately, the thing was a loud as a jackhammer and almost as heavy. The sound and vibration were so forceful, that as soon as I plugged it in Mary and the three cats jumped off the bed and fled the room in sheer terror.

Then along comes this coffee yoga, which I grudgingly stuck with until, lo and behold, it more or less got rid of the problem. Coffee yoga proved to be the gentler, softer way of pain relief for my bone spur.

Having done coffee yoga now for well over a year, I am a firm believer in its effectiveness and find the practice essential. I strive to do it twice a day, morning and night. It keeps my legs from getting sore after bicycling, especially on days when I pedal 20 or 30 miles at a stretch. It helps me to relax and wind down so that I go to sleep faster and feel more rested when I wake up. I do bits and pieces of the routine throughout the day, whenever I feel stiff or if an opportunity arises such as when I take a writing break or while standing in a line at the bank or a store. Opportunities are endless, if you don't mind too much what other people might think about your impromptu yoga in unconventional places. It also helps to maintain a rebellious spirit and be willing to deviate from cultural norms.

Activities and Solutions

How would you define a *midlife crisis*? Do you believe you've had one or are you going through one now? Have you experienced a major health problem or crisis? How did it affect your life? Review the basic principles of reaching bottom, discuss them with a friend, spouse, fellow church member, spiritual guide, or other trusted person. Read one of the books mentioned in this chapter.

Notes:

_____

_____

_____

_____

_____

_____

_____

Chapter 8

Dare to Be Inconvenienced: Exercise as an Act of Cultural Rebellion

Who wants a life imprisoned in safety? Amelia Earhart

If you really want to be a cultural rebel, try riding a bicycle half the distance you drive your car for commuting to work and leisure activities. There are many opportunities in our daily lives to become more active, so be creative about it. Dare to be inconvenienced. Go against the flow of modern society's ease and expediency. Discover the rejuvenating power of exercise and fitness. Taking better care of your body will automatically improve your mental outlook and restore your emotional health. The good news is that you don't have to wait for a personal calling to become motivated. Anger and guilt can be potent motivators for change. Sometimes we can do the right thing for the wrong reasons, and that counts, too.

Lifestyle Diseases and Car Culture

We have come to crave as absolute necessity comforts and conveniences that didn't even exist a few years ago. Dr. Kownacki's Journals

Inactivity is a lifestyle problem, a disease of modern civilization. It stems directly from three factors: cities, cars, and industrialization.[1] Obviously, progress and civilization are mixed blessings. As our modern way of life spreads around the world, so do the diseases of inactivity.[2]

Only 8 percent of the people in the world own cars. People in the United States own 25 percent of all the cars in the world but represent only 5 percent of the world's population. In China most people in urban areas ride bicycles; there are 250 bicycles for every car on the road. Compare that to the United States, where it's just the opposite. In many parts of the country, adult bicycle commuters are a fluke. While I was growing up, the only adult

I ever saw riding a bicycle regularly was a mentally challenged man. In some of the more progressive cities and suburbs, you will see a few adult bicyclists. However, in most regions of the United States commuter bicycle riding is still an anomaly. I've ridden my bicycle to work twice a week for the past year and a half, and rarely have I seen another adult commuting on a bicycle. There are plenty of mature cyclists who ride recreationally on the city's bicycle trail. I see a few children riding bicycles to school. But I've only met two adults who regularly rode a bicycle to work. One man was mentally challenged and pedaled out of necessity because he couldn't pass the examination to get a drivers license. The other rode a bicycle because he'd lost his driver's license after driving under the influence of alcohol.

Exercise as an Act of Cultural Rebellion

When I see an adult on a bicycle, I do not despair for the future of the human race. H.G. Wells

It's easy to lapse into cynicism and despair when we look at the gloomy statistics about our nation's poor health. You can get depressed just looking in the mirror if you're grossly overweight and out of shape. Many people have given up hope for a better life. They watch the evening news, get jaded by the latest inhumanities and negative sensationalism, and then retreat further into overeating and escapism. Some send away for the newest exercise machine after watching an infomercial, with plenty of good intentions, but only use it a few times before retiring it to the spare bedroom to collect dust in a corner before the monthly payments are all made. I've been there and done all that myself, and so have many people I've known.

Fortunately, there is a way out. It is possible to work out a solution despite being firmly entrenched in our habits of convenience—if you are willing to try something different and dare to be inconvenienced.

Lifestyle Change from the Inside Out

I think the most successful changes come about when we incorporate new behavior patterns into our current lifestyle.

Don't try to stop doing something, but rather begin doing something different. Practice the substitution rule of behavior change. Focus your effort on developing a new habit, and the old habit will fade away from attrition. For example, don't give up eating junk food. Instead, surround yourself with healthy foods and start eating only things that are good for you. Substitute fresh fruits and vegetables for the unhealthy snacks and junk food in the house. Starve yourself into eating healthy. Don't try to quit being a couch potato. Instead, start living an active lifestyle. Go for a walk around the block for 30 minutes after dinner, instead of sitting down to watch a TV show. You can always find ways to incorporate more physical activity into your daily schedule, no matter how crowded your agenda may be.

Life Imitates Art

In his 1970 comic farce *Bananas,* Woody Allen plays the part of a product tester who converts an office desk into an exercise station. The *Exec-usizer* is advertised as "a device to help busy executives get in their daily exercise without ever pausing in their crowded work schedule." The desk chair is a stationary bicycle, equipped with a seat belt so you don't fall out when answering the telephone, which is spring activated, or when working out your back and shoulder muscles using springs mounted on the wall behind the desk. The drawers are connected to weights, so you can exercise your biceps when opening them. There's a basketball hoop above the filing cabinet, and the ball drops from the basket into the top drawer, where a mechanism throws it back to you at your desk. The whole set up is a prop for Woody's slapstick madness, and the fun begins when the machine goes out of control, pelting Woody repeated with the basketball, beating him nearly senseless until he's finally knocked off the bicycle.

The whole concept is meant as a joke, but there's deadly seriousness at play here. It took thirty years, but corporate American has finally gotten the message. A financial firm in Minneapolis, SALO, conducted a six-month study designed to combat office obesity by testing the effectiveness of "state-of-the-art treadmill desks."[3] The strategy is based on the following facts:

walking two and one-half hours burns up 350 calories a day, which results in a loss of 30 to 50 pounds a year. It saves the company more money in the long run to have healthy employees.

The treadmill desk is essentially a normal exercise treadmill, except that instead of handgrips there's a modified desktop with a computer console and keyboard. The treadmill only runs at two mph, which is enough to help you burn off 100 to 150 calories an hour. The company started with four treadmill desks, but they proved so successful that twelve more were added. Some of the treadmill desks were installed in a conference room, so employees can have walking meetings. At the end of the six-month trial, office staff lost nearly 200 pounds. One woman was 70 pounds overweight when the study began. At the end of six months she had lost 12 pounds and went down 3 dress sizes.

The treadmill desks were designed by Dr. Jim Levine, an obesity expert from the Mayo Clinic. The desks are not cheap and cost about $4,000 each. But how much money would that save in long-term health care bills, lost productivity, and related business losses? Mary and I recently bought a treadmill for home and another for the office. For a few dollars, you can buy a bookstand or an adaptor to set your laptop on the treadmill. Special desktops that fit over a conventional treadmill are also available for sale for a few hundred dollars, but you can improvise one with a plank and clamps.

ABC News, which interviewed Dr. Levine and SALO employees, met a woman from Texas who designed her own "walking desk" with an extra leaf from her dining room table. She experienced skyrocketing weight after giving birth to triplets. Working out of her home on an Internet consulting business, she lost nearly 50 pounds in a year and a half with her walking desk.[4]

Corporate Recess

I think that instead of coffee breaks where people gather to drink coffee, smoke cigarettes, and eat junk food, we need to have mandatory recess in the workplace. That's what they do in the elementary schools, and I know from long experience that you don't want to mess with a kid's recess or there's hell to pay.

Whenever I spend the morning at a local school, I make a point to never take the kiddos out of recess for counseling sessions. It's that important, especially for the ones with ADHD. They need all the monkey bar and swing set activities they can get during those long classroom mornings. Adults aren't really any different than kids in their need for activity breaks—except that we've been around a lot longer to develop bad habits that we substitute for exercise. We drink caffeinated beverages and devour sugar products to pep us up, instead of getting our energy boosts from exercise or physical activity and eating healthy, nutritious foods.

If we train ourselves to incorporate fitness into our daily activities, we will come to depend on it, need it, and miss it when we don't have it. After several months of bicycle commuting, I couldn't ride my bike for nearly two weeks because of bad weather. I had to drive my car instead, which seemed oddly unfamiliar. I felt out of sync, increasingly restless at the office, edgy in the afternoons, and fidgety in the evenings. I drank more coffee those days, struggled with greater cravings for sweets, and didn't sleep as well. When the weather cleared up, and I could finally pedal my way to work, it was liberating. I could feel the calming effect almost immediately. I was relaxed and could cope more easily with work stressors. I slept better at night and felt fully rested the next day. And I wasn't pestered as much by cravings for caffeine and sweets.

I think it would be a good idea to put jogging trails in large factories and institutions, or else have hallways and corridors marked off for walking—a sort of corporate mall walking. Sell fresh fruits, vegetables, and herbal teas instead of potato chips and candy bars in the vending machines. Provide tangible incentives for employee fitness. Offer in-service training on health and fitness. A good start is a policy they had at the state hospital where I did my postgraduate training. You got a bonus day off if you didn't use any sick time for six months.

Fitness Makes Sound Business Sense

Businesses have an incentive to encourage employee health and wellness: decreased health insurance premiums. My wife and I own our own business, Big Sky Counseling & Assessment, and our health insurance premiums actually decreased twice in the past four years since we enrolled in a new health savings plan. The philosophy of health savings plans is to have a high up-front deductible, which encourages you to stay in better health so you don't have to use it. The insurance premiums and deductible are tax write offs, and ultimately you can roll over the unused deductible savings into an IRA to build retirement savings. Apparently, the other people who bought into our health plan were also health conscious, and they haven't had to use as much health insurance, which resulted in the lowered premiums. A pretty good deal for everybody involved. For this and many other reasons, improving employee health makes good economic sense.

Company promotion of exercise and fitness is already a common practice in the United Kingdom. My Internet search disclosed dozens of British companies that either offer free gym membership or provide a gym on the premises. The idea seems to be catching on more slowly in the United States, where the need is tremendous. The Centers for Disease Control estimates that U. S. industry loses 39 million work days a year from obesity-related illness, and 1.58 trillion dollars a year is spent on chronic diseases that are largely preventable.[5] Most Americans (62%) are insured through their employer. Accordingly, the CDC is promoting corporate wellness programs because "workplace obesity prevention programs can be an effective way for employers to reduce obesity and lower their health care costs, lower absenteeism and increase employee productivity."[6] A corporate wellness program can result in a 3.5 to 1 cost ration savings and 6 to 1 return on investment from the reduced costs and improved productivity that occurs because of the program. These figures are based on a review of five program outcome evaluations. Good health makes good business sense.

The CDC's LEAN Works program (Leading Employees to Activity and Nutrition) provides businesses with guidelines on how to establish and maintain a successful corporate wellness program. Research indicates that five components result in optimal effectiveness: 1) employee involvement in program development and maintenance, 2) a convenient schedule for times and places of activity, 3) rewards to employees for goal achievement, 4) a variety of program activities for different needs of employees, and 5) "change the workplace environment to support healthy lifestyles"—healthy selections from vending machines, low fat cafeteria foods, pictures of successful employees in the corporate newsletter, etc.[7]

In 2008 the Cleveland Clinic, which employs 27,000 health care workers, began offering free membership in fitness centers. Employees also get a monetary bonus if they attend the gym regularly. Gym membership expands the company wellness incentives, which began with a free smoking cessation program and free Weight Watchers memberships. Dr. Michael Roizen, who is chief wellness officer of the clinic, said in a press release that the goal is "to serve as a role model of prevention and wellness while reducing the costs associated with preventable conditions. We challenge other health care organizations to take a proactive, leadership position in transitioning our roles from providing 'sick' care to promoting 'health' care."[8] The clinic's chief human resources officer, Joe Patrnchak, sees that "we're removing the barriers of cost and conveniences that keep people from exercising. We believe that as people feel better and more balanced, they can bring more of themselves to work everyday."

You don't have to be a Fortune 500 corporation to implement a successful company wellness program. Ray's Boathouse, a Seattle seafood restaurant with 150 employees, has been offering free gym memberships to its employees for over 25 years. Eleven years ago they started their annual Fitness Challenge "to help crewmembers stay connected and motivated through the slower winter months." The prize is $1,000 for the best "overall physical improvement." Their motivation is twofold: 1) healthy people take better care of themselves and are less likely to become ill, and 2) people who work out at the gym look healthier, and this "reinforces the positive image" the restaurant wishes to convey to customers. Ray's goal is to "turn casual fitness routines into religious habits." According to general manager Maureen Shaw, "this contest has motivated many of our staff to change their lifestyles long-term, not just for four months [the duration of the contest]. The winners have inspired others to make positive changes, too." Ray's owners' philosophy is "a healthy crew is a productive, happy crew."[9]

High School Workout Programs

Of course, we need to start health consciousness training with our children. Fortunately, this is already beginning to happen. High schools in the Lower Hudson Valley began offering free gym membership to entice underprivileged students to improve their academic performance.[10] They tried it out on three students in 2007, and it was so successful that services were expanded to include 30 students for 2008. The principal reported a highly enthusiastic reception, where "kids are running up to us in the halls saying, 'I want to get into Work2Workout.'"[11]

This would be a good practice for all of our schools—but we should start it at the elementary school level. How many times are children punished for misbehavior by taking them out of recess or extracurricular recreational activities to attend in-school suspension classes?

Make Exercise or Increased Activity Part of Your Lifestyle

The only way to effectively change old behaviors is to consistently practice new behaviors. Albert Ellis, psychologist (1912-2007)

The only way I know of to successfully get physically (and mentally) fit and stay that way is to make behavioral changes a permanent part of your lifestyle. As I have mentioned earlier, you have to learn to eat in a manner with which you will be comfortable for the rest of your life and find a type of activity you enjoy and are willing to stick with for the rest of your life. In this sense healthy eating and physical activity are linked to successful aging like the bride and groom in the traditional marriage vows—until death do we part. It may be overwhelming to face the immensity of such a lifetime commitment. The good news is that you don't have to do it all at once. You can take the approach like in AA with one day at a time, or if need be, one meal or one exercise routine at a time. Which, logically, is all you have to work with anyway—right here and right now. The important thing is to stick with it. Find what works for you and keep doing the same thing. One step at a time is not too difficult, literally.

How To Become a Stair Master

Regular exercise has been shown to be one of the best predictors of successful weight maintenance. K. J. McInnis, obesity researcher[12]

Last year the elevator in our office building broke down. Everybody was complaining about what a hassle it was to have to walk up and down the stairs to get to our office, which is on the second floor of a two-story building. The elevator was out for about six weeks. After about a month my wife Mary began to comment about changes she was noticing. Her pants were looser, she felt better, the pain in her hips was less severe, and she even slept more soundly. She even lost a couple of pounds. When the elevator was finally fixed, Mary decided to keep walking up and down the steps to our office. Now it's a habit. I started doing the same thing. It might not seem like a lot of exercise—and it really isn't, but small steps add up to big time improvements over the long haul.

Begin Making Changes Right Now!

Here are a few examples of things you can change immediately. Cut down on TV watching and computer time and increase walking, exercise, and active time. You can build physical activities into your regular routines at home, in the office, or around town. Use the stairs instead of the elevator in your office or apartment building. If you're in a tall building, you can walk a flight or two of stairs and take the elevator the rest of the way. Ride a bicycle to work one day a week, if possible. When I go shopping, I always park quite a distance from the entrance; initially I was trying to protect my new sports car from nicks and dents due to careless parkers, but now I do it as a health habit. When I worked at the state hospital, I gave myself mandatory breaks to walk the grounds—15 minutes in the morning and

15 minutes in the afternoon. The institutional scenery was rather drab, so I entertained myself by identifying the different species of birds in the area and observing their habits. There's always something you can do to slip in a little exercise (and intellectual stimulation). Make your own list of ways to add more physical activity to your daily life's schedule—then start doing them.

Things to Do Besides Watching TV All the Time

I've always valued staying active one way or another. John Glenn, astronaut and statesman[13]

The good news is that you don't have to join a gym or buy an expensive piece of exercise equipment to get into shape. There are plenty of things you can do to increase your level of physical activity and derive the benefits of improved health. You can burn up a lot of calories with everyday household chores or recreational activities. All it takes is a commitment to replace one 30-minute TV show a day with some type of physical activity. The following figures are derived from Harvard Medical School's *Heart Letter*[14] and are estimates of the number of calories burned by a 185-pound person engaging in various activities for 30 minutes. If you weigh 126 pounds, you will burn about one-third fewer calories for the same activity.

Activity	Calories Burned
Sleeping	28
Watching TV	33
Standing in line	56
Cooking	111
Shopping for groceries	155
Walking 3.5 mph	178

As you can see from the numbers, watching television isn't much of a step above being asleep in terms of calorie consumption. Almost any daily activity is a major improvement over being a couch potato. Just standing in line nearly doubles the calories burned. Pushing a cart while shopping for groceries uses almost as much energy as a brisk walk. (Just don't fill the cart up with junk food and eat it all when you get home.)

Yard work pays off in energy consumption. Planting seedlings or shrubs uses 178 calories, as does raking the lawn and bagging the leaves. Weeding your garden burns 200 calories, and chopping wood or shoveling snow, 266. Turn housework blues into calorie burns. Wash the car and clean the windows of your house to burn off 200 calories; you'll use the same energy with chores that involve painting, carpentry, or plumbing. Moving furniture around is even more exerting, burning 266 calories— good news if you're a compulsive rearranger who needs to lose weight. Taking care of children can help you take off weight. You will burn up 155 calories bathing or feeding the children. Playing with the kids at moderate exertion uses 178 calories, increasing to 222 with more vigorous play like hopscotch.(If you're an overweight teenager or retiree who wants to trim down, you can do a lot of babysitting and try to find those kids with ADHD.)

You can always get yourself a video and exercise in the comfort of your own home. You will burn 178 calories with 30 minutes of Hatha yoga stretching, Tai chi, or low impact aerobics. Work up to high-impact aerobics and the calorie burn increases to 311. You can get similar results with simple calisthenics, burning 200 calories with a moderate level workout or 355 at a vigorous level. Playing badminton will burn off 200 calories and riding a horse consumes 178 calories. Playing golf using a cart consumes 155 calories, but if carry your own clubs that increases to 244 calories.

Ballroom or square dancing burns 222 calories, as does playing softball. Sign up for dance lessons with your spouse or significant other. Join a softball league at the office, church, or in your community. If you want to really defy age stereotypes, borrow your kid's skateboard and ride it for 30 minutes; that will burn off 222 calories. In-line skating consumes a whopping 311 calories. I seriously thought about buying myself a pair of Rollerblades and digging out my old French language tapes after reading about *Pari Roller.*[15]

Skate Around the Eiffel Tower

Every Friday night at 10:00 P.M., anywhere from ten to fifteen thousand people put on their roller skates and take off through the streets of Paris for the weekly Friday Night Fever skating tour. *Pari Roller* is the organization behind the event. It started out with a few dozen skaters making unauthorized treks through the heart of Paris "to skate for pleasure, discover the city, and meet other people—in other words, for freedom."[16] It has evolved into a government sanctioned, internationally acclaimed happening that promotes skating "as a leisure activity, as a sport, or as a means of transportation." Today skaters have police escorts (six officers on motorcycles, four on motor scooters, and twenty on skates) and ambulance chasers—the cobblestone streets of scenic, old Paris can be treacherous. The route is 18.6 miles long and takes about 3 hours to complete.

Find yourself a basketball court and shoot some hoops to burn off 355 calories. You'll expend the same amount of energy with breaststroke swimming, cross-country skiing, and mountain bicycling, or playing hockey, touch football, or beach volleyball. Soccer and tennis use up about 311 calories.

Buy yourself a bicycle—I paid $150 for a decent quality standard brand (Huffy's Magellan Commuter model). You can pay thousands of dollars for a fancy-smantzy model, but I've put 3,000 miles on my bike over the past year and still have the original tires and chain.[17] Depending on how fast you want to pedal, you can burn off massive amounts of calories riding a bicycle for 30 minutes:

12-13.9 mph	355 calories
14-15.9 mph	444 calories
16-19 mph	533 calories
20 mph plus	733 calories

Unless you're Lance Armstrong racing in the Tour de France (where racing speeds average around 24 mph through the Alps!) you won't likely be racing a bicycle at maximum velocity. At the top end of the calorie-burn list, we find running 10 mph or more—which also burns up 733 calories every 30 minutes—here you're talking about Boston Marathon speeds.

As a point of reference, you need to burn up about 3,000 calories in order to lose one pound of body fat. That means you could lose one solid pound by running 26 miles in a marathon or riding a bicycle for two hours in the Tour de France. You could get the same results by puttering around in your garden, playing softball, or going ballroom dancing for about one hour every day for a week. You decide what's best for you.

In conclusion, there's a level of exercise for everybody and every need or inclination. There's some type of exercise or physical activity that just about everybody could work into their schedule at home, at the office, or in the community.

Can One Survive Without a Car?

In the summer of 2008, I had to put my car in the shop and was annoyed beyond all belief that it would take several days to fix. How was I going to get around without my car for two or three days? Never mind the fact that my wife also has a car, and we both work together in the same office which is only about five miles from home. I wanted my car! I had a tantrum on the spot. I mentally cursed out our financial adviser for convincing us to eliminate the rental car coverage on our insurance policy. I was already fuming about gas prices doubling, and I was feeling very much like a victim of forces beyond my control.

Well, I'll show those blankity-blanks! I'll buy a bicycle so I won't have to spend over $4.00 a gallon, and then I can thumb my nose at the big oil companies every time I pedal past a gas station! I already was considering alternative transportation. For years, I'd been arguing that Wichita Falls would be a perfect town for bicycle commuting. There are few hills, it hardly ever rains, and the winters are mild. It's a small town, so you can pretty much get anywhere you want to go with a five- to seven-mile drive. But I never did anything about it.

I had recently written the section of this book describing an 84-year-old woman riding in the World Naked Bike Race (chapter 2: Why Should I Jog?), and was feeling the influence of this spunky elder. See, you can't even read about them without some of it rubbing off! Plus the Hotter'N Hell 100 annual bicycle race was coming up, and I'd never ridden in the race.

To make a long story short, I went out and bought a bicycle. Then I realized I hadn't been on a bicycle in 40 years. So I decided to see if I could handle an extended ride, and I marked off a route around my neighborhood where I could ride 10 miles nonstop. Afterwards, my butt was so sore I swore I'd never get on the thing again—even though I had replaced the original rock-hard seat with a custom designed, gel-foam padded model. However, after 15 to 20 minutes of R&R I could feel my lower extremities again and was much relieved—especially when I read that I could ride 25 or 50 miles in the Hotter'N Hell and not the full 100 if I chose, plus the fact that there are rest stops every 8-10 miles with free water and fresh fruit. So I decided to take my own advice and practice what I'm preaching in this book.

After a week or two of pedaling and getting my legs and rump adjusted to the new routine, I discovered that I really loved bicycling, and now it has become my preferred form of exercise. Cycling is easier on my knees, doesn't annoy the bone spur on my big toe like jogging, and I get a nice aerobics workout. I routinely get some of that endorphin high or positive addiction discussed by Glasser. I've worked it into my weekly schedule. I committed to riding my bicycle to the office twice a week—about 5 miles each way, and then added two weekend treks of 15 or 20 miles along the city's official bicycle trail that runs alongside Lake Wichita. I was surprised to find many other cyclists, quite a few of them gray-haired guys like myself—and most of them were in surprisingly good physical condition.

Not Too Old to Be in Good Shape

In the summer of 2009, 72-year old Oliver Seikel arrived on the campus of MIT, where he graduated half a century earlier. He traveled 800 miles to visit his alma mater, all the way from Cleveland, Ohio, in order to attend the 50th reunion of his graduating class. That might not seem like much of a journey from our modern jet-set vantage point, but Seikel didn't fly. Nor did he drive or take a bus. He pedaled the entire distance on a bicycle. It took him three weeks. Why would an elderly gentleman do such a thing? "I had to do something to prove to myself that I wasn't getting that old," he told reporters.[18]

Seikel, an attorney, is an avid cyclist. He rides his bike four days a week and exercises with his wife three mornings each week. He spent six months getting ready for the trip, and he carefully planned his rest stops and mapped a route along the famous Erie Canal. His strategy for not overdoing it was to bicycle 50 miles a day for four days and then use each fifth day for rest and recovery.

In commemoration of his cross-country trek, Seikel's classmates crowned him "Fittest of the Fiftieth." Upon completion of the journey, he conveyed his sense of fulfillment to reporters: "It was a great thing. It's hard to put into words, but just a great feeling of satisfaction that I had done it."

Two Wheels Keep on Spinning

I am 94 four years old and I believe I am the world's oldest cyclist. Rev. Frederick Hastings

"How many of us here will be able to cycle when we near the century?" So begins a 1932 newsreel film narrated by Rev. Frederick Hastings, of Eastbourne, Sussex, England. He was a firm advocate of physical fitness long before it became fashionable: "In my opinion, if there were more cyclists today there would be more men and women of my age and health in 50 years' time."[19] Rev. Hastings boasted that a recently purchased bicycle "should carry me up to the century, if I live, and past." He narrowly missed the century mark, serving as minister of South

Street Free Church in Eastbourne from 1918 until his death in 1937 at age 99.

Centenarian Cyclist

At his 107th birthday celebration, Larry Haubner of Fredericksburg, Virginia, flexed his biceps and hollered at the *Washington Post* reporter interviewing him, "Exercise! I think we should all exercise more than we do."[20] The centenarian is a "self-described health nut" who takes no medication and works out daily with a homemade weight: seventeen and one-half pounds of lead in a basket. He invited the reporter to lift it but cautioned her to "start with five times." Haubner lifts the weight himself at least 20 times each day. Although he needs a walker to get around, he still has the strength to lift the walker over his head. He also "remains vigilant about exercise and diet." Although he ate a piece of his birthday cake, he said, "I don't believe cake is good food."

Haubner lived in his own apartment and rode his bicycle all over town until he was 102 years old. He was known to locals as "the older fellow often seen cycling around town." After he fell off his bicycle and got hurt, he could no longer live on his own and entered an assisted living facility.

Health Benefits of Cycling

The health benefits of cycling are so great—and the health injuries from driving so great—that not cycling is really dangerous. British Medical Journal[21]

As part of its global strategy on diet, physical activity and health, the World Health Organization is encouraging government leaders to "create environments that promote physical activity."[22] This is especially important in the cities and suburbs, where health and well-being are compromised by sedentary lifestyle and lack of opportunities to exercise. To promote citizen health, WHO encourages local governments and urban planners to "ensure the provision of safe and accessible cycling and walk pathways."

Bicycling is an excellent form of aerobic exercise, which provides wonderful health benefits. Research published in the *British Medical Journal* and related sources indicates that "cycling reduces the risk of serious conditions such as heart disease, high blood pressure, obesity and the most common form of diabetes."[23] Even cycling short distances can reduce your risk of death by as much as 22 percent. Cycling is a good way to lose weight. Riding your bicycle to work 30 minutes, 5 days a week, will burn about 11 pounds of fat in one year's time. A survey of nearly 7,000 Australian men found that "men who cycled to work were significantly less likely to be overweight and obese (39.8 percent) compared with those driving to work (60.8 percent)."[24]

Lifetime fitness begins at an early age, and children should be encouraged to commute actively to school. K.K. Davison and colleagues from the University of Albany made a review of scientific research on the subject, and they concluded that "children who walk or bicycle to school have higher daily levels of physical activity and better cardiovascular fitness than do children who do not actively commute to school."[25]

Cycling is a good way to make up rapidly for lost time if you have been inactive and decide to start exercising to get into shape. A pilot study from the British Department of Transport found that nonexercising individuals who began riding bicycles significantly improved their fitness. "In just a few months, they went from the lowest third to the fittest half of the population."[26] British United Provident Association, one of the largest independent health insurance agencies operating out of the United Kingdom and 200 other countries, strongly promotes bicycling as "one of the few physical activities which can be undertaken by the majority of the population as part of a daily routine."[27] At the Centre for Neuromuscular and Neurological Disorders of the University of Western Australia, patients with sporadic IBM, a degenerative muscle condition similar to MS, were able to "improve aerobic capacity and muscle strength" through a 12-week program of aerobic stationary cycle three times a week.[28]

Even simulated bicycling is beneficial. Using a virtual-reality-based exercise bicycle, Chen and colleagues at the National

Central University in Taiwan found that patients suffering from spinal chord injuries became less tense and calmer than a control group who went through conventional therapy.[29]   Scientists from the Swiss Paraplegic Research Institution used electrically stimulated cycling on patients who had paralyzed limbs due to spinal chord injury. Patients increased "aerobic capacity, muscle strength, and functional capacity" after 12 months of training.[30]

Bicycle Safely Tips

Bicycling is a lot of fun, good exercise, and a fine means of transportation. Follow a straight line and avoid being run down. U.S. Public Safety newsreel from the 1950s[31]

Bicycling is "the safest, cleanest, most efficient, healthy, and fun means of personal transport that exists," according to Malcolm Wardlaw, writing in the *British Medical Journal.*[32] In "Three Lessons for a Better Cycling Future Wardlaw cites statistics from Great Britain to show that "the inherent risks of road cycling are trivial." As a result of improvements in road safety "the risk of death per mile cycled fell by 60 percent between 1971 and 1994." Controlled scientific studies have shown that when a cyclist develops "skill and a sense of caution" the risk of serious injury is reduced by 80 to 90 percent. The single best way to increase bicycle safety, ironically, is to increase the number of people on the roads riding bicycles. That makes sense because when more bicyclists are present, drivers learn to anticipate them and compensate by driving with greater care. Research from around the world shows that bicycle safety is greatest when cyclists ride on the roadways together with cars; this is true even in countries like the Netherlands, which has completely separate roads or pathways for bicyclists. Everybody benefits when bicyclists are treated like drivers of motor vehicles, and motorists can learn to share the road.

My own experience with commuter bicycling has been surprisingly pleasant. I really think that drivers treat me better when I'm on my bicycle than when I'm driving my car. For one full year, I rode my bicycle 50 miles a week that I ordinarily would have driven my car, and I only had one guy in a pickup truck come close to running me down in a crosswalk at an intersection. I experience more close calls like that with motorists pretty much every time I take my car out on the road—even if it's only for a short jaunt to the grocery store. While pedaling my bicycle about town, I've even had drivers back up out of the crosswalk at an intersection to allow me to pass. More drivers slow down when I'm cycling, yield me the right of way, and show me more basic driver's courtesies than when I'm in my car.

I suspect this is because when you're riding a bicycle, people assume you're a child—since the overwhelming majority of people who pedal bicycles in the United States are children. And most drivers are more careful around children and quicker to extend them courtesies. (I also pass through two school zones on my way to and from the office.) So I would add this to my list of benefits of riding a bicycle instead of driving a car: not only can you enjoy the childlike delight of bicycling, but you can experience the extra caution and courtesy that people extend to the kiddos.

Adult Cycling Is Not a Child's Pastime

You know you're getting old when you start window shopping at medical supply stores. Dr. Kownacki's Journals

And you know you're getting old when you start coming up with your own "you-know-you're-getting-old" jokes. Shortly after writing the section above, I had an experience that caused me to reevaluate the issue of bicycle safety. The *British Medical Journal* boasts that bicycling is so safe and clean and healthy and planetary conscientious, and I would agree that this is certainly true—except when you wreck your bike, break the tip off your elbow, and put yourself out of commission for six weeks. A brief malfunction of my headlight was all it took to go sailing like Evel Knievel over a barrier and skid across the pavement—easing the fall with my right elbow. I knew something was seriously wrong because of the profuse bleeding and a piece of loose bone where my elbow used to be. X-rays revealed a compound fracture of the elbow that required emergency surgery. The prescription for aftercare was six weeks without riding my bicycle.

Here's another irony of this minor tragedy. I successfully rode my bicycle over 3,000 miles during the previous year. I also raced in the Hotter'N Hell 100 twice—all without getting a scratch.[33] Then I was put out of commission on a short four-mile commute to the local gym for my daily workout!

My spirit perked up considerably when I began researching the prevalence of my injury. It turns out that elbow injuries of my kind, olecranon fractures, occur most often in childhood, typically when a kid falls off the monkey bars at the local playground. So now I feel vindicated. My accident proves that following my program for successful aging really works, because at age 55, I experienced a childhood injury! Who says you can't go back and do it all over again? (Although I advise that you don't get too literal about it!)

At the hospital, I struck up a conversation with a staff worker who was also a cycling enthusiast. We must have sounded like war veterans comparing battle scars as we exchanged anecdotes of our injuries. He related a sad tale of shattering his kneecap to avoid running over a woman walking her Pekingese around a sharp curve in the local bicycle trail. I was in the hospital again two weeks later because the pins installed to keep my elbow bone in place were migrating north into my arm. The pins were removed and a screw put in their place. So since then I can tell everybody, and it's official—I'm all screwed up! I told the doctor that maybe he should have put in a zipper instead of stitches on that right elbow, in case I need another tune-up. And I don't know now whether I should schedule my next follow up visit with the bone surgeon or the local hardware store.

Obviously, any type of athletic or sports activity contains an element of risk. The fact is that the more active you are, the greater the risk of suffering some type of injury. Some might conclude from this that it's not worth it. A radical alternative is to stay at home with your head under the covers, but even then you might be killed by a tornado, earthquake, or flash flood. Athletes and exercise enthusiasts are willing to take the risk of possible injury because of the tremendous benefits of physical fitness, greatly improved health, and the enormous sense of well-being.

My experience with a broken elbow taught me the need for greater caution. I learned a valuable lesson about the difference between sensible risk and reckless bravado. Today I no longer ride my bike to the gym when it's pitch black at 4:30 in the morning (over roads where they're doing construction work, with bad brakes and a faulty headlight). I make sure that all of my equipment is in good operating condition, and I practice extreme caution when riding at dusk or in the dark. I told Mary the other day that if I installed any more flashing lights I'll have to get registered as a Christmas tree instead of a bicycle rider. I maintain a healthy respect for my bicycle—which is clearly not a child's toy but rather a potentially dangerous form of mechanized transportation.

How About That Hotter'N Hell 100?

In a recent review of scientific research from around the world on the subject of exercise and health, the World Health Organization summarizes: "Available experience and scientific evidence show that the regular practice of appropriate physical activity and sports provides people, male and female, of all ages and conditions, including persons with disability, with a wide range of physical, social and mental health benefits."[34]

I witnessed the truth of this statement first-hand in August 2008 as a participant in the twenty-seventh Annual Hotter'N Hell Hundred bicycle race. Every year over 10,000 bicycle enthusiasts gather in Wichita Falls, Texas, to pedal 100 miles in the 100-degree plus Texas summer heat. They come to the race from virtually every state and several foreign countries, and they comprise every age group, from toddlers who need training wheels (not everybody rides the whole 100 miles) to spunky eldsters who need specially constructed tricycles to accommodate their frailty. Cyclists represent a cross-section of body types and states of fitness or lack thereof: thin and anorexic, fit and trim, buff and beautifully muscular or bodybuilder physique, nondescript, flabby and out of shape, extremely overweight, and even morbidly obese. One guy was so huge that he dwarfed his bicycle, and I kept waiting for the tires to explode. There were a few curiously designed custom cycles pedaled by individuals with various types of disabilities.

I registered late, and my entry number was 11,030! I kept wondering how 11,000-plus bicyclists would look lined up on the narrow downtown streets of Wichita Falls. Surprisingly, it was not sheer chaos; the organizers knew their business. While waiting for the 7:00 A.M. start, highlighted by the national anthem and a flyover of five jets from the local air force base, I struck up a conversation with the gentleman next to me. Several things about the man captured my attention: his age, the unique design of his bicycle, and his state of health—but more than anything else, my eyes were drawn to the cane strapped to the rear of his bicycle. He told me he was 76 years old and had gone through back surgery, hip replacement, triple coronary bypass, and two other major operations over the past several years, which left him unable to ride a conventional bicycle. So he had one specially built, a tricycle low to the ground, with a padded seat that had a high back, smaller custom-designed wheels, and pedals out in front so he could work them back-and-forth instead of up-and-down. We were both in the group planning to pedal 25 miles, and he told me he had made the ride before, despite increasingly poor health. He was no slouch, either. About 10 miles down the road, he passed me by! I'm certainly no speed demon, and admittedly I was in the Hotter'N Hell just for the ride and not to race anybody. Even still, I jog ten miles a week and lift weights, and frankly it was embarrassing to be passed in a bike race by a 76-year-old with a bad back and artificial hips, who can't even walk without a cane! However, the worst humiliation was yet to come. About 15 miles down the course, while slowing down to negotiate another of the gentle rolling hills along the route, I was passed by a man who looked to be about 80. He was pedaling a classic 1950s Schwinn Roadster. (Do you remember those big, heavy contraptions with only one gear speed—too hard to pedal? I developed strong leg muscles pedaling one of those up and down the mountains of western Pennsylvania growing up.) The guy was cycling along calmly as he passed me, neither winded nor even getting up out of his seat to climb the hill. The fact that I later passed him up going down the hill doesn't take away from the embarrassment of being passed on the hill. There was even a bevy of teenage girls on Rollerblades. Imagine traveling 25 miles on roller skates! But they did it, and none the worse for wear and tear as they skated across the finish line several hours later. A couple of days after the race, the clerk at a local store told me that his grandfather races every year in the Hotter'N Hell Hundred. A retired naval officer, he flies in from a small Texas town in the Rio Grande Valley.

I think you get my point: It doesn't matter if you are young or old, male or female, healthy or sickly, able or disabled. You really don't have any excuse not to exercise—unless you're a quadriplegic who's paralyzed from the neck down, and even then you need to have somebody move your arms and legs around a little to protect your body from atrophy.

You can benefit from a little cycling, even if you're suffering from Alzheimer's in a nursing home. Long-term care residents with dementia from Fort Meyers, Florida, were treated for depression in a novel fashion—with a wheelchair bicycle. Linda Buettner, PhD, found that therapeutic biking significantly reduced levels of depression in as little as two weeks.[35] Improvement was maintained for up to 10 weeks. Bike riding patients also slept better and engaged in more activities. Treatment included one-to-one bicycle rides with a staff member and small group therapy activity. (Dr. Buettner holds the intriguing title of Professor of Recreation, Tourism, and Hospitality Management at the University of North Carolina at Greensboro.)

You can never become too decrepit to benefit from exercise. Exercise can be an avenue for rejuvenation and renewal. You name the condition, and chances are somebody did a scientific study about it to show that this condition, too, is subject to improvement with exercise and increased physical activity.

Don't Feel Guilty—Get Active!

The spunky eldsters can serve as both positive and negative reinforcers. By studying the lives of aging athletes and physically fit elders, I was inspired to get in shape and feel better about myself. Part of my motivation was feeling a little ashamed and guilty about being in such pathetical physical condition—when guys 20, 30 and even 40 years my senior looked better than I have since high school! That's okay. Motivation is like that. In fact, we are often more inspired by the negative reinforcers. Guilt, shame, regret, embarrassment, and similar negative emotions can be very educational. Guilt may be an indication that you're doing something you shouldn't be doing, so you need to stop doing it and do something else. Or that you're not doing something you should be doing—so you need to start doing it.

If, after reading the preceding chapters, you still are not exercising or taking part in some sort of physical activity regularly, then you have probably felt some degree of guilt. Don't deny your feelings. Let them inspire you to change. The best way to overcome your guilty feelings for not exercising and being out of shape is to go out and start exercising and get back into shape. A six-month German study was conducted to see how obese individuals cope with being overweight. Conradt and colleagues concluded that individuals who felt most guilty about being obese were more likely to exercise and use positive ways to cope such as by following a diet plan than obese individuals who felt less guilt.[36]

The bottom line is that whatever motivates us to make and sustain major positive changes to enhance our lifestyle is useful. Do whatever it takes to stay motivated and get yourself in the best possible state of physical and mental health because the older you get the more your life depends on it—literally.

Multipurposing Instead of Multitasking

People talk a lot about multitasking, which is basically doing several things at the same time to obtain one overall objective. *Multipurposing* is just the opposite; you do one thing at a time in order to obtain multiple objectives. My bicycling 50 miles a week is a good example of multipurposing. What does this accomplish?

1. It saves about three gallons of gas a week, high test, which costs about $600.00 a year.

2. I drive 2,600 miles less each year, saving x-amount of wear and tear on the car.

3. It benefits others. I donate the money I save to the local Meals on Wheels program, allowing someone with limited funds to drive those 50 miles delivering meals to shut-in elders.

4. I'm doing my part for the environment. How much less pollution and environmental damage is being done?

5. I get to write off the charitable deduction from my income taxes, so that's several hundred dollars less I am paying each year to build weapons of mass destruction and support other antihumanitarian governmental projects.

6. I'm improving my health, stimulating my immune system, and decreasing the chances of chronic illness, which could lead to a) reduced productivity, b) increased medical costs, and c) possible disability, which would make me a drain on the economy instead of an asset.

7. Perhaps more importantly, I've gained a more jubilant spirit. I experience tremendous satisfaction and empowerment from being part of a solution rather than remaining stuck in the problem (global warming, high price of gasoline and automotive costs, motor vehicle accidents, traffic jams, parking nightmares, auto insurance, etc.)

8. Also, I'm satisfying the inner rebel, which rejoices every time I ride past a gas station and symbolically thumb my nose at the big oil companies. Whenever negative thoughts enter my mind while I'm riding, I take in a deep breath and peddle faster, so I stay absorbed in the present.

9. Close to half the time I'm cycling in scenic territory— the bike trail by a large lake and slough, with abundant natural beauty. Several times a week I get to spend 30 to 45 minutes watching barn swallows, stalking herons and egrets, roosting flocks of migrating pelicans, seagulls, and other birds. A lot of the time I'm cycling at dawn or dusk, so I get to enjoy the picturesque Texas plains country big sky during the most stunning time of the day. The sunrise

and sunset are categorically different in the "big country," and may last close to 45 minutes.

10. One other much welcomed, but not overtly sought benefit of bicycling has been considerable weight loss and improved physique. When I began riding a bicycle in the Summer of 2008, I weighed 215 pounds. I had plateaued there for quite awhile, and nothing I did seemed to make a difference—even eating an exceptionally healthy low-fat vegan diet. After six months of bicycling, I weighed in at 201 pounds in February of 2009 during a routine visit to my physician. I'd lost a little over two pounds a month with the extra physical activity—notwithstanding the Christmas season, when the national average is a seven- to ten-pound weight gain. Three months later I was down to 190 pounds when a nurse weighed me during a physical for a life insurance application. I wasn't particularly trying to lose weight but just increased my activity level and the pounds seem to melt off. When I went back to Pennsylvania for a funeral later that month, I was rather embarrassed by everybody's continual oooing and ahhing about how much I had slimmed down and how great I looked. My brother later told our mother that if he had seen me in a grocery store, he probably wouldn't have recognized me!

Multipurpose Mindfully

I have so very much to do today that I must spend an extra long period of time in prayer and meditation. Anonymous

Multipurposing is a good alternative to multitasking for aging baby boomers. If you're anything like me, trying to do too many things at once can become a workaholic's nightmare and end up driving you to a frenzied pace. In contrast, multipurposing is amazingly efficient and a good practice for those of us who have a history of trying to burn the candle at both ends. One of the greatest benefits I've discovered from multipurposing is being able to stay more fully present in the moment. It can be a form of meditation practice. When I'm riding my bicycle, I can focus fully on the task at hand. It's easier to dismiss negative thoughts and unpleasant images. I become one with the bicycle, with the rhythmic pedaling and motion, and I get more in tune with the environment.

There's an old Hindu metaphor about the mind being like a monkey. Yes, the mind is like a monkey. The mind is like a drunken monkey. The mind is like a drunken monkey with St. Vitus dance. The mind is like a drunken monkey with St. Vitus dance that's just stepped onto a hot griddle and been stung by a wasp. It goes on and on. My mind quickly becomes like that drunken monkey when I focus on multitasking and try to keep up with too many things going on at one time. With multipurposing, I can devote all my attention to the task at hand, which frees my mind to focus exclusively on the present moment in order to enjoy life and live it fully without the annoyance of that drunken monkey.

Activities and Solutions

Stop to think about your daily schedule and make a list of small changes you can make in order to increase your activity level. If you have a significant other or family, meet with them plan some shared activities.

What would you do if you didn't have to worry about what other people thought about what you were doing? Would you be willing to ride a bicycle to work? Why or why not? Would you be willing to use the steps instead of taking the elevator? Park at the far end of the parking lot instead of near the building entrance? How might you go against the grain of modern conveniences in order to increase your activity level and improve your health?

Notes:

_____

_____

_____

_____

_____

_____

Chapter 9

Conquer Over-the-Hill Syndrome

Once you see a grandmother on a Harley, you'll never think about getting old the same way again. David Lipschitz, MD, gerontologist[1]

I don't care how old I live; I just want to be LIVING while I am living! Jack LaLanne,[2] age 90-something

Over-the-hill syndrome occurs when we use age as an excuse to not live our lives fully. Spunky eldsters can shock us into sensibility and help us develop a new attitude towards aging as a remarkably creative, productive and socially valuable time of our lives.

I asked my mother-in-law Joseta why she decided to jump out of an airplane for her eighty-fifth birthday. She told me, "I just wanted to do something to surprise the children at Christmas." It certainly was a surprise, and it continues to surprise her family members and anybody else who sees the picture of her skydiving. I chose that photo for the cover to shock you into adjusting any outdated concepts you may have about aging.

When Joseta said that she was going to do something different for her eighty-fifth birthday, we all thought she meant taking her first ride on a Harley Davidson. She sent us the picture of her ride shortly after her birthday, and we assumed that was the end of the matter. That's Joseta in the photo above, riding shotgun on a fully dressed hog and waving to the crowd during her hometown's annual Teapot Parade.[3] Later she sent us a do-not-open-until-Christmas package that contained a video of her skydiving adventure. We were shocked speechless when we watched it because we all thought of Joseta as a little old lady who leads a quiet, conventional life in a small town and does all the things conventional elderly women in small-town America do.

Shocking Sensibility

For strange effects and extraordinary combinations we must go to life itself, which is always far more daring than any effort of the imagination. Sir Arthur Conan Doyle[4]

Novelist Tom Clancy once complained that the difficulty of writing fiction in contrast to nonfiction is that fiction has to make sense! I'm glad *Do Not Go Gentle* is nonfiction. That's one of the enticements of these spunky eldsters—their accomplishments are so unexpected and out of character that we hardly believe it to be true, even though we've just seen it happen.

I've made a point of mentioning some outrageous and extreme cases of spunky eldsters throughout this book because I want to shake up your thinking about aging and help you realize that it's never too late to do the things you've always wanted to do. I want to share the enthusiasm I've found by adopting a fresh outlook on aging, to help everybody realize that the early twenty-first century is an exciting time to be alive and the best time ever in which to be growing old. If we don't take advantage of the precious hours of life, we'll be missing out on a great adventure.

You Can Teach Old Dogs New Tricks

Ever since I turned 100, life has been busy. George Dawson[5]

George Dawson of Dallas, Texas, didn't learn to read and write until he was 98 years old. I have his picture in the waiting area of my office to serve as inspiration to all those I see for learning disability assessments; I test adults of all ages who didn't do very well in school and either dropped out or never got the hang of reading and writing. Most of them can't keep jobs and feel like a failure. They tell me they're too old to learn. I take them over to look at the picture of George Dawson, who's smiling broadly and holding up a yellow tablet with a sample of his penmanship; in the caption, he's quoted saying, "Every morning I get up, and I wonder what I might learn that day. You just never know."[6]

Dawson outlived four wives, four siblings, and two of his seven children. He did finally die, by the way. (Spunky eldsters are extraordinary but not immortal.) But not before publishing a book, *Life Is So Good,* which was quite amazing because until he was 98 years old, the only writing he ever did was to sign his name by making an X. "I've seen it all in these hundred years," he wrote. I'm sure he did, and I'm glad he decided to share it with us. As a spunky eldster, he motivates us to realize that it's never too late to do something you've always wanted to do. Considering Dawson's example, how can anybody ever imagine there's an age limit to learning?

What We Can Learn from the Spunky Eldsters

Death is not the greatest loss in life. The greatest loss is what dies inside us while we live. Albert Schweitzer

Most of us don't really understand what normal aging is, and few of us have great expectations about getting old. They don't teach courses about healthy aging in high school or most colleges. The media is full of negative images of aging, and we're left with a lot of cultural biases and misunderstandings.

Much of what we assume to be true about growing old is either false or only partially true. Every day brings new discoveries about aging. Perhaps more than anything else, most of us don't realize how much control we really have over the quality of our own aging experience. As we've seen, lifestyle choices can have a profound impact. For instance, strokes, heart disease, prostate cancer, arthritis, and many other so-called diseases of old age are often more the result of poor lifestyle choices than the aging process itself, according to a growing number of gerontologists.

I realize that few of us will be as healthy as Jack LaLanne when we get to be 95 years old. Then again, few of us will ever be as healthy as Jack LaLanne at any age. So what? The point is that you can always do something to improve your physical, mental, and spiritual health no matter what your age or how out of shape you have become. The more effort you put into improving yourself, the greater the results you'll get. And it doesn't matter how poor your condition may be. There are scientific studies showing how people in nursing homes can get stronger with weight training and that people developing Alzheimer's can derive some benefit from taking college courses. If these elders can do something to improve their condition, then you can do something, too. Sometimes you're going to improve a lot, and sometimes only a little. However, until the very day you die, there is always room for improvement. And even when they call in the priest for Last Rites, don't rule out the power of deathbed confessions and last-minute amends.

In the movie *The Bucket List*, two old men who have terminal cancer are each given six months to live; they share a hospital room and decide to make a list of all the things they want to do before they "kick the bucket." Then they go out and do those things. It turns out that one of the guys is a billionaire, so cost is no object, and they literally can do anything and everything they've ever fantasized about doing.

The truth is that you don't need to be rich, and you don't have to wait until you're dying to start doing the things you really want to do with your life. You can start right now. Don't wait for your ship to come in because it might sink before it gets to port.

Why Can't I Start Tomorrow?

The risk of missing out on opportunities through procrastination becomes greater as we age. This is just plain mathematics: the older you get, the less time you have to put things off. Time becomes what economists call a dwindling resource. And everybody knows that the way to deal with a dwindling resource is to use it more wisely. For aging individuals, time is our most precious commodity, but we're running short. So we can't afford to waste it. It makes logical sense to start living the kind of life you want to live right now and without delay.

Fortunately, many older people seem to develop a greater appreciation of life. These spunky eldsters are not anomalies. The increasing awareness of our own mortality and dwindling time reserves makes our time more precious. This seems to be a sort of natural law of human development. When Sigmund Freud was 65 he wrote to his daughter about the inevitability of death, calling it "something all we old people know, which is why life for us has such a special quality. We refuse to allow the inevitable end to interfere with our happy activities."[7]

Unfortunately, old age in itself is no guarantee of wisdom. Sure, you can wait until you're on your deathbed or experience a life-threatening illness because there's nothing like the imminence of death to help you set your priorities. As Samuel Johnson once wrote, "When a man knows he is to be hanged in a fortnight, it concentrates his mind wonderfully."[8] The only problem is that by then it may be too late.

I knew a guy who worked hard all his life, made a sizeable fortune, and kept putting off taking a vacation until he retired. Unexpectedly he got seriously ill, spent all his money on medical bills, and never got to go anywhere. Now bitter and despondent, he sits in a nursing home. As a complication of his illness he went blind, so he can't even enjoy watching the travel channel on the small television set in his room.

Cultivate a Zest for Living

Whereas ye know not what shall be on the morrow. For what is your life? It is even a vapour, that appeareth for a little time, and then vanisheth away. James 4:14

We don't have to wait for trauma to strike us, however. I think we all should adopt the mindset of my Aunt Margie—when you get to be 65, you don't know if you're going to live another 20 minutes or 20 years. We can find renewed zest for living by contemplating the imminence of your own demise. Wake up to the truth that life is short and start doing the things we need to be doing with our lives right now. Don't put it off another day, because "ye know not what shall be on the morrow." You ignore facing the truth about mortality at your own psychological and spiritual peril. When you truly appreciate how little time you have left—how very short life really is—then you can genuinely begin to appreciate your life.

Strangers in Good Company

One of the most exhilarating movies ever made about people who've grown old but remain ageless inside. New York Newsday

Although I'm old, I'm not really old inside of me. I don't take any notice of my age because inside of me I still feel young. Aging actress discussing her role in *Strangers in Good Company*

When eight elderly women find themselves stranded in the Canadian wilderness after their tour bus breaks down, they use the opportunity to discover the importance of being fully alive in the present moment. *Strangers in Good Company* won the 1991 Most Popular Canadian Film award at the Vancouver International Film Festival. Director Cynthia Scott selected nonprofessional actors, who could just be themselves without any pretense of being somebody different or anything other than what they were.

My favorite scene is when the women gather on the porch of a deserted farmhouse at sunrise, shouting out across the lake and into the distant woods, "I'm alive! I'm alive!" Indeed, these 70-, 80- and 90-year-old women, initially strangers on a bus, discover a level of genuine intimacy with each other and with themselves that many of us would envy at any age. They don't get caught up in worry about being lost out in the middle of nowhere, not knowing when or even if they will be rescued. They convert a potential crisis into an opportunity for joyous discovery of the world all around them. They catch and cook frogs and fish from a lake, and they occupy their time by singing, dancing, and sharing intimate details of their lives, loves, hopes, fears, ambitions, and frustrations. All the while they display a playful, cheerful, and creative spirit of ageless youth.

The movie is an allegory of how we should all be living our lives, and it convinces us that we can begin living life fully in the present moment any time we choose to do so, starting right here and right now.

We all seem to need an experience from time to time to help us wake up. It's like the old Zen parable about a man being chased by tigers through the jungle. To escape, he jumps off a cliff. Clinging to a vine, he looks up to see the snarling beasts swatting at him with their claws. Below there is a pool of hungry crocodiles. Meanwhile, a mouse is gnawing at his vine. Suddenly, he notices a wild strawberry growing on the side of the cliff. He plucks it in his mouth and says, "Ah! How delightful!"

I first heard this story in an Asian religions class, when I was in my twenties. At that age I found this story to be morbid, annoying, and pretty much irrelevant to my life. The prospect of death, especially my own, was far from my consciousness at the time. It's interesting how our perspectives change as we get older. Today I can appreciate the parable as a reflection of my own real-life predicament; having faced addiction issues and cancer (my own tigers), at age 55 I'm much closer to the hungry crocs of death. Now that I'm a mature man, this story has become one of my favorites. I can appreciate the poignant metaphor about the shortness of life and the precariousness of human existence (which can be interpreted on many levels—disease and personal crises, wars, global warming, etc.). I really love the vividness of the imagery (but still find it a bit creepy). Reflecting on it helps me to focus on priorities, awaken a little more, and rekindle my desire to live life fully in the moment. The older I get the more closely my life becomes exactly like that of the man in the story. I'm also convinced that my Aunt Margie must have been a practicing Zen master without realizing it when she gave me her philosophy of enjoying life as you age because you don't how much time you have left. Many aging individuals seem to naturally develop greater wisdom about the meaning of life. With maturity, the imminence of our own demise encourages us all to become more spiritually astute.

Awaken to a Higher Life

Why look to the insipid without when the inspired within forever sparkles with the vintage of eternal youth, health, wisdom, life? Charles Fillmore, founder of the Unity School of Christianity[9]

The ultimate truth, of course, is that nobody, not even the very young, knows how long they will live. The only difference with elders is that death becomes a much more imminent concern. The good news is that we can awaken to a higher life and a dynamically renewed zest for living at any point in our lives. It can even happen when you are very young. I'm thinking of Brother Lawrence, the thirteenth-century Carmelite monk. He had a spiritual awakening when he was only 18, not from a major crisis in his life or a near-death experience, but from the simple activity of contemplating a tree stripped of its leaves during winter. "He knew that they would soon reappear, followed by blossoms and then fruit. This gave him a profound impression of God's providence and power, which never left him," according to his biographer.[10] Brother Lawrence became a monk and joined a monastery, where he lived to a ripe old age working as a cook. I've always been deeply impressed by his prayer, "Oh Lord of all pots and pans and things, make me a saint by scrubbing up the kitchen and fixing lunch." Lawrence emphasized that time spent praying in church and taking Communion didn't differ from the time when he was scurrying about in the kitchen doing mundane tasks. He saw everything in life as holy and special, and each moment of life was vibrant and alive. He could appreciate every second of time as a precious commodity. The beatniks, and their spiritual heirs the hippies and new age devotees of the sixties, sought this type of spiritual renewal. Jack Keroauc did an interesting short film called *Pull My Daisy*, a slice-of-life vignette about a day in the life of some of the early beat poets. I remember some of the dialogue: "Is baseball holy? Is the umpire holy? Is the outfield holy?" To view everything in life as sacred and holy is a worthy vision for healthy living and successful aging.

That's what living fully alive in the moment is all about. Humanist psychologist Abram Maslow used the term *self-*

actualization to describe the experience of being fully alive, and it's not the exclusive domain of saints or deeply religious people. All of us experience fleeting moments of *peak experience*, when we have "feelings that one's boundaries as a person are suddenly evaporated and feeling that one has become a part of all humanity or of all nature."[11]

According to Maslow, one of the qualities of self-actualized people is a continually renewed sense of appreciation for life. This is what people in twelve-step programs call developing an attitude of gratitude. The goal of living, especially as you get older, is to enjoy the highest quality of life that you can. Don't end up like the man described by author Geoffrey Madan: "He is alive, but only in the sense that he can't be legally buried."[12]

Never Settle for Average

When we hear that the average life expectancy of Americans is about 78 years, we usually assume that we're all going to live to be 78. This is simply not true; some will die long before 78 and some will live well beyond that age.

The average life expectancy is derived by calculating how long everybody will live, and then dividing by the total number of people. It's a statistical average, technically the *mean* average, which is a mathematic concept. Sometimes the statistical average doesn't even exist in reality. (For example, according to the 2000 U.S. Census, the typical American family had an average of 1.86 children. What's with that .86th kid–stunted growth?)

In a normal distribution, the average is called the mean, and it is the dead center—which means that half the population falls below and half is above. Therefore, if the average American lives to be 78, then as many as half of us will be dead before we reach that age. That's a sobering thought.

We have to be careful about making personal expectations based on averages. Statisticians call this the *tyranny of the mean*. It is our tendency to put faith in expectations about groups rather than about individuals.

Don't assume that you are necessarily going to live to be 78. The Apostle James' "Ye know not what shall be on the morrow" is not just prudent spiritual philosophy, but a mathematical truth as well.

So the real issue isn't planning what you're going to do when you get to be a certain age—nobody can predict the future. The real issue is to start making the best use of the time you have RIGHT NOW. Don't put things off any longer.

What Is Over-the-Hill Syndrome?

What's keeping you from living your life as fully as you would like? Perhaps you have *over-the-hill syndrome?*

Do you accept a negative image of being old because you don't know anything different? Do you believe that growing old is strictly a matter of decline and that the best years have passed you by? Do you feel like the aging process is totally out of your control—either because there's nothing you can do about it or because you can't have enough influence to make change worth the effort? Perhaps you are using age as an excuse rather than an opportunity?

Over-the-hill syndrome is not an official diagnosis or a term commonly used by psychologists and gerontologists. It's just a concept I'm using to help us deal with our unfavorable attitudes about aging. I invite you to explore your attitude about aging and see what's preventing you from getting what you want out of life. My hope is that after you read this book, you'll never again be able to use the excuse "I'm too old."

Take a few moments and answer the following questions to find out if you are suffering from over-the-hill syndrome.

Over-the-Hill Syndrome Questionnaire

1. Have you given up on taking care of your body? Is your view of aging that you just have to let nature take its course?
2. Do you believe that health and longevity are all in your genes?
3. Are you appalled by elders who fail to act their age?
4. Do you think the best time of your life was when you were young?

5. Do you refer to yourself as an old geezer, over the hill, a coot or a biddy, or use other disparaging terms to describe your age?

6. Are you waiting until you retire to start having fun and do all the things you've always wanted to do?

7. Do you think that everybody will get Alzheimer's or end up in a nursing home if they live long enough?

8. Do you find yourself using your age as an excuse when you don't want to do something?

9. Have you given up on doing things because you don't seem to have the energy or interest? (Note: This might be a sign of depression.)

10. Do you believe you're too old to go to the gym or exercise? Do you avoid going to the beach or gym because of how badly you're out of shape?

11. Do you keep putting off taking that trip of a lifetime until you get in better health?

12. Do you pretty much do whatever you want and then when you get sick, wait for the doctors to fix you up? Do you think your state of health is totally dependent on the pills you take? Do you passively accept whatever medication your doctor gives you?

13. Do you think sex and love are only for young people? Have you given up on romance?

14. Do you believe that heart disease, strokes, arthritis, bone loss, cancer, and similar illnesses are just part of the normal aging process?

15. Do you get angry and self-pitying when you see younger people having fun and doing things you wish you could do?

If you have answered *yes* to several of these questions, then you may be suffering from over-the-hill syndrome.

What can you do about it? Plenty! There are many ways to conquer over-the-hill syndrome, some of which are discussed throughout this book. Consider this chapter your call to action. Read the rest of this book and others like it to discover more truth about successful aging.

The fact that you are reading this book is proof that you have taken an active interest in the subject of your own aging by learning more about it. This means that your chances of aging successfully are probably above average. Dr. George Vaillant found that education was one of the predictors of successful aging.[13] And it's not just having greater knowledge, but the fact that better-educated people are more motivated to learn, to try new things, and to improve their lives. That's why I'm confident that you won't stop with reading, but go on to practice the principles you read about.

Start right now to update some of your outdated concepts about aging by pondering the following general principles of the new gerontology. Then do the exercises at the end of this chapter.

Update Your Concepts of Aging

Comedian Jerry Seinfeld jokes that the law requires you to move to Florida when you reach retirement age. Ironically, the truth about aging is probably more startling than comedy, because it's totally the opposite from some of our most commonly held notions about aging.

1. You don't have to become decrepit and incapacitated. Only about 5 percent of Americans are in nursing homes, and the percentage is decreasing every year.
2. You can remain active all your life. There are some senior citizens' baseball teams in Florida that you can't join unless you're at least 80 years old!
3. You can keep your body in tip-top shape. Just turn on your television to watch exercise guru Jack LaLanne, who is now 95 years old, still fit and trim, and brimming with health.
4. You can stay healthy. Cardiovascular disease and cancer, the two top causes of disease, disability, and early death, are not only preventable but in many cases reversible. Exercise, physical activity, a healthy diet, and similar lifestyle changes are the unhidden secret to healthy aging.

5. You don't have to become senile. Only about 5 percent of Americans have Alzheimer's or some form of dementia.
6. You don't have to become depressed. Depression is actually less common among the elderly than in other age groups.
7. You never have to stop learning. George Dawson (1898-2001) of Dallas, TX, didn't learn to read and write until he was 98 years old.
8. It's never too late to have a happy childhood. British novelist Aldous Huxley said, "The secret of genius is to carry the spirit of the child into old age." Repeatedly, studies of elder attitudes demonstrate that most are satisfied and believe they have a high quality of life.
9. And, by the way, you don't have to move to Florida. You can move to New Mexico or Arizona instead! It's true; an increasing number of older folks are retiring to the southwestern United States these days. However, in a few years' time nobody's going to have to move anywhere when they retire. That's because of the Florida-ization of the nation. Pretty soon the whole country is going to be overrun with senior citizens. Right now Florida has the highest proportion of people age 65 and over of any state in the country—18 percent, based on the latest U.S. Census Bureau report from the year 2000.[14] However, Florida won't be able to hold onto its status as the Senior Fun Capital of the country for very much longer. The U.S. Census Bureau estimates that by the year 2030, senior citizens will comprise nearly 20 percent of the entire United States population—that's one in five Americans![15] So by then, every state will be Florida.
10. The fate of a curmudgeon doesn't have to be part of your destiny. Developing a mature sense of humor will actually help you to age better, and it is a component part of good coping skills. As people grow older, the sadistic and immature laugh-at-somebody-being-hurt-or-humiliated sense of humor "can evolve into the mature humor that permits people to laugh at their own misery

rather than at the misery of their victims,"[16] according to Vaillant. "With the passage of time adolescent jerks can evolve into paragons of maturity." Like diamonds in the rough, we're ground down by the vicissitudes of a long life. Mature humor serves a healing purpose, to help sublimate suffering into a nobler passion. "Miraculously, humor transforms pain into the ridiculous," says Vaillant. The good news is that most seniors develop a mature sense of humor, so it looks like we're all going to have a lot more fun when we get old.

Activities and Solutions

Make up your own bucket list of things that you'd like to do before you die. Then pick one and do it. Make a gratitude list. Write down everything you can think of that you appreciate—things about which you are thankful. List at least 10 items. Developing an attitude of gratitude helps to transform the ordinary into the extraordinary. Expressing gratitude regularly can help turn your whole life around.

Notes:

_____

_____

_____

_____

_____

_____

_____

Chapter 10
Don't Be An Old Fuddy-Duddy

You're never too old to raise a little hell! Doris "Granny D" Haddock, 94-year-old political activist[1]

I can't afford to die—it will wreck my image! Jack LaLanne, age 90-something[2]

An old fuddy-duddy is someone who doesn't live up to his or her potential, regardless of age. Spunky eldsters can serve as positive role models for the aging baby boomers. Human behavior is largely imitative, and we learn by modeling our behavior after the example of others. Spunky eldsters can help us overcome the negative image of old age and not use age or decrepitude as excuses for failure to live a full, productive, and happy life as long as we are alive.

Anything in Life Is Possible

Life after 50 was no longer to be a staircase leading down but a path leading outward. George Vaillant, MD, *Aging Well*[3]

In 1954, Jack LaLanne turned 40 years old. To commemorate the event, he swam the entire length of San Francisco's Golden Gate Bridge—underwater, with 140 pounds of equipment—which remains a world record. Twenty-five years later he swam across a Japanese lake while pulling 65 boats, also wearing handcuffs and with his feet shackled. Why 65 boats? That's one boat for each year of his life.

I've always wondered what motivated LaLanne to pull off these seemingly impossible stunts. In his recent book, *Celebrating 90 Years of Healthy Living*, LaLanne says that he began his remarkable exploits after he turned 40, because everybody says that you're over the hill when you turn 40. So he wanted to emphasis his philosophy of healthy living "to prove that anything in life is possible."[4]

In a 2006 interview for *Muscle & Body Magazine,* LaLanne announced plans to celebrate his ninety-fifth birthday by swimming underwater from Los Angeles to Catalina Island, a distance of about 20 miles. "But my wife says she would divorce me if I do it," he told reporters, adding: "I'm almost 92 now, so I still have three years to convince her to let me."[5]

My wife, Mary, once said I talk too much about Jack LaLanne during my presentations on successful aging. Perhaps I do, but I'm not going to stop. Jack LaLanne inspired me to get in shape when I was a kid, and he inspired me again when I hit a middle-age slump. He's been a powerful, positive role model over my whole lifetime. He also has a healthy sense of humor, which is hard to come by today. A reporter once asked LaLanne if he thought he'd live to be 100. "I might live forever or it may seem like that," LaLanne replied. "I tell people I can't afford to die— it will wreck my image!"[6]

I freely admit that the spunky eldsters are a minority. This makes them all the more desirable as role models because as a boomer I never did like to follow the crowd. Sometimes it can be difficult to find positive role models in the world today, especially for those of us who became cynical after the political assassinations of the sixties, the Vietnam War, and the subsequent eclipsing of counterculture ideals. It's important that we choose positive and healthy role models—let's say Jack LaLanne and not Homer Simpson. We need role models who set a standard toward which we may strive, and who are basically living the kind of life we wish to live.

The Inspiration of Role Models and Mentors

If you deliberately plan on being less than you are capable of being, then I warn you that you'll be unhappy for the rest of your life. Abraham Maslow, humanistic psychologist[7]

I've always been fascinated by people who perform exceptional work in their field of expertise—people like Jack LaLanne, championship weight lifters, Olympic athletes, classical musicians, and other talented people. There's something very moving about a finely executed display of talent, whether in sporting events or another area. Have you ever seen a piano or violin recital that really knocked your socks off or watched somebody carve a delicate sculpture from a block of ice using a chain saw? What about an Olympic figure skater who performs an amazingly difficult and complex routine with such grace and artistry that you hold your breath with excitement? It's a joy to watch exceptional performances because it stretches the limits of human possibility. We are forced to believe that something that we scarcely believe is possible is truly possible. That's the way I feel when I read about the exploits of these spunky eldsters, and that's why I talk about them so much in this book. I hope you will share some of the enthusiasm of living an exceptional life.

Exceptional people inspire us with hope, set an example of greatness to which we may aspire, and help us recognize the potential that is within all of us. They can motivate us to work a little harder to develop our own talents. This is the reason why people read the Bible and other scriptures or study the lives of saints, political martyrs, and famous people—to help inspire them to become better human beings.

We all need mentors, heroines, and positive role models. Sometimes we find them in our lives, sometimes in religion, literature, or art. Some of us have been blessed by the serendipitous appearance of a mentor to help us through a difficult phase of our life. Sometimes we have to go out of our way to find one. That mentor may be an AA sponsor, a therapist, a teacher, an elder coworker, or even a neighbor. A mentor provides the kind of nurturing and growth experience that might be given by the ideal parent. We all watched such role models on TV, with *Ozzie and Harriet* and *Leave it to Beaver*, but only a fortunate few lived in homes with anything close to such idyllic parentage. However, having a mentor can help to make amends for what we may have missed in our family of origin. In his study of the lives of nearly 1,000 elders, George Vaillant[8] found that mentoring during young adulthood or middle age can play a major role in a person's late life development. Some of the elders came from underprivileged or abusive backgrounds, yet went on to enjoy successful and happy retirement years due to the influence of mentors they had met along the way.

Exceptional people can serve us as mentors. Mentors act as tutors or personal trainers—bringing their experience and wisdom up close and personal, adding the vital element of active social support. Traditionally a mentor is somebody who befriends you, serves as a positive role model and teaches you things that you don't learn in school—knowledge of the real world, life, and practical experience.

Elders have traditionally played key mentoring roles. Many professions have apprenticeships, where elders pass on the trade to new members of the guild. Medical schools have discovered the effectiveness of elders as mentors, as a way to train doctors to be more understanding about the problems of aging. In one program at the University of Southern California, elderly volunteers from the community were assigned to undergraduate medical trainees. Several years later as residents, the new doctors were better prepared for working with the elderly than residents who hadn't received mentoring.[9]

Record numbers of the elderly are involved in mentoring through a variety of volunteer programs. Everybody knows that President John F. Kennedy started the Peace Corps, but not many know that he also started the Senior Corps program, which includes the Foster Grandparent Program, Retired Senior Volunteer Program, and Senior Companion Program. The objective of these services is "meeting the needs of children and youth through teaching, tutoring and mentoring."[10] The Senior Corps program currently employs nearly 600,000 elders aged 55 or more in volunteer service throughout the United States. (That's more than the number of active duty soldiers in the U.S. Army!)

As we age, we naturally tend to become more concerned for the well-being of future generations. Franz found, in his developmental research, that "between the ages 30 and 45 our need for achievement declines and our need for community affiliation increases."[11] Vaillant discovered that the men and women who successfully mastered the generativity stage of life were much happier in their seventies than those who didn't.[12] It's no coincidence that much volunteer work is done by mature and senior individuals, and "seniors are volunteering at a higher rate than ever before" for volunteer projects throughout the United States, according to a recent survey of Independent Sector.[13]

Monkey See, Monkey Do

Learning would be exceedingly laborious, not to mention hazardous, if people had to rely solely on the effects of their own actions to inform them what to do. Fortunately, most human behavior is learned observationally through modeling: from observation. Albert Bandura, psychologist[14]

One of my earliest memories involves going to the Highland Park Zoo in Pittsburgh, when I was about four years old. Dad's driving us in that old '49 Studebaker with the spaceship front end and no heater. I'm looking over his shoulder from the backseat as somebody pulls out in front of the car. Dad hollers, "Get out of my way you blankity-blank-blank! Why don't you learn how to drive?" Forty years later, I'm driving my own car down the road. Somebody pulls out in front of me and I holler, "Get out of my way you blankity-blank-blank! Why don't you learn how to drive?" It's rather scary to experience this type of developmental déjà vu. Multiply childhood learning experiences like this by a thousand, and you have our basic programming for life.

The psychological principle behind role models and mentoring is called *modeling*, which is part of social learning theory. Developed by Dr. Albert Bandura, social learning theory basically says that we learn by watching other people and imitating their behaviors. This is the way we learn most of our behaviors as human beings. When we are young, we learn from our parents and siblings; as teenagers we learn from each other, and as adults we learn from our children, friends, associates, and elders.

There Are No Age Limits to Learning and Teaching

It is one of the most beautiful compensations of life that no man can sincerely try to help another without helping himself. Ralph Waldo Emerson

We never outgrow our need to learn new things. We continue to learn from others as long as we are alive, and we also continue to teach others through modeling of our own behavior. Learning and teaching have no age limits and don't depend on our state of health, either physical or mental. For example, recent research shows that even elders with senile dementia can provide mentoring to benefit themselves and others. This is because dementia destroys short-term memory, meaning that you can't learn new things, but you still remember what you already knew before your memory went bad. Dr. Cameron Camp and colleagues from the Myers Research Institute linked up memory-impaired seniors from nursing homes to work with children from day care centers.[15] The seniors provided educational experiences along the Montessori lines in a very structured setting. The elders got a chance to use social skills and share knowledge, which increased their social interaction and decreased their solitary behaviors. The children benefited by learning new skills and prosocial behaviors from the elderly.

A Different Kind of Health

We looked into the abyss and we came out believing in life more than ever. Blair Justice, PhD, psychologist and stroke survivor[16]

We need positive role models not just to demonstrate that physical fitness is possible at all ages in life but also to show us how to persevere even when we aren't as healthy as we'd like to be. The first time I went on an ocean cruise, I was taken aback by the poor physical condition of some of the passengers. Some of them looked like they should have been in the hospital or a retirement home. How could such sickly looking people be going on a cruise to Alaska? But there they were right in front of me, laughing, smiling, and talking with their friends and family, out on the deck marveling at icebergs, splashing around in the pool, and filling up their trays at the buffets. In other words, doing everything everybody else was doing on the cruise. I saw eldsters pushing themselves along in wheelchairs, little old ladies who could barely walk, and bent-over grandpas creeping along on walkers trying to keep up with their scampering grandkids.

They were all out there, active participants despite their illnesses, handicaps, or limitations.

They are spunky eldsters. They are exceptional people because they don't let life get them down. They may have sickness or disability, but they don't act sick or disabled. They get out there instead of sitting at home feeling sorry for themselves. They don't give up but decide to keep on going no matter what. They show us that the quality of effort we put forth into living our lives is just as important as our outward accomplishments— sometimes more so. In the face of sickness and disability, they continue to inspire us with their persistence, stamina, and pure spunk.

Dr. Govindappa Venkataswamy, an 87-year-old Indian physician, has performed over 100,000 cataract surgeries after being crippled with arthritis.[17] Dr. V meditates daily then shows up at the office every morning at 7:00 A.M. "You need to be at work, not sitting meditating," he said. His goal is to eliminate curable blindness among India's poor by the year 2020. He has treated 70 percent of his patients for free.

Today I get inspired when I see an elderly gentleman inch his way into the gym with a walker. When I started going to the gym again at age 50, I was surprised to see a lot of older people. Some of them arrived as early as 6:00 A.M., including a group of three or four white-haired men who hang out together in the pool and hot tub. (Will *you* be going to the gym 6:00 A.M. when you retire?) Sometimes the pool is full of white-haired ladies doing water aerobics. One old gal routinely shows up with her walker! An 87-year-old man told me he was not trying to put on muscles, but "just maintain." Admittedly, most of these spunky eldsters aren't in tip-top shape like Etta Clark's aging athletes, but they show up on a regular basis and are doing something to improve their health and well-being. And it sure beats the alternative, as the saying goes. One thing is certain: I don't see many sourpusses among these eldsters. Everyone is surprisingly content, as evident from the ubiquitous smiles, laughter, and joking I observe. I told one of the hot tub crew that he looks like Sid Caesar, and he laughingly replied that he has never looked as good as Sid Caesar, especially now that he's 84 years old. The satisfaction with oneself and one's life that comes with age is terribly misunderstood by young people in America today. It's sometimes mistaken for senility, when, in fact, it is the radiance and vitality that we can all experience when we decide to live fully alive in the present moment—regardless of outward circumstances.

When I was delivering my *Do Not Go Gentle* presentation at the Texas Psychological Association (TPA) Conference in November 2007, I met Dr. Blair Justice, a colleague of distinction.Dr. Justice presented on a subject with which he was intimately familiar—stroke survival. As a stroke survivor himself, he discovered there were many, many other people like him, who were sick but not sickly, even disabled but not down for the count. He wrote a book about the subject, which he calls *A Different Kind of Health.* According to Dr. Justice, "many persons with chronic disease or disability gain a sense of well-being in the very presence of their disorder."[18] These are people who are happy, hopeful, and enthusiastic about life. They stay connected to other people and become active participants in life. These individuals have discovered that "inner health" and a "sense of well-being" don't depend on your outer circumstances, including even the condition of your body or the state of your health. They don't let infirmity keep them from deriving full meaning and purpose in life. On the contrary, such individuals have found that the disease itself motivates them to change, and that "because of illness or disability they reach deep inside themselves to find ways to be whole."[19]

Nursing Home Fishermen

Some elders refuse to let their circumstances keep them from being spunky. The other day I was jogging around a small lake by the gym where I work out. I spotted an elderly man in a walker approaching the water—something you don't see very often. I watched as he got out of his walker and sat down on the bank. Then he unhooked a fishing rod he had strapped to his walker and cast his line into the lake. Another man was approaching the lake in a wheelchair, obviously struggling. Fortunately a nearby attendant came to his assistance. As it turns out, both men were residents of a nursing home located next to the lake. I've passed by that nursing home for five years, and this was the first time I saw any of the residents approach the lake—even though it's only about 30 yards away. I guess the two old guys just decided they wanted to go fishing, so they went out and did it! I admire their spunk. The sun was just appearing on the horizon, and as I jogged by I could see the eldsters' beaming smiles as they prepared for a pleasant early morning at the neighborhood fishing hole. I sure hope they caught something.

Spunky Eldsters as Role Models of Successful Aging

I've hung a small poster of Dr. John Turner, the weight-lifting psychiatrist behind the desk in my office. When people ask who he is, I tell them, "Somebody I want to look like when I'm 67 years old!" And that's the truth. He has a muscular physique that most men would love to have at any age. What does Dr. Turner's image represent to me? It is a symbol of hope. He proves that it's possible for an aging person to remain in a state of peak physical fitness. Furthermore, if it's possible for him, then perhaps it's possible for you and me as well. Although I've never met him, Dr. Turner is a positive role model for me through the inspiration of his active lifestyle. I have a refrigerator magnet-sized poster of Dr. Turner pumping iron on my home refrigerator, and another on the small office fridge. There's a matching magnet of 73-year-old Marie Wilcox-Little, photographed by Etta Clark posing in her swimsuit, still fit and attractive, with the Growing Old Is Not for Sissies caption. (These magnets are available from stickergiant.com for $3.49 each.) I bought copies of *Growing Old is Not for Sissies* for my brother Ron, who lifts weights and is approaching age 50, and for my buddy Bill, who joined the gym with me when we were in our early teens. I keep copies in the waiting room of my office. I encourage everyone to buy a copy of these books and get inspired by studying the achievements and enthusiasm of these spunky eldsters.

In her second book, *Growing Old is Not for Sissies II*, Etta Clark followed up on Dr. Turner. His muscular physique was as well-defined at age 79 as it was 12 years earlier. He told Clark that "there is no age limit to exercise."[20] Three times a week he walks 15 minutes, exercises on a Stairmaster 15 minutes, and then lifts with free weights one hour. He also keeps abreast of scientific studies on successful aging and talked with Clark about research showing that people of advanced years can still benefit from weight lifting.

I'm drawing attention to weight lifting in the elderly because most people consider it a very strenuous sport and certainly not a pastime commonly associated with senior citizens. In that sense, it is very much a part of the *Do Not Go Gentle* theme. It's important to realize that not all old people are gathered at the local senior citizens' center to play dominoes.

What can be more not-going-gentle than a 79-year old weightlifting psychiatrist? Well, how about a 91-year old weight lifting grandmother? Helen Zechmeister works out three times a week, can lift double her body weight, and is still flexible enough to do a full split and touch the floor with her palms without bending her knees. She turned down an invitation to compete in Italy because she was "too busy." Happily married for 68 years to a man she met at a dance at the University of Vienna, Austria, she described her marriage as "the greatest pleasure in my life."[21] As we'll see later, a warm marriage is a strong predictor of successful aging and longevity. Etta Clark records her impression while photographing Helen dead lifting 230 pounds, which made her "gape with awe" and impressed most of the young men at the gym, who were gathered around her. Then she asked her husband to add 10 more pounds to the barbell!

Recent research demonstrates the benefits of resistance training for people of advancing age, whether in their seventies, eighties, or even nineties. Resistance training, which includes weight lifting, sit-ups, push-ups and similar exertion exercises, builds muscle strength and stamina. Your current state of health doesn't matter. You can always improve.

I hope that you start thinking differently about aging after reading the stories of these spunky eldsters. I am optimistic that you will change your image of old age by seeing the scientific evidence. The truth is that growing old does not have to be an inevitable downward spiral into helplessness and decrepitude. You can never be too old to improve your physical fitness. It's never too late to get into better shape and enhance your health. If a 91-year-old grandmother can go to the gym and make the young men "gape with awe" at her barbell exploits, then maybe you can draw a stare or two by doing something unexpected for your own age.

Spunky Eldsters as Cultural Rebels

In contemporary American society, elders are not often respected and honored, unlike in most traditional societies. The obsession with youth deprives elders of the opportunity to release their full potential, and it robs youth of the nurturance and wisdom that can come from an elder's lifetime of experience. Many of us who are members of the baby boom generation rebelled against our parents and the elders of society. Now that we are growing older ourselves, it would be a good time to have a change of heart and recognize that there is a lot we can learn from our elders.

These spunky eldsters are so far beyond the crowd that they are geriatric rebels because they are defying the traditions of what it means to get old. They are rebels against the conventions of old age. Many of us can identify very well with nonconformists. That is by definition what the counterculture was all about: a whole generation rose up to challenge the conventional ways of believing and behaving. Most of us boomers have idolized at least a few rebels against the conventions of youth in our younger days, like Marlon Brando in *On the Waterfront,* James Dean in *Rebel Without a Cause* or Peter Fonda in *Easy Rider*. Now that boomers are aging, we need new role models. What could be better than spunky eldsters who are defying the conventional standards of what it means to be old?

Harold and Maude–A Cinematic Spunky Eldster

The 1971 film *Harold and Maude* portrays the unconventional romance between a 75-year old woman and a 21-year-old man who looks like a teenager. I first saw the film in my twenties at one of the Los Angeles rerun theaters, and even then it challenged my preconceptions about what it means to be old. There's an ironic switching of roles that tickles your funny bone. Even though Harold is young and rich, he has a morbid view of life and is obsessed with death. He drives a hearse, attends funerals in his spare time, and stages suicidal stunts to rebel against his overbearing mother. In total contrast, Maude is antediluvian, but she is energetic and obsessed with life—she is a septuagenarian teenage rebel. She "borrows" other people's cars, drives recklessly, and shows blatant disregard for authority figures—even making off with a policeman's motorcycle in one scene while he's writing her a speeding ticket. (You should take this film as a parable of how to age successfully and not become a senior delinquent![22]) Maude lives her life fully in the moment, enjoying all the gusty— savoring the sights, sounds, smells, and sensations of being fully alive. Maude's love of life transforms Harold from a premature curmudgeon into a vigorous participate in life, with real feelings and joie de vivre.

Why Spunky Eldsters are Not Old Fuddy-Duddies

Nuts to being old! Casey Stengel

1. Spunky eldsters do not use age as an excuse. They continue to do what they want to do, as long as they can do it. Casey Stengel was a spunky eldster. He continued to coach the New York Yankees until he was forced to retire at age 70 because the team owners thought he was too old to manage. His response to them was: "Nuts to being old! I'll try to manage as long as I don't have to go to take a pitcher out in a wheelchair."[23] The Rolling Stones have been together as a group for 45 years and all the members of the band are now more than 65 years old. Although officially senior citizens, the Stones are as spunky as ever and show no signs of slowing down. I remember when the Stones were doing their Steel Wheels Tour in 1989-90, how some of us jokingly called it the *Wheel Chair Tour* or the *Nursing Home Tour*. Ironically, in a recent interview Stones guitarist

Keith Richards told an Associated Press reporter that he was not planning to quit the music scene any time soon, and if necessary, "I'll do it in my wheelchair."[24]

Seventy-Five Plus!

You've got to have guts to grow old. Walter Bortz II, MD, gerontologist[25]

Seventy-five-plus is the fastest growing age segment of the U.S. population.[26] If you are a boomer, there is a strong likelihood that you will live into your seventies and beyond. What can you accomplish at such an advanced age? Plenty!

- Ronald Reagan was 74 years old when he ran for his second term of office as president of the United States. When 56-year-old Walter Mondale suggested he was too old to get reelected, Reagan replied coyly, "I will not make age an issue in this campaign. I am not going to exploit for political purposes my opponent's youth and inexperience."[27]
- Benjamin Franklin invented bifocals when he was 78 years old.
- Winston Churchill was elected to his second term as prime minister of Great Britain when he was 77. He grew up with a speech impediment, and he worked for years to overcome his stuttering.
- At age 71, Nelson Mandela was released from prison, where he had been held a political prisoner for 27 years. At age 74 he was awarded the Nobel Peace Prize for his struggle against apartheid. At age 75 he became president of South Africa.
- Jimmy Carter won the Nobel Peace Prize at age 78 for worldwide humanitarian work—20 years after retiring from service as the thirty-ninth president of the United States.
- John Glenn became the oldest astronaut in October 1998, with his flight at age 77 on the Space Shuttle Discovery.

Up until the time of his septuagenarian space flight, he had served 25 years as a United States senator.

2. Spunky eldsters are full of vitality. They keep physically and socially active throughout their lives. "You need to ensure that each minute of your life is crowded with active participation," says Stanford University gerontologist Walter Bortz II, MD, in *Dare to Be 100.* [28]

- My wife's Aunt Ruth (an older sister of Joseta, the skydiving granny) was a spunky eldster.   Aunt Ruth organized a family trip to a botanical garden in Hot Springs, Arkansas, shortly after Mary and I got married. I took a picture of Aunt Ruth on that trip that I like to show in my presentations on successful aging. In the photo she's way out in front of everybody on the trail and appears fit, trim, spry, and vigorous. She's looking back with a bit of chagrin and hollering, "What's keeping ya'll?" She was always on the go, and she stayed that way right up until the day she died. At age 89 she went into the hospital for heart surgery. She had her bags packed and her clothes all laid out for yet another family gathering as soon as she got out. But unfortunately, she died during surgery.
- At age 92, Les Paul (born July 7, 1928), inventor of the electric guitar, still performs a regular Monday night gig in New York City at the Iridium Jazz Club. He was inducted into the National Inventor's Hall of Fame in Akron, Ohio, alongside Thomas Edison, Eli Whitney, and a troop of other creative geniuses. For his ninetieth birthday, he recorded a new album and performed live at Carnegie Hall.
- Well into his ninth decade, Charles E. Williams, founder of the renowned Williams-Sonoma kitchen specialty store, still goes to work every day. At his ninety-fourth birthday party he told a CBS *Sunday Morning* reporter, "If you love what you do, then the world will fall in love with you."[29]

Run Granny Run

When she was 89 years old, Doris "Granny D" Haddock became deeply depressed by the death of her husband. "Death took my husband and then my best friend and I thought I was next. I needed a reason to live, and I found that reason."[30] She got her new lease on life through political activism, combined with vigorous exercise. Doris decided to walk across the entire United States to protest the influence of big business and money on elections. Beginning in California, she headed for the East Coast. Along the way, she stopped people on the streets, signed them up to vote if they weren't registered, and protested her state senator's support for the war in Iraq: "What in the world was he thinking when he supports military misadventures?" She walked across the Mojave Desert, spent four long months traversing Texas, and hiked across the Appalachian Mountains in the dead of winter. Eighteen months after leaving Los Angeles, she arrived back in her native New Hampshire. She walked a staggering 3,200 miles.

When she was 94 years old Granny D decided to enter politics. She ran for state senate in New Hampshire against incumbent and former governor Judd Gregg. As part of her campaign, she pledged to walk across New Hampshire—which she did. She ended up with 34 percent of the vote—pretty good for a 94-year-old woman who only had $200,000 in campaign funds and couldn't even afford a TV commercial. She remains a political activist. To celebrate her ninety-seventh birthday, she spent the day advocating for public funding of elections at the New Hampshire State House. At the time I wrote this, she was still alive at age 98 and politically active.[31] The *Run Granny Run* video ends with one of her ubiquitous walking excursions and a statement of her personal motto for a life well spent: "I for one am certainly going to continue to raise a little hell. I want to plant a few more seeds here and there before they plant me."[32]

3.   Spunky eldsters remain creative and innovative throughout their entire lives. Advancing age does not cause any lose of the imagination. On the contrary, like fine wine and cheese, mature individuals can get better with each passing year. Some famous people in history didn't even reach their full potential of creativity until well into advanced age. During her own lifetime, Grandma Moses obtained renown as a painter, her output was prolific, and her paintings were sought throughout the world. However, she didn't even start painting until she was 76 years old, and she took up the palette only because she could no longer embroider because of crippling arthritis! How's that for coping with a disability and turning your adversity into a source of strength? Grandma Moses lived to be 101 years old (1860-1961), and she continued to turn out paintings until the very end. At age 100 she illustrated the *Night Before Christmas*, which is still a popular Christmas gift item. (I recently ordered a copy from Amazon. com). Her 100th birthday was proclaimed Grandma Moses Day by New York Governor Nelson Rockefeller.

Creativity has no known age limits. Pablo Picasso lived to be 91 years old (1881-1973), and he produced more artwork during his final 20 years than in any other period of his long life. "Picasso became more daring, his works more colorful and expressive" and "the sense of the artist's race against time is made clear."[33] His final output was "marked by a great restlessness whose aim must be to exorcise death itself."[34] Picasso remained intensely sensual into his waning years. Among the output from these 20 years were over 400 portraits of his second wife, whom he married in 1961 when he was 80 years old. Picasso died in April 1973, while he and his wife were entertaining friends. His last words were "Drink to me, drink to my health—you know I can't drink any more."[35]

4.   A spunky eldster makes the best of diminishing resources. He never gives up but has a staggering amount of persistence and fortitude. You can be sure to experience major losses as part of the aging process—cancer takes a breast, family members die, etc. But the spunky eldster surmounts these obstacles and seems to do even better than before the loss. He learns to roll with the punches and develops to his full potential at every age of life regardless of the vicissitudes of time, fortune, and even declining health. I can't think of a better example here than Stephen Hawking. Hawking is another guy I looked up on the Internet to find out when he died like I did for Jack LaLanne. I discovered Stephen Hawking was not only still alive, but he continues to reach new heights of achievement—literally.[36] At age 65, Hawking set a unique record: he became the first paraplegic senior citizen in free-fall orbit around the earth!

Many people consider Hawking to be a scientific genius of equal status with Isaac Newton and Albert Einstein. In 1988, he wrote a best-selling book on astrophysics, *A Brief History of Time*, which has sold more than nine million copies and was on the *Times* of London's best-seller list for four years. (Which is quite amazing for a book on such an esoteric subject like astrophysics and cosmology.) Hawking routinely travels all over the world to give lectures. He went to China in June 2006 to give a lecture on the origin of the universe to 6,000 people. The following year he was at U.C. Berkley addressing a standing room only audience— that large a crowd usually only appears for a major rock concert. He's been a guest star on *Star Trek: The Next Generation* and *The Simpson's* TV show, and he's probably the only quadriplegic to have his own action figure and wheelchair video game. Recently he coauthored a children's book with his daughter.

These might not seem like major accomplishments for a university professor who has written a popular book. The really amazing thing is that Hawking has made these achievements *despite* the fact that he has been confined to a wheelchair and profoundly disabled for over 40 years due the early onset of Lou Gehrig's disease (ALS). He hasn't been able to speak for over 30 years. Currently, the only voluntary motor control he has is to blink his eye, which he uses to operate a voice synthesized computer. Somehow, he found the will to live life fully, despite having a condition that most people would consider to be hopeless—and he's made all of his accomplishments seemingly with sheer spunk and willpower.[37]

If you visit Stephen Hawking's official Web site, you will find the following testimony: "I am quite often asked: How do you feel about having ALS?" Hawking replies to his rhetorical question: "The answer is, not a lot. I try to lead as normal a life as possible, and not think about my condition, or regret the things it prevents me from doing, which are not that many."[38]

Hawking's declaration astonishes me every time I read it. Here's a man whose body is over 99 percent paralyzed and who is totally dependent on other people for all of his basic physical and daily needs. Yet he claims to lead a pretty normal life and states flatly that there are "not that many" things he can't do! Talk about learning to cope and adjust to one's limitations! Hawking's attitude reflects the quintessence of coping and of successful aging. He wastes no time regretting what he has lost and what he can no longer do. Instead, he focuses all of his energy on what he can do: think, reason, and use his mind to develop his mental genius.

Hawking is truly a spunky eldster, and he can show us all that it is possible to surmount even the most disabling conditions with tenacity and courage.

Activities and Solutions

Have you ever been inspired by another person who has accomplished something you would like to do? Do you currently have any positive role models or heroes and heroines in your life? Take some time to explore your own attitudes about aging. Talk to other people your age and share your experiences. List at least 10 positive things about growing older. Find yourself one or more positive role models of people who are aging successfully. Read about what they've done and start doing those things yourself.

Notes:

_____

_____

_____

_____

_____

_____

_____

Chapter 11

Real-Life Space Cowboys

Despite our stereotypes, getting older doesn't mean you have to become decrepit. People age at different rates for many reasons. Traditional gerontology focuses on the negative factors like genetics, disease and disability, and that can encourage a fatalistic outlook. The new school of gerontology focuses on lifestyle factors and emphasizes the positive aspects of aging, which promotes hope, personal responsibility, and increased control over our own destinies. All of us can improve the quality of our lives as we age by making healthy lifestyle choices. For example, regular exercise, physical activity, and good nutrition can have a very potent antiaging effect. Although we can't literally turn back the clock in the number of years, healthy lifestyle choices can make us look younger, feel younger, and enjoy greater physical health and happiness.

Age Is No Barrier to Fitness

At 85, John Glenn was invited to write the foreword to *Fitness over Fifty: An Exercise Guide from the National Institute on Aging.* A lifelong advocate of physical fitness, Glenn declared: "Exercise and proper nutrition are crucial for staying healthy as we age. You are never too old to get in shape."

John Glenn's health and longevity are proof that he practices what he preaches. At age 77, he became the oldest astronaut in history with a 9-day mission on the Space Shuttle Discovery. Ironically, that was his second 'world's oldest astronaut' record. He set the first record in 1962, at age 40, when he became the first American to orbit the earth for the Mercury Project. So much for being over the hill after age 30, as many of us used to think during the sixties!

This is one of those situations where real life is stranger than fiction. I remember how deeply impressed I was by the movie

Space Cowboys, in which four aging ex-astronauts are brought out of retirement for a special mission. They're a bit out of shape, but still spunky and spirited enough to meet the demands of astronaut training, by hook or by crook. I later learned that John Glenn was older than any of the *Space Cowboys* actors when he went on his final mission into space—which ironically occurred **two years before** *Space Cowboys* was released (Aug. 4, 2000). When the film appeared Clint Eastwood was 70, James Garner was 72, Donald Sutherland was 66, and Tommy Lee Jones was the young whipper-snapper of the bunch—only 53.

Dare Not to Be Decrepit

The trick is growing up without growing old. Casey Stengel

I don't want to give the misleading impression that John Glenn, aging athletes, or anybody else is immune to the ravages of time. As Glenn grew older, he found in necessary to modify his exercise routine because of age-related decline and disease. Because of osteoporosis, his doctors advised against jogging, one of his lifelong activities, to reduce stress on his knees and joints. Rather than slow down, he took up speed walking instead.[2]

Successful Aging Is Largely a Matter of Attitude

Physical health is certainly important. However, successful aging does not mean that you will not get sick or suffer health problems. As Dr. George Vaillant points out, it's not so much your state of health as your state of mind about your health. Valliant coined the term *psychosocial health*, which means "being both contented and vigorous, as well as being not sad or sick or dead."[3] I can understand the importance of attitude from my clinical psychology practice. Most of the patients I evaluate have some type of serious physical or mental health problem; often it's a combination of back injury or other physical disability or disease, chronic pain, major depression, anxiety, and frequently alcohol and drug addiction. All of my patients' problems seem to be essentially of the same magnitude—extremely severe. However, some of them are applying for disability while others are out looking for jobs in the community. Attitude is obviously important. According to Vaillant, the key to strong psychosocial health is "experiencing the biological ravages of age without feeling 'sick.'" He concludes that "there's a big difference between being 'ill' and feeling 'sick.'"[4]

Don't Let the Fact That You Can't Do Something Stop You from Doing It

The secret to staying young at heart is staying fit. Ida Kline, 100-year-old aerobics instructor[5]

Successful aging does not require you to be a NASA astronaut or lifelong sports enthusiast. All that's really necessary is to keep up a moderate level of physical activity on a regular basis. The American Heart Association, for example, reported that as little as 45 to 75 minutes of exercise per week can result in "lower risks of cardiovascular disease."[6] Even nonstrenuous forms of activity like yoga can be tremendously beneficial. I had a yoga teacher once tell me that yoga is *exercise without exertion.* "Yoga is associated with a wide range of physical and psychological benefits that may be especially helpful for persons living with chronic illness," according to the Arthritis Center of Johns Hopkins University.[7] The American Diabetes Association and the American Heart Association both recommend yoga because it has been proven effective in combating arthritis and other diseases associated with aging, such as high blood pressure, diabetes and cardiovascular disease.

The bottom line is that physical limitations are not a good excuse to stop being active.

At 100 years of age, Ida Kline continued to teach aerobics and stretching classes every day. The fact that she couldn't stand up for the whole class didn't stop her; she just brought along a chair and led the exercises while sitting down. Kline also took good care of her mental health. She told Etta Clark, who photographed her one day in class that "the key to a long life is to control your worries. I don't worry about tomorrow. ... So many people waste time worrying when they could be thinking pleasant thoughts."[8]

This is very good cognitive coping, for any age. Dr. George Vaillant's *Aging Well* reports that effective coping was a major predictor of successful aging.[9] It can make a difference between whether you stay independent or end up in a rest home.

Mary Kownacki has a good definition of coping: "Being able to get through a crisis and not lose your ability to function." Through coping, you develop skills to process your negative emotions and thoughts, identify what you need, and find a way to get it. Or, as I like to put it, don't let the fact that you can't do something stop you from doing it. Find some way to do what you want to do, even if it's unconventional and makes people think you're not acting your age.

Don't give in to making excuses. Get out and do something. There's always something you can do to make any situation better. If you have arthritis so bad that you can't jog anymore, then you can perhaps join a water aerobics class or senior swim club. Let the stories of these spunky eldsters help to motivate you because some of them may be in worse shape than you, but they are still doing something to try and improve their lives. If an 89-year-old woman with arthritis and emphysema (Granny D) can walk across the entire United States, maybe you can walk around the block or sign up for an exercise class at the local YMCA.

Tom is the oldest member of the gym I attend. He shows up almost every day and is done working out around 7:00 A.M., so he can return home and join his wife for breakfast. At 87 years of age, he looks fit and trim. He knows his way around the gym with seasoned experience, and the other day he helped me fix one of the machines I had accidentally broken. Tom started going to the gym about 15 years ago, in his mid seventies, when knee problems interfered with his tennis and jogging. When I asked what motivates him to keep coming to the gym, he said, "It makes me feel better."

Where There's a Will, There's a Way

In February 2005, Shelby Stepp of Wichita Falls, Texas, died quietly at age 69 only five weeks after being diagnosed with cancer.[10] His death was unremarkable, but his life inspired many local residents with a sense of awe at the power of human beings to overcome adversity. In 1936, Shelby Stepp was born without hands or feet. He didn't have a mouth, either, until an incision was made so he could eat. The doctors told his family flatly that he would be better off dead. The family disagreed, and despite his handicap, Stepp went on to live a full life. He learned to write using his wrists and by age eight could walk on his stubs. He learned to play the marimba. He graduated from high school and completed an accounting program at a business college, but because of speech problems, he worked as a janitor at a local church. He held a job throughout his lifetime, got married, and drove himself all around town on a specially-designed three-wheeled bicycle. He attended services at several churches, played the marimba for nursing home residents, and went to concert performances of the Wichita Falls Symphony and basketball games at Midwestern State University. He continued to ride his bicycle and remained active until shortly before his death. I saw him on his bike from a distance a couple of times, but I never realized the extent of his handicap until reading about him in the paper. (I'm sorry that I never knew him while he lived and have to remain amazed at his spunkiness only after his death.)

We need to keep people like this in mind when we start complaining about having to park too far from the entrance to the shopping mall, or when an elevator is out of service in a two- or three-story building. We generally take for granted the fact that we do have arms and legs. Even worse, many Americans have no physical disability yet allow themselves to atrophy through years and years of inactivity. It's a sad fact that inactivity has become either the direct cause or a major contributing factor to so many of our elderly woes. The good news is that it's never too late to get back into shape and improve the quality of your life.

Old Age Stereotypes

As spunky eldsters, John Glenn, Ida Kline, and Shelby Stepp epitomize a major theme of this book: continued vitality and physical fitness should be the normal course of aging. Even if you have serious health problems like osteoporosis, arthritis, or a severe disability, you can remain active and minimize the impact of your condition. Decrepitude is not an inevitable consequence of getting old. Disease and sickness are not acceptable excuses for failure to live a full and meaningful life, at any age.

Unfortunately, we tend to stereotype older people as being all the same. The truth is that there are even more differences among older people than among younger people. Susan Whitbourne, a developmental psychologist, describes the popular prejudice: "Individuality fades as the aging process takes its toll on the body and the mind."[11] We tend to lump all older people together into some anonymous mass of sagging flesh, a corporeal decline of reduced capacity that we call old age—all of which is presumably tucked safely out of sight, perhaps in some gigantic, shopping mall-sized nursing home. Out of sight, but not out of mind because we all secretly dread our own impending decomposition. Our stereotypic view of old people as decrepit and in full physical decay flourishes in the media and is vigorously alive in the perception of the general public, especially of younger people. In general, the youthful view of middle age and beyond is summarized well by Australian psychologists Roland and Juliette Goldman: "The overall picture tends to be one of unrelieved gloom—death, decay, disease, broken bones; increasing illness and accident proneness; irritability, senility and loneliness are seen to be the major characteristics."[12]

Senior Angst

And ye shall know the truth, and the truth shall make you free. John (8:32)

One of my motivations to write this book was to share the hopefulness of a positive outlook on aging and to help others overcome their old, negativistic views about getting old. Thinking about aging and our own mortality can be frightening. David Gutmann makes the poignant observation that "we study what we are afraid of, and gerontologists are no exception."[13] Feminist psychologist Betty Friedan began her research on aging "in growing personal dread, because in my fifties I didn't even want to think about age."[14] Reviewing the scientific literature "confirmed my suspicion that the science of gerontology itself was perpetuating the fear and dread of age."[15]

I've been plenty scared more than once about growing old. Dealing with health issues, the increasing aches and pains of aging, losing hair and other more or less important body parts, confronting potentially fatal diseases, not being able to do everything you used to do so easily—it's definitely enough to alarm you out at times. And the more you age, the more you experience signs of your body's transience. Confronting your own mortality head on can be a terrifying ordeal. That's why so many people try to avoid it. Anthropologist Ernest Becker goes so far as to say that the fear of death "is a mainspring of human activity."[16] In his Pulitzer-prize-winning book, *The Denial of Death*, he argues that much of our behavior is designed to avoid having to deal with our own mortality.

The future is scary because it is unknown, and fear of the unknown is one of the greatest terrors. That's why the old style horror movies, which rely mainly on suspense and our imagination, can be more frightening than modern horror films, despite their graphic displays of gruesomeness.[17] However, we don't need to watch scary movies or media disasters and listen to the hyperbole of gloom and doom on the evening news. The truth is, our imagination can sometimes be our worst enemy. Each of us is fully capable of conjuring up fearful images of our own future demise, especially when dealing with aging issues like health threats and disease. Like one day, I discovered an unsightly mole on my back that I swear wasn't there the day before. The next thing you know, I'm imagining that I have skin cancer, and it's spread through my whole body; I'm dying a miserable death, agonizing in the hospital with all those tubes sticking out of my body and worried about whether I've updated my living will! I know I'm not the only person with an active imagination about these things.

Uncertainty and unpredictability can generate intense fear and anxiety. In his guidebook on stress management, *Stress & Health*, psychology professor Phillip Rice explains that "unpredictability is both psychologically and physically debilitating. When we have no way of predicting an event, we experience chronic arousal."[18] We suffer "a feeling of helplessness or futility" that can be overwhelming. To make matters worse, fear, worry, and unresolved stress produce wear and tear on our bodies that increases the risk of heart attack, stroke, and other diseases, shortens your life and reduces the over all quality of the aging experience.

Overcoming Fear of Aging

Fortunately, we're not helpless against the onslaught of senior angst. The good news is that knowledge can liberate us from fear. According to Dr. Rice, "information seeking is one of the most important coping resources a person can develop" because "it both reduces uncertainty and increases the perception of personal control."[19]   One of Dr. George Vaillant's findings from *Aging Well* is that "education predicts healthy aging"— independently of social class and intelligence.[20]

Educating ourselves about successful aging can help us to overcome our fear of aging. Sometimes we get an education without conscious intent, and despite our stereotypes about growing old. In a *National Geographic* feature on centenarians, correspondent Dan Buettner candidly discussed his own feelings about interviewing extremely old people. "I didn't expect to enjoy meeting centenarians. In fact, I associated them with my own eventual frailty and the smell of retirement homes."[21] He described his meeting with 112-year-old Lydia Newton, who still lived in her own mobile home in Sedona, California. Her clarity of mind impressed him vividly and helped change his views of aging. "She had 107-year-old memories she could recall with the clarity of much younger people remembering what they had for lunch. She possessed wisdom and a sense of satisfaction with her life that made me actually look forward to the twilight years."

Sir Francis Bacon (1561-1626) said that "knowledge is power," and that is certainly true when it comes to learning about successful aging. Studying the lives of spunky eldsters provides us with positive role models from which we gain a sense of direction. We can confront our stereotypes and negative views about aging, and replace them with healthy, positive images; this improves our self-esteem and increases our sense of hopefulness and personal empowerment. Learning about new research on successful aging shows us what works, so we can avoid mistakes and spend our time doing things that we know are good for us.

We are just beginning to understand the truth about aging, and it often stands in marked contrast to the pessimistic view that prevails. In *The Fountain of Age* Betty Friedan talks about how surprised she was to find that only five percent of Americans over sixty-five are in nursing homes and fewer than five percent are senile. "You think from the image that that is what awaits us all," she writes.[22] Learning the facts about aging reduced Friedan's fear of the unknown, in the same way that learning the truth about aging can help the rest of us allay our fears. That's what this book is all about; that's why you're reading it and applying what you learn.

Once we take action and start practicing the principles of successful aging, then we will see positive change occur in our lives. This gives us a tremendous sense of power and mastery. We are no longer blind victims of fate but knowing participants in our own future well-being, helping to make our senior years better through responsible action.

Research on death anxiety shows that "self-confident individuals with a clear sense of purpose and control over their lives express less fear of death."[23] Having a strong commitment about the meaning of life, rather than religious faith per se, is instrumental in reducing fear of dying. According to a study by Purdue psychologist Victor Cicirelli, "both devout Christians and devout atheists viewed death as less threatening than did people with ambivalent religious views."[24]

There's encouraging news from developmental psychology that fear of aging and death anxiety decrease for most people as they get older—even if we don't go out of our way to read and study more about the aging process. Erik Erikson argued that the resolution of death anxiety occurs naturally during the final stage of life, *maturity*, which occurs roughly between age 65 and death. During the maturity stage, we resolve the tension between ego integrity and despair, learning to cope with our mortality and the waning years of our lives. We learn to be comfortable in our own skin and find meaning and value in our life's experience. Erikson described this stage as "an experience which conveys some world order and spiritual sense."[25] Mature elders are also driven to pass on their experience to the next generation. "Erikson suggests that one of the life tasks of Integrity is for the old to show the young how not to fear death," according to Vaillant.[26]

I remember when my father was dying of cancer. When I first saw his disease-wracked body, he looked like an Auschwitz prisoner, and there was a hollow look of sheer terror in his eyes. A relatively short time later, however, he underwent an extraordinary transformation. He became confident and serene. In high spirits, he rhapsodized like an Indian holy man about the mysteries of life, how nothing ever gets destroyed because the atoms of our bodies dissolve into the vastness of the universe, and we become a part of it all. I didn't understand fully what he was talking about, even though I had earned my master's degree in religious studies. That's because I was only 32 years old at the time and not developmentally prepared to understand the existential mysteries beyond the intellectual level. Since then I have aged a bit and stared out into the great void myself. Today I can see that Dad had found his inner peace and successfully resolved the final stage of life of which Erikson speaks.[27]

Senescence vs. Chronological Age

Biologically, one can be young or old for one's chronological age.
George Vaillant, MD, *Aging Well*[28]

Seventy-eight-year-old mountaineer Dick Elton climbed the highest peaks in 48 states to stay in top physical condition. One day he was giving a lesson to a group of Girl Scouts, all dressed up in his backpacking outfit as he explained the intricacies of hiking and camping safety. When he stopped for a break one of the girls asked him a question, but not about outdoor life. She wanted to know "how can we get a pair of legs like yours?"[29]

When Etta Clark took his picture for her book on aging athletes, Elton shared this anecdote and jokingly suggested that she should be taking a picture of his legs and not show his face, which reveals how old he really is. Ironically, Clark actually used the incongruence test to select pictures for her book. She showed her photo proofs to family members, and if they gasped "that man's head does not fit on his body," she knew to include the picture in her book. If they had no reaction to the picture, she knew it would not convey the desired image.[30]

Despite the negative stereotypes about growing old, the reality of aging is that the physical, mental, and emotional effects differ remarkably from person to person. Why does one 78-year-old man have legs that are envied by teenage girls, while another refuses to be seen publicly in short pants? How come one 85-year-old woman is depressed and confined to her bed in a nursing home while another is joyously jumping out of airplanes? Why is there often such discrepancy between a person's chronological age and the way he or she looks, feels, and behaves? Gerontologists explain this incongruity with the term *senescence*, which refers to the way age impacts on a person's body—the biological and physical changes, as distinguished from the chronological passage of years. Senescence is the wear and tear on our bodies that occurs as we grow older; to put it bluntly, it's a measure of decrepitude.

Let's look at something straight forward and seemingly obvious–physical appearance. Some people who are 65 years old hardly have any gray hair or wrinkles, while others are already graying and wrinkled by the time they're 35 or 40. Awhile back I was asked to evaluate an elderly woman for dementia. As soon as I walked into her room at the rehab hospital, I thought there had been a mistake. The patient was clearly no senior citizen. She had the face of a young-looking middle-aged woman, perhaps in her early forties. I was astounded to discover that she was really 93 years old! This vividly taught me a lesson of how difficult it can be to estimate a person's age by physical appearance alone.

This sort of shocking double take is familiar to modern gerontology researchers. Etta Clark recalls her photographic interview with Els Tunzing, a runner in the Dipsea mountain trail race, a grueling trek from a beach north of San Francisco to a path that climbs 4,500 feet and winds its way across two mountain ranges. Double Dipsea runners return over the same rugged course back to the ocean. Tunzing earned her nickname "Dipsea Grandma," because she was 61 years old and routinely ran the Double. Clark, who was in her forties at the time, was anxious to get a look at this grandmother who took part in such an arduous race. She wrote about being disappointed after seeing Tunzing's youthful demeanor. "This woman was certainly not 61! She looked my age—not someone who could be a *senior* athlete."[31]

Can You Really Turn Back the Clock?

While looking through a catalog of meditation and yoga paraphernalia, I came across a DVD titled *Stop the Clock*, which as advertised will show you "how to prevent and reverse the signs and effects of aging."[32] The author of the DVD demonstrates exercises to improve posture and control your breathing, so you look more fit and trim, stand erect and don't hunch, etc. The idea here is that when you improve your physical appearance, you are going to look and feel younger.

You hear a lot of talk about stopping the clock, growing younger, taking years off your age, etc. Obviously, no drug, exercise, or medical breakthrough can literally do that. However, you can influence the course of your own senescence. You can take the edge off of age-related decline and improve the quality of your life by making positive lifestyle choices, especially with exercise, physical fitness, and dietary changes. But you'll still have to put one more candle on the birthday cake each year.

When gerontologists talk about senescence they generally mean biological and physical traits. However, there is a psychological dimension to senescence that deserves equal attention. The way I see it there are three faces of senescence:

1. Appearance. There is the snapshot physical appearance like the graying or loss of hair, wrinkles and sagging skin, and changes in body posture.
2. Physical fitness and health. This includes body mass index, endurance level, vascular, and organ health.

3. Psychological disposition. This is your emotional and mental health—how you feel and think about your age. Are you young at heart or over the hill?

All three realms of senescence are important, and they are all interrelated. For example, if you exercise and take care of your health, then your body will look younger and you will feel better and enjoy higher self-esteem and suffer less depression. It's important not to neglect any one area. If you focus exclusively on your physical appearance, and neglect diet and exercise, then you may look good but not feel well and suffer from a poor-lifestyle-induced illness. There seems to be a hierarchy of needs here. To some extent, physical fitness and health have primary importance. Unfortunately, physical appearance is often the sole focus of many aging individual's efforts to thwart the ravages of time. Antiaging remedies have become a big industry in modern society. The sad truth is, even though you look young and have great self-esteem, if your heart and arteries are old and you die of a heart attack, then only the mortician is going to appreciate the fact that you don't need a major makeover when you're laid out in the morgue.

Staying Young in Spirit

Youth is a matter of attitude, not of calendar age. Clara May Rowland[33]

In my opinion, the worst form of senescence is to grow old in spirit, to be conquered by over-the-hill syndrome. Don't use age as an excuse to stop learning new things, stay stuck in old habits, or avoid taking risks. Instead, continue to grow socially, mentally, emotionally, and psychologically. (See chapter 9: Conquer Over-the-Hill Syndrome.) Do you remain young at heart or have you become an old fuddy-duddy? (Chapter 10)

When we are young in spirit, we transcend time. We are in the flow, living in the here and now, and fully in the present. To the extent that we do that, time and physical age are irrelevant. We have to make the most of our lives at any age—especially as we get older. Unless we want to end up like Mrs. Munchnik.

Mrs. Munchnik is the character played by Madeleine Kahn in the offbeat Christmas movie *Mixed Nuts.* She's an attractive but distinctly middle-aged woman, and in one scene an elderly gentleman addresses her as "young lady." Mrs. Munchnik furrows her brow and warns him not to call her a young lady, because "I am not young. I have never been young!" Sadly, many people grow old before their time. Fortunately, attitudes about aging can change—at any time and at any age. Even curmudgeonly Mrs. Munchnik enjoys an epiphanous about face and celebrates a yuletide tryst on the sands of Venice Beach, California.

How Long Can You Live?

According to Walter Bortz II, MD, a professor at Stanford University Medical School, "there is now a virtual consensus that the maximum human lifespan is around 120 years."[34] That's how long we can live without making genetic modifications.

Jeanne Calment of Arles, France, lived to be 122, and she holds the record for longest-lived human.[35] She was born February 21, 1875 and died August 4, 1997; her lifespan is extremely well documented. Calment outlived her husband (by 49 years), her daughter, and one of her grandsons. She attributed her longevity to olive oil, port wine, and chocolate (she ate about two pounds a week!) Although she smoked cigarettes, she also led a very active life, playing tennis, swimming, roller skating, and riding a bicycle. At age 85 she took up fencing, and she was still pedaling her bicycle at 100. She lived independently until she was 109, and then moved into a nursing home after starting a fire in her apartment while cooking.

Genetic science is rapidly moving from the realm of science fiction to reality, so what will be the average human lifespan a century or two in the future is anybody's guess. "I think it's virtually a certainty that we'll discover, within the next few decades, ways to substantially slow down aging," says Steven Austad, a comparative zoologist who specializes in gerontology.[36] Laboratory research has shown that by manipulating just one gene, an animal can live up to six times as long as normal,[37] and "as many as 7,000 of our 100,000 genes may influence some aspects of the aging rate" according to Austad.[38]

The Natural Superiority of Women

I want to die young at a ripe old age. Ashley Montagu (1905-1999)

The prospects for survival into a truly ripe old age are greater than ever before, but about four times better for women than men. About 15 percent of American women will live to be 90, but only 4 percent of American men.[39] Women live longer than men in almost every society on earth. Even in Okinawa, which has a higher percentage of centenarians (100-year-olds) than anywhere else, women outlive men an average of eight years.[40]

Why do women live longer? It's not because they age slower, but rather because men die at higher rates throughout their lives. Male behavior accounts for some of this; men smoke and drink more heavily than women, men engage in more stressful and dangerous activities, and men die by violence—murder and suicide, three times as frequently as women. Men also die at higher rates from almost every disease—heart attacks, strokes, cancer, and even infancy conditions or the flu. This is explained in part by biological differences; women have more effective immune systems. According to biologist Steven Austad, "it's difficult to escape the conclusion that women are simply better designed biologically for survival."[41] Hormones are an important factor; testosterone suppresses immune system functioning, speeds up artery wall deterioration, and plays a role in prostate cancer development. Male animals that are castrated live longer. Men in a state institution who were castrated for eugenics purposes (in the early twentieth century) lived 14 years longer than noncastrated men in the same facility. Austad concludes, "although castration may be one remedy for some of the causes of aging, it probably will not catch on as a popular remedy."[42]

Ashley Montagu was one of the most well-read and respected anthropologists of the twentieth century. In *The Natural Superiority of Women*, he marshaled compelling scientific evidence against the social prejudice of women being considered "the weaker sex." His seminal work was ahead of its time. First published in 1952, it was serialized in the *Saturday Evening Post* and inspired the formation of the National Organization of Women in 1966. Montagu brought out the fifth edition in 1999, shortly before he died young at the ripe old age of 94–defying the averages of male life expectancy.[43] He did not go gentle, but battled social prejudices like racism and sexism throughout his long career.

What Are Normal Aging Processes?

Everybody knows that with age our bodies begin to wear out, and we experience reduced physical capability in most areas. There are distinct and measurable changes that gerontologists consider to be part of the normal aging process. Most noticeably, our hair grays, whitens, thins out, or falls out. Our skin wrinkles, sags, and gets thinner. Our body height decreases, and we lose bone mass, more so for women than men. Bone loss can be significant—between 5 and 12 percent for every decade of our life from the twenties through the nineties. Body mass increases because we lose lean muscle and accumulate fat around the hips and waist. Motor skills decline, so our bodies move slower, and our sensory skills decline—you can't see and hear as well, and your taste and smell are worse. Reflexes get slower. Cardiovascular performance weakens due to loss of heart muscle and hardening or clogging of the arteries. We become more susceptible to diseases associated with aging, like osteoporosis, heart disease, stroke, and Alzheimer's.[44]

There's no question that age brings about a decline in appearance, bodily processes, and level of functioning that can be quite substantial. Aging results in "generalized deterioration," according to Austad.[45] The key questions are: How bad is it going to get, and what can we do about it, if anything? The answer to these questions depends on whom you ask.

The Traditional View of Aging

The elderly are depicted as a figurative ball and chain holding back an otherwise spry collective society...Acknowledging the truth about aging in America is critical...if we are to move ahead toward successful aging as individuals and as a society. Rowe and Kahn, *Successful Aging*[46]

Sadly, the field of gerontology has been dominated by a degeneration model. Here's a typical example from the *Handbook of the Biology of Aging*: "Biological aging may be defined as a process of intrinsic, progressive, and generalized physical deterioration that occurs over time, beginning at about the age of reproductive maturity."[47] So basically, it's pretty much all downhill after puberty. That's a pretty gloomy forecast. The *Handbook's* cover highlights the silhouette of a man and woman standing beside a tranquil lake—both hunched over and using canes to prop themselves up. I obviously don't subscribe to such a view. That's why I chose the picture of a sky-diving granny to put on the cover of *Do Not Go Gentle*—to help promote a new, positive view of aging.

Unfortunately, the morbid, pathological view has also dominated the research and opinions of mental health professionals, including psychologists. "The conventional psychology of aging is almost completely devoted to a study of its discontents; aging as depletion, aging as catastrophe, aging as mortality," according to Dr. David Gutmann, a psychologist and gerontologist. "At best the aged are deemed barely capable of staving off disaster, but they are certainly not capable of developing new capacities or of seeking out new challenges... The weak face of aging...currently dominates conventional thinking on gerontology."[48]

The old school of gerontology doesn't give us much hope for aging successfully. One might conclude that if it's going to get that bad, then we might as well all reserve rooms at the local nursing home when we're out purchasing our burial plots! Fortunately, new research has begun to emphasize the strong face of aging to challenge the gloomy old view.

A Different Kind of Age

My research on aging, and the time I've spent with thousands of patients, have made it abundantly clear that many of our assumptions about aging are, to put it bluntly, wrong. David Lipschitz, MD, PhD[49]

Many researchers have changed their attitude about aging by studying the lives of healthy seniors. Betty Friedan says, "I had to break out of my personal denial before I could truly take in and exult over the stories of the surprisingly many women, and also men, whom I found in their sixties, seventies, eighties, and even nineties continuing to grow, and living with vitality a different kind of age."[50] Friedan argues for "the study of age as a state of becoming and being, not merely an ending." She feels that our aging population needs to find "a new meaning" and "a new wholeness," and we should recognize old age as the culmination of your life's journey, a time finally to solve the jigsaw puzzle of life. She concludes *The Fountain of Age* with her own epiphanous experience: "It took me all these years to put the missing pieces together, to confront my own age in terms of integrity and generativity, moving into the unknown future with a comfort now, instead of being stuck in the past. I have never felt so free."[51]

In *Reclaimed Powers: Toward a New Psychology of Men and Women in Later Life* Dr. David Gutmann goes so far as to argue that human longevity is "a matter of evolutionary design."[52] In contemporary society, elders are seen as weak and mere by-products of our affluent, technologically advanced societies, who exist only because of advances in medical care and nutrition. Gutmann points out, however, that "the aged were a recognized part of human existence long before social scientists or nutritionists came into being." He draws upon anthropological studies and historical records to conclude: "The aged are acknowledged as a regular part of the social scene in almost every human community from the most primitive to the most advanced." Elders are "an integral part of the total human life cycle."[53] Furthermore, "elders are necessary to the well-being of all age groups, particularly the young." In summary: "We do not have elders because we have a human gift and modern capacity for keeping the weak alive; instead, we are human because we have elders." Dr. George Vaillant derives a similarly bold conclusion from his longitudinal study of the elderly in America: "Without the old there would be no culture."[54]

Dr. David Lipschitz changed his medical specialty to gerontology after he had a heart attack, turned fifty, and faced "tangible evidence of my own mortality."[55] Through the experience of being a patient himself, he saw "how poorly older patients—those in their fifties, sixties, and beyond—are served by their doctors."[56] Dr. Dave (as he prefers to be called these days) resolved to treat all of his patients personally, with dignity and respect, as "living, breathing people" rather than as "bundles of symptoms." He hosted the award-wining *Aging Successfully* PBS series and wrote *Breaking the Rules of Aging* to refute some of the old stereotypes about aging. "My patients travel, work, play sports, have sex, go out to dinner, see new movies. They're one of the main contributing forces in the economic engine of our society." More than 25 years of geriatric experience has helped him to see aging in an entirely different light, and he has been inspired by the lives of his patient's who are aging successfully. "One of my patients holds the over-60 world record for running the 1,500 meter. Another, at 75, just earned his doctorate degree. Another, in her 80s, rides a motorcycle. When I see her pulling on her helmet as she leaves my office, I'm reminded that my job isn't merely to prolong her life, but to strengthen the quality of her life."[57]

What is the secret to successful aging? Dr. Dave summarizes his findings: "The only way you're going to live a long time, doing all the things you want to do, is to stay healthy. Forget age. It's just a number. But your health, in a very real way, is who you are."[58]

A Real-Life Shangri-La: Okinawa

At seventy you are but a child, at eighty you are merely a youth, and at ninety if the ancestors invite you into heaven, ask them to wait until you are one hundred...and then you might consider it. Okinawa proverb[59]

Okinawa has been called the real-life Shangri-La, because the elders there "seem to have beaten the aging process."[60] Doctors Bradley Willcox, Craig Wilcox and Makota Suzuki have studied aging Okinawans for more than 25 years to discover the secrets of extended life. Their description of traditional Okinawan culture sounds like an excerpt from *Lost Horizon*, James Hilton's classic novel about the mythical lost paradise: "Energetic great-grandparents live in their own homes, tend their own gardens, and on weekends might be visited by grandchildren who, in the West, would qualify for senior citizen pensions. People are active, and appear youthful beyond their years...They have slim, lithe bodies, sharp clear eyes, quick wits, passionate interests, and the kind of Shangri-La glow of youthfulness that we all covet."[61]

Okinawa is home to the longest-lived and healthiest people in the world. There are more 100-year-olds in Okinawa, as a percentage of the population, than anywhere else on earth–34 per 100,000. This is nearly three and one-half times higher than in the United States, which has 10 centenarians per 100,000. Diseases traditionally associated with aging like heart disease, stroke and cancer occur with a lower frequency in Okinawa than anywhere else on earth. The word for retirement doesn't even exist in the older Okinawa dialect.

Upon meeting their first centenarian, Doctors Willcox and Suzuki were greeted on the porch by "a sprightly man of about seventy" who "greeted us with a wave and a winning smile." They assumed this was the son and "imagined that the old man was quietly resting in the house" because it was already very hot outside from the "scorching" sun.[62] They watched the man sorting through gardening tools and getting ready to go to work in the fields, and asked him where they could find his father. They were pleasantly embarrassed to discover that "the energetic man, dressed in the kind of clothes we in North America might wear on weekends to putter around the garden, was not seventy, he was one hundred—and gardening was exactly what he was preparing to do."

The Secret to Not Going Gentle: Study the Survivors

Old age is a minefield. If you see footprints leading to the other side, step in them. George Vaillant, MD, *Aging Well*, Harvard gerontologist[63]

I certainly want to enjoy a long and healthy life like that 100-year old Okinawan who was subjected to vigorous physical examination by Willcox and Suzuki. They found "there was basically nothing wrong with his body!"[64]

It makes perfect sense that attitudes about aging will continue to change as the baby boomers confront their own aging issues. We grew up with the progressive, future-oriented idealism of *Star Trek*, after all, and who doesn't want to "live long and prosper," to quote Mr. Spock?

Studying the lives of Okinawans who seem to be healthier than I am, yet twice my age gives me hope for aging successfully. Reading about how many new cases of Alzheimer's disease were diagnosed last year in nursing homes just gets me depressed. (I usually diagnose one or two patients with dementia every week.) I'm going to stick with the spunky eldsters, because I want to find out what they're doing right. After all, successfully aging elders are survivors. As Dr. George Vaillant points it, they've survived the conditions that killed off those who died before them. Therefore, "if we are to understand successful aging, we need to ask very old people about the road they travel."[65]

Creative Blossoming in Old Age Begins in Midlife

Dr. George Vaillant's *Aging Well: Surprising Guideposts to a Happier Life* contains a wealth of information that challenges the decrepitude model of aging and portrays a much more inviting picture of old age. Vaillant was surprised to find that "healthy aging or lack of it is predicted by factors already established before age 50. What seemed even more astonishing was that these factors are more or less controllable."[66] The six strongest predictors are:

1. Having a warm marriage. Ironically, a good marriage at age 50 predicts successful aging and happiness at age 80 better than low cholesterol. I suspect that the important factor here is probably not being married, per se, but having strong social support. If you can boast of a happy marriage, then you also probably have good social skills

and know how to get your interpersonal needs met, and vice versa. Regardless, this demonstrates that social and psychological factors are sometimes more important to successful aging than medical and genetic factors. An extensive body of research confirms that social support is beneficial in many areas.

2. Good adaptive or coping skills. You have to be flexible and go with the flow. Change careers, find new interests, learn to do things differently. In *Aging Well*, Dr. George Vaillant looked at Sigmund Freud's ego defense mechanisms as an explanation of how we deal with the trials and tribulations of our lives. Creativity, humor, and perseverance are positive means of coping and are considered to be healthy and mature. On the contrary, negative coping included repression, isolation, and projection are immature or unhealthy forms of coping. "If our brain stays free of disease, we are able to use these mechanisms more gracefully at 75 than we did at 25," says Vaillant.[66] He goes on to say, "A test of successful living becomes learning to live with neither too much desire and adventure nor too much caution and self-care."[67]

If this sounds surprisingly like the age-old advice of the Greek and Roman philosophers for moderation, it is just that. It's interesting how contemporary social research often proves the truth of ancient wisdom. Nearly 3,000 years ago the Greek historian Hesiod (*Works and Days*) wrote: "Observe due measure; moderation is best in all things." Dr. George Vaillant rightly acknowledges our debt to antiquity, and notes that "the sweet emotional freedom preached by the Woodstock generation has worked no better than dour rationality. We must go back to Aristotle and Plato to find the Golden Mean."[68] I'm glad he does, because one of my pet peeves about psychologists and social science researchers is that they sometimes think they invented every new psychological principle just yesterday!

The next four predictors are germane to the core content of the *Do Not Go Gentle* philosophy, and they are an integral part of living a successful life, as discussed throughout this book—so they will not be covered in detail here:

3. Not smoking heavily.
4. Not abusing alcohol.
5. Getting ample exercise.
6. Not being overweight.

Activities and Solutions

Watch movies about successful aging like *Space Cowboys, Second Hand Lions,* or *Young at Heart,* preferably with a group of people your own age. Read more about the life of John Glenn, Jack LaLanne, or another spunky eldster. Has there been a spunky eldster in your own life? Apply the concept of senescence to yourself. What age-related changes have you noticed in yourself? What would you like to see different about yourself, to improve your age image?

Notes:

_____

_____

_____

_____

_____

_____

_____

Chapter 12

The Real-Life Fountain of Youth

Retirement at age sixty-five is ridiculous. When I was sixty-five I still had pimples. George Burns

You can discover the real fountain of youth by practicing a lifestyle that promotes optimum physical, mental and spiritual health. Writing this book helped me to lose 75 pounds, adopt a healthier diet, and exercise more vigorously than I did in my teens. At age 56, I look and feel years younger. In my experience, when you surround yourself with examples of healthy aging, you cannot help but have a little bit rub off on you. Let some of it rub off on you, too. My hope is that you will experience important changes in your own life by studying the lives of spunky eldsters and practicing the principles of successful aging.

He Still Has That Youthful, Boyish Look

There's a cartoon about class reunions that I've shared in my successful aging seminars. One guy says something like, "Gee, Mickey, you haven't changed at all over the years!" A social nicety we've all heard from time to time, but in this case it's literally true. Everybody at the reunion looks distinctly middle aged, except for Mickey, who still looks exactly like a schoolboy— complete with the short pants and beanie cap! (This reminds me of AC/DC lead guitarist Angus Young, who just turned 55 years old and still wears a traditional English schoolboy uniform during concert performances.[1])

Wouldn't we all like to stay young forever? Of course we would, and the pursuit of youthfulness has become an obsession for many Americans—especially for the baby boomers. The quest for youth extension has generated a major industry, a description of which makes fascinating reading in books like Stephen Hall's *New York Times* bestseller *Merchants of Immortality: Chasing the Dream of Human Life Extension*. The longevity business is summarized well in a critique by two gerontology professors from the University of Chicago, S. Jay Olshansky and Bruce A. Carners in *The Quest for Immortality: Science at the Frontiers of Aging*: "A multi-billion-dollar industry today offers a bewildering array of herbs, vitamins, hormones, or lifestyle changes that are supposed to slow aging, prevent disease, and lengthen life. These 'discoveries' are big news to the aging baby-boom generation. Unfortunately, the touted benefits of many of these treatments are either unproven, grossly exaggerated, or just plain false."[2]

The Real-Life Fountain of Youth

Do you think you are just a puny form, when the whole universe lies raveled up within you? Sufi proverb

There is some truth to the legends of the fountain of youth, because we really can experience rejuvenation. However, it's not going to come from some magic pill invented in a laboratory or an elixir to be discovered out there. The real fountain of youth is the gold mine of your own inner development, manifested outwardly through simple lifestyle changes that result in physical fitness and improved health of our body, mind, and soul.

We really can slow down the rate at which we age. Exercise or increased physical activity, good nutrition, and other lifestyle factors can help to slow decline and reduce the degeneration of old age, and in some cases actually reverse disease and repair damage. Gerontologists use the term *plasticity* as a measure of how "the rate at which we age is modified by health behavior habits and by psychosocial factors such as personality processes and social context."[3]

The rate at which we age can be altered by lifestyle choices. Scientists have identified *age accelerators,* which speed up the rate at which we age, and *age inhibitors,* which slow down the aging process. This means that if you practice healthy habits, then you will look younger and live longer; but if you practice unhealthy habits you will look older and die younger. *Age accelerators* include bad habits like smoking, abusing alcohol and drugs, overeating, and not exercising. For example, people who smoke throughout their lifetime die an average of 12 to 15 years earlier than people who don't, according to the Centers for Disease Control.[4] Psychological age accelerators include negative emotions like depression, anxiety, and hostility.[5] *Age inhibitors* include exercise and physical activities, healthy diet and good nutrition, social support, and psychological factors like forgiveness, laughter, and positive emotions. For example, regular aerobic exercise throughout middle age "can slow or reverse functional deterioration, lowering biological age by at least 10 years," according to Alzheimer's researcher Laurie Barclay, MD.[6]

Senescence and age plasticity are the keys to understanding that rejuvenation really is possible, despite chronological aging. In this sense, you literally can get better with age in some areas. Even though you keep adding candles to your birthday cake, you'll be in much better shape to blow them out. Healthy lifestyle choices can make you look younger, feel younger, and enjoy greater physical health and happiness.

Senior Olympian Case Study

You can never be too old to experience rejuvenation through fitness and lifestyle improvement. When he retired, Jim Law described himself as "an overweight, chain-smoking fast-food junkie with a serious cholesterol problem."[7] Law was determined to improve his lifestyle, so he joined the Senior Olympic Games. Getting in shape required "a radical shift in diet and the substitution of regular exercise for my forty years of sedentary existence." He also gave up his 49-year habit of smoking cigarettes. The payoff was enormous. Over a period of seven months he lost 25 pounds and reduced his cholesterol level from 322 to 188. He became so physically fit and healthy that he set six National Senior Olympic records for sprinting. At age 69 he modeled his spandex running suit while being photographed by Etta Clark in her book on aging athletes. "As a result of these changes," he told her, "I felt better, looked better, and had less stress and more energy. I was more productive, and life was more fun."[8]

My Personal Midlife Renaissance

It is remarkable how ones wits are sharpened by physical exercise.
Pliny the Younger (Roman lawyer, 61-112 AD)

I've had a similar experience through my own lifestyle changes. My personal rejuvenation through exercise, fitness, and healthy eating has been a major inspiration for writing this book.

At age 56, I'm healthier than I was at age 50 on several objective measures: drastically lower weight and BMI, below normal levels of cholesterol and triglycerides, and blood pressure that causes everybody who measures it to comment favorably. I need less sleep, and yet feel more rested and energetic. I spend about 8 to 10 hours a week exercising—going to the gym three days a week, jogging, and bicycling for 50 miles—and I still get more work done in less time. I have fewer aches and pains, and I seldom use over-the-counter pain meds. I recently found a half-full bottle of time-release acetaminophen that was lodged behind some books on my desk, with an expiration date three years past. It used to be I couldn't keep enough of that stuff around. After several years of healthy living, I'm more organized and efficient but less of a workaholic than ever before. I'm less depressed, anxious, and worried, and I enjoy better emotional balance than ever in my life. I think clearly and make better decisions. I have a more positive attitude and greater hope for the future. It don't get no better than this, to quote the old beer commercials—except it doesn't require any mind-altering substances—only 100% pure, natural and healthy ingredients and good honest exertion, which are readily available to everybody. Furthermore, it does get better. My personal midlife renaissance is the evidence for this.

All these benefits came from taking the principles of successful aging seriously, practicing a natural lifestyle of simple exercise, physical fitness, low-fat vegan diet, and good social and spiritual support—without deep psychotherapy, obsessive self-help work, or heavy doses of psychotropic medications. After reading the stories of spunky eldsters in this book, you know that my experience is far from unique and supported by an ever-increasing body of scientific research.

Enjoy a Healthy Spirit of Rejuvenation

Life should be a happy adventure, and to be happy you need to be healthy. Jack LaLanne[9]

In August 2009, I went to see my physician, Dr. Tadros, for a routine annual physical exam. After the nurse weighed me in, we reviewed my chart. I was excited about losing more weight since my last visit six months earlier. That added up to a total of 75 pounds lost over a five-year period since I got interested in the principles of successful aging and began applying them to my own life.

Dr. Tadros was initially wary of my preference for simple lifestyle changes instead of state-of-the art pharmaceuticals. So I kept taking blood pressure medication until I lost weight through exercise and a nutritious diet. I bought a blood pressure cuff and took readings twice a day, recording the results in an old college chemistry lab book. It was a pleasant surprise to watch the levels go down until my blood pressure was completely normal. Dr. Tadros was a bit perplexed when I brought in my lab book full of blood pressure readings for him to examine and suggested that perhaps I could stop taking the medication. However, he warmed up to the idea because every time I went to his office, I shared some of the latest research I was uncovering about lifestyle changes and improved health—and he certainly couldn't ignore the evidence of my own improved physical health. When my triglyceride level skyrocketed, he suggested medication but sent me home with nutritional guidelines instead of a prescription—and they worked. My triglyceride levels went down and stay low, so long as I keep eating healthy and exercising heartily.

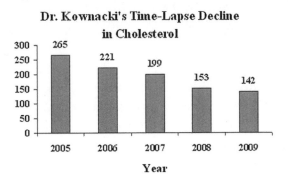

Dr. Kownacki's Time-Lapse Decline in Cholesterol

So in August 2009, when Dr. Tadros came into the exam room and asked why I was there, I replied: "To show you the benefits of healthy living!" He smiled and asked if I was still going to the gym. I outlined my exercise routine, bicycle riding, and vegetarian eating habits. He reviewed my chart, looked me over, and then said with a big grin, "Well, you certainly look younger!"

That shot up my enthusiasm more than any medication he could have given me. You don't normally think of a visit to your doctor's office as an exciting experience, but let me tell you, I was pumped up! I felt vindicated by the demonstration of the power of positive lifestyle changes. All this stuff I'd been researching about the healing power of exercise and healthy eating was coming true in my own life. Suddenly, it was no longer just a theory, a lot of facts and figures and words on paper, but a flesh-and-blood reality in my own life. That was by far the most delightful visit to the doctor's office, ever!

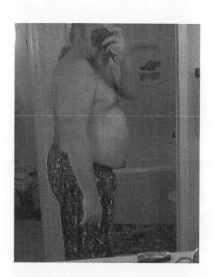 

Five years ago, I took my picture in front of the mirror because I was too embarrassed to have anybody else see my fat stomach. Today I take my picture because I'm proud to be seen in fit condition.

I repeatedly tell people that the solution to successful aging is quite simple but not very easy. That is a recurring theme of this book: simple behaviors practiced on a consistent basis can yield big results. When it comes to getting fit and healthy, the solution is to exercise and be more active while eating fewer calories. These are very simple behaviors, but far from easy to adopt as a lifestyle in our convenicncc-laden society of leisure and abundance. My goal is to provide the facts and information you need to help motivate you to age successfully.

It Just Keeps Getting Better and Better

And in the end, it's not the years in your life that count. It's the life in your years. Abraham Lincoln

Here are some of the positive changes that occurred in my health and body fitness as a result of major lifestyle changes—regular exercise (weights and gym workout, jogging, bicycling, and a lot of yoga-type stretching), good social support, meditation and spiritual discipline, and especially a vegan diet.

1. Relief from Irritable Bowel Syndrome (IBS) with a high-fiber, low-fat vegan diet. I finally threw out the psyllium dietary fiber supplement, which I took faithfully since I was first diagnosed with IBS in my early twenties.

2. Relief from chronic back pain with three-minutes of simple stretching exercises in the morning, which I learned from a book recommended by my massage therapist: *Somatics: Reawakening the Mind's Control of Movement, Flexibility, and Health* by Thomas Hanna.[10]

3. Relief from restless leg syndrome by doing 5 to 10 minutes of *Coffee Yoga* stretches before going to bed.

4. Relief from snoring so loudly that sometimes Mary was driven in desperation to sleep in the spare bedroom (sometimes embarrassment drove me there). I tried nose sprays and nasal strips—with only limited relief. Today I almost never snore, and I only retire to the spare bedroom when I wake up a little too early and want to lie around, stretch, or read a bit before getting up.

5. Relief from wintertime flu and cold symptoms. I routinely got sick with the flu or a cold two or three times a year,

and the symptoms sometimes dragged on for weeks. Now I seldom get sick, and during the winter of 2009-2010, for the first time in my entire life, I didn't even get a cold or the flu.

6. Relief from acid indigestion and gastric reflux. I used to go through antacid tablets like they were candy. Even though I season everything with hot sauce and sometimes consume massive amounts of hot peppers, I seldom suffer from acid indigestion and I haven't bought any antacids in several years.

7. Relief from nasal spray addiction. Most of my life I've suffered from severe nasal congestion, sometimes so bad I had trouble sleeping at night. Since I substituted soy milk for dairy products, that's a thing of the past. I occasionally use some saline nose drops during the allergy season, and jokingly say that eating Chinese hot mustard works better than OTC nasal sprays.

8. Relief from lung problems. It seems I was always coming down with or recovering from bronchitis. I used a lot of OTC expectorant and cough syrups. I went to the doctor at least twice a year for antibiotics, worried I was developing a lung infection.

9. Relief from the middle-aged spread—the dreaded potbelly. My pants waist size decreased from 44 inches to size 34—my just-out-of-high-school size. I've even taken to wearing a sports coat (sometimes) instead of my typical Hawaiian shirts, because I don't have to cover up my big stomach anymore.

10. Relief from bleeding hemorrhoids and improved colon health. A colonoscopy done before my healthy lifestyle changes showed a couple of polyps. One done last year, five years later, showed everything was completely clear.

11. Relief from chronic fatigue, which in the past I treated with pots of coffee and handfuls of sugary treats. Now I don't even take my customary Sunday afternoon naps,

unless it's been an exceptionally busy day at the office the previous week.

12. Relief from obesity and sustained weight loss. Healthy living virtually eliminated the lifelong weight yo-yoing. I'm still giving away old clothing. Some of my old shirts and pants can only be worn if I dress like a teenager going to a grunge concert. For the longest time, I would buy only pants with stretch or elastic waistbands, and I never tucked in my shirts in (so as not to reveal my distressingly large stomach). Now I often tuck in my shirts (which helps a lot in the winter when the office is chilly!) and have to wear a belt so my older pants don't fall down. One day I went to put on a Hawaiian shirt I hadn't worn in years, and it was so big I joked with Mary that both of us could fit into it. Well, seeing is believing, so I asked Mary to stand in front of me; sure enough, we both were able to fit into that gargantuan shirt and even fasten the buttons!

13. Five years after I was diagnosed with prostate cancer, I applied for a life insurance policy, which required a physical exam, blood tests, and extensive review of my medical records. After several months of carefully scrutinizing my health risk, the insurance company offered me a high-dollar policy. This may be the best proof of all that the principles of successful aging really work. I had become so healthy through exercise, good nutrition, and wholesome living that I had a much lower risk of dying prematurely.

Unfortunately, there is a down side to this business of shaping up your body and your lifestyle. Not everybody will share your enthusiasm for health pursuits. The 2006 TPA gathering was held at a conference center next to the Dallas Galleria mall. As I walked through the mall at a brisk pace about 5:00 A.M., all the security guards began to follow me. Finally, one of them approached and not so tactfully told me to leave, saying that walking was not permitted until the shops opened—7:00 A.M. or so, when a couple of the bakeries and breakfast spots unlock their doors. It was rather distressing to have to hoof it through the Galleria parking lot, which is at a major interstate of dangerous freeway entrance and exits—but fortunately it was still too early for hazardous levels of morning rush-hour traffic.

Conclusion

Spunky Eldsters Live Longer and Better

Age may wrinkle the face, but lack of enthusiasm wrinkles the soul.
Danish Proverb

When I was nearly done writing this book, a coworker phoned and told me to turn on the evening news. The human interest story for October 7, 2009 was Jack LaLanne celebrating his ninety-fifth birthday. He was ceremoniously driven through the streets of San Francisco in a fire engine. Then he jumped off the truck and did 95 jumping jacks and 95 push-ups. At age 95, most people would probably settle for the fire truck ride. I'd certainly like to be able to do 95 push-ups at age 95.

Spunky elders like Jack LaLanne, John Turner, the weight-lifting psychiatrist, and my mother-in-law Joseta, the skydiving granny, can serve as role models of successful aging to boomers who are resisting the process of getting older. They have an inner motivation, a drive, a lust to live life fully, no matter what their age. They can help us reduce negative stereotypes of old age and show us that you may be retired, but you're "never too old to rock," says *New York Times* drama critic Steven Holden, in describing the Young At Heart Chorus.[1]

Young at Heart is a group of two dozen feisty senior citizens, average age 80, who tour the country singing songs from the sixties. Although young in spirit, Chorus members display the typical infirmities of aging. The lead singer carries an oxygen tank with him onto the stage, and one of their videos was made in a nursing home—a parody of the Ramone's "I Wanna Be Sedated." However, the Young at Heart Chorus members allow neither disease nor disability to prevent them from living a full life in their senior years. The 2009 video release *Young at Heart: You're Never Too Old to Rock* documents their inspirational adventures in successful aging.

Fortunately, you don't have to jump out of an airplane or swim across San Francisco Bay in your eighties to age successfully. And even if you don't keep your body in tip-top shape, you can still age well despite your infirmities. It's certainly desirable to keep active despite infirmities and to remain robust and lively even while suffering chronic illness. This is without doubt a big part of successful aging and one way to surf the silver tsunami.

However, it's even better not to develop the illnesses or chronic diseases associated with old age, if at all possible, or to reduce their severity and try to eliminate them—if it is in your power to do so.

I'm not trying to say that if you exercise your tail off and eat the healthiest diet imaginable then you're going to live forever. You may have a charmed life and get up every day at the crack of dawn to exercise, yet still get run over and killed by a delivery truck while you're out on your morning jog.

Numerous reporters have asked Jack LaLanne if he thinks he'll live to be 100, and he always replies that he doesn't know how long he's going to live, but that as long as he's alive he wants to keep living. I take this to mean that the overall quality of life is just as important as how long you live. Some people are alive but barely living to their full potential. What's the point of living a long life if you're going to be deathly unhappy or so sick and miserable that you can't wait to check out?

You have a choice to make. You can look at the gloomy statistics about our nation's declining health and inadequate healthcare system and conclude that what you do doesn't really make any difference. Scientists who study disease trends (epidemiologists) look at it like this, and that's why they encourage us to prepare for the worst—train more gerontologists and build bigger and better nursing homes, etc. Health care professionals tend to assume that most people are going to continue to do things the way they've been doing them and not change to practice healthy lifestyle behaviors. They probably will. So what's that have to do with you and me? This attitude is fatalistic and based on the averages. The *Do Not Go Gentle* philosophy encourages you to defy the averages and choose to be exceptional.

My job as a psychologist is to try to bring out the best in people. I take the orientation of the optimist in the parable of the starfish on the beach. Two friends are walking along a beach full of washed up starfish. The optimist picks up a starfish and throws it back into the ocean. The pessimist looks at the masses of beached starfish, shakes her head and says it won't make any different. The optimist picks up another starfish and throws it back in the ocean, smiles and replies, "It makes a difference to that one!" Sometimes very small changes can make a big difference.

There's only one person who can ultimately cause a change in your own life, and that is you. You can choose to be average, or you can choose to be an exception to the rule. I encourage you to rebel against the averages! Rebel against the status quo and start practicing principles of healthy living and successful aging right now. Become a rebel with a cause!

Don't Be an Old Stick in the Mud

And be not conformed to this world: but be ye transformed by the renewing of your mind. I Cor. 12:2

When all is said and done, it gets down to a matter of choice. You can call it faith, perspective, attitude, or disposition—but the bottom line is that you can make choices. You have a choice in what you believe, how you think, what you do, and how you live your life. It's like the old Peace Corps commercials of the sixties: Are you the kind of person who sees the glass as half empty or half full? This book is obviously written from the half-full perspective. I freely admit to having a definite bias about successful aging—I'm all for it! I'm fully committed to the outlook of the new gerontology and principles of successful aging not only because of the rapidly increasing scientific evidence, but also because they've worked for me and many others who inspired me to continue with this book.

I chose a skydiving granny for the cover of my book with the clear intention of sharing my zeal for the *Do Not Go Gentle* philosophy. Of course it's a matter of style and taste. You have to decide for yourself what you'd rather be doing when you're 85: tottering by the lake with your cane and trying not to fall in or jumping out of an airplane and not minding the fall.

In the movie *Second Hand Lions*, Robert Duvall and Michael Caine play two aging adventurers who have retired to a rural Texas farm. Rich and eccentric, they chase off door-to-door salesman with shotgun blasts, purchase an old zoo lion to have a backyard safari, and build their own airplane for stunt flying. Forced to take care of a 14-year-old nephew for the summer, they regale him with tales of past exploits and overseas adventures. When the nephew is leaving at the end of summer vacation, he tells his uncles to take care of themselves and not do any airplane stunts or hunt any lions. Robert Duvall gets a long face and exclaims, "What do you expect us to die of—old age?" At the end of the film a deputy sheriff informs the nephew, now an adult, that his two 90-year-old uncles apparently died while trying to fly their stunt plane upside down through their barn.

Don't Go Gentle is not a denial-of-aging or a denial-of-death philosophy. There's no getting around the fact that human life is a temporary state of affairs. We're all getting older, and eventually we're going to die. Successful aging requires that you "abandon the myth of perpetual youth and eternal life," according to Harvard gerontologist Muriel Gillick, MD, in her book *The Denial of Aging*.[2] One element of successful aging is, therefore, to come to grips with decline, loss, and diminishment in major areas of living, including the deteriorating condition of your own body over time.

I have no pretensions that if you follow the principles of successful aging then you will somehow be immortal. However, the scientific research and evidence clearly demonstrate that lifestyle factors influence both the length and the quality of our lives. Therefore, I am totally confident that if you practice healthy lifestyle behaviors, then you will extend your life and improve its quality. And as an added bonus for taking care of yourself, as I found out the other day, you can be 56 years old, go down to the gym, buy a new muscle shirt, and have some sweet young thing come up to you smiling and say, "You're really looking buff today!" I let Mary read this passage after I wrote it, and she asked, "What sweet young thing!?" and then she added, "from now on I guess I'm going to have to go to the gym with you to fight the young women off you!"[3]

Epilogue

Surfing the Silver Tsunami

A good diet is the most powerful weapon we have against disease and sickness. T. Colin Campbell, PhD, *The China Study.*[1]

    Exercise is king. Nutrition is queen. Put them together and you've got a kingdom. Jack LaLanne[2]

    Illness and suffering can be powerful catalysts for changing not only behaviors such as diet and exercise, but more important, for helping to transform more fundamental determinants of health, including the patient's values, relationships, self-perceptions, and self-esteem. Dean Ornish, MD[3]

Exercise Is Not Enough

Reading *Do Not Go Gentle* may give you the impression that I think exercise is the quintessence of human existence. I'll admit that when I began writing this book I was in a lot more denial about aging than I am now. In my heart of hearts, I think I was still hung up on the myth of eternal youth, magically believing that exercise and physical fitness are a panacea for all the problems of aging, and that if you just take good enough care of your body you should never get sick, suffer any problems or God forbid, die.

I learned the hard way that exercise and a moderately healthy diet are not enough. During a routine annual physical examination, my physician discovered a high level of PSA (prostate specific antigen). Follow up testing and a biopsy revealed early stage prostate cancer.

My struggle with prostate cancer helped me to develop a more realistic sense of mortality. I came to learn that, even if you seem to be doing all the right things, you can get blindsided by an unexpected health problem or other life crisis. The cumulative effects of a lifetime of bad eating and unhealthy lifestyle practices can still take their toll, even after you decide to turn your whole life around.

My journey through the fear of dying from cancer and the ordeal of treatment led me to discover the importance of diet, nutrition, and other lifestyle factors for successful aging. I learned that prostate cancer, like other so-called diseases of aging, is strongly influenced by the choices we make. I discovered the power of *integrative medicine*—combining state-of-the-art medical care with healthy diet, nutrition, exercise, and other lifestyle factors. I learned to let food be my medicine. I learned that to surf the silver tsunami, I had to become a counter-counterculture rebel.

Become a Counter-Counterculture Rebel

The sequel to *Do Not Go Gentle* discusses how to surf the silver tsunami by becoming a counter-counterculture rebel.

1. Rebel against the health care system by staying so healthy that you don't become overly dependent on it.
2. Avoid going into a nursing home and maintain independence throughout your lifetime by adopting a healthy lifestyle that promotes physical fitness and good nutrition.
3. Rebel against the 'Great American Steak Religion' and eat modest amounts of nutritious foods—preferably a low-fat, vegan diet. Take such good care of your body that you won't be ravaged by the diseases of aging. (Nutritionist Francis Moore Lappe coined the term Great American Steak Religion in her 1965 classic, *Diet for a Small Planet.*[4])
4. Rebel against convenience and overcome resistance to change by doing the things you think you cannot do.
5. Rebel against excess and overindulgence by practicing moderation.
6. Rebel against know-it-allism and learn to trust competent authorities and practice integrative health care.

7. Rebel against the obsession with youth culture and learn to mature with dignity.
8. Rebel against middle-aged complacency and materialism to become a philanthropist. Learn why developing humanitarian interests is a natural part of mature human development and an excellent way to surf the silver tsunami.

Preview of Topics of Interest

Here's a glimpse of some chapter titles and subheadings from *Surfing the Silver Tsunami*:

The Graying of America
Where Have All the Hippies Gone?
Let Food Be Your Medicine
Things to Do Besides Eating All the Time
The Psychology of Weight Loss: What Really Works?
How to Stay Out of a Nursing Home
Rebel Against the Establishment of Aging
Psychological and Health Benefits of Altruism
Senior Shock and the Psychology of Aging
Surviving Senior Angst
Do Your Genes Fit Your Lifestyle? Truth About the 'Fat Gene'
Laughter Really Is the Best Medicine
Become the Hero of Your Own Life's Story
Aging Is Mind Over Matter
More Psychology for the Health of It

Excerpt from Surfing the Silver Tsunami:

Where Have All the Hippies Gone?

Was the hippie movement merely a curious anachronism, or was it a preliminary stage of growth, with greater development yet to come as the boomer generation fully matures through the life cycle? Has the counterculture lain dormant, like a butterfly in a cocoon, awaiting its spectacular emergence and a brilliant future flight of maturity?

My reply to those rhetorical questions is resoundingly affirmative, and this book will demonstrate why I believe it is true. I hope to show that the counterculture was the youthful paroxysm of the baby boom generation. An image comes to mind of one of those outlandishly festooned caterpillars with all the gaudy colors, patterns and spikes, which was followed by dormancy, akin to the bland and boring cocoon stage, during which time the baby boomers have been living middle-aged lives raising families and pursuing economic productivity. As boomers move into the final stages of advancing age, becoming grandparent boomers, they are preparing properly to finish what they started. I expect them to emerge as a mature butterfly, fulfilling their developmentally appropriate task of giving back to the community and discovering true peace, both inner and outer.

The Counterculture Redefined

There were great hopes for the baby boom generation and the counterculture, or hippie movement, which challenged the traditional ways of thinking and behaving during the 1960s and early 70s. In *The Greening of America* published in 1971, Charles Reich, a Yale law professor who was both a mentor and convert to the counterculture lifestyle, wrote "a paean of praise to the counterculture of the 1960s and its values."[1] Reich prophesied a revolution of consciousness, which was "not a passing fad" but rather a widespread social transformation. "It is now spreading with amazing rapidity, and already our laws, our institutions and social structures are changing in consequence," Reich wrote.[2] "It is both necessary and inevitable, and in time it will include not only youth, but all people of America."

Unfortunately, I'm afraid Reich's enthusiasm was misplaced. From what we know about human development, it was inappropriate to expect young people to significantly change the world. The task of youth and early adulthood is to find an identity and learn intimacy—which were certainly dominant themes of the time. How many of us were trying "to get our heads together" or learning to "love one another"? However, the members of the counterculture were absorbed back into the system they rejected. From a psychological perspective, this so-called "selling out to the system" really was the baby boomers growing up into the next developmental phase: marriage or stable relationships, raising families, and developing career. (Unfortunately, there are many in middle age who still have not successfully achieved those developmental milestones. As Garrison Keillor put it: "Age does not always bring wisdom. Sometimes age comes alone."[3])

Fortunately, research on human development gives us reason to hope that most boomers will successfully make the transition into the senior stages of development. All boomers are technically now in the stage of middle adulthood (ages 40-65), which involves the developmental task of *generativity*. Generativity means the passing on of your knowledge and experience to society at large and to future generations. Dr. George Vaillant explains that this involves "demonstration of a clear capacity to unselfishly guide the next generation."[4] This is definitely not something young people do, as a general rule. However, it is a task that comes easily and as a matter of course to most elders. Just ask any child who is being spoiled rotten by a grandparent's lavish generosity.

We need to look toward the graying of America, because in the process of earning their gray hair boomers may gain true wisdom, combined with a developmental readiness to make a real difference in the world on a vaster and broader scope than was possible by cadres of youth, no matter how fiery their energy and idealism.

We can see some clear indications of a promising future in this regard. Elton John established an AIDS foundation as amends for his promiscuous past. Bill Gates left Microsoft and dedicated his life to charitable service, donating hundreds of millions of dollars. There are many more examples like this. I don't believe these behaviors are anomalies; we can expect to see a lot more over the next two to three decades. These scattered behaviors are like the first efforts of the wrinkly butterfly emerging from its cocoon of dormancy. What will we see once the wings are fully unfurled and ready for flight?

"To every thing there is a season, and a time to every purpose under the heaven" proclaims the preacher in Ecclesiastes (3:1). The year has its seasons and our lives have their cycles, moving inexorably from birth to death. Yet we tend to lose sight of that fact because of our cultural obsession with youth and our avoidance of old age. The aging boomers will as a matter of course learn to put things in their proper perspective.

No, the counterculture was not a false start; it was only a beginning, just one stage of the baby boomer generation's developmental lifetime. Will we boomers rise up to the challenges ahead of us or will we remain stagnant? Each stage of life presents us with a challenge. If we meet the challenge successfully, we pass on to the next stage. If not we get stuck. The middle-age stage is conceptualized as *generativity vs. stagnation.* Stagnation is typified by Ebenezer Scrooge, the archetypal curmudgeon. The point is that we either learn to give more of ourselves, realizing the benefits involved, or we mummify in our own selfishness. In our senior years, we either find integrity—get our heads together as we used to say, making peace with ourselves and the world—or else suffer the involutional depression of old age.

I prefer to be hopeful, and I predict that we will see more and more seniors as mentors, guides, and motivators of the younger generations. As the baby boomers mature, they will become spunky eldsters themselves and work for the regeneration society. I think the research points to a bright future. However, it depends on us. Look at our first two baby boomer presidents. One tried to carry us into the twenty-first century with human rights and social reform, and the other sent us back to the nineteenth century in terms of foreign policy and civil liberties. What will the next few decades reveal?

Notes

Preface

1. Trenton, Tennessee, is a small town of about 5,000 people located 108 miles northeast of Memphis, Tennessee. It is a little like Mayberry on *The Andy Griffith Show* and although you won't find a Barney Fife-type deputy, a former mayor once changed the citywide speed limit to 31miles per hour—and that's how it stays to this day.

2. One reviewer pointed out an inconsistency: this book is about fitness and exercise and good nutrition, things to which Joseta doesn't devote any special attention. It's not that Joseta doesn't take care of herself—she doesn't smoke or drink or have any bad habits, she keeps very active without a formal exercise program, and she's always eaten a lot of vegetables and fruit. However, until recently she didn't do anything extra in the areas of diet and exercise like many of the elders I will talk about in this book. Shortly before I finished writing this book she signed up for a yoga class. Some people seem to age well without any special effort—and in some cases despite unhealthy lifestyle practices—like Jeanne Calment, the 122-year-old French woman who smoked all her life (actually, until she was 117 years old!). Good genes is no doubt one factor in the equation for successful aging, but most of us really have to work at it.

3. Vaillant, 2002, p. 160.

4. Buie, 2006.

Introduction

1. Olshansky, et al, 2005.

2. Quoted in Durant, 1935, p. ix.

Chapter 1: Growing Old Is Not for Sissies

1. Clark,1986.
2. Ibid., p. 14.
3. Clark, 1998.
4. Clark, 1986, p. 40.
5. Clark, 1995, p. 54.
6. Austad, 1997, p. 9.
7. Clark, 1986, p. 106.
8. World Triathlon Corporation, 2007.
9. Haddock, 2003, p. 252.
10. *Time*, 1948.
11. Tuttle, 2006.
12. Todd, 1992, p. 4.
13. Burns, 2006, p. 195; oldtime.com, 2010; digitaldeli, 2010.
14. LaLanne, 2005, p. 15.
15. Clark, 1995, p. 51.
16. Abu Bakr (573-634), First Muslim Caliph, was also the first convert to Islam. Quotation obtained from Brainyquotes. com. Online at http://www.brainyquote.com/quotes/quotes/a/ abubakr219641.html

Chapter 2: Why Should I Jog When There's a New Car in the Garage? Exercise for Disease Prevention

1. Worldnakedbikeride.com, 2006.
2. List of 28 countries that host World Naked Bike Rides: Argentina, Australia, Austria, Belgium, Brazil, Canada, Czech Republic, Denmark, France, Germany, Greece, Ireland, Israel, Italy, Japan, Latvia, Mexico, Netherlands, New Zealand, Peru, Poland, Russia, South Africa, Spain, Sweden, Switzerland, the United Kingdom, and the United States.
3. Worldnakedbikeride.com, 2006.
4. Rowe and Kahn, 1998, p. 28.
5. Ohio Department of Aging, 2008.
6. thinkexist.com.
7. CDC, 2010, May 10.
8. World Health Organization, 2008, 2003.

9. LaLanne, Jack. (2010, Mar 8).
10. Aldwin et al, 2006, p. 85.
11. Shephard and Shek, 1994.
12. Appalachian State University, 2008.
13. Bledsoe, 2009.
14. Farzanaki et al, 2008.
15. Bledsoe, 2009.
16. What's the difference between a cold and the flue? Both the cold and flu are respiratory illnesses, with similar symptoms, but the flu is generally worse.
17. BCBS, 2005, p. 2.
18. CDC, 2008, Aug. 12.
19. CDC, 2005.
20. Cited in LifePower, 2010.
21. Birren, 2006, p. 90.
22. Horber et al, 1996.
23. American Diabetes Association, 2010.
24. American Hospital Association, 2007.
25. American Federation for Aging Research, 2007.
26. Kung, 2008.
27. Masoro and Austad, 2001, pp. 304-307.
28. American Diabetes Association, 1999.
29. World Health Organization, 2003, p. 2.
30. Sigal et al, 2007.
31. AARP, 2004, Nov. 8.
32. Ibid.
33. Rowe and Kahn, 1998, p. 88.
34. American Heart Association, 2007.
35. Ogden, 2004, p. 170.
36. Jones et al, 2003.
37. CDC, 2008, Sept. 28.
38. Cited in Barnes, 2004, p. 38.
39. World Health Organization, 2003, p. 3.
40. Ogden, 2004, p. 170.
41. Cited in Lunde, 2008.
42. Bullitt et al, 2009.
43. Lunde, 2008.

44. Centers for Disease Control, 1999, Nov. 17.
45. AARP Bulletin, p. 43.
46. CDC, 1999, Nov. 17.
47. Tully et al, 2006.
48. Ham and Epping, 2006.
49. Motooka et al, 2006.
50. Giaquinto and Valentini, 2009.
51. Thorpe et al, 2006.
52. Culos-Reed et al, 2008.
53. Nguyen, 2008.

Chapter 3: Psychology for the Health of It

1. Matarazzo, 1980, p. 815.
2. Hamlet act 1, scene 5, pp. 159–167.
3. Bortz, 1982.
4. Sheehan, 1975, p. 4.
5. Ogden, 2004, p. 181.
6. Ibid, p. 5.
7. Sheehan, pp. vii-viii.
8. Ibid, p. 17.
9. Karlinsky and Harper, 2009.
10. Baron, 1989, p. 379 and 397.
11. Quoted in *Surfing for Life* video, Brown, 2002.
12. Plante and Rodin, 1990.
13. Callaghan, 2004.
14. King, 1992.
15. Miller et al, 1996.
16. Vaillant, 2002, p.5.
17. Ibid.
18. MedlinePlus, 2008.
19. Whitbourne, p. 354.
20. Sheehan, 1975, pp. 3-5.
21. Blumenthal et al, 1999.
22. Random assignment means everybody had an equal chance of being selected for any of the three groups, and it is considered the gold standard of scientific research.
23. MailOnline.com. (2008).

24. Salovey, 2000.
25. Ogden, 2004, pp. 260-283.
26. Salovey, 2000, p. 110.
27. Ibid, p. 111.
28. Labott and Martin, 1990.
29. Dillon et al, 1989.
30. Labott et al, 1990.
31. Laughter Yoga International, 2010.
32. Madrid, 2000.
33. Merck. (2010). Merck manual of geriatrics. Online at: http://www.merck.com/mkgr/mmg/sec10/ch75/ch75a.jsp.
34. Rowe and Kahn, 199, p. 133.
35. Sheehan, 1975, p.5; p. 19.
36. Karlinsky and Harper, 2009.
37. Preece and Hess, 2008, p. 5.
38. Preece, 2008, p. 35.
39. Ibid.
40. Ross and Thomas, 2010.
41. Yanek et al, 2001.
42. Hacker, 2009.
43. Cited in Sheehan, 1975, pp. 43-44.
44. Crisp, 2006, p. 2.
45. FitCommerce.com, 2002.
46. Cited in Seniorjournal.com, 2007, Aug.6.
47. World Health Organization, 2003.
48. Shephard, 2008.
49. Shephard et al, 1996, p. 246.
50. Ogden, 2004.
51. Barnes, 2004, p. 43.
52. Vaillant, 2002.
53. Shouler, 2002.
54. Vaillant, 2002, p. 209.
55. Ibid.
56. U.S. Dept. of Health & Human Services, 2004, Jan. 21, p. 2.
57. Ibid.
58. Inspirational-quotes-and-quotations.com, 2010.

59. Summarized in Bandura, 1997, p. 102.
60. Ibid.

Chapter 4: The Couch Potato Nation

1. Sheehan, 1976, p. 15.
2. DeGroot, 2008, p. 11.
3. White, 1996, p. 156.
4. Ibid.
5. Galbraith,1969, p.29.
6. DeGroot, 2008.
7. Potter, 1954, p. 84.
8. Vaillant, 2002, p. 3.
9. CDC, 1999.
10. Rowe and Kahn, 1998, p. 7.
11. Ibid., p. 5.
12. Berk 2004, p. 7.
13. U.S. Census Bureau, 2004.
14. U.S. Census Bureau, 1999.
15. U.S. Census Bureau, 2004.
16. Bortz, 1996, p. 19.
17. Hobbs and Damon, 1996, p. 20.
18. World Health Organization, 2000.
19. Ornish, 2009.
20. Olshansky et al, 2005.
21. *The New York Times*, Aug. 2008.
22. *CIA World Fact Book*, 2008.
23. RAND Corporation, 2008.
24. Keisernetwork.com., 2007; OECD 2009. American health care spending is more than double the average of the 30 members of the Organization for Economic Cooperation and Development.
25. Ayres,1996, p. xii; Vladeck, 2002.
26. Institute of Medicine, 2004. According to its official Web site, "the Institute of Medicine (IOM) is an independent, nonprofit organization that works outside of government to provide unbiased and authoritative advice to decision makers and the public." The IOM was chartered in 1863 during the presidency of Abraham Lincoln.

27. *The New York Times*, 2007.
28. World Health Organization, 2000, pp. 152-155.
29. Vladeck, 2002.
30. United Nations Development Programme, 2008.
31. U.S. Census Bureau, 2008b. The World Health Organization ranks life expectancy in the United States as twenty-fourth in the world: 67.5 years for males and 72.6 years for females.[32] This ranking is based on the concept of "healthy life expectancy" for babies born in 1999, which means the number of years lived in "full health," with years of ill health or disability subtracted from the overall average.
32. World Health Organization, 2000, June 4.
33. OECD Health Data 2005, cited in Nationmaster.com, 2008.
34. CDC, 2007, Nov. 28.
35. Ogden et al, 2007.
36. Galson, 2007.
37. Fuhrman, 2003, p ix.
38. CDC, 2007, Nov. 23.
39. Ogden et al, 2007. Technically boomers were aged 43 to 61 in 2007; but these are the closest age-group stats available.
40. Leveille et al, 2004.
41. Fontaine, 2003.
42. U.S. Department of Labor, 2008.
43. CDC, 2008, Dec. 17.
44. Ogden, 2004, p. 169.
45. CDC, 2009, Feb. 22.
46. National Council on Aging, 2002.
47. Bouchez, 2005.
48. Moschis and Mathur, 2007, pp. 29, 31, 65. George Moschis, PhD, is professor of marketing at Georgia State University in Atlanta. He has been researching boomers and their parents' generation for the past 20 years.
49. CDC, 2007, Nov. 23.
50. 2007, Nov. 23.
51. U.S. Census Bureau, 2005.

52. CDC, 2007, Nov. 23.
53. Moschis and Mathur, 2007, pp. 64-65.
54. Cited in Bouchez, 2005. The time period was between 1987 and 2003.
55. Ibid.
56. Cited in Stein, 2007.
57. Bee, 2007.
58. Stein, 2007
59. Ornish, 2001, p. viii.
60. National Institute on Aging, 2007.
61. Stein, 2007.
62. Lakdawalla et al, 2001.
63. Australian Bureau of Statistics, 2003.64. Moschis and Mathur, 2007, pp. 64-65.
65. Fuhrman, 2003, p. x.
66. Prochaska and DiClemente, 1983.

Chapter 5: The Lap of Luxury is Way Too Soft

1. World Health Organization, 2008.
2. Ibid.
3. Centers for Disease Control, 2008, Nov.
4. Bee, 2007.
5. Department of Transport, 2009.
6. Ruiz, 2008, p. 2.
7. Pace, 2006.
8. World Health Organization, 2003, p. 1.
9. Mokdad, 2004.
10. Cited in Melville, 2004.
11. Seniorjournal.com, 2004.
12. Fuhrman, 2003, p. x.
13. *USA Today*, 2008.
14. Moynihan et al, 2002.
15. World Health Organization, 2006.
16. World Health Organization, 2003a.
17. Bosely, 2008.
18. FitCommerce.com, 2002.
19. NHTSA, 2008.

20. World Health Organization, 2008b, p. 29.
21. Novotney, 2009, p. 32.
22. Vanderbilt, 2008, p. 60.
23. Dunning et al, 2004.
24. Alcoholics Anonymous, 2001, p. 44. The actual quotation is "To be doomed to an alcoholic death or to live on a spiritual basis are not always easy alternatives to face."
25. Ornish, 1990.

Chapter 6: It's Never Too Late to Change Your Whole Life Around

1. Rowe and Kahn, 1998, p. 23.
2. CDC, May 4, 2009.
3. *GMAC Quest Magazine*, April 1988, p. 13.
4. Summerbell et al, 2008.
5. *GMAC Quest Magazine*, April 1988, p. 13.
6. silvaslifesteps.com, 2008.
7. Ibid.
8. Tuttle, 2006.
9. Cooper, 1998, p. ix.
10. Ibid, p. 25.
11. Ibid, p. 37.
12. Ibid, p. 6.
13. Ibid, back cover.
14. See mastersweightlifting, 2007; Baron, 2007; 40plussports. com., 2010.
15. Clark, 1995, p.4.
16. Ibid, pp. 14-15.
17. Clark, 1986, p. 18.
18. Ibid, p. 51.
19. Haddock, 2003, p. 12.
20. Rowe and Kahn, 2003, p. 23.
21. Cicero, 2006.
22. Ibid.
23. National Institute on Aging, 2006.
24. Galson, 2007.
25. brainyquotes.com.
26. thinkexist.com.

27. World Health Organization, 2000, p. vii.
28. fitness.gov, 2010.
29. Jakicic and Otto, 2005.
30. Doug Ross @ Journal, 2006.
31. CDC, 2008, Dec. 17; National Guidelines Clearinghouse, 2009.
32. Ibid.
33. Barnes, 2004, p.43.
34. Pennington, 2006.
35. Bee, 2008.
36. Harding, 2009.
37. Clark, 1986, p. 56.
38. Glasser, 1985, p. 38.
39. Ibid, pp. 38-40.
40. Sheehan, 1975, p. 17.
41. CDC, 2008, May 21.
42. McInnis, 2000.

Chapter 7: Make Your Midlife Crisis Work for You

1. quotationspage.com, 2007.
2. Egger, 2008.
3. Lasch, 1979, p. 29.
4. Ibid, p. 30.
5. Sheehan, 1975, p. 3.
6. Clark, 1986, p. 54.
7. Fox, 2002, p. 4.
8. Ibid, p. 6.
9. Ibid, p. 2.
10. Siegel, 1986, pp. 176-177.
11. Frankl, 1973, p. 6.
12. Fox, 2002, p. 238.
13. James, 1994, p. 228.
14. Ibid, p. 230.
15. Freud, 1961, p. 10-11.
16. James, 1994, p. 91.
17. Walker, 2008.
18. Tedeschi and Calhoun, 2001.

19. Gould et al, 1999.
20. Schultz, 1999.
21. De Laine, 2009.
22. Li et al, 2008.
23. U.S. Dept. of Health and Human Services, 2004, p. 2.
24. Mandino, 1968, p. 64.
25. World Book Encyclopedia, 1993, Vol. E, p. 78.
26. Hanus et al, 1977.
27. Trechsel, 1998.

Chapter 8: Dare to Be Inconvenienced: Exercise as an Act of Cultural Rebellion

1. According to the World Health Organization (2008): "industrialization, urbanization, and mechanized transport."
2. There seem to be no emotionally neutral synonyms for inactivity. The thesaurus gives either negative synonyms like laziness, lethargy, idleness, and sloth or positive synonyms like calmness, serenity, peacefulness, and tranquility.
3. Tabacoff, 2008.
4. Ibid.
5. CDC, 2010, June 21.
6. CDC, 2010, Jan. 4.
7. CDC, 2010, June 21.
8. Cleveland.com, 2008.
9. Ray's Boathouse, 2009; Karmer, 2002; conversations with Ray's crew members.
10. Costello, 2008.
11. Ibid..
12. McInnis, 2000.
13. National Institute on Aging, 2006, foreword.
14. Harvard Medical School, 2009.
15. I did buy those Rollerblades, much to Mary's chagrin, while still wearing the sling from my elbow surgery after wrecking my bicycle.
16. Pari Roller, 2009.

17. After I wrecked my bike, I took it in for a tune-up and discovered the gears were basically shot, so I bought a Giant brand hybrid model that can be ridden on or off the road, for about $350.
18. WKYC-TV, 2009.
19. British Pathé, 2010
20. Brown, 2009.
21. Wardlaw, 2000.
22. World Health Organization, 2003.
23. BUPA, 2009.
24. Wen et al, 2008.
25. Davison et al, 2008.
26. BUPA, 2009.
27. Ibid.
28. Johnson et al, 2009.
29. Chen et al, 2009.
30. Frotzier et al, 2009.
31. Cited in *Indecent exposure: The story of the World Naked Bike Ride.* www.WorldNakedBikeride.org, 2007.
32. Wardlaw, 2000.
33. In the 2009 Hotter'N Hell 100, I witnessed three major accidents during the first 30 miles, a disturbing turn of events as I watched the ambulances speeding away carrying mangled bicyclists to the nearest hospital.
34. World Health Organization, 2003.
35. Buettner, 2002.
36. Conradt et al, 2008.

Chapter 9: Conquer Over-the-Hill Syndrome

1. Lipschitz, 2002, rear cover.
2. Dennis, 2003.
3. Photo of Joseta Barker riding with Carl Wyatt.
4. Brainyquotes.com. Also from "The Red Haired League" in *The Adventures of Sherlock Holmes.*
5. Dawson, 2001.
6. Ibid.
7. Cited in Rowe and Kahn, 1998, p. 45.

8. BrainyQuotes.com.
9. Fillmore, 1998, p. 3.
10. Brother Lawrence, 1982, p. 11.
11. Jourard, 1980, pp. 6-7.
12. agehumor.com.
13. Vaillant, 2002.
14. U.S. Census Bureau, 2001, Oct., p. 7.
15. U.S. Census Bureau, 2005, April 21.
16. Vaillant, 2002, pp. 62-63.

Chapter 10: Don't Be An Old Fuddy-Duddy

1. Haddock, 2001.
2. McManis, 2003.
3. Vaillant, 2002, p. 50.
4. LaLanne, 2005, p. 15.
5. Also see Scandigital.com, 2009; and Squires, 2007.
6. Dennis, 2003.
7. BrainyQuotes.com.
8. Vaillant, 2002.
9. Wieland et al, 2008.
10. Senior Journal.com, 2003.
11. Franz, 1994.
12. Vaillant, 2002.
13. Independent Sector, 2000.
14. Bandura, 1976.
15. Camp et al, 1997.
16. Justice, 1998, p. 98.
17. *The Hindu*, 2006, July 8.
18. Justice, 1998, p. xi.
19. Ibid, p. 3.
20. Clark, 1995, p. 62.
21. Ibid, pp. 24-25.
22. I've often joked about how both the very young and the very old tend to be more sociopathic or antisocial—the young because they don't know any better and the old because they no longer care. There may be more truth than fiction here. Japanese are the longest-lived people in

the world, with a very large and growing aging population. There is presently concern about the sharp increase in crime among the Japanese elderly.

23. Stengel et al, 1992.
24. Associated Press, 2007, June 6.
25. Bortz, 1996, p. 17.
26. Rowe and Kahn, p. 5.
27. Neikirk, 2006.
28. Bortz, 1996, p.18.
29. *CBS Sunday Morning,* Jan. 10, 2010.
30. Poras, 2007.
31. I wrote this August 18, 2008. Granny D's date of birth is January 24, 1910.
32. Poras, 2007.
33. Wikipedia 2009.
34. Goodreads.com 2009.
35. Wikipedia 2009.
36. At the time I wrote this—August 31, 2008.
37. Hawking was diagnosed with Lou Gehrig's disease (ALS) in January 1963, when he was only 21 years old and studying physics as Cambridge University. Doctors didn't expect him to live more than two years. Despite the grim prognosis, he got married in July 1965—"somewhat past the expected date of [his] death," as a fellow scientist put it (Schaefer, 2001). So far, he has lived more than 45 years past the date of his expected death! In 1974 he was inducted into the Royal Society, the oldest and most venerated scholarly organization on Earth. In 1980 he was appointed Lucasian Professor of Mathematics at Cambridge University, a position once held by Isaac Newton.
38. Hawking, 2008.

Chapter 11: Real-Life Space Cowboys

1. National Institute on Aging, 2006, foreword.
2. Men average three to five mph when walking; speed walking is over five mph. Olympic race walkers may log in

at nine mph! Jogging speeds vary considerably, because jogging is halfway between walking and running. What is the speed of marathon runners? The Boston Marathon record was set April 22, 2008—2:07:46, to run 26 miles, 385 yard distance; which is about twelve and one-quarter mph. Sources: Litzky, 2008, and Bloom, 2008.

3. Vaillant, 2002, p. 187.
4. Ibid, p. 186.
5. Clark, 1995, p. 108.
6. Seniorjournal.com, 2007, May 30.
7. Haaz, 2009.
8. Clark, 1996, p. 108.
9. Vaillant, 2002, p. 256.
10. McGinnis, 2005.
11. Whitbourne, 2005, p. 5.
12. Goldman, 1982, p. 93.
13. Cited in Friedan, 1993, p. 72.
14. Ibid, p. 9.
15. Ibid, pp. 71-72.
16. Becker, 1973, p. ix.
17. "The unseen is much scarier than the seen," says A.O. Scott (2002) in a *New York Times* review of *Wes Craven Presents: They*, aptly titled "For the Scariest Monsters: A Little Glimpse'll Do Ya." Scott praises the 2002 horror film's director for relying more on atmosphere and imagination than graphic gore and high-priced special effects. The film appealed to lovers of H.P. Lovecraft, but didn't do well at the box office and generated mixed reviews from "the worst, dumbest movie I have ever seen" to "a criminally underrated film." (Amazon.com. 2009)
18. Rice, 1992, 73; the whole book addresses this issue.
19. Ibid, p. 74.
20. Vaillant, 2002, p. 210.
21. Buettner, 2005.
22. Friedan, 1993.
23. Berk, 2004, p. 626.
24. Summarized in Berk, 2004, p. 626.

25. Cited in Vaillant, 2002, p. 49.

26. Vaillant, 2002, p. 57.

27. I remember asking Dad, who had always been a devout skeptic about the mysteries of life after death, that if he found something to be sure and tell me. He responded, "Don't worry, Dick, you'll be the first one I tell." That reply seemed ominous, especially after I received no overt communiqué from the spirits in the Great Beyond. I feared that I would be the next one to die in our family, since I was the eldest son. However, a short while after Dad's funeral, I encountered a series of uncanny events that led to a major life transformation. I was able to give up the heavy drinking, returned to college to get an advanced degree, and fell in love with a beautiful woman with whom to spend the rest of my life. "We will surely show them the signs of God in themselves and the world," to paraphrase a verse from the Qur'an.

28. Vaillant, 2002, p. 186.

29. Clark, 1995, p. 50.

30. Clark, 1986, p. viii.

31. Ibid, p. 50.

32. *Spirit*, 2008, p. 9.

33. Rowland, 1956, p. 215.

34. Bortz II, 1996, p. 21.

35. Wikipedia, 2010.

36. Austad, 2010.

37. Ibid.

38. Austad, 1997, 47.

39. Bortz, 1996, p. 23.

40. Willcox et al, 2001, pp. 217-18

41. Austad, 1997, p. 50.

42. Austad, 1997, p. 104.

43. Montague, 1999.

44. Data summarized from Whitbourne, 2005, pp. 87-129.

45. Austad, 1996, p. 181.

46. Rowe and Kahn, 1998, pp. 12-13.

47. Austad, 2001, p. 3.

48. Gutmann, 1987, p. 5.
49. Lipschitz, 2002, p. xix.
50. Friedan, 1993, p. 9
51. Ibid, p. 638.
52. Gutmann, 1987, p. 4.
53. Ibid, p. x.
54. Vaillant, 2002, p. 57.
55. Lipschitz, 2003, p. xviii.
56. Ibid, p. xix.
57. Ibid, p. xxi.
58. Ibid, p. xxiv
59. Willcox et al, 2001, p.1.
60. Ibid.
61. Ibid, pp. 1, 3.
62. Ibid, pp. 13-14.
63. Vaillant, 2002, p. 4.
64. Willcox et al, p. 14.
65. Vaillant, 2002, p. 4.
66. Ibid, p. 60.
67. Ibid, p. 61.
68. Ibid.

Chapter 12: The Real-Life Fountain of Youth?

1. My understanding is that Angus began wearing the uniform when AC/DC first formed, upon the recommendation of his sister, because he was only 15 years old and still in high school at the time.
2. Amazon.com, 2009b, editorial review summarizing the book.
3. Birren et al, 2006, p. 85.
4. CDC, 2006, p. 885.
5. Birren, et al 2006, p. 85.
6. Barclay, 2008.
7. Clark, 1995, p. 52.
8. Ibid.
9. Tuttle, 2006.
10. Hanna, 1988.

Conclusion: Become a Spunky Eldster to Live Longer and Better

1. Holden, 2008.
2. Gillick, 2006, p. 10.
3. This seems like an appropriate place to end. I decided to ake my wife's advice: "At some point it might be a good idea to stop writing the book." Amen! (June 7, 2010)

Epilogue: Surfing the Silver Tsunami

1. Campbell, 2004, p. 3.
2. Squires, 2007.
3. Ornish, 1990, p. 26.
4. Lappe, 1985, p. 10.

Excerpt from *Surfing the Silver Tsunami*

1. Wikipedia, 2008.
2. Reich, 1971, p. 18.
3. QuoteDB, 2005.
4. Vaillant, 2002, p. 47.

References

Where Do You Find All This Stuff?

AARP Magazine. (May/June 2006). Paul is 64. Cover story.

AARP. (2004, May 28). Suing to get out in the world. *AARP Bulletin Today*. 14:54:00-04:00.

AARP. (2004, Nov. 8). Beating diabetes each and every day. *AARP Bulletin Today.* http://www.aarp.org/health/conditions/articles/beatingdiabetes.html

AARP. (2008, Aug. 7). Marathon woman. (Video). *AARP Bulletin Today.* http://bulletin.aarp.org/yourworld/reinventing/articles/multimedia__marathon.html

AARP Bulletin. (2009 issue). Walking 50 miles a month, Jan-Feb, p. 43.

Ackermann, Sheri. (2008, Jan. 29). 100-year-old local woman reborn through exercise. The Tampa Tribune. Cited in Tampa Bay online (TBO.com). http://www2.tbo.com/content/2008/jan/29/me-100-year-old-b-day-girl-is-reborn-through-fitness

Alcoholics Anonymous. (2001). *Alcoholics Anonymous [The big book].* New York City: Alcoholics Anonymous World Services, Inc.

Aldwin, Carolyn M., Spiro III, Avron, and Park, Crystal L. (2006). *Health, behavior, and optimal aging: a life span developmental perspective.* Chapter Five in Birren, James E., and Schaie, Warner K., Eds. *Handbook of the psychology of aging, 6th edition.* Amsterdam: Academic Press (Elsevier), pp. 85-104.

Amazon.com. (2009a). Reviews of Wes Craven Presents: They. Online at: http://www.amazon.com/Craven-Presents-They-Laura-Regan/dp/B00005JLHF/ ref=sr_1_1?ie=UTF8&s=dvd &qid=1237726246&sr=1-1

Amazon.com. (2009b). Editorial review of *The quest for immortality: Science at the frontiers of aging.* www.amazon.com/gp/product/product-description/0756761026/ref= dp_proddesc_0?ie=U TF8&n=283155&s=books

American Association of Health Education. (2009). Aging: Promotion of a positive perspective within health education.   http://www.aahperd.org/aahe/advocacy/positionStatements/loader.cfm?csModule=security/getfile&pageid=19435

American Diabetes Association. (2009). Small steps. Big rewards. Prevent type 2 diabetes. Online at: http://www.diabetes.org/weightloss-and-exercise/exercise/ overview.jsp

American Diabetes Association. (2010). Fitness. http://www.diabetes.org/ food-and-fitness/fitness/

American Federation for Aging Research. (2007). How is diabetes related to aging? http://websites.afar.org/site/PageServer/PageServer?pagename= IA_d_diab_9_aging).

American Heart Association. (2007). *Physical activity and public health: Updated recommendation for adults from the American College of Sports medicine and the American Heart Association.* Obtained online at: http://circ.ahajournals.org/ cgi/reprint/CIRCULATIONAHA.107.185649

American Heart Association. (2010). Body Mass Index Calculator. Accessed Mar. 10. http://74.125.47.132/search?q=cache:jaTKlOIJtVMJ:www.americanheart.org/

presenter.jhtml%3Fidentifier%3D3048134+american+heart+association+bmi+calculator&cd=1&hl=en&ct=clnk&gl=us

American Hospital Association. (2007). *When I'm 64: How boomers will change health care.* Chicago, Illinois.

Appalachian State University. (2008, Jan. 25). Flu arrives at Appalachian. *University News* online. http://www.news.appstate.edu/2008/01/25/flu/

Associated Press. (2007, June 6). Rolling stones kick off Euro leg of tour. AP Press Release, NineMSN News online. http://news.ninemsn.com.au/article.aspx?id=271530

Austad, Steven N. (1997). *Why we age: What science is discovering about the body's journey through life.* New York: Wiley & Sons.

Austad, Steven. (2001). Concepts and theories of aging. Chapter One of *Handbook of the biology of aging*, 5th ed. Eds. Masoro, Edward J., and Austad, Steven N., Eds. Academic Press: San Diego, CA.

Austad, Steven. (2010). Transcript for *State of tomorrow, Episode 9, Aging with dignity.* http://www.stateoftomorrow.com/stories/transcripts/ AustadInterviewTranscript.pdf

Australian Bureau of Statistics. (2003). *Western Australia's baby boomers a high priority for planners.* http://www.abs.gov.au/ausstats/abs@.nsf/ mediareleasesbyTopic/FA9A04281D0E14F0CA256D570005199E? OpenDocument

Ayres, Stephen M. (1996). *Health care in the united states: The facts and the choices.* Chicago: American Library Association.

Bandura, Albert. Psychologist. (1976). *Social learning theory.* Upper Saddle River, New Jersey: Prentice-Hall.

Barclay, Laurie. (2008, April 29). Regular exercise through middle age may delay biological aging. *Medscape Medical News* online. http://cme.medscape.com/ viewarticle/573636

Barnes, Darryl. (2004). *Action plan for diabetes.* Champaign, Illinois: Human Kinetics.

Baron, Richard Laurance. (2007, March 21). "Weightlifter Bob," Signal Writer, http://signalwriter.blogspot.com/2007/03/weightlifter-bob.html

Baron, Robert A. (1989). *Psychology: The essential science.* Boston: Allyn and Bacon.

BCBS– Blue Cross Blue Shield of Rhode Island. (2005). The common cold costs big money. *Today's Healthcare Costs* newsletter. Online at: https://www.bcbsri.com/BCBSRIWeb/pdf/THC/THC_November_2007.pdf

Becker, Ernest. (1973). *The denial of death.* New York: The Free Press.

Bee, Peta. (2007). The baby boomers who are in worse health than their parents, June 26). *MailOnline.* http://www.dailymail.co.uk/health/article-462906/The-baby-boomers-worse-health-parents.html

Berk, Laura. (2004). *Development through the lifespan, third edition.* Boston: Allyn & Bacon.

Birren, James E., and Schaie, Warner K. (2006). *Handbook of the psychology of aging, 6*[th] *edition.* Amsterdam: Academic Press (Elsevier).

Bledsoe, Jim. (2009). Saliva & illness prediction - Can clues regarding your risk of infections be found in your saliva?

Sports Injury Bulletin. http://www.sportsinjurybulletin.com/ archive/saliva-illness-prediction.html

Blumenthal, James A.; Babyak, Michael A.; Moore, Kathleen A.; Craighead, W. Edward; Herman, Steve; Khatri, Parinda; Waugh, Robert; Napolitano, Melissa A.; Forman, Leslie M.; Appelbaum, Mark; Doraiswamy, P. Murali; and Krishnan, K. Ranga. (1999). Effects of exercise training on older patients with major depression. *Archives of Internal Medicine,* 159: 2349-2356. Article obtained online at: http://archinte.ama-assn. org/cgi/content/full/159/19/2349

Bloomer Consumer blog. (2008). *Valuable insights into the hearts, minds and wallets of today's baby boomers.* http:// boomerconsumerbook.blogspot.com/2008/06/ five-things-retailers-need-to-know.html

Bortz, Walter M. II. (1996). *Dare to be 100.* New York: Fireside Books (Simon & Schuster division).

Bortz, Walter. (1982). Disuse and aging. *Journal of the American Medical Association,* 248(10), 1203-1208.

Bosely, Sarah. (2008, Feb. 22). Obesity rates start badly and get worse at primary school. *The Guardian.* http://www.guardian. co.uk/society/2008/feb/22/children.health).

Bouchez, Colette. (2005, Nov. 11). Baby boomers are flocking to fitness centers in record numbers. http://www.medicinenet. com/script/main/art.asp?articlekey=56354

BrainyQuotes.com. (2009). www.brainyquote.com/quotes/ quotes/p/ peterustin161731.html

British Pathé. (2010). The world's oldest cyclist (video newsreel film).http://www.britishpathe.com/record.php?id=8974

Brother Lawrence. (1982). *The practice of the presence of God.* New Kensington, PA: Whitaker House.

Brown, David. (2002). *Surfing for Life* (video). David L. Brown Productions.

Brown, Emma. (2009, July 2). Va. Man, 107, Finds blessings and burdens in longevity. *The Washington Post* online. http://www. washingtonpost.com/wp-dyn/content/article/2009/07/01/ AR2009070103861.html

Buettner, D. (2005, Nov.). The secrets of longevity. *National Geographic Interactive Edition.*

Buettner, Linda. (2002). AD-Venture Program: Therapeutic biking for the treatment of depression in long-term care residents with dementia. *American Journal of Alzheimer's Disease and Other Dementias,* 17(2), 121-127.

Buie, J. (2006, August 30). Jim Buie's Blog. www.jimbluie. net;http://jimbuie.blogs.   com/journal/2006/08/ maxines_living_.html#more] The original source may be unidentifiable; there are many versions on internet blog sites. This is the oldest reference I could find.

Bullitt, E.; Rahman, F.N.; Smith, J.K.; Kim, E.; Zeng, D; Katz, L.M.; & Marks, B.L. (2009). The effect of exercise on the cerebral vasculature of healthy aged subjects as visualized by MR angiography. *Bulletin of the American Journal of Neuroradiology.* [Epub ahead of print] Abstract obtained from PubMed, online at: http://www.ncbi.nlm. nih. gov/pubmed/19589885?ordinalpos=2&itool=EntrezSys tem2.PEntrez.Pubmed.Pubmed_ResultsPanel.Pubmed_ DefaultReportPanel.Pubmed_RVDocSum

BUPA. (2009). Cycling and health. *British United Provident Association   website.*   http://www.bupa.co.uk/health_

information/html/healthy_living/lifestyle/exercise/
cycling/cycling_health.html

Burns, Eric. (2006). The smoke of the gods: A social history of tobacco. Philadelphia: Temple University Press.

Bush, George W. (2002, June 21). President promotes physical fitness to senior citizens. Texas of speech from The White House website, online at: http://www.whitehouse.gov/news/releases/2002/06/20020621-1.html

Butterworth, Eric. (1984). *Celebrate yourself.* Unity Village, Mo.: Unity School of Christianity.

Callaghan, P. (2004). Exercise: a neglected intervention in mental health care? *Journal of Psychiatric and Mental Health Nursing,* 11, 476–483.

Camp, C. J., Judge, K. S., Bye, C. A., Fox, K. M., Bowden, J., Bell, M., Valencic, K., & Mattern, J. M. (1997). An intergenerational program for persons with dementia using Montessori methods. *The Gerontologist,* 37(5), 688-692

Campbell, T. Colin, with Campbell II, Thomas M. (2004). *The China study: The most comprehensive study of nutrition ever conducted and the startling implications for diet, weight loss and long-term health.* Dallas, Texas: Benbella Books.

Carter, Abby. (2003). *My hippie grandmother.* Cambridge, MA: Candlewick Press.

CBS. (2009, April 12). Sunday Morning show public broadcast.

CBS Sunday Morning Show. (2010, Jan. 10). Bringing sophistication to the kitchen. http://www.cbsnews.com/video/watch/?id=6078893n&tag= contentMain;contentBody

CDC – Centers for Disease Control. (1999). *Morbidity and Mortality Weekly Report,* July 30, 48(29), 621-629.

CDC – Centers for Disease Control. (1999, Nov. 17). The benefits of physical activity.   http://www.cdc.gov/nccdphp/sgr/ ataglan.htm.

CDC – Centers for Disease Control. (2005). *Impact of influenza vaccinations on seasonal mortality in the U.S. elderly population.* Simonsen et al. A statement by the Centers for Disease Control and Prevention (CDC) and the National Instituttes of Health (NIH). Online at: www.cdc.gov/flu/pdf/ statementeldmortality.pdf

CDC – Centers for Disease Control. (2006). *Surgeon general's report—The health consequences of involuntary exposure to tobacco smoke,* p. 885. Obtained online at: http://www.cdc.gov/ tobacco/Data_statistics/sgr/sgr_2004/00_pdfs/chapter7. pdf

CDC – Centers for Disease Control. (2007, Nov. 20). Prevalence of regular physical activity among adults — United States, 2001 and 2005. Online at: http://www.cdc.gov/mmwr/ preview/mmwrhtml/mm5646a1.htm

CDC – Centers for Disease Control. (2008, May 21). *Obesity and overweight: Contributing factors.* http://www.cdc.gov/ nccdphp/dnpa/obesity/contributing_ factors.htm

CDC– Centers for Disease Control. (2008, Aug. 12). *Flu season is here: Learn how to protect yourself and your loved ones.* http:// www.cdc.gov/Features/flu

CDC – Centers for Disease Control. (2008, Aug. 20). *Fast stats A to Z.* CDC online at: http://www.cdc.gov/nchs/fastats/ overwt.htm

CDC—Centers for Disease Control. (2008, Sep. 28). Diabetes and Me: Prevent Diabetes. http://www.cdc.gov/diabetes/consumer/prevent.htm

CDC – Centers for Disease Control. (2008, Nov.) *Physical activity and the health of young people.* http://www.cdc.gov/healthyyouth/physicalactivity/pdf/facts.pdf

CDC – Centers for Disease Control. (2008, Dec. 17*). How much physical activity do older adults need?* http://www.cdc.gov/physicalactivity/everyone/guidelines/   olderadults.html#Aerobic

CDC – Centers for Disease Control. (2009, May 4). *Number of U. S. adults reporting a disability is increasing.* CDC Website. http://www.cdc.gov/Features/DisabilityCauses/

CDC – Centers for Disease Control. (2010, Jan. 4). Environmental and Policy Strategies. http://www.cdc.gov/leanworks/build/environmental.html

CDC – Centers for Disease Control. (2010, Feb. 22). *Physical activity and health: A report from the Surgeon General.* CDC Center for Chronic Disease Prevention and Health Promotion. http://www.cdc.gov/ NCCDPHP/sgr/ataglan.htm

CDC – Centers for Disease Control. (2010, May 10). How much physical activity do older adults need? Physical activity is essential to healthy aging. http://www.cdc.gov/physicalactivity/everyone/guidelines/olderadults.html

CDC – Centers for Disease Control. (2010, June 21). CDC's LEAN Works! - A workplace obesity Prevention Program. http://www.cdc.gov/leanworks/

Center for Mindful Eating. (2009). *Principles of mindful eating.* Online at: http://www.tcme.org/about.htm

Chen, C.H.; Jeng, M.C.; Fung, C.P.; Doong, J.L.; & Chuang, T.Y. (2009). Psychological benefits of virtual reality for patients in rehabilitation therapy. *Journal of Sport Rehabilitation*,18(2), 258-68.

CIA. (2008, August 7). Central Intelligence Agency. *The world fact book: United Sates.* Online at: https://www.cia.gov/library/publications/the-world-factbook/geos/us.html

Cicero, Marcus Tullius. (2006). *On a life well spent.* Delray Beach, FLA: Levenger Press.

Clark, Etta. (1986). *Growing old is not for sissies II: Portraits of senior athletes.* . New York: Pomegranate Communications.

Clark, Etta. (1995). *Growing old is not for sissies: Portraits of senior athletes.* New   York: Pomegranate Communications.

Clark, Etta. (1998). My grandfather can swim laps around you! Portraits of senior athletes. *Natural Health,* Jan-Feb. http://findarticles.com/p/articles/mi_m0NAH/   is_n1_v27/ai_20152684

Cleveland.com. (2008, Oct. 27). Cleveland clinic gives employees free gym membership. City of Cleveland website. http://blog.cleveland.com/medical/ 2008/10/in_final_phase_of_wellness_eff.html

Conradt, Matthia; Dierk, Jan-Michael; Schlumberger, Pia; Rauh, Elisabeth; Hebebran, Johannes; Rief, Winfried. (2008). Who copes well? Obesity-related coping and its association with shame, guilt, and weight loss. *Journal of Clinical Psychology,* (64)1129-1144.

Cooper, Kenneth H. (1998). *Regaining the power of youth at any age.* Nashville: Thomas Nelson Publishers.

Costello, Diana. (2008, Dec. 3). Free gym membership entices students to hit the books. *The Hall Monitor.* LoHud.com internet blog. http://hallmonitor.lohudblogs.com/2008/12/03/ \free-gym-membership-entices-students-to-hit-the-books/

Crisp, Simon. (2006, Aug.). Taking a risk for adolescents: Wilderness adventure therapy. *Australian Psychological Society website. InPsych Bulletin.* Online at: http://www.psychology.org.au/publications/inpsych/wilderness_therapy/)

Crocker, Richard. (2007). *The boomer century: 1946-2046. How America's most influential generation changed everything.* New York: Springboard Press.

Culos-Reed, S. Nicole; Stephenson, Lynette; Doyle-Baker, Patricia K, and Dickinson, James A. (2008). Mall walking as a physical activity option: Results of a pilot project. *Canadian Journal on Aging,* 27(1), 81-87.

Davison, K. K.; Werder, J. L., & Lawson, C. T. (2008). Children's active commuting to school: current knowledge and future directions. *Prevention of Chronic Disease,* 5(3); A100. Epub June 15.

Dawson, George. (2001). *Life is so good.* New York: Penguin Putnam.

DeCurtis, Anthony. (2006). You say it's my birthday? *AARP Magazine,* May & June.
Online archives. http://www.aarpmagazine.org/entertainment/my_birthday.html

DeGroot, Gerald. (2008). *The sixties unplugged: A kaleidoscopic history of a disorderly decade.* Cambridge, Mass.: Harvard University Press.

De Laine, Michael. (2009, Feb. 9). New cells for old in Parkinson's trials. *Times Higher Education.* Online at: http://www.timeshighereducation.co.uk/ story.asp?storyCode=1513 59&sectioncode=26

Dennis, Hughes. (2003). Interview with Jack LaLanne: Legendary fitness expert, health pioneer, diet and nutrition innovator. *Share guide: The holistic health magazine and resource directory.* Online at http://www.shareguide.com/LaLanne.html

Department of Transport. (2009). The environmental impacts of road vehicles in use. Online at: http://www.dft.gov.uk/ pgr/roads/environment/cvtf theenvironmentalimpactsofro a3793?page=2). (Data is for the United Kingdom, which is presumed to be similar to the United States, for which data was not found.)

Digitaldeli.com. (2010). The Digital Deli Online. http://www. digitaldeliftp.com/ DigitalDeliToo/dd2jb-Mystery-In-The-Air-1945.html

Dillon, Kathleen M.; and Totten, M.C. (1989). Psychological factors, immunocompetence, and health of breast-feeding mothers and their infants. *Journal of Genetic Psychology,* 150(2), 155-62.

Dillon, Kathleen M.; Minchoff, Brian; Baker, Katherine H. (1985-1986). Positive emotional states and enhancement of the immune system. *International Journal of Psychiatry in Medicine,* 15(1), 13-18.

Doug Ross @ Journal. (2006, Jan. 15). Jack LaLanne Quotes. Internet Blog. Online at: http://directorblue.blogspot. com/2006/01/jack-lalanne-quotes-fitness-godfather.html

Dunning, David, Heath, Chip, and Suls, Jerry M. (2004). Flawed self-assessment: Implications for health, education, and the workplace. *Psychological Science in the Public Interest,* 5(3), 69-106.

Durant, Will. (1935). *The story of civilization Vol. 1: Our oriental heritage.* New York, MJF Books.

Ebookmall.com. (2010). Life is so good summary. http://ebooks. ebookmall.   com/title/life-is-so-good-dawson-glaubman-ebooks.htm

Egger, Garry. (2008). Shame on you, generation excess. (Sep. 6). *Sydney Morning online.* http://www.smh.com.au/ news/national/shame-on-you-generation-excess/2008/ 09/05/1220121526791.html

Farzanaki, P.; Azarbayjani, M. A.; Rasaee, M.J.; Jourkesh, M.; Ostojic, S. M. & Stannard, S. (2008, Oct.). Salivary immunoglobulin A and cortisol response to training in young elite female gymnasts. *Brazilian Journal of Biomotricity,* (2)4, 252-58.

Fillmore, Charles. (1998). *Talks on truth.* Unity Village, MO: Unity Books.

FitCommerce.com. (2002). Jack LaLanne chosen as IHRSA's "Person of the Year," http://www.fitcommerce.com/ Blueprint/Jack-LaLanne-Chosen-as-IHRSA-Person-of-the-Year_page.aspx?pageId=276&announcementId= 387&tabId=87&tabIndex =0&portalId=2&cid=112

Fitness.gov. (2010, Mar. 7). HealthierUS and steps to a HealthierUS. The President's Council on Physical Fitness. http://www.fitness.gov/about_overview.htm

Fontaine, Kevin R.; Redden, David T.; Wang, Chenxi; Westfall, Andrew O.; & Allison, David B. (2003). Years of life lost due to obesity. *JAMA,* 289,187-193.

40plussports.com. (2010). Sports competition for adults over 40. http://www.40plussports.com/index.php

Fox, Michael J. (2002). *Lucky man.* New York: Hyperion.

Fox, Michael J. (2009). *Always looking up: The adventures of an incurable optimist.* New York: Hyperion.

Frankl, Viktor E. (1973). *Man's search for meaning.* New York: Pocket Books.

Franz, C.E. (1994). Does thought content change as individuals age? A longitudinal study of midlife adults. In T. F. Heatherton J. L. Weinberger (Eds.), *Can personality change?* 1993, Cambridge, MA: Harvard University Press.

Freud, Sigmund. (1961). *Civilization and its discontents.* Translated and Edited by James Strachey. New York: W. W. Norton.

Friedan, B. (1993). *The fountain of age.* New York: Simon & Schuster.

Frotzier, A.; Coupaud, S.; Perret, C.; Kakebeeke, T.H., Hunt, K.J.; & Eser, P. (2009). Effect of detraining on bone and muscle tissue in subjects with chronic spinal cord injury after a period of electrically-stimulated cycling. *Journal of Rehabilitative Medicine,* 41(4), 282-285.

Fuhrman, Joel. (2003). *Eat to live: The revolutionary formula for fast and sustained weight loss.* New York: Little, Brown and Company.

Galbavy, Renee. (2004). *Influences on the effectiveness of mentoring at-risk youth.* Dissertation Abstracts International: Section B: The Sciences and Engineering. 65(4-B), 2125.

Galbraith, John Kenneth. (1969). *The affluent society, second edition.* New York: New American Library

Galson, Steven K. (2007, Nov. 5). Encouraging exercise as a prescription. Luncheon address for exercise is medicine conference. U. S. Department of Health and Human Services website. http://www.surgeongeneral.gov/news/speeches/11052007.html

Giaquinto, S. and Valentini, F. (2009). Is there a scientific basis for pet therapy? *Disabil Rehabil.*, 31(7), PP. 595-8.

Gillick, Muriel. (2006). *The denial of aging: Perpetual youth, eternal life, and other dangerous fantasies.* Cambridge, Ma.: Harvard University Press.

Glasser, William. (1985). *Positive addiction.* New York: Harper.

Goldman, Ronald and Juliette. (1982). *Children's sexual thinking: A comparative study of children aged 5 to 15 years in Australia, North America, Britain and Sweden.* London: Routledge & Kegan Paul.

Goodman, Susan. (1988). Step by step to a better life. *GMAC Quest Magazine,* April, p. 13.

Goodreads.com. (2009). Picasso: Painting against time. Book review. Goodreads online. http://www.goodreads.com/book/show/977482.Picasso_ Painting_Against _Time

Gould, Elizabeth; Reeves, Alison, J.; Graziano, Michael S.A.; & Gross, Charles G. (1999). Neurogenesis in the neocortex of adult primates. *Science,* 286(5439), 548-552.

Gutmann, David. (1987). *Reclaimed powers: Toward a new psychology of men and women in later life.* New York: Basic Books.

Haaz, Stephany (2009). Yoga for people with arthritis. *The Johns Hopkins Arthritis Center* website. http://www.hopkins-arthritis.org/ patient-corner/disease-management/yoga.html#benefits

Hacker, E. (2009). Exercise and quality of life: Strengthening the connections. *Clin.J.Oncol.Nurs;* 13(1), 31-9.

Haddock, Doris; & Burke, Doris. (2003). *Granny D: A memoir.* New York: Villard Books.

Ham, S. A., and Epping, J. (2006). Dog walking and physical activity in the United States. *Prev. Chronic Dis.* 3(2), A47.

Hanna, Thomas. (1988). *Somatics: Reawakening the mind's control of movement, flexibility, and health.* Reading, MA: Addison-Wesley Publishing Company.

Hanc, John. (2008, Aug. 7). Going strong: Older adults swell the ranks of endurance athletes. *AARP Bulletin Today.* Online at: http://bulletin.aarp.org/yourworld/ reinventing/ articles/ going_strong__older.html

Hanus, Steven H.; Homer, Terri D.; & Harter, Donald H. (1977). Vertebral artery occlusion complicating yoga exercises. *Arch Neurol,* 34(9), 574-575.

Harding, Anne. (2009). Boomeritis hits aging athletes. *Reuters Medical online.* http://www.reuters.com/article/healthNews/ idUSTRE56103J20090702

Harvard Medical School. (2009). Calories burned in 30 minutes for people of three different weights. *Harvard heart letter.* (Harvard Health Publications.) Online at: http://www. health.harvard.edu/newsweek/Calories-burned-in-30-minutes-of-leisure-and-routine-activities.htm)

Hawking, Stephen. (2008). *Stephen Hawking's official website. Online* at: http://www.hawking.org.uk/home/hindex.html

Hay, Louise L. (1999). *You can heal your life.* Carlsbad, CA: Hay House, Inc.

Hellmich, Nanci. (2008, Apr. 21). Mother of 5 takes time for her own fitness. *USA Today* Online. http://www.usatoday.com/news/health/weightloss/2008-04-20-weight-loss-reuter_N.htm

Hellmich, Nanci. (2008, Sept 21). He woke up to a big problem and shed 100 pounds. *USA Today* online. http: http://www.usatoday.com/news/health/weightloss/2008-05-04-dieter-eilering_N.htm

The Hindu: Online edition of India's National Newspaper. (July 8, 2006). G. Venkataswamy passes away. Staff writer. http://www.thehindu.com/2006/07/08/stories/   2006070806771200.htm

Hobbs, Frank B. & Damon, Bonnie L. (1996). *65+ In the United States. U.S. Bureau of the Census. In Current population reports, special studies*, P23-190. Washington, D.C.: U. S. Government Printing Office.

Holden, Stephen. (2008*). Retired, yes, but never too old to rock. New York Times*, (October 14). http://movies.nytimes.com/2008/04/09/movies/09youn.html

Horber, Kohler, Lippuner, & Jaeger, (1996). Effect of regular physical training on age-associated alteration of body composition in men. *Eur. J. Clin Invest*, 26(4), 279-85.

Howell, Cynthia Lake. (2004). *Resilience in adult women students in higher education: Implications for academic achievement and persistence*. Dissertation Abstracts International Section A: Humanities and Social Sciences. 65(1-A), 86.

Independent Sector. (2000). *America's senior volunteers. A national leadership forum to encourage philanthropy, volunteering, and not-for-profit initiative and citizen action.* Washington, DC.

Institute of Medicine. (2004). *Insuring America's health: Principles and recommendations.* Synopsis obtained online at: http://www.iom.edu/Reports/2004/ Insuring-Americas-Health-Principles-and-Recommendations.aspx

Jack LaLanne Show. (2010). Jack Lalanne Show Week1 Monday Part1. Accessed from YouTube Mar. 24, 10. http://www.youtube.com/watch?v=4WsMcfxCw2g

Jakicic, John M. & Otto, Amy D. (2005). Physical activity considerations for the treatment and prevention of obesity *American Journal of Clinical Nutrition,* 82,1, 226S-229S.

James, William. (1994). *The varieties of religious experience.* New York: New Library (Random House).

Johns Hopkins. (2009). *Medicine health alerts–Yoga therapy.* Onlineat:http://www.johnshopkinshealthalerts.com/alerts/back_pain_osteoporosis/JohnsHopkinsHealthAlertsBack PainOsteoporosis_2942-1.html

Johnson, L. G.; Collier, K. E.; Edwards, D. J.; Phillippe, D.L.; Eastwood, P.R.; Walters, S.E.; Thickbroom, G.W.; & Mastaglia, F.L. (2009).Improvements in aerobic capacity after an exercise program in sporadic inclusion body myositis. *Journal of Clinical Neuromuscular Disorders,* 10(4), 178-84.

Jones, G; Bennell, K; & Cicuttini, F. M. (2003). Effect of physical activity on cartilage development in healthy kids. *British Journal Of Sports Medicine,* 37, 382-3

Jourard, Sidney M., & Landsman, Ted. (1980). *Healthy personality, 4th edition: An approach from the viewpoint of humanistic psychology.* New York: Macmillan.

Justice, Blair. (1998). *A different kind of health: Finding well-being despite illness.* Houston: Peak Press.

Karmel, M. (2007). The boomers are coming! Prepare their care. *Eye Net Magazine,* May. American Academy of Ophthalmology, http://www.aao.org/ publications/ eyenet/200705

Karmer, Ari. 2002, (Aug. 2). Free gym memberships keep employees healthy, happy. *Puget Sound Business Journal (Seattle).* Online at: http://www.bizjournals.com/ seattle/ stories/2002/08/05/focus9.html

Karlinsky, Neal; and Harper, Eloise. (2009, May 26). The iron-nun: Sister Madonna Buder balances her love for faith and fitness. ABC World News. http://abcnews.go.com/WN/ story?id=7671970&page=1

Keisernetwork.com. (2007, Jan.). Health care spending in the United States and OECD countries. http://www.kff.org/ insurance/snapshot/chcm010307oth.cfm

Kessler, David. (2009). *The end of overeating: Taking control of the insatiable American appetite.* New York: Rodale.

King, Abby C.; Blair, Steven N.; Bild, Diane E.; Dishman, Rod K.; Dubbert, Patricia M.; Marcus, Bess H.; Oldridge, Neil B.; Paffenbarger, Ralph S. Jr.; Powell, Kenneth E.; Yeager, Kim K. (1992). Determinants of physical activity and interventions in adults. *Medicine & Science in Sports & Exercise, 24*(6), 221-236.

Kung, Hsiang-Ching; Hoyert, Donna L.; Xu, Jiaquan Xu; Murphy, Sherry L. (2008). Deaths: Final data 2005. National Vital StatisticsReports, 56(10), April 24. http://www.cdc.gov/ nchs/data/nvsr/nvsr56/nvsr56_10.pdf

Labott, S. M., Ahleman, S,, Wolever, M. E., & Martin, R. B. (1990). The physiological and psychological effects of the expression and inhibition of emotion. *Behavioral Medicine,* 16, 182-189.

Labott, S. M., & Martin, R. B. (1990). Emotional coping, age, and physical disorder. *Behavioral Medicine,* 16, 53-61.

Lakdawalla, Darius, Goldman, Dana, and Bhattacharya, Jayanta. (2001, April). Are the young becoming more disabled? RAND Corporation abstract. *Social Science Research Network.* Online at: http://papers.ssrn.com/sol3/papers.cfm?abstract_ id=267434

LaLanne, Jack. (2005). *Celebrating 90 plus years of healthy living.* Fairfield, NJ: Tristar Products, Inc.

LaLanne, Jack. (2010, Mar 8). Jack Lalanne Show Week1 Monday Part1. Video clip from YouTube. http://www.youtube.com/ watch?v= 4WsMcfxCw2g&feature=player_embedded#

Lappe, Frances. (1985). *Diet for a Small Planet: Twentieth Anniversary Edition.* New York: Ballantine.

Lasch, Christopher. (1979). *The culture of narcissism.* New York: Warner Books.

Laughter Yoga International. (2010). Laugh yourself young again. *The official website of Dr. Kataria.* http://www.laughteryoga.org/ index.php?option=com_ content&view=article&id=673:laugh-yourself-young-again-&catid=229:articles-for-publishing& Itemid=472 Alzheimer's Information at: http://www. laughteryoga.org/ index.php? option=com_content&view= article&id=213:laughter-yoga-and-alzheimers&catid= 97:alzheimers-and-senile-dementia&Itemid=288

Li, J.Y.; Englund, E; Holton, J.L.; Soulet, D; Hagell P, Lees AJ, Lashley T, Quinn NP, Rehncrona S, Björklund A, Widner H, Revesz T, Lindvall O, Brundin P. (2009). Lewy bodies in grafted neurons in subjects with Parkinson's disease suggest host-to-graft disease propagation. *Nature Medicine.* 14(5), 483-5.

LifePower. (2010). Internet fitness blog by Nigel Brown. http:// blog. lifeplanningmatters.com/my_weblog/2009/08/never-too-old-to-compete.html

Lipschitz, David. (2002). *Breaking the rules of aging.* Washington, D.C.: Lifeline Press.

Lunde, Angela. (2008). Preventing Alzheimer's: Exercise Still Best Bet. Online at: http://www.mayoclinic.com/health/alzheimers/MY00002

Madrid, Dina Rebeca. (2000). *Sense of humor, pessimistic explanatory style and immune system response in healthy, non-depressed older adults.* Doctoral Dissertation obtained from Dissertation Abstracts International: Section B: The Sciences and Engineering. 61(6-B), 2974.

MailOnline.com. (2008). Walking the dog beats loneliness and depression, research reveals. Nov. 8. Online at http://www.dailymail.co.uk/news/article-415305/Walking-dog-beats-loneliness-depression-research-reveals.html

Mandino, Og. (1968). *The greatest salesman in the world.* Hollywood, Fl.: Frederick Fell Publishers, Inc. (Bantam Books).

Masoro, Edward J., and Austad, Steven N., Eds. (2001). *Handbook of the Biology of Aging.* Academic Press: San Diego, CA.

Masters Weightlifting Results. (2007). 2007 National Masters Weightlifting Championships. www.mastersweightlifting.org/results/2007nm/Men.pdf

Matarazzo, J.D. (1980). Behavioral healthy and behavioral medicine: Frontiers for a new health psychology. *American Psychologist,* 35, 807-17.

McDougall, John. (1991). *The McDougall Program: 12 days to dynamic health.* New York: Plume Books (Penguin).

McGinnis, Judith K. (2005, February 25). Man touched many in city during life. *Wichita Falls Times Record News.* Pages 10-11A.

McInnis, K. J. (2000). Exercise and obesity. *Coronary Artery Disease,* 11(2),111-6.

McManus, Steve. (2003). Raising the bar: At 88, fitness guru Jack LaLanne can run circles around those half his age. San Francisco Chronicle, Jan. 19. SFGate.com online at: http://articles.sfgate.com/2003-01-19/living/17474209_1_jack-lalanne-show-golden-gate-bridge-jenny-craig

MedlinePlus. (2008). Medical Encyclopedia: Depression – Elderly. Online at http://www.nlm.nih.gov/medlineplus/ency/article/001521.htm

Melville, Kate. (2004, March 10). Poor diet, physical inactivity set to overtake tobacco in death stakes. *Science a Go* online at: http://www.scienceagogo.com/ news/20040209171802data_trunc_sys.shtml

Miller, T.Q., Smith, T.W., Turner, C.W., Guijarro, M.L., and Hallet, A.J. (1996). A meta-analytic review of research on hostility and physical health. *Psychological Bulletin,* 119(2), 322-48.

Mokdad, A.H., Marks, J.S., Stroup, D.F, & Gerberding, J.L. (2004). Actual causes of death in the United States, 2000. *JAMA,* 291(10), 1238-45.

Montagu, Ashley. (1999). *The natural superiority of* women, 5th ed. Lanham, MD: AltaMira Press.

Moschis, George P. & Mathur, Anil. (2007). *Baby boomers and their parents: Surprising findings about their lifestyles, mindsets, and well-being.* Ithaca, NY: Paramount Market Publishing.

Motooka, M., Koike, H., Yokoyam, T., and Kennedy, N.L. (2006). Effect of dog-walking on autonomic nervous activity in senior citizens. *Med. J. Aust,* 184(2), pp. 60-63.

Moynihan, Ray; Heath, Iona; & Henry, David. (2002). Selling sickness: The pharmaceutical industry and disease mongering. *British Medical Journal,* 324, 886-891.

National Council on Aging. (2002). *American's perceptions of Aging in the 21st Century: The NCOA's continuing study of the myths and realities of aging.* Washington, DC: National Council on Aging.

National Council on Aging. (2008). Senior fitness program shown to reduce healthcare costs. NCOA Website, https://secure.my-websites.org/supporter/ casematerial. do?n=gg@5C&cmdbid=1051169&or=ld

National Guidelines Clearinghouse. (2009, June 20). Physical activity and public health in older adults: recommendation from the American College of Sports Medicine and the American Heart Association. Obtained online at: http://www.guidelines.gov/ summary/summary.aspx?ss=15&doc_id=11691&nbr=6038

National Institute on Aging. (2006). *Fitness over fifty: An exercise guide from the national institute on aging.* New York: Healthy Living Books.

National Institute on Aging. (2007). *The health and retirement study: Growing old in America.* Bethesda, MD: NIA (U.S. Dept. of Health and Human Services). NIH Publication No. 07-1752.

National Institute of Medicine. (2010). About the IOM. Accessed Mar. 14. http://www.iom.edu/About-IOM.aspx

Nationmaster.com, 2008. *Health statistics: Obesity by country.* http://www.nationmaster.com/graph/hea_hea-obe-health-obesity.

Neikirk, William. (2006, July 6). Ageless quotes for aging presidents. The Swamp: Tribune's Washington Bureau. http://www.swamppolitics.com/news/politics/ blog/2006/07/ageless_quotes_for_aging_presi.html

New York Times. (2007, Aug. 12). World's best medical care? Editorial. http://www.nytimes.com/2007/08/12/opinion/12sun1.html

Nguyen, Anna. (2008, Jan. 3). Older women walking for exercise ease anxiety, stress and depression. Senior Journal.com. http://seniorjournal.com/NEWS/Fitness/2008/8-01-03-OlderWomen.htm

NHTSA. (2008). National Health and Traffic Safety Administration, a division of the U.S. Department of Transportation keeps these statistics, available from their website: http://www-fars.nhtsa.dot.gov/Main/index.aspx

Novotney, Amy. (2009). Dangerous distraction. *Monitor on Psychology,* Feb, 40(7), 32-36.

OECD—Organization for Economic Cooperation and Development. (2009). *OECD health data 2009: How does the United States compare?* http://www.oecd.org/dataoecd/46/2/38980580.pdf

Ogden, Jane. (2004). *Health psychology: A textbook, third edition.* Berkshire, England: Open University Press/McGraw-Hill Education.

Ogden, Cynthia L, Caroll, Margaret D., McDowell, Margaret A., Flegal, Katherine M. (2007, Nov.). Obesity among adults in the United States—No statistically significant change since 2003-2004. U.S. Department of Health and Human Services. http://www. cdc.gov/nchs/data/databriefs/db01.pdf

Ohio Department of Aging. (2008) Ohio State University Extension, Senior Series website. Online at http://ohioline. osu.edu/ss-fact/0101.html

Oldtime.com (2010, Feb. 27). Doctors recommend smoking camels. http://www.old-time.com/commercials/1940's/ More%20Doctors%20Smoke%20Camels.html

Olshansky, Jay; Passaro, Douglas; Hershow, Ronald; Layden, Jennifer; Carnes, Bruce; Brody, Jacob; Hayflick, Leonard; Butler, Robert; Allison, David; and Ludwig, David. (2005). A Potential Decline in Life Expectancy in the United States in the 21st Century. *New England Journal of Medicine.* 352,1138-1145.

Ornish, Dean. (2009, Feb. 26). Integrative care: A pathway to a healthier nation. Testimony of Dean Ornish, M.D. Senate Health Reform Testimony. Senate Committee on Health, Education, Labor and Pensions. Senate Dirksen Building, Washington, D.C.

Ornish, Dean. (2001). *Eat more, weight less: Dr. Dean Ornish's life choice program for losing weight safely while eating abundantly, revised and updated.* New York: HarperCollins.

Ornish, Dean. (1990). *Dr. Dean Ornish's program for reversing heart disease.* New York: Ivy Books (Random House division).

Overeaters Anonymous. (2001). *Overeaters Anonymous, second edition.* Rio Rancho, New Mexico: Overeaters Anonymous, Inc.

Pace, Gina. (2006, Mar. 1).   Obesity bigger threat than terrorism? CBS News online at http://www.cbsnews.com/stories/2006/03/01/health/main1361849.shtml

Pari Roller website. (2009). Online at: http://www.pari-roller.com/index.php?p=101)

Pennington, Bill (2006, April 16). Baby boomers stay active, and so do their doctors. *The New York Times* online.http://www.nytimes.com/2006/04/16/sports/ 16boomers.html

Plante, Thomas G.; Rodin, Judith. (1990). Physical fitness and enhanced psychological health. *Current Psychology: Research & Reviews,* 9(1), 3-24.

Poras, Marlo. (2007). *Run granny run.* DVD recording. Marlo Poras Productions/Arts Alliance America.

Potter, David. (1954). *People of plenty: Economic abundance and the American character.* Chicago: University of Chicago Press.

Preece, Gordon. (2008). 'When I run I feel God's pleasure.': Towards a Protestant play ethic.   Chapter Two in *Sport & spirituality.* Preece, Gordon, and Hess, Rob, Eds. Adelaide, South Australia: ATF Press. Reprint of *Interface: A forum for theology in the world,* Vol. 11, No. 1.

Preece, Gordon; and Hess, Rob. (2008?) *Sport & spirituality.* Adelaide, South Australia: ATF Press. Reprint of *Interface: A forum for theology in the world,* Vol. 11, No. 1. [The book contains no date of publication; Amazon.com indicates 2006, but intext references exist for Autumn 2007, so I estimate a publication date of 2008.]

Prochaska, James O.; DiClemente, Carlo C. (1983). Stages and processes of self-change of smoking: Toward an integrative model of change. *Journal of Consulting and Clinical Psychology,* 51(3), 390-395.

Publishers Weekly. (1999). Review of *John Glenn: A Memoir.* Cited on Amazon.com at http://www.amazon.com/John-Glenn-Memoir/dp/0553110748/ref=sr_11_ 1?ie=UTF8&qid=1215 626106&sr=11-1

Quotationspage.com. (2007). The Quotations Page. http://www.quotationspage.com/quote/2704.html.

QuoteDB. (2005). Online at http://www.quotedb.com/quotes/1971.

Quotegarden.com. (2007, Oct. 14). Quotations about Exercise. http://www.quotegarden.com/exercise.html

RAND Corporation. (2008, June). U.S. still leads the world in science and technology; Nation benefits from foreign scientists, engineers. http://www.rand.org/ news/press/ 2008/06/12

Ray's Boathouse. (2009). Ray's boathouse 11th annual fitness challenge winners announced! Press release, June 16, 2009.

Reich, C. (1970). *The greening of America: The revolution of the new generation.* New York: Bantam.

Rice, Phillip L. (1992). *Stress & health, second edition.* Pacific Grove, Ca: Brooks/Cole.

Roget's Thesaurus. (1977). New York: Harper & Row.

Rollingstone.com. (2008). The Rolling Stones: Biography. *Rolling Stone Magazine* Online at http://www.rollingstone. com/artists/therollingstones/biography

Roosevelt, Eleanor. (1960). *You learn by living.* Westminster: John Knox Press.

Ross, Philip D; Norimatsu; Hiromichi, Davis, James; Yano, Katsuhiko; Wasnich, Richard D; Fujiwara, Saeko; Hosoda,

Yutaka; and Melton, L. Joseph III. (1991). A comparison of hip fracture incidence among native Japanese, Japanese Americans, and American Caucasians. *Am J Epidemiol,* 133, 801-9.

Ross, A; Thomas S. (2010). The health benefits of yoga and exercise: a review of comparison studies. *Journal of Alternative and Complementary Medicine,*16(1),3-12

Rowe, John W., & Kahn, Robert L. (1998). *Successful aging: The MacArthur Foundation study. New* York: Dell Trade Paperbacks.

Rowland, Clara May. (1956). How to be young—Spiritually, mentally, physically. In *The Unity Treasure Chest,* pp. 212-215. Fillmore, Lowell, Ed. Lee's Summit, MO: Unity School of Christianity.

Ruiz, Rebecca. (2008) America's most sedentary cities. Forbes.com. http://www.forbes.com/2007/10/28/health-sedentary-cities-forbeslife-cx_rr_1029health_print.html

Salovey, Peter; Rothman, Alexander, J.; Detweiler, Jerusha B.; & Steward, Wayne T. (2000). Emotional states and physical health. *American Psychologist.* 55(11), 110-121.

Scandigital.com. (2009, Sept 24). What's your story, Jack LaLanne? (Happy 95th Bday too!). http://www.scandigital.com/blog/scandigital/ what%E2%80%99s-your-story-jack-lalanne-happy-95th-bday-too/

Schaefer, Henry F. (2001). *Stephen Hawking, the big bang, and god.* Lecture Notes http://www.leaderu.com/offices/schaefer/docs/bigbang.html

Schwarzenegger, Arnold. (1977). *Pumping iron: The 25th anniversary edition.* DVD. Home Box Office 2003 release.

Schultz, Steven. (1999). Scientists discover addition of new brain cells in highest brain area. New from Princeton University, Online at: http://www.princeton.edu/pr/ news/99/ q4/1014-brain.htm

Scott, A.O. (2002, Nov. 28). For the scariest monsters, a little glimpse'll do ya. review of Wes Craven presents: They. *New York Times* Online. http://www.nytimes. com/2002/ 11/28/ movies/film-review-for-the-scariest-monsters-a-little-glimpse-ll-do-ya.html?pagewanted=print

SeniorJournal.com. (2003, Feb. 3). President calls for more senior volunteers in 2004 budget. Washington, D.C. http:// seniorjournal.com/Volunteers.htm

Seniorjournal.com. (2004, Mar. 10). Study shows poor diet, inactivity close to becoming leading preventable cause of death: HHS launches new strategies against overweight epidemic. http://seniorjournal.com/NEWS/Health/4-03-10causesofdeath.htm

SeniorJournal.com. (2007, May 30). Growing frail with aging can be avoided with aerobic exercise. http://seniorjournal. com/NEWS/Fitness/2007/7-05-30-GrowingFrail.htm

SeniorJournal.com. (2007, Aug. 6). Senior citizens get advice on exercise from heart association, sports docs. Online at http://seniorjournal.com/NEWS/Fitness/2007/ 7-08-06-SenCitGetAdvice.htm

Shakespeare, W. (1997). *As you like it.* Act II, Scene 7. New York: Washington Square Press.

Sheehan, George. (1975). *Dr. Sheehan on running.* New York: Bantam Books.

Shephard, R. J., and Shek, P. N. (1994). Potential impact of physical activity and sport on the immune system—a brief review. *British Journal of Sports Medicine,* 28:4, 247-55.

Shephard, Roy J., and Shek, Pang N. (1996). Chapter 6: Exercise training and immune function, pp. 93-120. In *Exercise and Immune Function,* Ed. Laurie Hoffman-Goetz. Boca Raton, Florida: CRC Press.

Shephard, Roy J. (2008, April 10). Maximal Oxygen Intake and Independence in Old Age. *British Journal of Sports Medicine,* Online http://bjsm.bmj.com/cgi/content/ abstract/bjsm.2 007.044800v1?maxtoshow=&HITS=10&hits=10&RESULTFO RMAT=&author1=shepherd&fulltext=independence+in+old +age&andorexactfulltext=and&searchid=1&FIRSTINDEX=0 &sortspec=relevance&resourcetype=HWCIT

Shouler, Kenneth. (2002). Review of *Aging well: Surprising guideposts to a happier life from the landmark Harvard Study of Adult Development.* http://www.bookpage.com/ books-9543-Aging+Well: +Surprising+Guideposts+to+a+H

Shouler, Kenneth. (2002). If I'd known I'd live this long, I'd have taken better care of myself. Book Review of Aging Well. Online at: http://www.bookpage.com/0201bp/ george_ vaillant.html

Siegel, Bernie. (1986). *Love, medicine, and miracles.* New York: Harper & Row (Perennial Library).

Sigal, R.J., Kenny, G.P., Boule, N.G., Wells, G.A., Prud'homme, D., Fortier, M., Reid, R.D., Tulloch, H., Coyle, D., Phillips, P., Jennings, A., & Jaffey, J. (2007). Effects of aerobic training, resistance training, or both on control of blood sugar in type 2 diabetes. *Annals of Internal Medicine,* 147:6, 1-16.) From the Abstract online at: http://www.annals.org/cgi/content/ summary/147/6/357

Silvalifesteps. (2008). Website online at http://www.silvaslifesteps. com/about.html

Silversneakers. (2009). Healthways Silversneakers fitness program. Online: http://www.silversneakers.com/ Default.aspx?section=About&subsection=AboutMain), or =SuccessStories

Spirit. (2008, Summer). *Acacia products catalog.*

Squires, Sally. (2007). A fitness icon keeps his juices flowing. *The Washington Post,* June 12. http://www.washingtonpost.com/wp-dyn/content/ article/2007/06/11/AR2007061101919.html

Stein, Rob. (2007, April 20). Baby boomers appear to be less healthy than parents. *Washingtonpost.com* online. http:// washingtonpost.com/wp-dyn/content/article/2007/ 04/19/AR2007041902458_pf.html

Stengel, Casey; Berkow, Ira; and Kaplan, Jim. (1992). *The gospel according to Casey: Casey Stengel's inimitable, instructional, historical baseball book.* New York: St. Martin's Press.

Summerbell, C. D., Cameron, C., & Glasziou, P. P. (2008. Withdrawn: Advice on low-fat diets for obesity. *Cochrane Database Syst Rev.* 16;(3):CD003640. Abstract online at: http:// www.ncbi.nlm.nih.gov/pubmed/18646093?ordinalpos=4&it ool= EntrezSystem2.PEntrez.Pubmed.Pubmed_ResultsPanel. Pubmed_DefaultReportPanel.Pubmed_RVDocSum

Tedeschi, Richard G. & Calhoun, Lawrence. (2001). Posttraumatic growth: A new perspective on psychotraumatology. *Psychiatric Times,* 21(4). Obtained online at: http://www. psychiatrictimes.com/display/article/10168/54661

Thinkexist.com. (2010). Online compilation of quotations. Accessed March 1, 2010. http://thinkexist.com/quotation/

to_me-old_age_is_always_fifteen_years_older_ than/199956. html

Thorpe, R.J. Jr, Kreisle, R.A., Glickman, L.T., Simonsick, E.M., Newman, A.B., and Kritchevsky, S. (2006). Physical activity and pet ownership in year 3 of the Health ABC study. *J Aging Phys Act*, 14(2), 154-68.

Time. (1948). The press: Highly irregular, Jun. 21. http://www. time.com/time/ magazine/article/0,9171,798803,00.html

Trechsel, Jane. (1998). *A morning cup of yoga*. Crane Hill Publishers.

Tully, M.A.; Cupples, M.E.; Hart, N.D.; McEneny, J.; McGlade, K.J.; Chan, W.S.; and Young, I.S. (2006). Randomized controlled trial of home-based walking programmes at and below current recommended levels of exercise in sedentary adults. *Journal of Epidemiology and Community Health*, 61(9), 778-83.

Tuttle, David. (2006, August). "'Godfather of Fitness' Still Going Strong at 91." *Life Extension Magazine* . Online: http://www. lef.org/magazine/mag2006/ aug2006_report_lalanne_01. htm

United Nations Development Programme. (2008) *Human development report, 2007/2008.* http://hdrstats.undp.org/ countries/country_fact_sheets/cty_fs_USA.html)

U.S. Census Bureau. (1999). *Table 1. Nativity of the Population and Place of Birth of the Native Population: 1850 to 1990.* http://www. census.gov/population/www/ documentation/twps0029/ tab01.html

U. S. Censure Bureau. (2004, Mar. 18). *U.S. interim projections by age, sex, race, and Hispanic origin.* Online at: http://www. census.gov/ipc/www/usinterimproj/

U. S. Censure Bureau. (2005, April 21). *U.S. population projections. Table 5: Interim projections: Population under age 18 and 65 and older: 2000, 2010, and 2030.* Online at: http://www.census. gov/population/www/projections/projectionsagesex.html

U. S. Census Bureau. (2008a). Statistical Abstracts of the United States: 2008. *Table 200. Percentage of adults engaging in leisure-time, transportation- related and household-related physical activity: 2005.* Online at: www.census.gov/compendia/ statab/ tables/08s0200.pdf - 2008-01-10

U.S. Census Bureau. (2008b). *Births, deaths, marriages, & divorces: Life expectancy. Table 98. Expectation of life at birth, 1970 to 2004, and projections, 2010 and 2015.* Online at: http://www.census. gov/compendia/statab/tables/08s0098.pdf

U.S. Dept. of Health & Human Services. (2004, Jan. 21). *Healthy people 2010 progress review: Nutrition and overweight.* Online at: http://www.healthypeople.gov/ data/2010prog/focus19/ Nutrition_Overweight.pdf

U.S. Department of Labor. (2008). Spotlight on statistics: Sports and exercise. Online at: http://www.bls.gov/spotlight/2008/sports

USA Today. (2008). Let the cholesterol fight begin, at age 8, July 8, p. 4D.

Vaillant, George E. (2002). *Aging well: Surprising guideposts to a happier life from the landmark Harvard study of adult development.* New York: Little, Brown and Company.

Vanderbilt, Tom. (2008). *Traffic: Why we drive the way we do (and what it says about us.* New York: Knopf.

Vladeck, Bruce. (2002). Universal health insurance in the United States: Reflections on the past, the present and the future. *American Journal of Public Health,* (93)1: 16-19.

Walker, Lyndal. (2008). *The relationship of self-esteem, spirituality, negative emotional symptoms, and locus of control to posttraumatic growth in older, middle class adults.* Dissertation Abstracts International: Section B: The Sciences and Engineering. 68(11B), 7681.

Wardlaw, Malcolm J. (2000). Three lessons for a better cycling future. *British Medical Journal,* 321(7276),1582–1585.

Wen, L. M. & Rissel, C. (2008). Inverse associations between cycling to work, public transport, and overweight and obesity. *Preventive Medicine.* 46(1), 29-32.

West, Jessamyn. (1957). *To see the dream.* New York: Harcourt Brace.

Whitaker, Bill. (2009). Star power: How Hollywood saves the world. *CBS Sunday Morning Show.* Dec. 20. Online at: http://www.cbsnews.com/stories/2009/12/20/ sunday/main6001183.shtml

Whitbourne, Susan. (2003). *Adult development & aging: Biopsychosocial perspective,* 2nd edition. Hoboken, NJ: John Wiley & Sons.

White, Donald W. (1996). *The American century: The rise and decline of the United States as a world power.* New Haven, CN: Yale University Press.

Wieland, D, Eleazer GP, Bachman DL, Corbin D, Oldendick R, Boland R, Stewart T, Richeson N, Thornhill JT. (2009). Does it stick? Effects of an integrated vertical undergraduate aging curriculum on medical and surgical residents. *J Am Geriatr Soc,* 56(1):132-8.

Wikipedia. (2008, July 11). The Greening of America. *Wikipedia,* the Free Encyclopedia, Online at http://en.wikipedia.org/wiki/The_Greening_of_America

Wikipedia. (2009). Pablo Picasso. http://en.wikipedia.org/ wiki/ Pablo_Picasso

Wikipedia. (2010). Jeanne Calment. http://en.wikipedia.org/ wiki/ Jeanne_Calment

Willcox, Bradley J., Willcox, D. Craig, & Suzuki, Makoto. (2001). *The Okinawa program: How the world's longest-lived people achieve everlasting health—and how you can too.* New York: Three Rivers Press.

WKYC-TV. (2009, Aug. 23). Local man bikes 800 miles to 50th college reunion. Cleveland TV station website. http:/222. wkyc.com/news/local/news_article.aspx?storyid-120203

Word, Sheela. (1996). Mortality awareness and risk-taking in late adolescence. *Death Studies,* 20(2);133-48.

World Health Organization. (2000). *The World Report 2000—Health systems: improving performance.* Geneva, Switzerland: WHO. Online at: http://www.who.int/whr/2000/en/whr00_en.pdf

World Health Organization statistics (2000, June 4). WHO issues new healthy life expectancy rankings. WHO website, online at: http://www.who.int/inf-pr-2000/en/pr2000-life.html

World Health Organization. (2002). Keep fit for life: Meeting the nutritional needs of older persons. http://whqlibdoc. who.int/publications/9241562102.pdf

World Health Organization. (2003a). *Health and Development through Physical Activity and Sport.* Geneva, Switzerland: WHO Document Production Services.

World Health Organization. (2003b). *WHO global strategy on diet, physical activity and health: Western pacific regional consultation meeting report.* Online at: http://www.who.int/hpr/NPH/docs/regional_consultation_report_wpro.pdf

World Health Organization. (2006, Sept. 11). Largely preventable chronic diseases cause 86% of deaths in Europe. WHO Online at: http://www.euro.who.int/mediacentre/PR/2006/20060908_1

World Health Organization. (2008). *World health statistics: 2008.* Geneva, Switzerland. Available in electronic format online at WHO website. http://www.who.int/whosis/whostat/EN_WHS08_Full.pdf

World Health Organization. (2008). *Risk factor: Physical inactivity.* WHO website http://www.who.int/cardiovascular_diseases/en/cud-atlas-08-physicalactivity.pdf

World Health Organization. (2008b). *World health report. 50 facts: Global health situation and trends 1955-2025.* http://www.who.int/whr/1998/media_centre/50facts/en/

WorldNakedBikeride.org. (2007).*Indecent exposure: The story of the World Naked Bike Ride*[film]. Canada.

World Triathlon Corporation. (2007). Sister Madonna goes after another Kona record. http://ironman.com/events/ironman/ironman-world-championship/sister-madonna-goes-after-another-kona-record

Worldnakedbikeride.com. (2006). http://www.worldnakedbikeride.org/ uk/london/2006/index.html

WTOPnews.com. (2007, Oct. 15). *Md. woman becomes first boomer to file for social security.* Federal News Radio website. http://www.wtopnews.com/index.php?nid= 598&sid=1268141

WPXI.com. (2009). McKeesport man starts walking, sheds 146 pounds. Online at: www.wpxi.com/print/19386908/detail. html

Xinhua News Agency. (2006, June 22). Stephen Hawking enjoys China trip. *China Internet Information Center.* http://www. china.org.cn/english/scitech/172341.htm

Yaffe, Kristine; Barnes, Deborah; Nevitt, Michael; Lui, Li-Yung; & Covinsky, Kenneth. (2001). A prospective study of physical activity and cognitive decline in elderly women. *Archives of Internal Medicine,* 162, 1703-1708.

Yamori, Yukio. (2006). Food factors for atherosclerosis prevention: Asian perspective derived from analyses of worldwide dietary biomarkers. *Experimental Clinical Cardiology,* 11(2), 94–98.

Yanek, L.R.; Becker, D.M.; Moy, T.F.; Gittelsohn, J.; & Koffman, D.M. (2001). Project Joy: Faith based cardiovascular health promotion for African American Women. *Public Health Rep,* 116 Suppl 1:68-81.

Yoeman, A. (1999). *Now or Neverland: Peter Pan and the myth of eternal youth : A psychological perspective on a cultural icon (Studies in Jungian psychology, 82).* Toronto: Inner City Books.

Young, Greg, Director. Gorman, Amy, Project Director. (2007). *Still kicking.* (DVD video). Golden Bear Casting.

Young At Heart. (2009). Interview for the Jewish TV Network. Video on YouTube. http://www.youtube.com/ watch?v=bwvz5G9zAXg

Young at heart: You're never too old to rock. (2008). DVD, directed by Stephen Walker. Fox Searchlight Pictures.

Index

About the Author

Dr. Kownacki and his wife, Mary

Richard Kownacki grew up in Pittsburgh, Pennsylvania, as the oldest son of Italian and Polish parents. He is currently married and enjoys traveling with Mary, his wife. When he's not busy with research on successful aging, he likes to spend his time (growing old) while listening to rock-and-roll music, watching 1950s monster movies, reading science fiction, playing with the cats, cooking vegetarian gourmet meals, and soaking in the Jacuzzi. On Sunday mornings, he tries to find the proper balance between hugging his wife, lying on the couch, watching the garden grow, and doing absolutely nothing at all.

Dr. Kownacki is a clinical psychologist licensed in the state of Texas. He maintains a private practice in Wichita Falls, with

Mary, who is a psychotherapist. His practice mainly involves psychological evaluations of adults and children.

Dr. Kownacki earned his doctorate in clinical psychology from the University of Memphis in 1997. Before that he earned a master's degree in counseling psychology from Angelo State University (1992). In a previous career incarnation, he was a historian and obtained a master's degree in history of religions from UCLA (1979) and undergraduate degrees in both religious studies and history from California State University at Fullerton (1978).

Besides being overeducated, Dr. Kownacki has nearly thirty years of experience in the field of mental health or human services: 1) six years in vocational rehabilitation, as a vocational evaluator and rehab counselor; 2) eight years in community corrections, as a probation officer, alcohol and drug counselor, and program evaluator; and 3) fourteen years as a clinical psychologist (1996 onward). He is a certified rational emotive therapist, with a cognitive-behavioral orientation and experience in twelve-step program work.